Wedding Belles

ALSO BY HAYWOOD SMITH

The Red Hat Club

Queen Bee of Mimosa Branch

The Red Hat Club Rides Again

Ladies of the Lake

PRAISE FOR H

"Haywood Smith's brilliant new novel hits all the right notes because of its authentic Southern voice, but will satisfy readers everywhere because of its heartfelt message for mothers, daughters, and yes, even mothers-in-law. Smith is hilarious and wise. *Wedding Belles* is perfect for book clubs."
—Dorothea Benton Frank, author of
The Land of Mango Sunsets and *Return to Sullivans Island*

"Fun and moving, *Wedding Belles* is a Southern treat serving up love, friendship, and family."
—Linda Francis Lee, author of *The Ex-Debutante*

"In *Wedding Belles*, five savvy fifty-something friends find themselves faced with a daughter who just might be marrying the wrong man. Haywood Smith's lively, caring characters help one another deal with the complications of many different kinds of love and marriage with common sense and kindness, and best of all, lots of laughter."
—Nancy Thayer, author of *The Hot Flash Club*

"Smith's fizzy exploration of enduring friendship and family signals more changes ahead for Georgia, her family, and the red hat matrons. Fans of the series will enjoy and look forward to the next."
—*Publishers Weekly* on *Wedding Belles*

"A joyous, joyful ode." —*Booklist* on *The Red Hat Club*

"Belly laughs and tears." —*Omaha World-Herald* on *Wedding Belles*

"A tribute to women who emerged victorious through divorce, menopause, spreading waistlines, and other tribulations."
—*Chicago Tribune* on *The Red Hat Club*

"An engaging ode to the lasting bonds of Southern sisterhood and life-begins-at-fifty optimism."
—*Kirkus Reviews* on *The Red Hat Club Rides Again*

Wedding Belles

· · · · · · ·

HAYWOOD SMITH

 ST. MARTIN'S GRIFFIN ❧ NEW YORK

WEDDING BELLES. Copyright © 2008 by Haywood Smith. All rights reserved. Printed in the United States of America. For information, address St. Martin's Press, 175 Fifth Avenue, New York, N.Y. 10010.

www.stmartins.com

The Library of Congress has catalogued the hardcover edition as follows:

Smith, Haywood, 1949–
    Wedding belles / Haywood Smith.—1st ed.
        p. cm.
    ISBN 978-0-312-32973-0
    1. Middle-aged women—Fiction.   2. Female friendship—Fiction.   3. Mothers and daughters—Fiction.   4. Georgia—Fiction.   5. Domestic fiction.   I. Title.
    PS3569.M53728W43   2008
    813'.54—dc22   2008020997

ISBN 978-0-312-57388-1 (pbk.)

First St. Martin's Griffin Edition: September 2009

10 9 8 7 6 5 4 3 2 1

This book is dedicated to precious Mama,

who smiled through my wedding anyway,

and who still drives like a New York cabbie,

shares her keen mind and talents to help others,

and is always there for me as consoler,

traveling companion, and friend.

· 1 ·

Nobody's perfect. So, a lot of the people on the beach are skinnier than you. Big deal. There's always somebody older and fatter out there, too, so you might as well wear your bathing suit and enjoy yourself.
— MY BEST FRIEND, LINDA MURRAY

. . . .

*L*IKE MOST PEOPLE, I've always thought of the word *perfect* as an absolute, but there's nothing like a wedding to prove otherwise, especially when the wedding's your daughter's and you know it's a big mistake. Then the term is relative—like *disaster*.

All her life, my second-born, Callie, had been a mother's dream: smart as her physicist father, outgoing as her big brother Jack, principled and salt-of-the-earth sensible as my precious mother-in-law, and gorgeously athletic as my mother—who is still a handsome woman at eighty-four and walks three miles a day, and drives like a New York cabbie in Atlanta traffic.

Callie was our perfect daughter. Never in her life had she given us serious cause to worry.

But the word *perfect* can also mean "completed." Little did I know that my obedient daughter was saving up all her bad-behavior credits to cash them in on one giant bombshell of a boo-boo that would redefine "perfect wedding" in biblical terms, meaning finished, thank-God-it's-finally-over-with.

Oh, for a crystal ball! If I could have been absolutely sure my instincts were right, I would have gunnysacked her to keep her from the altar. As it was, I was the one who got gunnysacked.

The present. Second Tuesday in January. 10:55 A.M. Muscogee Drive, Atlanta.
. . . .

NORMALLY I LOVE January's sweet, silent stillness after the glittering clutter and excitement of Christmas. Stripped of wretched excess (the only way to decorate for the holidays), my house seems clean and sleek and tranquil. I bask in the new year's quiet order with a long, relaxing breath and look forward to the high spot in my monthly routine, lunch with my lifelong best friends.

For the past thirty-something years, since we were pledges in our high school sorority, Linda, Diane, Teeny, and I (and lately Pru, our prodigal) have tended the ties that bind on the second Tuesday of every month at the Swan Coach House Restaurant, where we share laughter, fun, fellowship, frozen fruit salad, and generous doses of "Poor Baby" on a scale of one to five (the only allowable response to whining of any kind).

When we all started turning fifty, we decided to wear red hats and purple in honor of Jenny Joseph's wonderful poem "Warning," a delightful declaration of independence for midlife and beyond. Governed only by our own Twelve Sacred Traditions of Friendship, our luncheons have become a welcome refuge of acceptance and sanity—or occasional insanity, none of which was ever *my* idea—in this crazy world. And every month, we take turns bringing a joke that's not woman-bashing, and preferably not man-bashing, either.

For the past thirty-something years, I've always gotten to the Swan Coach House Restaurant early so I could sip my iced tea or hot lemonade in our regular banquette in the back corner of the main dining room and savor the anticipation of seeing my friends.

Until that gray morning last January, when—for the first time ever—I was seriously considering skipping the whole thing. Disconnecting the phone, turning off my cell, taking one of the four sleeping pills I had left from a trip to England five years ago, and pulling the covers up over my head.

Not that it would do any good to postpone the inevitable, but I couldn't stand the idea of telling anybody, even my best friends, about the dumb thing my brilliant daughter was about to do. Not until I absolutely had to.

If I stayed home and took the sleeping pill, it would knock out my internal Chicken Little along with me. She'd been dithering away in hyper-drive ever since Callie's New Year's Day announcement.

Not that I'm mental or anything, but when it comes to my psyche, I have this constant internal dialogue with pieces of myself that just won't shut up. Chicken Little, my drama queen, and my scolding Inner Puritan hog up the whole house, relegating my Sensible Self and Creative Inner Child to the shed out back.

It occurs to me that some people might think it odd, especially when I argue with myself aloud, but it works for me. I mean, it's not like I believe I'm hearing voices. I know it's all me. I talk to machines, too—all the time—but that's not crazy. It's only crazy when you think they talk back. Unless they really do, which happens more and more often these days.

Nevertheless, on that second Tuesday morning last January, my Sensible Self managed to push her way into the parlor and urged me—for the fiftieth time since Callie's announcement—to look at the big picture and remember how blessed my family was.

We were all healthy and productive. Callie had finished her doctorate in theoretical mathematics and landed a job teaching at Oglethorpe in the fall. Our twenty-nine-year-old son Jack was happily building Home Depots all over America. My husband John and I had a fabulous love affair going that had waited till midlife to burst into flame. John had tenure teaching physics at Georgia Tech. We had finally paid off the mortgage. God was in His heaven. And I had four steadfast friends to help get me through this.

Maybe I ought to go to the luncheon after all.

As usual, Chicken Little ignored all the blessings, only to squawk, *Callie's making the mistake of her life! She has no idea what she's getting into! Linda and Teeny and Pru will know the minute they slap eyes on you that something's seriously wrong.*

All I've ever wanted to do was keep a low profile, but no such luck. It's a curse, having a face that hides nothing.

I could always call an MYOB (Mind your own business: Sacred Tradition of Friendship Number Five). But then my loyal friends would probably worry up all kinds of drastic things.

If I simply played hooky, they'd send out the bloodhounds. But if I called to cancel, they'd expect an explanation. When it came to our monthly friendship fix, the only acceptable excuses were foreign travel, jury duty, chemo, moving away, or hospitalization.

Standing at the mirror in the foyer of my little house on Muscogee Drive, I reapplied my nonfeathering red lipstick for the third time and prayed with as much conviction as I could muster for the grace to accept Callie's choice. But God and I both knew my heart wasn't really in it. So I ended up reminding Him yet again that this whole thing couldn't be a good idea.

The Lord and I have that kind of a relationship. I speak my mind, and He loves me anyway and runs the Universe as He sees fit, whether I agree with Him or not.

Things could certainly be worse. Linda's daughter Abby had quit Agnes Scott six months short of graduating with honors to become a hairdresser and move in with (and later marry) her Jewish mother's nightmare: a lapsed-Moslem Rastafarian tattoo artist whose student visa had expired.

Which meant that Linda would certainly be able to empathize, but that offered cold comfort. Nobody really wants to hear, "It could be worse."

I sighed in resignation. As the Beatles said, "Oh-blah-dee, oh-blah-dah, life goes on," so I decided to suck it up and go to my luncheon.

I picked up my red felt picture hat. Maybe just this once, I could keep from blabbing everything.

Other people's secrets, I could keep, but not my own. Still, just because I hadn't ever been able to do it before didn't mean I couldn't do it now. There's a first time for everything.

Grabbing my red pocketbook, I resolved to develop a pleasant, impenetrable mask on the way. I could do this. After all, I'd managed to keep from telling Mama so far.

Oh, lord. How would I ever tell Mama?

· 2 ·

Bad news is like a dead fish. The longer you keep it hidden,
the worse it stinks up your whole life.
—LINDA'S RUSSIAN GRANDMOTHER *BUBBIE*

Same day. 11:35 A.M. Swan Coach House, Atlanta.

I WAS SO late I had to use valet parking, then maneuver my honkin' big hat through the crush of waiting women crammed into the foyer. I could tell they were staring at me behind their polite smiles, and I cringed at the overwhelming (and ridiculous) feeling that they had somehow sniffed out my bad-fish bad news.

It didn't even occur to me that they were probably just taken aback by my huge red hat and purple gabardine overcoat.

When I got to the dining room, I looked toward our regular corner booth and saw that I was the cow's tail.

There they were, my four best friends, resplendent in red hats and purple outfits.

Teeny, who looked like a blond little Audrey Hepburn with big blue eyes, was our Miss Melly, but with one major difference: She was our keeper of secrets. Beneath her impeccable manners and gentle ways hid a hard-headed businesswoman. A devout Catholic, she'd compensated for being stuck in a bad marriage by eavesdropping on her abusive mega-developer husband when he and his powerful father talked shop over their bourbon. Then, for the next thirty years, she'd used what she heard to secretly invest every cent she could scrape up. Only when her two sons were grown and gone—and she'd amassed a fortune of twenty million—did she file for divorce and an annulment from the Vatican.

Now Teeny's pet project was Shapely Clothing, a break-even operation that employed needy women to make comfortable, flattering, classic clothes for real-women shapes and sizes. We all wore them (she'd had dress forms made to our exact measurements), and she paid us a thousand dollars apiece for any of our design ideas she could use.

Next to her sat Diane in deep purple slacks and a red cashmere sweater that accented her slim build and brunette hair. The organizer in our group, Diane had marshaled our help to get the goods on her cheatin' lyin' lawyer husband who planned to leave her penniless. And we got him good, yes we did. Now very happily divorced (with a cowboy on the side, but we'll get to that later), she runs the design division of Shapely from the penthouse office next to Teeny's, just a few blocks away on West Paces Ferry.

Beside her sat Pru, our prodigal. Tall and rawboned, Pru was a size sixteen from the knees to her waist, and a size twelve everywhere else. Back in the hippie era, she and her pot-smoking husband had tuned in, turned on, and dropped out, sacrificing each other and all Pru's self-respect to drugs and alcohol over the long, lost years. Then Teeny had found her and brought her back to us. After a promising beginning, Pru had fallen off the wagon so hard that we'd had to go to Vegas to stage a spectacular intervention (with the help of Cameron "the Cowboy"). Then we acted as her family in rehab whether she liked it or not, and Pru had pulled through with flying colors. For more than a year now, she'd showed up clean and sober every day for work as Diane's assistant at Shapely.

Last but not least was Linda, our heart and our humor, but she didn't look very happy. Her plump face was drawn down into an uncharacteristic frown. Maybe I wasn't the only one with bad-fish bad news.

The two of us had been confidantes since our high school days as Mademoiselles, when Friday-night sleepovers meant services with her family at the Temple and *shul* on Saturday morning. Once trim and athletic, Linda had married the love of her life, a wonderful urological surgeon named Brooks, and both of them had grown fluffy and contented. Until their only child Abby did her own dropout and shacked up with Osama-damned-boyfriend (yes, his name is really Osama), but as the Bible says, "The rain falls on the just and the unjust."

Of all of us, Linda was the only one confident enough to let her hair go silvery white. (Not me. I've warned my children that I plan to be the redheaded old lady with *way* too much makeup, who talks too loud and pokes people with her cane.)

Watching my girlfriends scrutinize my approach, I could see their concern and braced myself for the inevitable questions they would ask about why I was late.

Hang in there. You can do this, my Sensible Self encouraged in optimistic denial of my lifelong inability to keep from telling on myself.

My smile grew more fixed with every step as I worked my way between the brightly tulipped underskirts of the white-clothed tables in the Coach House's main dining room. When I reached our corner banquette, Teeny stood for an air kiss, her tiny, slender hands cold as she took my big, garden-scarred warm ones. "Glad you made it," she said without recrimination. "I was about to send out a search party to blanket the city." Which she could literally afford to do. She cocked her head at me. "Are you okay?"

"I'm fine," I lied, anxious to shift the attention somewhere else. "Linda, you look miserable," I said as I sat in my usual place. "What in the world's the matter?"

"Not now," she snapped, then got me off the hot seat with a grumpy, "Who's got the joke? Somebody make me laugh, *please*."

Almost invariably, whoever called for the joke wanted to get it out of the way so she could discuss something urgent, so the others promptly shifted their concern from me to Linda.

Pru signaled it was her turn to tell the joke by reluctantly waving her long fingers. "Me."

"Okay," Linda grumbled. "Get on with it."

It wasn't easy finding funny jokes that met our criteria, and even when Pru found one, she had shown no talent for the telling. In the past year, she'd made two well-meaning tries, but failed miserably. Not that we cared. We laughed anyway and complimented her on the consistency of her terribleness.

Teeny couldn't tell a joke right to save her life, either, but her lame efforts were often funnier than a lot of ours that went off without a hitch.

"Remember, now," Pru cautioned. "I'm awful at this."

"Remember, now," I said with affection, "that doesn't matter."

Pru responded with a welcome glimmer of spunk. "Trust me. That doesn't make it any easier." She composed herself. "But this time, I really practiced. So here goes:

"One day, when she was on her way to visit her mama in Florida, Mavis stopped for gas in a tiny little south Georgia town, right across the street from a cemetery and a funeral home. While she was gassing up, a hearse came out of the funeral home down the way and slowly rolled toward the graveyard, followed by a woman in a red dress walking a huge rottweiler on a leash. Behind her came another hearse, then at least thirty more women, single file."

Rapt, the four of us hung on Pru's every word as she went on.

"As the woman in red came by her, Mavis can't resist asking, 'Please excuse me for intruding on your grief. I'm sorry for your loss, but could you please tell me what happened here?'

"The woman in red stopped. 'My husband got drunk and tried to kill me, so our dog, here, attacked and killed him,' she answered without the slightest hint of remorse.

"Mavis looked at the other hearse behind the widow. 'So who's in there?'

" 'My mother-in-law,' the widow said. 'She was trying to help my louse of a husband finish me off, so the dog killed her, too.'

" 'Wow.' Mavis thought about her own lousy husband and mother-in-law and asked, 'Could I borrow your dog?' "

We started to laugh in delight, but Pru raised her palm to indicate the joke wasn't over.

" 'Sure,' " she went on. "The widow cocked her head toward the long procession behind her. 'But you'll have to get in line.' "

Stunned by Pru's perfect delivery, we waited for a heartbeat, then burst out laughing—along with several people at nearby tables.

"That was perfect!" I told her. "And *funny*." I lifted my hands and did a polite opera clap, fingertips patting the other palm. "*Brava*."

Linda arched a silver eyebrow, "I'm in a bad mood, and you still made me laugh," she said. "Even though there was a widow in it."

What was that supposed to mean?

"Traitor," Teeny said in mock indignation. "Now I'm back to being the only one who can't tell a joke."

Pru flushed with pride. She looked really happy, a rare and special state for her. "I practiced on Bubba"—her grown son—"till I got it right."

"It was great," Diane said. Then she turned abruptly to Linda. "Okay, so what's wrong with widows, and why are you in such a rotten mood?" No preliminaries with Diane. She always cut straight to the chase.

Linda hesitated with a frown.

Taking advantage of the break in conversation, our regular waitress Maria put a fresh basket of mini muffins on the table, then pulled out her tablet and pen. "May I take your orders now, or would you ladies like me to come back later?"

"We'll order," Linda decided for all of us.

Maria waited patiently without the slightest hint of irony while we all perused our menus, then ordered the same choices we always did: the shrimp salad plate for Diane, the Favorite Combination plate for Linda and me, the grilled chicken green salad for Teeny, and a chicken salad croissant for Pru.

As soon as Maria headed for the kitchen with our orders, Linda told us, "I got a call last Friday from my Cousin Rachel Glass, the one from Manhattan."

Diane frowned. "I don't remember any cousin Rachel."

"Well, actually, we're not close," Linda said. Prodded by our Southern compulsion to identify relatives, she clarified, "Her mother was Daddy's sister Gladys, the one in Queens, but she and Daddy didn't get along, so we never visited. I've only met Rachel twice: once, when we were kids, sittin' *shiva* up there for my granddaddy; and once in our teens at a kissin' cousin's wedding in New York." She shook her head. "Trust me, twice was two times too many."

I frowned in sympathy. "She was that bad?"

Linda nodded, her tone ominous. "Imagine a grossly exaggerated stereotype of an obnoxious Upper West Side Jewish princess, then double it. That's Rachel."

"So, why did she call you?" Diane asked in the timeless rhythm we'd perfected for helping each other get the story out at our own pace.

"Seems she came home to her penthouse apartment overlooking Central Park four months ago and found her high-falutin' plastic surgeon husband dead of a cocaine overdose," Linda confided, "and when Rachel went through the files in his medical office looking for his will, she found out everything they owned was hocked to the gills, with huge debts besides. It was all joint assets, so her goose was cooked. He'd even stolen the money her parents left her. And switched out all her big diamonds with zircons."

"Now, that is *low,*" Teeny chimed in.

"Bummer," Pru said. "Coke'll do that to you." She knew all too well from her own experiences. "Makes you a slave. Anything for money to score that next hit. And I do mean anything."

Linda nodded. "Rachel really is desperate. She lost not only her husband but everything she thought they owned. The woman lived in a complete state of financial oblivion. Her husband handled everything from his office. Turns out the IRS had huge liens on their Manhattan penthouse overlooking the park and their 'cottage' in the Hamptons. The minute her husband was dead, they immediately seized all the properties and froze the bank accounts. And the lenders foreclosed on the equity loans he'd taken out to feed his habit. Creditors laid claim to everything else except her clothes. She doesn't even have a car."

"Whoa," Pru said. "That is *way* harsh."

Linda sighed. "She managed to stall things and stay in her apartment for the last four months, but apparently, yesterday was her drop-deadline to be out. And—surprise, surprise—none of her fair-weather friends would take her in."

"Uh-oh," Diane said, seeing where this was going.

"Turns out," Linda told us, "I'm the only living relative she has, since Daddy died."

"Double uh-oh," I added.

"You don't know the half of it." Linda moaned. "So she calls me Friday and pours all this out, then informs me—not asks me, mind you, but informs me—that she's coming to Atlanta to make a fresh start, and she plans to move in with us till she gets a job and finds a place! 'Because it's so cheap theah.' " Her imitation of a thick New York accent was right on the money. " 'And theah's no other place to go,' " she mimicked. " 'I'd be on the *street*!' "

I whistled low. "Man, that takes some nerve."

"Nerve," Linda said, "is the only thing Rachel has plenty of at this point."

Teeny's eyes widened. "Would she really be on the street?"

Linda scowled. "Unfortunately, yes. So I couldn't very well tell her not to come. Daddy would roll in his grave." So much for giving with a cheerful spirit, but I didn't blame her one bit for feeling taken advantage of.

Linda flopped back against her seat. "I figured she'd call me back to tell me when she was coming, but I went ahead and cleaned out the guest room. Good thing I did. Yesterday I'm vacuuming, and the doorbell rings, and who's standing there but Rachel?"

Whoa!

"With seventeen—count 'em, seventeen—Louis Vuitton suitcases of every shape and description, including trunks. She had to hire a van at the airport to hold it all, and expected me to pay him!"

"Good night, nurse," I said. A regular cab from the airport could cost fifty dollars. "How much was it?"

"One hundred and thirty dollars," Linda fumed. "Not including the tip. Good thing I had my State Patrol money tucked away, or I'd have had to go to the ATM while the meter was still running." (We all carry a hundred-dollar bill as cash bond so we won't have to surrender our licenses if we get a ticket out of our home county.)

Linda fluffed up even more. "While I was helping her unpack, I found out that two of the big suitcases were crammed with Pradas and Manolo Blahniks that looked brand-new. Sixty-five pairs of shoes, most of them black. I counted. The rest of her bags were chock full of real designer clothes, almost all dressy and mostly black. She must have gone on one last mother of a spending spree before anybody found out her husband was dead."

Her shoulders sagged. "Now she's crammed into our guest room with all her stuff, keeping us up till the wee hours with the TV blaring while she hollers over *my* cell phone to heaven-knows-who all night. Poor Brooks could barely keep his eyes open when he headed for his morning rounds." That would be at 6:00 A.M., sharp, fortified by a hot breakfast, compliments of Linda's genuine devotion.

"You gave her your cell phone?" I asked, surprised.

"No. She just took it out of my purse," Linda complained. "Along with my American Express card."

"No, no, no," Diane said. "That cannot be. You must get back your credit card immediately. And your phone. Do not pass go, do not collect one hundred dollars."

Linda unconsciously tugged at the bandeau of her bra through her sweater, a sure sign she was feeling trapped. "She swore she'd pay me back and get her own phone, but with what, I'd like to know."

"Linda," I chided, "she's probably ordering Beluga caviar and truffles even as we speak."

"No, she's not," Linda countered. "I checked as I was leaving, and she was out like a light. I doubt she'll be up before I get home."

"This is a recipe for disaster," Diane warned. "You and Brooks value your peace and privacy so."

Teeny lifted a finger. "I've got an idea. One of the condos I own just up Roswell Road is almost finished being renovated. I'd be happy to furnish it like a corporate rental and let her live there till we can find her a job and get her back on her Pradas. It shouldn't take more than a month to get the place ready."

"Oh, Teens!" Linda knocked Teeny's hat askew hugging her. "Thank you, thank you, thank you." She drew back. "I can handle anything for a month. You're a lifesaver."

Teeny repositioned her hat. "Old Spanish proverb: Fish and house-guests stink after three days. My favorite cause is helping displaced women. Obnoxious or not, Rachel certainly qualifies. We'll find something she can do at Shapely."

Linda pulled a face. "Oh, honey, I don't know about that. She hasn't even been here for twenty-four hours, and already, I wouldn't wish her on my worst enemy."

Teeny didn't flinch. "She'll come around. I know just the manager for her."

Linda still wasn't convinced. "Don't say I didn't warn you. And feel free to fire her."

The matter was settled with Teeny's cheery "Okay."

Our mistake—a natural one—was thinking only about Linda in all this. I mean, who in their right mind would turn down a job and a free condo? But we hadn't met Rachel.

Worried that my friends might focus on me now that we'd taken care of the Rachel thing, I changed the subject with, "So Teeny, how are things going with Shapely?"

Her eyes brightened. "Oh, I'm so glad you brought that up. I have checks for you and Linda. We're using those ideas you sketched for our spring line next year." She looked to Pru. "Did you think to bring those final drawings and the checks?"

"But of course," Pru said, reaching into her oversized bag for a manila folder. "Here." She handed Linda a thousand-dollar check and a color sketch of a cute jacket dress. "Just the way you described it."

"Perfect for all the little barrel-bodied biddies like me." Linda beamed at the check. "And this will provide a nice down payment on a used car for Rachel. Thank you, ma'am."

Pru handed me my check and a color rendering of a pretty pink drop-collar dress with short sleeves and an elastic waist. "The fabric's a poly-crepe with a little rayon, washable and dryable, as you requested," she said. "We added the faggoting on the collar and sleeves to make it more feminine, and the stitched-down tucks on the bodice."

Grateful that we were talking clothes instead of why I'd been late, I noted the improved design. "That turned out gorgeous." Then I looked at the check and let down my guard ever so briefly, just long enough to say, "I can use this to take John to Hawaii after the wedding."

Instantly, I went rigid, eyes wide. Oh hell! I didn't say that out loud, did I?

Four red-hatted heads swiveled toward me faster than Linda Blair in *The Exorcist*.

"What wedding?" Diane asked, her eyes narrow.

Calm. Stay calm! "One of John's cousins," I lied in what I hoped was a convincingly offhand tone. "It's June seventeenth, way down in Albany. We'll roast."

Linda tucked her chin. "Baloney," Diane said. "John doesn't have any cousins. You, yourself, told me his parents and grandparents were all only children."

Rats. Why, when I had such a talent for lying to myself, couldn't I manage to do it with anybody else and get away with it?

I hesitated, debating whether to invoke Sacred Tradition of Friendship Number Five with a terse "MYOB." But the concern in my friends' expressions made me think again. They were going to find out about Callie; it was just a question of when.

Did Chicken Little really need a couple more months to run amok in my mind? I could sure use some sympathy and support. "Okay." I stood. "But this is strictly classified for now. To the Board Room." Or the downstairs bathroom, as it was more commonly known. Despite the constant din of female voices in the restaurant, the brightly padded walls had ears. So whenever we had something truly confidential to share, we headed downstairs for a confab.

The moment we all rose and started toward the foyer, the atmosphere in the dining room went sharp as hatpins, and fifty Buckhead matrons turned to follow our progress. Every follicle of peach fuzz on my face cinched tight with a flaming prickle of self-consciousness.

The Buckhead grapevine would be abuzz with the truth soon enough when the engagement announcement came out. After that, my presence would be greeted with sympathetic glances, subtle whispers, and pity.

And pity is a mighty tough dish for any Southern woman to swallow. Not that I cared what anybody—beyond God and my family and my best friends—thought of me, but I cared very much what people thought about my daughter.

Once we reached the elegant faux-marble bathroom downstairs, we made pit stops till we were alone, then Linda took her post as watchdog at the door.

"Spit it out, sugar," Pru told me. "Trust me, you'll feel better afterwards."

They perched, all ears.

I tried my best to seem pleased. "Callie got engaged New Year's Eve."

Normally, this would have elicited a flurry of delight, but my Red Hats read the dire reservation between my words.

Linda's silver brows drew together in confusion. "Please tell me she didn't get back together with what's-his-name." A perfect designation for the boring boyfriend Callie had finally jettisoned the summer before.

"No," I said, reassessing the guy quite favorably in comparison to Wade. "What's-his-name married somebody else on the rebound just two months after they broke up."

"So, who's the lucky young man?" Diane prodded with exquisite irony.

Try lucky *old* man.

Why couldn't I just come right out and say it? "Actually, she's known him forever."

"Do *we* know him?" Pru asked.

"Umm-hmm." I felt the corner of my proper little smile begin to quiver, signaling a crack in the dam that threatened to release all my fears for my brilliant daughter.

It shouldn't have been so hard to tell them. Linda, of all people, would understand. Diane would assess the situation and offer a plan. Teeny would commiserate. And Pru would try to say something nice. They would all comfort me, then pitch in to do whatever I needed. Still, saying it aloud made the whole disaster *way* too real.

I took a deep breath, determined to tell them it was Wade, but instead I heard my voice say, "The wedding's the third Saturday in

June, the seventeenth, at St. Philip's Cathedral. They told us on New Year's Day. Everything's all arranged. They don't even want us to pay for the ceremony and reception. The service will be at four, the reception at Ansley. They're doing a buffet. With lots and lots of flowers."

Which figured. The groom was one of Atlanta's most respected florists. And my husband's best friend since they were college roommates.

Linda frowned slightly. "Okay, so the problem's not the ceremony or the reception. Or the money. Or the date. Which leaves the groom."

Might as well get it over with.

Suddenly the door to the bathroom flew open, silencing us all with a jolt of adrenaline. Linda had gotten so interested in what I was saying, she'd forgotten to stand guard.

Patty Habersham hurtled inside with an apologetic, "I am so sorry to intrude, y'all, but till I get that bladder tack next week, I cannot hold a thing."

Our bathroom powwows were legend and sacrosanct, but we couldn't very well let Patty suffer—I mean, almost all of us had experienced that particular brand of middle-aged torture—so despite the tension hovering in the air, we waited while she unloaded at least four glasses of tea, then washed up, still apologizing.

"It's okay, Patty, darlin'," I told her. "Been there, done that."

But the instant she left, the others zeroed in on me.

"Callie's not marrying a woman, is she?" Linda asked, a question that had only become conceivable of late.

"Of course it's not a woman," I retorted. Same-sex marriages were illegal in Georgia. If Wade were Wanda, that would multiply the horrified pity quotient from the lunch bunch upstairs by the power of ten. After all, this was the Bible Belt.

"So," Diane said. "Enough pussy-footin' around. Who's the groom?"

"Wade Bowman," I blurted out. There. I'd said it.

They all frowned in confusion. The truth was so inappropriate, they didn't process it.

"I thought Wade and Madelyn's son was named Scott," Teeny said.

Linda nodded. "Wasn't he, like, three years younger than Callie?"

My answer of, "He is," got lost as Pru digressed with, "Diane told me Wade and Madelyn had a really messy divorce."

"They did," Linda confirmed. "Madelyn hitched her wagon to a high-priced orthopedic surgeon at Emory, dumped Wade, took the kids, and told them it was all Wade's fault. She always was a mean, mercenary little thing."

A light went on in Pru's eyes. "I remember her! Mean Madelyn."

"Aka Madelyn the Mooch," Diane added.

"Didn't Wade marry some chickie-boom right after the divorce?" Linda accused.

"For about thirty minutes. Typical." Diane sneered the way we always did when men our age married a mere child.

Just the way all our Buckhead contemporaries who didn't know Callie would sneer when they gossiped about her and Wade.

My country grandmother's pragmatic Baptist voice echoed in my mind during the conversational vacuum. *Judge not, that ye be not judged, sweetie. It's the law of sowing and reaping. That means we'll be judged for the same thing we've judged in others, and face it, you've done your share of judgin' when it comes to young wives and older men.*

She was dead right, as usual. (No pun intended.) Maybe I did deserve it.

All that judgment now hovered, pulsing, waiting to fall on me in cosmic retribution.

But Callie was the one who would suffer for it. Every bitch in Buckhead would go around telling the world that my precious, intelligent Ph.D. was just another chickie-boom.

My only daughter was going to be wife number three to an alcoholic (albeit a dry one) old enough to be her father! And all I really knew about the middle-aged Wade was that he was a fabulous florist who had good manners and dressed well, and he played a fair round of golf and a hell of a doubles tennis game with John.

Linda frowned, finally processing what I'd said. "So it's not Scott . . . ?"

"No," I said quietly. "It's Wade."

A terrible light dawned in Linda's expression. "Not *John's* Wade!

Wild Man Wade from ATO? The one who is responsible for the most humiliating moment of my life?"

"Wade the florist, Wade?" Teeny said, the prejudices of her privileged upbringing rising from the dead.

"I can't believe she's fallen for *Wade*," Linda sputtered. "Talk about baggage! I know he's supposed to have quit drinking, but—"

"We're all well aware of his shortcomings," I said in an effort to get them to quiet down. The faux-marble walls of the bathroom magnified sound, and anybody waiting outside would get an earful. I dropped my voice and leaned in. "But it gets worse."

They halted in mid-reaction.

I forced myself to reveal the thing that had haunted me every second since Callie had told me. "She's moved in with him."

They blinked, stunned, knowing how this flew in the face of my—and Callie's—old-fashioned religious beliefs.

"Callie?" Teeny asked in disbelief. "Our model-child goddaughter, Callie?" (We're all godmothers to each other's children.)

"Hyper-Christian Callie?" Diane asked way too loudly. "Who's renewed her virginity-till-marriage oath every year at church since she was fourteen?"

I rolled my eyes. "Yep." Hard as it may be to believe in this Jerry Springer world, there are actually more than four million teens and singles who take the Pledge to remain sexually abstinent till marriage, and a substantial percentage actually keep it. As I said, this is the Bible Belt. As a devout Southern Baptist, Callie was stone serious about her personal commitment to Christ, and just as serious about her pledge to remain chaste till marriage. Not that it had been a difficult vow to honor; she'd been so consumed with her education and her thesis that dating had never been a priority. Frankly, she was such a Bigbrain, like her father, she had yet to meet her match.

Why she thought that match was college-dropout Wade Bowman, I couldn't imagine.

"All these years, she's been saving herself to give to the likes of *Wade*?" Linda protested. "The man's an animal! God only knows how many women he's slept with."

"Now, Linda, be fair," Teeny interjected. "Lots of guys sowed their wild oats. Wade's sixty now, and I haven't heard a word of gossip about the man since right after his divorce."

Linda shook her finger at Teeny. "Once an animal, always an animal." She turned to me. "Oh, you poor thing. No wonder you didn't want to tell us. This is awful. How long have you known?"

"Like I said, since New Year's Day."

Her eyes narrowed. "What does John think about all this?"

"He said, 'Callie's a grown woman' "—I could still hear my husband's wistful confidence as he'd spoken—" 'and she's capable of making her own decisions and living with the consequences.' "

"That's what he *said*," Diane countered. "But how does he *really* feel?"

"You know John. He doesn't talk about his feelings," I said. "He never has. Now Jack"—our son—"Jack's a lot more open, and he's appalled, but he refused to try to talk Callie out of it. He said it's her life and she has to learn for herself."

Worn out by the telling, I scrubbed the heels of my hands into my eyes, forgetting all about my mascara.

"Stop that!" Linda pulled my hands away. "Oh, good grief. Now you look like a raccoon." She grabbed a paper towel and started rubbing away the mess I'd made. "Hold still."

"Ow. Not so hard. Everybody will think somebody socked me in the eye."

Better they should talk about that than the truth.

"And they're *living* together?" Diane said.

I nodded. "You know how practical Callie is. She insists it's just to make sure they're compatible. She swears she's not sleeping with him. She says she's even redecorated her own room."

Linda's Abby had made no such pretense when she'd moved in with Osama-damned-boyfriend, now Osama-damned-son-in-law. "Well, we all know what's paved with good intentions," Linda retorted. "The girl's only human. He'll wear her down, just like he did me."

Diane zeroed in on her, aghast. "You slept with Wade Bowman! When?"

"Damn," Linda sputtered. "I cannot believe I just blurted that out."

She straightened, her mouth a tight line before she replied, "If any of you breathe a word about that to anybody, and I mean anybody, I will personally go on the Internet and tell everybody that you have an obscene tattoo on your twat."

Diane bristled. "Linda! I do not!"

Linda turned a smug smile on her. "I know you don't, and you know you don't, but nobody else does."

Pru raised her hand with a sunny giggle. "I have one just like that."

I switched the subject back to Callie. "I know my daughter," I said. "If she does sleep with Wade, her conscience will force her to marry him."

"Oh, honey," Teeny said to me. "It's so hard to let go when we see our kids headed toward a big mistake, isn't it?" Her two boys had certainly raised their share of Cain. "But the fact is, Callie's an adult, and like John said, her choices are hers to make, and the consequences are hers to live."

"I know it," I pouted out, "but I hate it!"

The others peered at one another, then turned as one to say, "Poor baby! Poor baby! Poor baby!" The only allowable Red Hat response when one of us needs to whine.

"Only three?" I complained.

"Poor baby, poor baby, poor baby, poor baby!" Teeny amended, raising the situation level to just below code red.

It was about time. "Thank you!" I pulled a paper towel from the dispenser and dabbed at a sole remaining smudge under my eye. "I was beginning to wonder about y'all."

"Now that you've had your *poor babies*," Diane said, "we need to talk turkey." She looked to me in sympathy. "Face it, sweetie, it's not the same world it was when we got married. Nothing's sacred anymore."

"Well, marriage should be," I countered.

Not that I had gone to my own marriage bed pristine. But Linda was the only one who knew I'd slept with my first love Brad in high school. I didn't want my children to use my mistake to justify their own, so Linda and I both would take that secret to our graves.

"I feel sorry for our kids' generation," Teeny said. "There are no more rules. Even guys our age think of sex as the next step after a handshake and dinner. It's so depressing."

The thought of Wade's taking advantage of my innocent daughter made me queasy. "Please do not mention guys our age and sex," I groaned, "or I might have a nervous breakdown."

"You can't even do that anymore," Diane fussed. "They stopped calling it a nervous breakdown years ago. Now it's a psychological break, which sounds more like, 'Oh, take fifteen minutes, a 7 Up, and a quick shock treatment.'"

Total meltdown reduced to a mental coffee break. I almost had to laugh at that one.

Teeny shook her head. "Heaven only knows what things will be like for our granddaughters."

Life is change, my granny used to say, *but that doesn't mean we have to like it. We just have to live with it.*

"So, Callie's human," Pru consoled. "Hardly a news flash. Why should she be different from the rest of the world?" She scanned the room. "Any perfect people at this meeting?" She zeroed in on me with a wry smile. "Last time I looked, the only perfect person was Jesus."

"Point taken," I admitted. I'd always been so proud of Callie. Maybe too proud.

Pride goeth before destruction and a haughty spirit before a fall.

"So," Teeny reasoned, "Callie's still the girl she's always been. This doesn't change that. Bottom line, she's great, and she loves you, and you love her. Y'all will get through this."

"I don't care about myself," I protested, but halted at a skeptical glance from Diane. "Okay, well, maybe I do care about myself a little. This is going to be *so* embarrassing. But Callie has no idea what she's getting into. She's twenty-seven and a ball of fire. Wade's almost sixty, and there's no telling when he might take that one next drink."

"Her life would definitely be simpler if he wasn't an alcoholic," Pru agreed, "but nobody comes with guarantees."

She had a point, but as a mother I wanted Callie to find someone without that stigma.

"Drinking aside," I went on, "Callie has no concept of what life at sixty looks like. It's Sunday afternoons in bed with the *New York Times* crossword puzzle and the football game on the TV. It's fighting your weight, and doctor's appointments, and Rogaine and BenGay. It's turning in at ten and reading till you both fall asleep. Callie's always been so active. How long before she's bored stiff with that?" I bristled further. "Not to mention all the baggage Wade has."

Teeny patted my arm. "Oh, sweetie, everybody has baggage."

"Yeah?" I said. They only knew the half of it. "Well, Wade has a whole warehouse full."

"What do we really know about this guy, anyway?" Diane asked. "I mean, really?"

Teeny glared at her. "Diane, this isn't helping."

Linda shook her head in disbelief. "Wade freakin' Bowman. Of all the people in the world, why *him*?" she asked rhetorically.

"How did this happen?" Diane asked. "I mean, I know Callie has been helping Wade out at the flower shop, off and on, since she was just a kid, but that was a father-daughter kind of thing. Wasn't it?"

"I sure thought so," I said, "or I never would have let her do it."

"How did they get from there to here?" Linda demanded.

"The same way Woody Allen did with Soon-Yi. Older man, trusting younger woman," I complained. "Callie did some arranging for him last September. She said they hit it off right away and started . . ."—I couldn't bring myself to say *dating*—"seeing each other."

"September?" Diane pounced on that. "So they've been hiding it from you, and no wonder why. Wade's old enough to be her father."

"Every girl goes through the older-man thing," Pru said. "Maybe she'll just get him out of her system."

It was too ironic. As parents, we'd stressed marriage as the honorable objective for any serious relationship, and now that had come back to bite us. "I've begged her to wait, get to know him better, have a proper courtship, but she won't hear of it. Says they have little enough time left together, as it is, because of his age. So she decided to play house." (My Episcopal grandmother's polite euphemism for *shacking up*.)

I could almost see a lightbulb go off over Pru's head. "Ohmygosh!" she blurted out. "You're gonna be Wild Man Wade's *mother-in-law!*"

I stared at her. "Thank you so much for pointing that out." My words bounced back at me from the pale green faux-marble stalls.

"Surely John knows what Wade's really like," Teeny offered.

I repeated the unsatisfactory whole of my husband's answer to that very question. "He said Wade's a straight-up guy now. That was it."

Diane shrugged. "He ought to know. Wade's been his best friend since college."

"Man friends," I qualified. "Neither one of them ever talks about important stuff, just sports or business. You know guys."

Pru frowned. "She's right."

"I don't know what to do," I confessed. "This is my only daughter. Do I just let her make what I'm convinced is a horrible mistake, or do I try to stop it? I've already warned her that couples who live together before marriage have a higher divorce rate, but she said that didn't apply to them, because they weren't sleeping together." I shook my head. "Should I go against everything I believe and tell her just to have a fling? I'd totally blow my credibility."

"I hate to say it," Diane said, "but living together first makes sense to me."

"One more crack like that," I warned her, "and you're off the case." How can a mother reason with a child who won't be reasonable? "She said she knew what she was doing, and everything would be fine."

Teeny's mouth went flat. "Just what I told Mama when she begged me not to marry Reid."

I stopped short. "I thought your parents were thrilled that you married Reid."

She shook her head. "They were terrified. They knew what a train wreck Big Reid was, and the acorn rarely falls far from the tree. But I was in love, just like Callie. I didn't listen, any more than she will."

Diane's expression went sly. "We can find out what kind of a man Wade really is." She turned to the others. "Y'all helped me get the goods on Harold. We could take turns trailing Wade for a while. See what he's up to."

I shook my head. "If he catches us, we're dead meat, especially me." But the idea had merit. I turned to Teeny. "Maybe you could have somebody check him out? Somebody discreet. I'd be so grateful."

Teeny clearly wasn't keen on the idea. "Only if you really want me to," she said. "But if Callie finds out, she'll be furious with both of us, and I can't say I'd blame her."

Pru nodded in agreement. "How do you think John would feel if he finds out you had his best friend investigated?"

"He wouldn't like it," I admitted. "John doesn't have an underhanded bone in his body, and he takes people at face value"— qualities I adored in him under most circumstances—"but if we use pros, there's no reason for anybody to find out. Or connect it to me."

Linda was skeptical. "And you're sittin' there telling me that you could keep something like that from John? I'll believe that when I see it."

I shifted uncomfortably. "There's a first time for everything."

"You might want to reconsider an investigation," Linda pressed. "Think it over for a while." After a pregnant pause, she finished with, "We had Osama investigated, and it backfired."

That was news to me! We all regarded her in surprise.

"When?" Diane challenged.

"When we found out Abby was living with him." Linda stepped away from guarding the bathroom door to look in the mirror and adjust her red knit cap. "I mean, we had to find out something about the man. Turns out he'd been booked for all sorts of minor offenses and convicted of two misdemeanors for pot. Plus, his student visa had expired, and marrying an American would keep him from being sent back to Iran. When we showed Abby what we'd found, she got furious with us and defended him. It only drove them closer."

"You never told us," I said.

She scowled. "I was too embarrassed."

Yet she'd shared it now, to help me.

Linda waggled my cheek the way I'd seen her *bubbie* waggle hers so many years ago. "At least Wade's not a nonpracticing Moslem Rastafarian tattoo artist without a square inch of unmolested skin."

The extent of tattooing was an exaggeration—not by much—but the rest was an accurate description of Abby's true love, who'd become Osama-damned-son-in-law (SIL) under a tie-dyed *chuppah* at their impromptu wedding last November at the pavilion on Lake Clara in Piedmont Park.

"I'm not pulling rank here," Linda said with the first hint of humor she'd shown about it since the bizarre nuptials, "but you've gotta admit, Wade looks like the second coming compared to Osama." (Though she and Brooks were active members of the Temple, Linda had picked up plenty of Christian idioms from us over the years.)

"Do not mention the word *coming* in the same breath as my future son-in-law," I warned in my own attempt to lighten up.

Teeny blinked, missing the point, but a bubbly giggle escaped Pru.

Trying to cheer me up, Linda recounted yet again her own nuptial nightmare as mother of the bride: "And Callie's wedding will be the soul of propriety compared to Abby's weird ceremony with a rabbi on one side and a six-foot-tall floral portrait of Haile Selassie on the other"—expertly rendered by none other than my future son-in-law—"not to mention the huge cloud of ganja weed from their weird friends. At least Callie's wedding guests won't end up stoned by secondhand smoke."

"I confess." Diane raised the Girl Scout salute. "I inhaled."

"I was sure we were all going to get busted," Teeny said as she always did whenever we talked about Abby's wedding. "Thank goodness it was raining, so there weren't any other people in the park."

At least I wouldn't have to worry about the Drug Enforcement Agency descending on Callie's nuptials. "Okay," I begrudged. "So it could be worse. Lots worse."

Linda nodded. "I'll say. And you won't have to worry about tiptoeing around the groom's family," she said, referring to the fact that Wade's parents were deceased. "Callie's lucky the Bowmans are long gone. Wade's mama was a real piece of work."

But parents aren't the only relatives of the groom. "Oh, yeah?" I retorted. "How do you think Wade's *kids* are going to feel about this?"

The others winced.

Just because Wade's kids and ours had grown up together didn't mean they would accept Callie as a stepmother. And it didn't take a lick of imagination to know what Wade's ex, Madelyn, would have to say about all this. My ears were already burning.

"Callie can handle Wade's kids," Teeny said with confidence. She motioned me toward the door. "Come on. Let's go back upstairs. I'm starving."

Linda pulled me by the elbow after her. "I wish *my* mother-in-law would die and leave us alone," she told me, "but like you always say about mean people, 'The good Lord wouldn't have her, and the devil's gettin' too much use out of her to take her.' "

Once we got back to our table, Maria stood waiting with fresh drinks and more hot lemonade. "Your plates will be right out."

Diane settled into her place. "I know what would be fun: We ought to get up a list of the twelve most terrible mother-in-law transgressions."

"Please, not now," I implored, already teetering on the edge of depression. "Oh, y'all. I'm about to become you-know-who's *mother-in-law!*" My Drama Queen conjured the strains of Ray Stevens's "I'm My Own Grandpaw." "I deserve a good sulk."

"Sulk away, honey," Diane said. "But mark my words, you are gonna come through this just fine, because we're gonna help you."

"Your mouth to God's ear." I looked to Teeny. "You'll have you-know-who checked out?"

She nodded despite her obvious reservations. "Consider it done."

"And if he comes up dirty?" Diane asked me.

"We'll cross that bridge when we come to it." Part of me was hoping Wade was truly the straight-up guy John thought he was. Regardless of my reservations about this May-December marriage, Callie loved the man, and I had no desire to see my daughter's heart broken.

But a broken heart isn't the worst thing that can happen to a woman. Blinded to my high school heartthrob's selfishness by raging hormones, I'd been besotted with Brad and devastated when he'd disappeared. Now, looking back, I was so grateful I hadn't married him. It would have been a disaster.

I turned to Teeny. "If your parents had had Reid investigated, and you'd known he used drugs and prostitutes, would you still have married him?"

Her eyes lost focus as she contemplated the question with a distant smile. "Probably. I knew Reid was no saint, but I truly believed my love could make things right." She focused on me. "There are no guarantees, not with anybody. Even under the best of circumstances, marriage is a gamble."

"Ain't *that* the truth," Pru said emphatically.

I frowned and took a blueberry mini muffin. "I just want to improve the odds for Callie."

Diane shook her head. "Aw, sweetie, don't we all? But last time I looked, none of us had a crystal ball."

Teeny sighed. "When it comes to marriage, we only have a mirror, for how it was for us."

"And what do you see in your mirror?" I asked.

Teeny smiled without regret. "The happiest day of my life. Reid and I really were happy at first, before the boys came. If I hadn't married him, I wouldn't have my boys. Or my precious granddaughters. Even if I'd known how sick Reid was, I wouldn't change it."

I moaned, head in hands. "I don't know what I should do."

Diane gave my shoulders a side hug, lifting me up. "Sit up and eat your chicken salad, sweetie," she said gently. "We'll worry about the rest later."

My daughter had moved in with Wild Man Wade from ATO. I was worried *now*.

Just then, a tiny wasp of a woman with a big bust line charged in wearing a black, belted Chanel suit with a wide black hat, giant sunglasses, an open-collared white silk blouse all but obscured by oodles of pearls, and black tights and stiletto heels. She took one look at us, pointed a long red fingernail our way, let out a cackle, then said in a thick New York accent that carried over the chatter, "Ohmygod! You look like clowns!"

Which was a case of the pot calling the kettle black if ever there was one, considering the fact that she looked like Natasha from *Rocky and Bullwinkle*.

She made a beeline for us.

"Oh hell," Linda groaned out. "How did she *get* here?"

Rachel. It had to be. She might have been pretty behind those glasses, but for her sour expression.

She stormed up to our table. "Jesus, Linda," she blared, causing every Christian within earshot to bristle. "How do people evah get anywhere in this town? I had to call three cab companies before I found one that took plastic, then they didn't come for an hour. One hour. And the dolt of a driver didn't even know where the Goose House Restaurant was. What an idiot. I had to tell him you were all wearing red hats before he brought me here. Jesus H. Christ!"

"Rachel," Linda growled out, jerking her cousin down into the empty chair beside her. "I've told you a dozen times, you cannot talk like that here. It offends people."

Rachel turned toward her, almost knocking Linda's knitted red hat off with the hard edge of her own. "Oh, get a life," she retorted loudly from behind her glasses as she straightened her jacket. "They're probably calling us kikes behind our backs right this minute."

Conversations all around us halted in outrage.

Mortified, Linda bit out, "Rachel, you have just insulted everyone in this room. Do not say another word."

Diane glared at Rachel as if the woman were a giant wood roach, but out of respect for Linda didn't square off with her.

But Teeny's reaction was one of concern. "What a shame, Rachel," she said with quiet intensity.

Rachel rounded on her. "What's a shame?"

"First impressions are so important, yet I don't think you realize how you've just embarrassed Linda, or the barrier you've put between yourself and all these other people, including us," she said in her gentle tone. "Why don't we just start over, with no name-calling or loud remarks that offend?"

The rest of us savored hearing Rachel get hers with a velvet glove.

"I know you're going through a terrible ordeal," Teeny continued quietly, "and this is a very trying time for you. But don't worry. We're glad you're here. We'll be happy to educate you in all the local customs, including things that get in the way of making friends."

Clearly unsure whether she'd just been criticized or complimented, Rachel frowned and cocked back her chin, but remained silent, so Teeny went on. "Atlanta and New York are very different places, but I'm sure you'll like it here, once you learn what does and doesn't work."

"Great," Rachel said. "I think." She took off her sunglasses, revealing the biggest, most thickly lashed deep-violet eyes I'd ever seen. The *only* deep-violet eyes I'd ever seen, and the dark lashes looked real. Suddenly the caricature of a woman turned into a slim Liz Taylor at her prime, times ten. The effect was mesmerizing.

All of us but Linda stared at her in awe.

"Are those color contacts?" I blurted out before putting my brain in gear.

"Absolutely not." A cold expression dimmed Rachel's beauty. "They're real—the only thing I got from my mother that my rat of a husband couldn't steal, may he burn in hell. Are those boobs real?" she shot back at me. "And how about those nice, straight teeth? Caps? Veneers?"

Linda stood. "Y'all, I'm so sorry for all this." She took firm hold of Rachel's elbow. "Come on," she snapped, drawing Rachel to her tiny feet with surprising force. "We're leaving before you offend anybody else."

"But I just got here," Rachel protested, "and your friend said she was glad I came."

"And I say we're leaving," Linda responded with deadly determination. "Don't forget your purse. And give me back my cell phone. We'll buy you a prepaid one on the way home. I'll need my American Express to pay for it, so you can give that back, too."

Yea, Linda!

She shot us a grim look of apology. "I promise, this will not happen again."

Which only sent Rachel into a huff of digging herself in deeper by trying to justify what she'd said, as Linda urged her forcibly toward the door, a buzz of critical asides in her wake.

"It better not happen again," I told the others in my official Red

Hat Club capacity as Stater of the Obvious. "Another humiliating spectacle like that, and we'll get ourselves kicked out, permanently."

Only when Rachel and Linda were out of sight did Diane venture, "Man. Poor Linda. What a horrid woman."

"Horrid, but not hopeless," Teeny qualified. "She clearly doesn't know better, but I'm sure she can learn. I taught my hard-headed boys to behave politely. It takes patience and positive reinforcement, but if they learned, anybody can."

"That was rich, what you said to Rachel," Pru complimented. "You are so smooth."

"Thanks," Teeny said. "But the bad habits of a lifetime take time and a willingness on her part to change. So the sooner we show Rachel it's to her advantage to be more considerate, the better for everybody."

"What are you suggesting?" Diane asked, skeptical.

"Criticism will only make her worse," Teeny explained. "She's got to be frantic and really lonely and really angry about what's happened. If we can befriend her and teach her how to make and keep friends, it will help her and Linda, both."

True to form, Diane came up with a plan. "How about each of us take her out once a week, so Linda can have a break, and we can work on civilizing her? Kill her with kindness. What do y'all think?"

"Great idea," Teeny said. "Pru, you can take her to lunch on the expense account."

Pru grinned. "Lady lunch, on the clock? I am *so* up for that."

"I can do something with her one night a week," Diane suggested. "Give Brooks some time alone with Linda."

"I'll find out what her favorite foods are and have her over for dinner," I volunteered.

With that, Maria arrived with our checks.

I stuck out my hand. "I'll pay Linda's. She had to leave." It was the least I could do, bless her heart.

Waiting for the valet outside, I told Diane, "Good idea, getting Rachel out of Linda's hair every week. Babysitting will help take my mind off Callie."

Teeny gave me a hug. "It's gonna be okay, I promise."

"Rachel or Callie?"

She smiled. "Both."

I wished I could share her confidence, but I couldn't—about either one.

And now, I had the investigation to keep from John.

This time, I would keep my mouth shut. Unless the detectives turned up something dire. Judging from the way things had been going, they would.

Wild Man Wade of ATO

"Bad Moon Rising"
— CREEDENCE CLEARWATER REVIVAL

The past. Friday, October 3, 1969. 6:55 P.M. College Circle, Atlanta.

ANE!" I HOLLERED through the locked bathroom door over the sound of "Sugar, Sugar" on my big sister's transistor. "Hurry up. I'm gonna wet myself!" A major peril of living in a two-bathroom house with seven other people. "You shouldn't even be up here!" Jane's bedroom was downstairs. "Go downstairs, where you belong."

"Can't. Taken," she said with her usual aplomb, her calm voice and the music echoing off the white and black tiles. "Just a few more eyelashes, and I'm done."

Eyelashes! Major violation of the Peyton house bathroom code. Cosmetics did not grant exclusivity from your sisters in the facilities.

I grabbed a letter opener from my desk and popped open the lock, then hurried past my oldest sister, who was wearing white lace bikinis and a French bra as she leaned toward the medicine cabinet mirror with acute concentration.

"You cannot lock the door for eyelashes," I scolded, barely getting my underpants, pantyhose, and girdle down in time to relieve my distended bladder. "It's seven o'clock. The last thing I want my date to do is look up the stairs through the front door and see me coming out of the bathroom. How embarrassing."

Jane remained unruffled, as always. "Relax. Guys are never punctual."

"John will be. He's a scientist. Scientists are very precise. And reliable. And we're doubling, so if he's late, we'll be late picking up Linda." I hoped John's best friend was as nice as he was.

I couldn't wait for Linda to meet John. I'd told her all about him, but I'd held out about the warm little glow I'd felt when he'd asked me out for coffee after the night class he was teaching at State. I'd been admiring him for a week while he explained basic physics in his laid-back, logical way, never dreaming he might be attracted to me. I mean, he was a professor, for heaven's sake. But then again, he barely looked five years older than the students he taught.

Who knew he was some kind of genius who'd graduated from MIT at nineteen and become the youngest full professor in the history of Georgia Tech? All I knew was, he was really cute and sort of sexy in a wonderfully lanky, self-conscious way.

The attraction was nothing so earth-shaking as what I'd felt for my bad-boy high school lover Brad, but John was the first guy who'd even put a hum into my chimes since. Better yet, he was completely stable and logical. I just knew Linda would like him, which was important, because my gang of best friends could be merciless about boyfriends—for our own protection, of course.

I wondered what it would feel like to kiss him.

I flushed the potty, then stood to carefully arrange my Eve's Leaves bikini pants and smooth the shirttail to my blouse underneath my suntan pantyhose so there'd be no visible lines. Then I pulled up my mandatory gut-sucker girdle from Lerner's that minimized my boxy hips and slight tummy pooch.

It was only years later that I realized Mama's mandatory girdle rule was her polite, repressed effort to discourage her daughters from impetuous sex. Not that it worked for me with Brad, but the rest of my sisters were less prone to throw caution to the wind than I.

I washed my hands as Jane inspected the last clump of lashes with a satisfied sigh. "There. What do you think?" She blinked at me.

Her hazel eyes looked as huge as Twiggy's, which was great, because they offset the fact that her chin wasn't quite as strong as it should be. I nodded. "Wonderful. But next time, do it in your bedroom."

"How can a person get any time alone in this house?" She slung on her short kimono robe, then reached for the doorknob.

"Wait!" I warned her. "What if John's down there now?"

If he saw my big sister coming out of the bathroom in her scant kimono, our relationship would be doomed before it started.

Jane patted my shoulder. "Do you actually think he's standing at the door, not ringing the bell, and peering up the stairs for a glimpse of the bathroom? He doesn't even know this is a bathroom."

"He will if he sees you," I shot back.

The doorbell rang, sending a mild shock of adrenaline through me. "See!" I hissed. "Now we'll have to wait here till he's in the living room."

I cracked the door and listened to hear who would let John in. Please, not one of my brothers. No matter how many times Daddy lectured them, they were invariably crude to our dates, especially first-timers. Then I heard the familiar creak of my father's steps on the wooden floor of the front hall. The door opened, and Daddy said, "Yes?"

"Hi. I'm John Baker," John said in a firm, man-to-man tone that carried easily up the stairwell. "I'm here for Georgia. May I come in?"

A+ on the greeting! Yes!

"Come right on in, young man," Daddy's baritone said with obvious approval. "I'm Georgia's father. Tech, class of '48. Take a seat. I'll tell her you're here."

It stung, knowing John was seeing our shabby, worn-out furniture ˙ ̣d stained, late-forties knotty pine paneling. But that was how we lived. No sense trying to hide it.

I cracked the door wider and saw Daddy stick his head into the stairwell. "Georgia, your young man is here," he said genially, then his smile turned to a glare of disapproval when Jane hurried into my room with her robe slung immodestly low.

"Tell him I'll be right down," I said, then waited, poised to eavesdrop. Daddy always liked some time alone to interview our new dates.

Jane stretched out on my bed and pretended to read my copy of *Seventeen*, but she was listening, too.

I whispered to her, "Put that back when you're finished with it."

She smirked at me.

"So," Daddy said when he plopped down with a squeak of protest from his red vinyl chair. "How did you and Georgia meet?"

John's answer was respectful, but direct. "She's one of my students in a basic physics night class I'm teaching at State."

"I thought she said you taught at Tech," Daddy said with deceptive mildness. I'd neglected to mention that John was my teacher, for fear Daddy might object. But it was out now.

"I do teach at Tech," John said, anything but defensive. "But I pick up a little extra income teaching night school at State when they need somebody. I've been so focused on work till now, I've never had much of a social life."

"Nothing wrong with that," Daddy said. "First things first, I always say."

I heard Mama come in from the kitchen, and the sofa groan as John rose.

"Hi," Mama said. "You must be John. I'm Georgia's mother. May I get you something to drink?"

It was a test. If he asked for anything alcoholic, he'd lose major points.

"No thank you, ma'am. I'm just fine. But thank you."

Daddy's voice hardened. "So, they let you date your students at State?"

"Walter!" Mama scolded gently. "Where are your manners?"

To his credit, John wasn't intimidated. "It's okay, ma'am. I'd rather hear what Mr. Peyton really thinks, straight out." He addressed my father. "Dating students is not forbidden, but it's not encouraged, either." Regardless of the Age of Aquarius and free love, this was Atlanta, after all, where we maintained the illusion, at least, of decorum. "Of course, we don't have many women at Tech yet," John clarified, "so the administration is still formulating policies for a co-ed environment."

Daddy let out a skeptical, "Mmmmmm."

John cut to the chase. "I assure you, sir, I will treat your daughter with the utmost respect and restraint. And I also assure you, Georgia won't get any special grade concessions from me just because we're seeing each other."

Caught off-guard, Daddy barked a laugh and relaxed. "Well, that's a shame, 'cause she's gonna need all the help she can get. Georgia never has been much of a science or numbers person. Makes hundreds in all her liberal arts courses, but those others . . ."

I cringed. *Please don't start with the anecdotes about my mathematical deficiencies!*

But John took it in good humor. "She's clearly intelligent. Maybe I could help her out with a few key concepts. I'm sure she'll do fine."

Before I could digest that, Daddy said in his hunker-down voice, "Listen, have I got a story for you . . ." Oh, no! "Last year when she took her checkbook and statements up to the bank to try to get them to help her straighten it out—"

Embarrassing stories were an inescapable part of a big family, but I didn't like being laughed at.

I raced downstairs, hoping the clatter would drown Daddy out, but I didn't make it to the living room till he was finishing with the punch line.

"So the bank guy told her to let the account die, then gave her two boxes of Sophie Mae Peanut Brittle if she'd promise to take her business to their competition."

John had just started to chuckle when I walked in with a frosty look on my face. He stood abruptly, a brief flash of embarrassment replaced by a look of raw appreciation. "Wow. You look . . . great. Really great."

I swear, he said it on the inhale, erasing my annoyance at Daddy.

"You look pretty good yourself." Oh lord, did I say that out loud?

But it was true. Nobody had ever picked me up for a regular date in a sport coat and tie. John's navy blazer and trim gray slacks showed off his tall, runner's physique, and his white button-down shirt with a subdued tie were classic and elegant without being pretentious. He even had on grown-up oxblood tasseled slip-ons . . . expensive ones . . . and socks. (College boys weren't wearing socks those days.) He looked very much the man, not the college kid.

Why hadn't I remembered him as this good-looking? Maybe it was the blazer. I've always been a sucker for a good-looking guy in a navy blazer.

Daddy took it all in, arching a wary eyebrow. When John stepped forward and offered his arm, Daddy clamped a hand on his shoulder. "This is one of my most precious, young man, even if she can't balance a checkbook, so I'm counting on you to make good on being a gentleman."

John's expression sobered as he met father's gaze. "Georgia's too fine a lady for me to do anything else, sir."

A+++ on the rebound!

Daddy clapped John on the back with a little more vigor than was necessary. "I like you, Jim."

John coughed. "It's John, sir."

"Ignore him," I told John. "Daddy does that to all our first dates."

Daddy just grinned and pushed open our patched screen door ahead of us. "Don't be a stranger."

"Thanks." John led me outside as if it were the most natural thing on earth to be subjected to an inquisition on a sofa with flesh-seeking coils. "I like your dad," he said as we walked up the driveway toward his slightly dented Plymouth. "Things wouldn't be so crazy in this world if there were more fathers like that."

He sounded sincere.

I took a chance and asked, "What's your father like?"

An irresistible smile lit his face. "A lot like yours."

"Do you have any brothers or sisters?"

"Nope." He cocked his head. "Engine and caboose, that's me: the only child of two only-child parents and four only-child grandparents. Haven't got a cousin to my name."

"I don't either, but I've got three sisters and two brothers."

He pulled a little face. "Wow."

John led me to the car's passenger door, but until I got there, I was too preoccupied with him to notice that there was a guy sprawled, slack-jawed, in the back seat, broadcasting whiskey fumes with every breath. When I turned to get in and saw him, I turned right back around and grabbed John's lapels. "Tell me this is not the best friend you had me get a date with Linda for."

For the first time, he withdrew into a closed expression. "I know it looks bad, but he swore he wouldn't drink. I didn't know he'd had a few till I picked him up."

"Had a few?" I growled out through a rigid grin worthy of the Joker, lest anybody see my outrage. "He's smashed. You bring a drunken sot to go out with my best friend? What happened to all that talk about respect?"

John colored. "He got in the car and refused to get out, and I didn't want to be late picking you up." John was so earnest, I decided to give him the benefit of the doubt. And I really, really wanted to go out with him.

"What's his name?" I asked, still smiling for public consumption.

"Wade Bowman."

"Any chance we could sober him up?"

"Definite chance. I swear, sometimes he just needs to hang his head out of the window for a few miles, then he's charming as hell."

Not an image I wanted to be any part of, but I didn't have a better idea.

I leaned into the open back window. Maybe he wasn't passed out. Maybe he was just napping. Dodging distillery breath, I hollered, "Wade!"

He popped bolt upright, took one look at me, gasped as if he were seeing the throne of God, and rasped out, "Nancy! You're alive!"

The next thing I knew, he'd dragged me halfway through the window and planted a huge, horribly wet and tonguey French kiss on me, muttering "Nancy" over and over again beneath it. Legs flailing, I was mortified to know my girdle was on display for the whole neighborhood as I tried to escape.

John did the only thing he could: He grabbed my waist and tried to pull me back out. "Wade! It's not Nancy! Let her go!"

Oh, lord, please don't let anybody be looking. But even as I prayed, I knew half the neighborhood had been summoned to their front windows by an extensive network of kid-spies who never missed a thing on our street.

The first chance I got, I filled my lungs with air, then pinched my assailant's nose shut and blew as hard as I could into his mouth, puffing out his cheeks like a toad and shocking him enough to let me go. Which sent me tumbling backwards atop John onto the pavement.

"Agh! Yacch!" I rubbed the backs of my hands across my plundered tongue as my date helped me up. "Gross! Gross! Gross!"

"God, Georgia, I am *so* sorry!" John glared bloody murder at Wade when we gained our feet. "He had this girlfriend, Nancy, before they sent him to Vietnam, and when he got back, he was so messed up that she—"

He didn't get to finish. Wade exploded out of the car, loaded for bear. "You son-of-a-bitch!" He took a wild swing at John and missed, almost hitting me. "You didn't even warn me! She looks just like her, and you didn't have the common decency to warn me." Even in a drunken rage, his accent was old-money Atlanta.

John shoved me out of harm's way. "Go back inside where it's safe. I'll come talk to you after I've gotten him settled down."

When I saw the curious faces peering at us from my neighbors' windows, I reacted on instinct and grabbed Wade by the front of his designer golf shirt. "Stop it!" I ordered, the way I did when breaking up my two lunk-headed brothers' fights. I clamped on to John's arm. "Get into the car, both of you. Now!"

I shoved Wade into the open rear-passenger door, then slammed it shut, heedless of appendages. Jerking open my door, I turned to John, livid. "I will not be further humiliated by a common street brawl in front of my house," I said through my fake smile. "Get us out of here before my daddy gets wind of this." I glared at John, "Or you, mister, will be history with this woman."

Nodding, he closed my door and hurried around to the driver's seat. To his credit, he didn't attract further notice with a screeching takeoff, but made smartly for Northside Drive.

After a few moments of sullen silence, both of them started yelling at each other at once. I opened my door and threatened, "Do I have to jump out? Is that what it's going to take for you two to stop acting like idiots?"

They lapsed into tense silence. John's neck and face was mottled with red, while Wade's had gone the even hue of a tomato.

"Now that I can be heard," I clipped out to John, "we have to talk about this double date. No way am I letting that guy within a mile of Linda."

"I swear," Wade protested, "I'll make this up to you. I'll be a perfect gentleman."

"Perfect gentlemen do not arrive drunk to pick up their dates," I snapped. "Or manhandle innocent strangers!"

"John should have warned me that you look so much like Nancy," Wade accused.

"She doesn't look like Nancy," John protested, glaring at Wade in the rearview mirror. "Nancy was brunette."

So was I, but I'd been putting peroxide into my shampoo since I was eleven. Blondes really do have more fun.

"It's her eyes," Wade said intensely, pinning me with a look that could have pierced my skull. "She has her eyes. And her chin. And her cheekbones. And her voice."

"No she does not," John countered. "You just think so because you're drunk."

"Please do not talk about me as if I am not present," I clipped out as we neared the intersection of Northside Parkway and Paces Ferry. "Pull over to the pay phone in that gas station. I've got to call Linda."

"Do you see what you've done?" John said to Wade in the rearview mirror. "You knew how important this was to me, and you ruined it." We halted with a lurch.

I stomped to the phone, then put in a dime and dialed Linda's number.

Her mother answered. "Helloooo."

"Mrs. Bondurandt, this is Georgia. May I please speak to Linda?"

"I'll get her," Mrs. Bondurandt said, then cupped her hand around the receiver and dropped her voice. "I so appreciate your getting her this date. All she does is sit around home and mope when she's not with the rest of you girls, but now she's in there singing like a lark, so happy to be going out with a nice Jewish boy. I can't thank you enough, sweetie."

Gulp.

"I hope you got her a smart one," Mrs. Bondurandt added before putting down the phone with a bonk. "Linda-lapinda," she called down the hallway, "it's Georgia." Even we had two phones, but the Bondurandts only had one in the hallway, which precluded private conversations, but eliminated the possibility for parental eavesdropping on an extension.

I heard brisk steps, then Linda said, "Hi. Please tell me nothing's gone wrong. I've had my hair and nails done, and I bought a new dress."

Much as I wanted to spare her, my best friends and I had long held a common pact that we would never lie to each other, even when it hurt. It was one of our sacred rules of friendship. "Honey, much as I hate to tell you this, there is definitely a problem. My date's fine, but yours was passed out in the back seat when we got to the car, and when I leaned into the back window to wake him up, he jerked me inside and put such a mash on me, calling me 'Nancy,' that I barely escaped with my life. He's so drunk, he thought I was an old girlfriend."

After an assessing pause, Linda asked, "Is he good-looking?"

"What?" I peered at the grimy receiver, then returned it to my ear. "I tell you this, and all you can say is, is he good-looking?"

"Well, is he?" She was serious!

I glanced back to the car, where both of the guys scrutinized my every motion between barbs at each other. "Extremely, in a dissolute kind of way."

"Is he nicely dressed?"

For the first time, I paid attention. "Black polo shirt, cotton tennis sweater over his shoulders, and dark gold slacks. Expensive." I tucked my chin. "What difference does that make? He's drunk."

I heard humor in Linda's voice as she cupped the receiver so her mother couldn't overhear. "He couldn't be any worse than my uncle Manny at every family wedding I've been to since I turned sixteen. I know how to handle a drunk. This one's eligible and gorgeous. Bring him on."

"Linda, have you lost your mind?"

"Nope," she said firmly. "But if he's too smashed to get by Mama, have John pretend he's my date. And remember to tell him that he's supposed to be Jewish."

At least he wouldn't have to face her father. Except for High Holy Days, Linda's daddy was hardly ever home. We all accepted without question Mrs. Bondurandt's explanation that he was traveling on business.

I had a bad feeling about this Wade and Linda thing. "I don't think this is a good idea."

"Was Brad a good idea?" Linda shot back, going for the jugular. "In case you've forgotten, we all warned you about him, but we let you make your own choices."

Touché.

"Don't you want to go out with John?" she challenged.

The question was rhetorical. I'd already told her how much I was looking forward to this. "You know I do."

"Well, I want to go out, too. And that's that. MYOB." Another one of our friendship codes: When one of us tells another to mind her own business, we are obliged to do so.

"Well, okay," I said against my better judgment, "but we are *not* leaving you alone with him, not for one second."

"Agreed," she said. "Where are y'all?"

"At the Gulf Station at Paces Ferry."

"Good. See y'all in a minute. I'll be waiting at the door."

I hung up and got back into the car. Once there, I turned to point the Finger of Judgment at Wade. "Do you solemnly swear to act like a gentleman, not have anything more to drink, and to treat my friend Linda like the lady she is?"

Already looking a lot more sober, Wade flashed me a 9,000-volt grin and raised the Boy Scout salute. "I do so solemnly swear," he said without a single slur.

I rolled my eyes at John. "Okay, then. Linda wants to go. Why, I cannot fathom, but she wants to go."

Wade grinned in triumph. I turned back around. "And if anybody asks, you're Jewish. Conservative. You made your bar mitzvah at twelve, and you go to Ahavath Achim," I said just to be safe, since the Bondurandts went to the Temple.

Wade tucked his chin in mock surprise and accused John, "You already told her I was Jewish?"

John looked at me. "He's not Jewish. He's Episcopalian."

"Trust me, the services aren't that different," I said, "but the Jewish ones are in Hebrew."

John glared at Wade in the rearview window. "Mess this up any worse, man, and I'll have to see you behind the Zesto afterwards." That was where the local hoods went to fight.

I couldn't see John's taking his professor self out behind the Dumpsters to get physical with his best friend, but who knew? We'd only known each other for a few weeks.

Fortunately, with the help of half a pack of peppermint Chiclets, a comb through his thick, sun-streaked hair, and a few strategic tucks of his clothing, Wade managed to look quite presentable when he went to the door to collect Linda. Both Mrs. Bondurandt and Linda immediately fell for his considerable charm. As he walked Linda back to the car, her eyes sparkled with happiness.

True to his word, Wade was attentive and charming all the way back down to Tech for the party. He and Linda made the usual blind-date small talk in low tones in the back seat, while John and I sat in awkward silence up front.

As we pulled into a crowded parking area behind a Craftsman bungalow just off Tenth Street, John turned back to his friend. "Ginger ale, bucko. Got it?"

Wade nodded without breaking the rhythm of the story he was telling Linda about Vietnam. Hand clasped over her heart in sympathy, she was eating it up.

What is it about the bad boys? Why are they so irresistible?

But not to me. Not anymore. After losing bad-boy Brad, I hardly had a heart left to care with.

"What are faculty parties like?" I asked John as he helped me out of the car.

"Like any other parties. Some are nice. Some are duds. We're dealing with a lot of brilliant, sometimes socially inept people here."

"This will be a good one," I predicted. "I'll have you to talk to."

We walked inside to a hodgepodge of Einstein and psychedelic posters, beaded doorways, and mismatched furniture full of people who looked like college kids, just a little older and heavier. And every single one of them checked me out when I came in beside John. Maintaining my cool, I picked up snatches of Bigbrain shop talk where the guys were clustered, while their dates or wives visited with each other about more mundane topics.

John led me to the ancient kitchen, where the linoleum counter served as a bar beside a sink full of iced-down beer. "What can I get you?"

"A tall tonic and lime on the rocks." No booze for me. Not on a first date. I talked too much when I was nervous to start with. Add a little alcohol, and my tongue got loose at both ends. I didn't want to blow this. Despite his drunken letch of a friend, I could already tell that John was a keeper.

"Tall tonic and lime it is," he said rooting around till he found the makings, then nabbing a beer for himself.

"I'd have thought you were a Scotch man," I said as he handed me my drink. "Being a professor and all."

He made a face and shook his head. "That stuff tastes like Mercurochrome." He tipped his beer bottle in my direction. "No, I just usually nurse a beer. Gotta watch what you say at these things. A lot of our research is classified, so it wouldn't do to get loose-lipped."

Sensible, with the Cold War raging.

"Then let's talk about nonclassified stuff," I said. "Tell me about growing up."

"Okay," he said, "as long as you do, too."

So we talked of our childhoods. His had been white-collar, solid middle class, in contrast to mine, which had been middle class only in concept as my parents struggled to provide for the six of us kids. Maybe it was the fact that John seemed truly interested in my life that made me feel comfortable to confide the frustrations of living in a tiny house with five siblings, where you always had to move something to sit down, and every penny was stretched till it screamed. "At the neighborhood Christmas party one year," I confided, "Daddy's gift was a coat of arms with the Latin motto: *Abundance made me poor.*"

"I think you're lucky to have such a big family," John said. "No, seriously. When you're an only child, there's nobody else to take the blame."

We shared a laugh that built a bridge between our differences.

After about an hour, I glanced over and saw Linda and Wade dancing, slow and seductive, to "Hurt So Bad" by the Lettermen. It worried me. "I think Linda has definitely taken to Wade. Please tell me he's not going to drop her after tonight."

John's expression clouded. "Wade's . . . complicated." He shot an empathetic look at his friend. "He and Nancy partied a lot, but nothing drastic. They were seriously in love. Then Wade flunked out and got sent to Vietnam. It did terrible things to him. I hardly knew him when he came back. Nancy was desperate to help him, but he just couldn't connect. Then she caught him with a hooker, and that was it. She didn't just dump him; she moved away and didn't give any of us a forwarding address."

Note to self: Warn Linda about the hookers.

John peered into the neck of his beer bottle as he spoke. "Ironically, that was what it took for him to hit bottom. He tapered his drinking down till he was just having a beer a day for a long time. Then, gradually, it started creeping back up to two beers, then three. But this is the first time in more than a year that he's gotten drunk." He cocked an apologetic half-smile my way. "Of all times. I could mop the floor with him, but it wouldn't do any good."

He looked to his friend. "I keep hoping he'll meet someone nice. Someone who can give him a reason to stay sober."

Linda was certainly nice—maybe too nice. I didn't want Wade to take advantage of her.

"Did he ever finish college?" I asked. At our house, that was right up there with the Ten Commandments.

John shook his head. "No. He couldn't focus anymore." He sighed. "I only told you all this so you could know what your friend might be getting into. But Wade's got a good heart. I can't tell you the things he's done for me." His expression lightened. "Including bugging me till I finally mustered up the courage to ask you out. I really owe him."

I looked at the thoughtful, compelling man beside me. "Then I owe him, too." I turned to watch Linda swaying, her petite cheerleader's body shaped to Wade's tall one. "I just hope he doesn't hurt her."

John put his arm around me, a warm, reassuring gesture. "Wade and Linda will have to work that out for themselves. But I can promise you one thing," he said gazing into my eyes. "I would never do anything to hurt you. Ever."

I relaxed against his shoulder, my head fitting perfectly below his chin. "I believe you."

It wasn't the love of a lifetime, but it was good and sure and safe. Just as good and sure as Wade was dangerous.

I hoped Linda would have enough sense to go slow, but I feared she wouldn't. The chemistry between them was undeniable. I remembered the passion I had shared with Brad. Even with the heartache that followed, it had been worth it.

I could hardly blame Linda for making the same mistake I had.

John and I got lost in conversation till Wade—clearly refortified—stood in a chair and started loudly accompanying Creedence Clearwater Revival in "Bad Moon Rising" in a halfway decent voice. Linda just laughed, then pulled him down when the song ended to a smattering of applause.

"Uncle Manny," she mouthed to me. "I can handle this."

Before I could get mad at Wade for breaking his word about the booze, John fixed on me with sobering intensity. "Georgia?" His breathing suspended. "I'd like to see you, if that's okay."

"Sure," I said casually, delighted that he wanted to go out again.

"I mean, a lot," he clarified as gingerly as if he were extending some renegade theory of the cosmos.

"Exclusively?" Not that I wasn't willing, but it seemed awfully quick.

"Any way you want," he conceded, "as long as I'm the one you end up with."

Truly a man, declaring his honorable intentions.

I warmed to him even more. "Exclusive is okay with me," I murmured, wishing he would kiss me, even though nice girls didn't kiss on the first date. Not in Buckhead. But we'd had coffee several times, so maybe that counted.

"But if it doesn't work out," I promised, "I'll tell you straight up."

John's smile held all the confidence of a man used to achieving what he wanted. "It'll work out."

I wasn't so sure, but it would do for the meantime.

When we got to Linda's house, John and I looked the other way while she and Wade made out in the shadows by her front door, then said a lingering good-bye. When Wade got back into the car, he sighed. "Now *that*, ladies and gentlemen, is one hell of a woman." Then he promptly went to sleep. Or passed out. It was hard to tell.

When John walked me to my door, I found myself wishing he wasn't quite as gentlemanly as he was.

I needn't have worried. When I turned my face up to say good night, he kissed me long and slow, gentle at first, then wrapping me in his arms and planting one on me that sent a surprising pang of longing where only warmth had been before.

Then he pulled back abruptly, as if afraid he might have gone too far. "Wow."

Reminded of what it felt like to want someone, I looked up at him and murmured. "Maybe this might work out, after all."

· 4 ·

John

"Hooked on a Feeling"
—B. J. THOMAS

The past. Friday, October 31, 1969. The Varsity, Atlanta.

ROM THE BEGINNING, dating John was like finding a long-lost friend. We laughed at the same things. Both liked comedies and thrillers. Both liked soft rock and classical. Both loved live theater—as long as it wasn't violent or confusing. Both enjoyed cheap dates, like riding up to Lake Lanier for a picnic or climbing Stone Mountain to watch the sunset.

I liked talking, and he liked listening—a huge plus. But when he had something to say, it was always well worth hearing.

John never pushed, but he treated me like someone wonderful and intelligent and worthy of his respect. Being with him felt like being wrapped in a cashmere blanket on a cold night, even if there were only embers instead of flames in my fireplace. We just fit. Not to mention the fact that he helped me understand physics for the first time. His enthusiasm for the subject was almost contagious.

I had no real worries about us. My worries were about Wade, to whom John was as unshakably loyal as I was to Linda, Diane, Teeny, and Pru.

"Order up in Snellville," the Varsity drive-in's dispatcher called from his little control tower behind us. "Flossie Mae, you've got a fan in Sandy Springs." Each drive-in area was named for a local burb, and the legendary Flossie Mae, a grizzled and indomitably cheerful little carhop, had been requested by somebody in the Sandy Springs section.

For as long as I could remember, the Varsity had been *the* place to go in Atlanta. Just across the Interstate Connector from Tech, it provided fresh-made, inexpensive food that hit the spot for native Atlantans and college kids alike. And like most Atlantans, I had acquired my addiction to it as a child—maybe because it was the only place Daddy could afford to take us on the rare occasions when we ate out.

Forget crispy fries. Back then, the fries were peeled and cut behind glass walls, providing entertainment and the assurance of cleanliness, then cooked in good old grease till the long ones would bow to the eater. And the onion rings—also peeled and sliced in sight—were lightly battered on the outside and sweet on the inside. True, the burgers were small, but like everything else there, they had a distinctive taste that was *the* quintessential taste of Tech games and our hometown.

Which was why I had suggested John and I go there before our movie at the Fox. I had a feeling his salary wasn't anything spectacular.

The carhop arrived with our order. "Raise your winda up a little, please." When John obliged, the man hooked the silver tray over the window, then called back the order. "We gotcha fries, 'rangs,' a Special"—a grilled sandwich for John with barbecue and slaw and who knew what-all else in it—"two Glorifieds"—lettuce, tomato, and mayo burgers, for me—"and two Big Oranges. That'll be . . ." He briefly turned his eyes toward the metal canopy. ". . . four seventy-five."

John handed him six. "Thanks. Keep it."

The carhop grinned. "Y'all let me know if you need anything now, hear?"

Thrifty though he was, John always overtipped the carhops, which I admired, since most of them looked at least forty under their jaunty red and white paper hats. How could anybody support themselves— much less a family—running orders at a drive-in?

But since it would have been rude and humiliating ever to ask one straight out about it, I never pursued the matter further, and just enjoyed the food.

After I'd scarfed down sufficient onion rings, fries, and both of my burgers, I felt fortified to broach the subject that was on my mind. "John, I'm really worried about Linda and Wade."

He turned and looked me in the eye, gently stroking back my hairline with a finger. "I know you are. And I know it bothers you that they never want to double. But do you really think there's anything we can do? They're free agents, and Linda's no fool."

"I think she is about Wade," I countered. "She's so . . . dazzled, that she excuses all his faults. Wade is nuts. She's going to be hurt, and I hate that."

"I didn't want Wade to be hurt, either," John said, "but he was, and it was his own doing. If he hadn't flunked out . . ." He shook off the should-have-beens. "Linda knew what she was getting into. All we can do is stand back and wait." His concern hardened to a protective frown. "The rest of you will be there for her when she needs you. Sacred Rule of Friendship Number Five: Mind Your Own Business."

I bristled. John remembered everything he saw like a snapshot, and whatever he heard—including the Seven Sacred Rules of Friendship—was tucked away in that Bigbrain of his along with jillions of images, scientific formulas, and ideas.

"That total recall of yours is gonna get you in trouble," I warned him. "Those rules are mine to invoke, not yours."

His perfect memory could cause some serious problems if this relationship went anywhere, because I had a much more casual arrangement with the truth. Like Mark Twain, I was a firm believer in the truth, and at least ten percent of everything I said was absolutely true. I was rock solid on what really mattered, but prone to embellish the fine points a bit around the edges, especially to make a good story.

I nudged us back to the subject of Wade. "Is there any chance Wade could reform? He seems happy around Linda, and I know she'd do anything to help him. But I'm really afraid that he's an *alcoholic*." I felt disloyal for suggesting that about someone Linda was quite probably *doing it* with. Not to mention that Wade was totally non-Jewish and directionless. "Is there any hope for him?"

John's expression closed. He pondered for a moment, then said, "Wade's demons aren't his fault. He has the same gift of total recall that I do. It's one reason we were drawn together at ATO. But I was the ant and he was the grasshopper, so when he started partying instead of going to class, Uncle Sam put a helmet on that sky-high IQ and sent him to Nam, where his brain got filled with unspeakable images that he didn't possess the capacity to erase. Every night when he closed his eyes after he got back, he relived it all in intricate detail. So he smoked weed and dropped acid and drank till the images faded. And he isolated himself from the people who loved him so he wouldn't 'taint' them."

"Oh, John." It hadn't occurred to me what a curse total recall could be.

I sent up an arrow prayer for Wade.

John laid down his sandwich and stared unseeing through the windshield. "At least he's quit the acid and the pot. Right now, the best I can do for him is be there to pick up the pieces, no matter what, just the way you will for Linda."

Linda had loyally stood by as I squandered myself on Brad, a boy who hadn't even thought enough of me to let me know he was alive after he moved to California and turned on and dropped out. Until I'd challenged her about Wade, Linda had never once even hinted at an "I told you so."

I sighed, losing my own appetite. "Boy, this best-friend stuff can be hard."

"You know it."

Speak of the devil, twenty minutes later we ran into them at the Fox, and all was not well. When we got into the long concession line, I couldn't help noticing that there was some kind of a disturbance near the front. Over the murmur of the crowd, I heard Linda's voice snap, "Take your hands off me." Then, "Wade, you're embarrassing me. Stop."

"Or what?" Wade's sullen voice retorted. "You won't sleep with me anymore?"

A collective gasp went through the G-rated movie crowd. Several men stepped forward in Linda's defense, but John launched himself past them, with me close behind. "I know him," he told the others. "I'll take care of this." We found Wade holding Linda hard against him, stroking her body in a way that should have never seen the light of day.

"Wade, stop this," she pleaded, her voice quivering with fear and shame.

"Let her go," John ordered with quiet fury.

Wade turned in surprise, and in a blink, I snatched Linda free while John got him into a proficient police choke hold, bending Wade's arm up behind his back. "You wish she would sleep with you," John said gallantly as he hustled Wade toward the exit. "Dream on."

Tears streaming down her face, Linda sprinted for the subterranean ladies' room, with me in pursuit. When we reached the musty, deserted parlor, she spun and wailed, "Go. Just go. I can't stand that you saw that. I can't stand your pity. You warned me, and you were right. Now leave me alone." Then she collapsed, sobbing into one of the ancient velvet couches.

I sat beside her and pulled her to my shoulder, saying the same soothing things she'd said to me after Brad had disappeared. "It's okay, sweetie. I don't pity you; I love you. It's gonna be okay. Just let it out."

"He knows I love him," she cried. "He said he loved me. How could he do that, act that way, betray our love in front of all those people like I was some kind of *whore*?" Her sobs deepened. In time, they'd subside, and we'd clean her up, and we'd call Pru or Diane or Teeny to come get us. But for now, I would just be there, holding on to the pieces.

I wondered what John was doing with Wade. Something drastic, I hoped, but nothing that would get *him* in trouble.

And in that moment, I hated Wade Bowman with a passion I had never spent on a fellow human being.

The next morning I was sorting ladies' blouses at Regenstein's downtown store when John's voice surprised me from behind. "You were right. I should have done something."

Easy for him to say . . . after the fact.

I checked to make sure my supervisor wasn't watching, then walked to the end of the counter. "I know he's your friend, but if you try to excuse this, we're through."

John's boyish face aged before me. "I didn't. I don't."

I was skeptical. "What did you do with him?"

John leveled his gaze with my accusing one. "I dragged him to the cop out front and said he'd just assaulted a lady, and if they didn't keep him in the drunk tank long enough to sober up, I'd hold *them* responsible for whatever he did next."

"Good," I said, only partially satisfied. "But what happens when they let him go?"

"This time, it's going to be different." I wouldn't have thought John could look so menacing, but he did. "I called the dean. I'm taking a leave of absence from work and dragging Wade's sorry ass up to a place for alcoholics out in the wilds of Habersham County. And when he's sober, I'm going to stay glued to him up there and take him to AA meetings till something gets through to him." His resolve faltered. "Something has to get through to him." He exhaled heavily, as if he was trying to expel all the frustration and anger at his friend. "If he doesn't straighten up, I'll make a citizen's arrest and testify to what he did to Linda. There are limits, even for a best friend."

"Let's just pray you won't have to." I knew how hard this would be, but I loved John for it. I grasped his hand in reassurance. "I'll sure miss you, but it's a good thing you're doing."

He looked at me with gratitude. "Thanks, but it's the last ditch. And I can't tell you how much I'll miss you."

I tried to lighten things up a little. "I'll probably flunk physics, but it's a minor sacrifice."

He cocked a welcome smile. "I wouldn't worry about that. I've spoken to my replacement, and she's promised to tutor you."

I wanted to hug him, but my supervisor strolled by with a scolding look on her face. "When do you think you'll leave?" I whispered, holding up a McMullen blouse with a Peter Pan collar as if he were looking to buy.

"Now. The jail just called me. The judge and I worked it out last night. They're releasing him into my custody."

My heart sank. In three short weeks, I'd gotten so used to having John there whenever I wanted him that I felt a looming void at the prospect of being without him. "Can I come up there and see you?"

He shook his head. "I'll call when it's over, one way or the other."

The sinkhole inside me got deeper. "Well, all I can say is, Wade better straighten up."

John glanced down. "I don't know how long it's going to take. Could be months, so it wouldn't be fair to ask you to sit home all that time." His eyes told me he wanted me to. "Just don't forget me. What we have."

I didn't hesitate. "I'll wait. Linda will need lots of distractions. I'll wait."

Relief washed over him. "Great. Great. That's . . . great." He scanned for my supervisor, and when he saw the coast was clear, he stepped into the gap in the counter and gave me one of those end-of-World-War-Two-in-Times-Square kisses, then set me back on my feet. "Just a little something to remember me by."

It was memorable, all right.

Without another word, he turned and left.

Missing him already, I swore that Wade Bowman damned well better straighten up and get better. Then I went back to sorting the blouses at my counter.

· 5 ·

The present. Tuesday, January 17. 9:00 A.M. Muscogee Drive, Atlanta.

THE MORNING SUN shone strong from a deep blue, cloudless sky, God's perfect gift wrap for one of those warm winter days Atlanta enjoys with increasing frequency, thanks to global warming. Even though there was a full week of January left, my King Albert daffodils bloomed gloriously and out of synch in the flower bed across the back yard from my kitchen window. Bolstered by the sight of them, I drained the last sip from my second cup of coffee, sent up a brief arrow prayer, then lifted the receiver and dialed my mother's number.

I'd debated telling Mama in person, but I'd chickened out at the prospect of seeing the look that implied all of Callie's transgressions were the result of my poor parenting.

Not that Mama had ever said a word to that effect, but the message came across loud and clear, a fact of which she was completely unaware.

Stay calm, I told myself as the first ring sounded. Callie is a grown woman, and this is her decision. I had nothing to do with it. She was brought up better.

Ring two.

Part of me wished Mama wouldn't be home, but I'd put off telling her for so long that I dared not wait any longer. God forbid she should hear it from somebody else.

By ring three, I knew she wasn't fiddling with her investments on the Internet. That message always picked up after I heard the second ring.

At ring four, I started to hang up without leaving a message, since she rarely checked them. My receiver was halfway to its cradle when I heard a breathless, "Hello?"

I snatched it back to my ear. "Oh, hi, Mama. Did I get you out of the north forty?"

"Sort of. I was hauling a wheelbarrow full of mulch to the back yard," she panted out. Even at eighty-four, she refused to give up the battle of the back yard, a contest she'd waged with our long, shady lot for more than half a century.

"Mulch?"

"Uh-huh." Her voice brightened. "Remember that huge oak I told you about that fell on Jane Healey's house during that last big storm? Such a shame, poor things, but thanks be to God, it hit on the other side of the house from their bedroom." I braced myself for the details—she'd related the story twice already, verbatim—but instead of another rehash, she surprised me with, "Well, the tree people came yesterday and chipped the whole thing up, and when I asked them what they planned to do with the chips, they said they were just going to take them to the dump." She paused for emphasis. "Can you imagine? Think of all the space that perfectly good mulch would take up in the landfill. Such a waste," she huffed.

For Mama, thrift had become an inextricable mix of habit and hobby. She'd pinched pennies for so long making ends meet for our family of eight that even after she was alone, she'd kept it up, full force. Daddy's life insurance had left her more than comfortable, yet she still washed out used plastic bags and hung them to dry over the swing arms of her vintage towel holder.

"So I talked the tree man into dumping it at the bottom of the driveway," she said in triumph. "All that mulch, for free. Imagine."

"How much mulch?" I asked, appalled at the prospect of her shoveling and hauling like a ditch digger.

"The whole truckload, of course." She let out a satisfied sigh.

"A pickup-truck load, or a dump-truck load?" I demanded, knowing that she'd never spring for manual labor to spread the lethally fresh chippings over the shady end of the yard.

"It was a dump truck."

I visualized a heap of sour-smelling chips the size of a Ford Navigator in front of her gently listing single-car detached garage. "Don't tell me you're planning to spread out that mountain of mulch yourself."

"Of course, I am. I managed twelve wheelbarrows yesterday, but I was wretchedly sore afterward, so I figured eight would be a better daily goal." Three barrows full would have laid me up for days! "At that rate," she boasted, "I'll be done in less than two weeks."

My interior Chicken Little screamed, *Ruptured disk! Sprained ankle! Torn rotator cuff! Nursing home!*, which prodded me into an all-too-familiar script. "Mama, I love you too much to let you do that. You could really hurt yourself. I'm sending over some muscle to handle it for you, and I don't want to hear another word about doing it yourself."

We both knew Mama would argue till the last shovel of mulch was moved, but my brothers and sisters and I had long since learned to ignore her protests and hire the labor anyway. Not that we weren't willing to help out, ourselves, but every one of us was either too decrepit or too busy. So we kept track of all our Mama-related expenses—which included her once-a-week maid and the lawn service—then split them six ways at our annual beach reunion.

"Don't be ridiculous," Mama shot back, right on cue. "The reason I'm in such good shape is that I've kept up my gardening and my walking. I'd like to see you walk three miles a day."

Ah, yes. The familiar reference to my lack of exercise.

"Mama, it's a done deal."

She went into duchess mode. "Might I remind you that I am in full possession of all my capacities, and I shall not be ordered about or interfered with by my own child."

I could just picture her standing bolt erect under the huge oak behind our house, dressed in denim pull-on slacks and a white shirt, Keds, her broad-brimmed straw hat, and flowered gardening apron with matching gloves. "Did you hear me?" she demanded.

"Yes." Considering the purpose of my call, the last thing I wanted to do was get her all riled up. So, since long phone conversations were the only thing Mama hated as much as "wasting" money, I decided to appeal to that. "Listen, Mama," I said, doing my best to sound cheerful. "Why don't we just skip this part? It takes up so much time, and you know I'm sending somebody over, so I really don't want to argue about it."

"I just can't stand for y'all to waste your money that way," she fumed, "when I'm perfectly capable of doing it myself."

I didn't bite. "There's something else I really need to talk to you about. Something important."

"Well, money is pretty darned important. And you're going to need yours with Callie's wedding coming up."

My brain got whiplash from my mental double take. Had she just said what I thought she said?

My carefully planned revelation about Callie's engagement poised for delivery, I felt as if somebody had sucker punched me in the gut. "You know about the wedding?"

"Callie told me in confidence ages ago. Thanksgiving, I think."

More than a month before she'd told us? Ouch!

I didn't know whether to be relieved that Mama already knew or mad at Callie for not coming to me first.

It hurt, knowing that my only daughter had felt safer telling my mother than me. A lot.

I gathered my crushed feelings in silence, wondering how in the world I should respond to such a thing. I couldn't lash out at Mama; it wasn't her fault. And Callie was off-limits. Alienating her would make it impossible to bring her to her senses. Not that I'd figured out how to make my daughter understand she was only going through a perfectly predictable older-man phase.

"Are you there?" Mama asked, clearly worried by my rare silence.

"Yes. I'm here." Then I promptly threw my better resolutions out the window with, "All this time, you've known, and not said a word to me about it?"

Mama ignored the accusation in my voice. "Sweetheart," she said with disarming softness, "this was Callie's to tell, not mine. And frankly, I was hoping she'd come to her senses and call it off."

"So you don't approve, either." At least we were in agreement about that.

"Are you kidding?" Mama said with uncharacteristic informality. "I'm horrified."

"What did you say when Callie told you?"

"I told her she'd lost her ever-lovin' mind," Mama said. "I sat her down and went over all the many good reasons why this couldn't possibly be the best thing for her. I explained that it was perfectly normal to go through an older-man phase, but that didn't mean she ought to marry him. And sober or not, Wade's an alcoholic! God only knows when that could blow up in her face."

She paused to collect herself. "But the child's besotted. Said he was a changed man, and this was true love, not some phase. I pointed out that she's just starting out her own life. The last thing she needs is to tie herself to somebody who's in the final stages of his. But did she listen? No. So I told her to sleep with him, live with him—whatever it took for her to get this out of her system and see things clearly—but for heaven's sake, put off marrying him for at least another year."

"Sleep with him?" I all but shouted. "Live with him?"

"As long as she promised to use condoms every time and be religious with her birth control pills," Mama said as matter-of-factly as you please.

This, from the same woman who couldn't bring herself to discuss my period with me, much less sex!

I was floored. "What happened to all those strict rules of conduct you held for me and the others? You'd have died if we admitted we were having sex out of marriage."

She let out a most unladylike snort. "Well, it was certainly no mystery which of you were, but what possible point was there in discussing it? I knew perfectly well you weren't taking those pills just to clear up your face. Ditto for Nina. The doctor and I had a confidential chat about it."

She'd known about Brad and me! And Nina and Peter! My world tilted on its axis.

"Are you there?" Mama tapped the receiver, the sound muffled by her garden glove. "Hello."

Talk about mixed emotions. Mama had raised all the objections with Callie I wanted to myself, but Callie hadn't listened to her, either. Still on the inhale, I said, "So it didn't do any good to tell her all those things, even though they're true."

"At her age, she thinks she knows everything. Just like you and that awful, selfish Brad boy in high school. A formula for disaster, if ever there was one. It killed me to see how he broke your heart by disappearing, but I have to confess, I was relieved." Mama paused.

If I hadn't found out that my first love had disappeared of his own free will, I might have wondered if my mother had arranged the whole thing.

"You know, that gives me an idea," Mama said. "Suppose we have someone take Wade out of the picture—not hurt him; just make him disappear for a few years. That could work."

"Mama! Bite your tongue!" I couldn't believe how blithe she was.

She sighed. "Just a pipe dream. We'd never be able to find someone to do it, anyway. Certainly not at St. Philip's."

My perverse sense of the absurd conjured an ad in the diocesan newsletter: *Wanted, one kidnapper to temporarily dispose of undesirable suitor, no violence allowed. Contact EKP at P.O. Box B549, Atlanta, 30327. Must take Visa or MasterCard.*

Mama's voice brightened. "But, then again, I might just be able to find somebody at the thrift shop. Our sorters are all from the homeless ministry, you know. Many of them are well acquainted with the criminal element, bless their hearts."

"Mama!" You think you know your mother . . .

"Oh, for heaven's sakes, Georgia, lighten up. I was only joking."

Mama, joking?

"This is my daughter's life we're talking about," I scolded, "and I am in no mood to joke about it."

"Welcome to the world of the mother of the bride," Mama said without sympathy. "You think I wanted Nina to marry Peter? The boy had no aspirations in life beyond watching sports in a recliner with his own pony keg." A goal he still indulged, to the detriment of his ability to make child-support payments to poor Nina for their three kids. "But your sister wouldn't hear of anything else, and she was of age. So I prayed daily that Peter would get struck by lightning, but gave Nina a wedding anyway."

Who was this person speaking? Certainly not my all-too-proper mother. "You prayed Peter would get struck by lightning?"

"Or a Mack truck." After a brief silence—appalled on my part and thoughtful on my mother's—I could hear the dreamy smile in her voice when she spoke next. "Your father and I used to lie in each other's arms after we turned out the light, making up ways to kill Peter and get away with it. It definitely helped."

Daddy? My gentle, controlled daddy?

Mama's voice sharpened. "Of course, after they divorced, we started thinking about offing the deadbeat louse in earnest, but the prospect of getting caught kept us from doing anything. It would only have made things harder for Nina and the kids."

I sat amazed on the phone. This was the longest, frankest conversation about Mama's personal life that she'd ever had with me, and it shattered my picture of her as the perfectly controlled Southern lady. It was almost too much to absorb.

"Georgia? Are you all right?"

"Yes . . . No. Mama, why couldn't we have talked this way a long time ago?"

She paused. "Well, frankly, I was afraid you wouldn't respect me anymore."

"Oh, Mama, I'd have respected you. We all would have. What made you think we wouldn't?"

Stricken, she employed the familiar giant emotional eraser she'd always used. "Nothing, honey. Y'all did nothing to make me feel that way. It was me, not y'all." Expecting her to smother me with apologies, I was surprised when her tone shifted to self-annoyance. "Listen to that. I try to open up, and the first thing out of my mouth is a half-truth." I could tell she was wrestling with herself, but fortunately, candor prevailed. "What I just said about not respecting me, that was just my rationalization. The real reason I've kept things to myself all these years is that it took so much of me just to make ends meet and keep y'all fed, clothed, tended, and chauffeured to all your activities that I hardly had anything left for me. I had to save something of myself, for myself, or I'd disappear entirely. By the time you were all grown, it had become a habit I didn't know how to break."

Hearing how it had been for her, I blinked, then opened my eyes to a whole new perspective about my mother. How could I have seen our relationship from such a selfish perspective? It all but took my breath.

Yet children do that, don't they? Assume that their parents owe them a happy childhood.

"What made you decide to tell me all this now?" I asked her gently. "What changed?"

"This mess with Callie made me realize how hard getting through a wedding to Wade would be for you. And how silly I'd been, keeping everything inside for so many years. I'm eighty-four years old, and I don't want to go to my grave at arm's length from my children."

"I love you so much, Mama," I said, choking back tears of gratitude for all she'd sacrificed, yet pricked by remorse for my failure to see things through her eyes, even once. I wanted to boo-hoo all over her, but I knew Mama well enough to know that she'd only get disgusted if I went all mushy. So I wiped my cheeks and made myself smile. "I may not say it often enough, but I am so grateful for all you and Daddy did for us. Especially now that you've let me see what it cost you to do it. I love you, Mama. That won't change, no matter what you tell me. I want to hear everything. Everything. You are brave and amazing and wonderful."

"Nonsense," she blustered, but I could tell she was pleased. "I did what I needed to do. Just like you've done for your children. And just like you'll do to deal with this ridiculous idea Callista has gotten into her head."

Ouch. Brought back to the present by a psychological hatpin.

Her voice crisped. "I have to go now. It's getting hot, and I still have four more loads of mulch left to haul. We'll talk again."

I wiped my eyes with a paper towel, then blew my nose. "Okay, but soon." I wouldn't forget.

"One more thing, sweetheart," Mama said. "Don't be afraid to let Callie see who you really are and how you really feel. As long as you let her know you love her no matter what, she'll be able to handle it." She took a long breath. "It's no excuse, but your Nana never let me in. I ached for her to do it, yet I repeated the same mistake with y'all, and I'm sorry. Can you forgive me?"

I flapped my hand to ward away more tears. "Of course I forgive you. And I thank you for opening up now. I plan to hold you to it."

An awkward pause was followed by, "Oh, good gracious. We've been talking for twenty minutes. I have to run."

I managed a soggy, " 'Bye, Mama."

" 'Bye," she chirped and hung up.

Phew! I lowered the receiver slowly, still taking in what had just happened. But it was too big to digest all at once. I'd have to think about it piecemeal, over time, for it to all sink in.

I, at fifty-six, was still discovering and being surprised by my mother. Suddenly it didn't matter anymore that she was tacitly critical, rigid in her habits, independent to her own detriment, took three times too long to do everything, and hopelessly beat around the bush with every sales clerk and service person she encountered. I finally loved her as she was, the way she had loved me. The way I loved Jack and Callie.

Even when Callie was hell-bent on making a marriage that probably wouldn't last.

I pulled out the classified phone book and tried to find a tree service to move the chippings in Mama's driveway, but even with my reading glasses, I couldn't read the fine print through my tears.

After wiping my eyes with a fresh paper towel, I did my imitation of an elephant blowing its nose (an unfortunate family trait), which drowned out the sound of John's arrival home.

"Okay, God," I said out loud. "So something good has come from this mess with Callie. I admit it. Thank you."

"What are we thanking God for this time?" my husband asked as he came up behind me for a rib-wrapping hug.

I wanted to explain, but at the moment, it felt too huge and personal to put into words. Instead, I turned and latched on to him, hard, suddenly very, very horny. "I'll tell you later. After we've made mad, passionate love."

"Here?" he asked with boyish hope, eyeing the solid-surface nylon "marble" on the kitchen island.

"Why not?" Never mind that we would both be decrepit in the morning. The passion we shared was proof that even a tepid beginning could have a happy ending.

So maybe there was hope for Wade and Callie, after all.

I backed up hard against the island. "Make me sing soprano, Big Boy."

And he did.

· 6 ·

What do you mean, call before I come over? I'm still your mother.
I should suddenly become premeditated, just because you left home?
—LINDA'S *BUBBIE*

The present. Thursday, January 26. 2:00 P.M. Buckhead, Atlanta.

. . . .

*L*INDA AND I were heading south on Peachtree on our way back
from shopping the sales at Lenox Square when she came up
with, "Hey, it's only two, and I'm not ready to go home to Rachel.
Why don't we check out Heeney's? It's been four months."

The Heeney Company was our favorite wholesaler. Linda had
kept her decorator's license active so we could all buy there, but we always got so carried away at the wholesale prices that we'd had to
limit ourselves to once-a-quarter trips. The silk flowers and ribbons
were so gorgeously inexpensive that I always saved myself out of at
least a hundred dollars.

"Great." Anything to distract me from obsessing about Wade and
Callie. I turned right onto West Wesley and headed for Howell Mill at
a neighborhood-conscious speed of thirty-five.

"How did you do it?" I asked Linda. "Keep your cool about Abby
and Osama when they moved in together?"

"You're kidding, right?" She peered at me in disbelief. "Or have you caught amnesia?" The question was rhetorical. "I went bonkers, and you know it. Obsessed twenty-four/seven for months and months. Drove Brooks crazy. Drove our rabbi crazy. Resorted to anti-depressants. Gained fifteen pounds comforting myself with mashed potatoes. Broke every rule of common courtesy with Abby, including hiring a detective to check out Osama, which backfired, as I told you."

"I think hiring a detective was a very smart idea," I defended. "I mean, who knew what he was really like? He might have been a ter-rorist."

"No way. Osama's too stoned to go on Jihad." She scanned the big, beautiful homes we passed. "Whoever would have thought there'd be a positive side to his ganja weed? The man might atrophy, but I can't see him getting violent."

"But you settled down about him eventually," I reminded her.

She sighed. "For a while. Till they announced they were getting married. Then I went hysterical all over again."

This was news to me. "You sure didn't act hysterical."

I turned left on Howell Mill, toward town.

"I figured I'd put y'all through enough angst already. But Mama sure got an earful, day in and day out."

"This is not what I want to hear."

Linda shook her head. "Sorry, but it's the truth. The good news is, I only wake up in a cold sweat about it once a week, now. That's progress, even though it's been three years." She pulled a lipstick from her purse and reapplied it perfectly to her chronically dry lips without having to look in the mirror, a skill I long had envied. "The ironic thing is, after Mother Murray was such a witch, may she rest in peace"—Linda's little wish, since Mrs. Murray was still alive and kicking—"I swore that I'd be the best mother-in-law in the world. But I didn't bank on Abby's ability to pick somebody so wretchedly wrong for her."

Driving on automatic pilot, I turned into my old neighborhood out of habit, heading for College Circle. "I hear *that*. But I think you've done a great job," I said, meaning it. "Especially considering."

"That's because I didn't tell y'all the stupid stuff I did. I was too embarrassed." She looked out the car window and frowned. "Where are you going, honey? This is not the way to Heeney's."

I swear, the steering wheel had done it, all by itself. We were only half a block from Wade Bowman's house. Callie's house, now. "Linda, I did not do this on purpose, but that white brick ranch up on the right is Wade's." The one with the pitifully neglected yard.

Callie's Dodge Neon was parked in the driveway.

I slowed. I'd put off seeing the scene of the crime, but with Linda there for moral support, I decided I might as well get it over with. "Since we're here, why don't we just hop in and say hello?"

"Not a good idea," Linda told me. "Abby hates it when I drop in. Not that I haven't—I have, way too many times—but she always asks me to call at least an hour ahead the next time."

"Just this once," I rationalized. When I turned into the driveway and pulled alongside Callie's car, I heard what sounded like a huge dog inside the house. Every deep *woof* sounded like a cross between a warning and an asthma attack.

Linda listened. "What is *that*?"

"I seem to remember Callie's mentioning that Wade has an ancient, senile, incontinent old golden retriever."

Did I mention, I'm allergic to dogs? And afraid of them—especially big ones. Not terrified, by any means, but definitely not comfortable. A German shepherd attacked me when I was twelve, and ever since, I haven't trusted any canine capable of getting a piece of me in its mouth, which includes all of them.

But motherly curiosity is stronger than fear, so I persevered. "She swears he's harmless. I'll be fine."

Eyebrows raised, Linda shot me a skeptical glance. "Suit yourself."

"I'll call and let her know we're coming." I shut off the engine, then retrieved my purse from behind Linda's seat and got out the cell phone.

"Calling from the driveway doesn't count," Linda chided none too gently. "I know it's a case of do as I say not as I do, but I really think you'll regret this later. What if the place is a mess? Callie will be embarrassed, and you're already negative enough about this without bad mental images to obsess about."

"Wade's store is always immaculate," I said. "And you know how particular Callie is about her environment. I'm sure it'll be fine."

Linda glanced at the neglected yard, skeptical. "I don't know . . ."

I hit speed dial numeral two for Callie's cell anyway. She was Pavlovian about answering it, so I rarely had to leave a message. "She could always ask us to come back another time," I excused, knowing she wouldn't.

"This is not a good idea," Linda murmured toward the window as I waited through three rings.

"Hi, Mom," Callie's voice said. "What's up?"

I still found it highly disconcerting that she knew it was me before I even said hello. "Well, actually, I'm sitting in your driveway. Linda and I were on our way over to Heeney's, and I wondered if you'd like to join us."

Linda rolled her eyes.

When Callie didn't respond, I said, "If you're not ready, we could come in and wait. Take your time."

Silence. There had never been any such guarded pauses between us before Wade.

Callie's answer was strained. "Thanks for the offer, but since Wade's a florist, I really don't need anything from there." Another of those awkward, assessing pauses. "But if you and Linda would like to come in, do so at your own risk." I could tell she regretted giving in the minute she said it. "Don't hold what this place looks like against me. I could've had everything spotless and organized in ten days, but Wade's got enough to adjust to right now, so I'm taking it easy about invading his turf."

Very smart on her part, and selfish on his. Baggage, baggage, baggage.

My comment about his having a warehouse full proved to be accurate—literally.

"Great. We won't get in your hair. Just a quick visit, then we're off. 'Bye." I should have been ashamed of myself, but I wasn't. Pulling the keys from the ignition, I said, "Ten minutes, tops. Time me."

"You're worse than I am," Linda said as she got out. "I waited two months before I dropped in on Abby. Not that it made any difference. The place was a pigsty, and still is, but it's not my fault. She was brought up better."

"Callie said the place is a mess, but I'm sure she was exaggerating." I took care not to ding Callie's car with my door as I got out. "You know what a neat freak she is. It would drive her crazy to live in chaos."

We headed up the overgrown slate path to the small slate stoop at the front door. Dormant Bermuda grass choked the azaleas on either side, and there was no protective overhang at the doorway, typical of the small, mid-fifties traditional brick ranches in the neighborhood. I rang the doorbell.

"Come in!" emanated from the back of the house.

I opened the door and eased into a miasma of dog and dust odors that permeated bachelor hell. No sign of the dog, thank goodness. She must have put him up.

I looked around me, appalled. Talk about negative visual images! "Callie?"

"Be there in a sec," she called from the bedrooms. "Have a seat."

I peered at the ancient, stained recliner sofa with its matching chair of indiscriminate dingy color. No way was I sitting on all that dog hair.

The place was worse than I ever would have imagined. Magazines, newspapers, and books were stacked haphazardly on every surface. Vintage pine paneling made a cave of what was probably a spacious room underneath the clutter and ugly, oversized furniture. Dead pothos vines cascaded from mismatched planters. (It takes some serious effort to kill a pothos.) Only the huge LED TV and elaborate sound system looked new. No surprise, considering Wade shared John's love of golf, tennis, and football on TV.

The only other thing out of place was a large, ornately framed (and recent) photo of Wade's youngest, Laurie, on the coffee table. Definitely a territorial marker.

"Good lord," I muttered, my eyes beginning to water from the dander. "How can a man who looks as natty as Wade live in a house like this?"

"It's a guy thing, I guess." Linda opted not to sit, either.

I took a clean hankie from my purse and covered my nose and mouth. "I need a gas mask," I whispered back. "I cannot believe my daughter is living in this."

Linda paused to listen for sounds of Callie before proceeding with a low, "But look at the bright side. Besides that conspicuous portrait of his daughter, I don't see any woman sign in here, probably not for decades."

"That doesn't mean he hasn't had one. It just means he was smart enough not to bring any of them here," I murmured back. "Moving in was Callie's idea. Wade just wanted to get married and sort things out later, but she wanted to make sure they could live together first." I'd been praying that reality would change her mind.

Not that any other obstacles had ever discouraged my daughter.

I leaned close to Linda. "Were you glad Abby didn't marry Osama right away?" I whispered.

"I would have been, if I hadn't been so hysterical about everything else." She sized me up. "Wipe that look of horror off your face before Callie gets here," she whispered. "And ditch the hankie."

Callie, come home, my darling daughter! my Drama Queen raved. *Don't live like this! Don't sell yourself short. Find a man who hasn't been marking his territory with old newspapers and dog pee for twenty years.*

All of a sudden, the woof-wheeze exploded directly behind me, launching me on a bolt of pure adrenaline to the other side of Linda. But not before dog pee splattered my calf and ankle. My scream only made the huge, fat, mangy dog bark louder, sending hair everywhere.

Woooof! Wheeze. Woooof! Wheeze. Wooooooof!

The lethal smell of its breath was exceeded only by the gas that came out of the other end. My heart pounding, I gripped Linda's upper arms from behind and used her as a shield. I'm not proud of it, but I did. "Callie! Help!"

"Oh no!" she called from the end of the hall. "Boone! Come!"

"Aaagggh!" Eyes watering, Linda held her nose and laughed with a definite edge of hysteria. "Gross. Down, Boone! Down! Back!" she commanded, but the dog ignored her, despite the fact that every woof sounded as if it might be its last. More gas. "Oxygen! Callie! Call your dog, before he or your mama expires on the spot."

Callie raced in, "Oh, I'm so sorry! He got the bathroom door open. I didn't even hear him escape." She grabbed his collar and tried to drag him away from me. But animals can sense when somebody is either afraid or allergic to them, which sets up an irresistible attraction, so he would not be deterred. "Poor old thing," Callie shouted over the ruckus. "Wade adores him, but he can barely see or hear. He's harmless, Mama, I promise."

"Not if you have to breathe in the same room with him," Linda laughed out.

"He peed all over my ankle!" I scolded. "And my favorite Papagallos."

"Oh, dear. Sorry," Callie said, her lips folded inward as she put her arms around Boone's shoulders and dragged him back toward the hall. "Come on, you bad old thing! Hup."

Laughter? Was she laughing? This was *not* funny.

"Let go of me," Linda told me, "so I can help her put him away."

I thrust her forward and retreated behind the recliner.

Linda and Callie wrestled Boone down the hall, laughing and yelling at the dog all the way. I heard a door slam, and the barking stopped. When my daughter and my best friend returned, Callie had her arm around Linda's shoulders and Linda had hers around Callie's waist.

"Whoo." Grinning, Callie blew a shock of hair out of her eyes. "Welcome to my world." She opened the front door and used it to fan fresh, cold air into the room. "Wade adores that dog, but I think the poor old thing is really in bad shape. I'm trying to convince Wade to take him to the vet, but he keeps"—she mimed quotes—" 'forgetting.' He's such an old softie. I don't know how he'll handle it if they say he should put Boone down."

So he lets the animal suffer? I bit my tongue and kept my views on responsible pet ownership to myself.

"Here, Mama," Callie said, heading for the kitchen. "Let me get you something to clean off your foot."

When she returned with several warm, wet paper towels and as many dry ones, I slipped out of my fake alligator flat and gingerly cleaned it, then wiped my foot and leg.

"I think there's a little on the hem of your skirt," my daughter pointed out, her barely concealed amusement saying, "That'll teach you to drop in," far louder than words.

Determined not to be negative, I tried to make polite conversation, but stuck my foot in my mouth, instead. "Well, I can see you've got your work cut out for you here."

No, no, no! I did *not* just say that!

Callie bristled. "Like I said, I'm going slow in the common areas." She eased a little. "Come look at my room. That much, at least, is done."

I shot Linda a glance at "my room," but she didn't react. The fact that Callie had her own room was a good sign. Three cheers for the virginity pledge!

Callie misunderstood my hesitation. "Don't worry. I locked Boone in Wade's room. He can't get out."

Wade's room. A very good sign. "Thanks."

"I really am sorry," she said with a spark of mischief that made me wonder for a split-second if she'd loosed the hapless old creature on me as payback for my unannounced visit.

Which of course, she hadn't. Callie was far too kind to do anything like that.

But when she and Linda exchanged lipless glances, I wasn't so sure.

I made another effort at small talk. "Where's Wade?"

Stupid question. At work, of course.

"He has a lot of deliveries this afternoon, but he'll be home when they're done. His daughter is covering the store."

"How's it working out with you and Laurie at the shop? Has she softened any about you and her dad?"

Linda's smile solidified as she discreetly pinched my arm to warn me away from the sensitive topic.

"She's still pouting," Callie said, "but she'll get tired of it eventually. We just keep being nice to her, without encouraging her bad behavior." Callie motioned us after her into the hallway. We passed a seriously cluttered home office, then headed for a closed door opposite another at the end of the hall.

A weary *"Wuff"* marked the one on the left as Wade's (and Boone's) room.

Callie opened the other door to a fresh space done all in white, the simple furnishings and bed linens complemented by brushed silver accents and accessories. "Ta-daaaah!" The only color was a white kimono splashed with pink cherry blossoms hanging on the wall opposite Callie's bed, and a huge dragon-leaf begonia loaded with the same shade of dark pink blossoms by the sunny window.

Callie's room smelled of paint and radiated light and hope. "Honey, this is gorgeous!"

Linda seconded enthusiastically.

Callie beamed. "I got all the furniture at that secondhand place near Chamblee Plaza, and the one on Cheshire Bridge near Buford Highway. I painted it in the garage. Took me a week to clear enough space to do it out there. I don't think Wade really wants to keep all that junk, but when it comes to throwing stuff out, he does all kinds of avoidance behaviors."

"Maybe he'd be more agreeable to tossing stuff if you applied to *Clean Sweep* on one of those cable decorating channels," I suggested.

Uh-oh. She didn't think that was funny.

Callie paused, then reverted to describing her room. "The accessories are mostly from Wal-Mart. The rest, I got at Ikea. Wade absolutely loves it, but I'm still going slow with his room and the living areas. Negotiating the junk out of there will really take some work. The kitchen's good, though."

Chicken Little piped up with, *This separate rooms arrangement is probably just a ruse to spare your feelings!*

As usual, my expression must have revealed my dismay, because Callie bristled. "Mama, I am still the same person I was before I fell in love with Wade. I'm just as serious about abstaining from sex outside of marriage as I ever was. We want each other as much as anybody ever wanted each other, but Wade respects my convictions. Sometimes, when it gets really tough, we go out to a midnight movie or the Waffle House till we both settle down. I told you, I moved in to see if our lifestyles were compatible, and that's it. Nothing more."

"I believe you," I said. I did. But I also knew temptation was only going to get stronger in the months to come. Who knew how long

Wade would stay the gentleman? Or Callie, the innocent? They were only human. "I think it's so wise that y'all get out of the house when temptation gets really strong."

Callie responded with a chilly, "Right."

Linda interjected a soothing, "Sweetie, your mama's still the same person she was before you fell in love with Wade, too. She loves and believes in you, and only wants what's best."

Callie arched an eyebrow, then changed the subject. "The kitchen's clean as a whistle. Let me fix y'all a decaf Diet Coke."

My favorite. "Diet Coke sounds great. Lead on."

I was dying for a glimpse of Wade's room, to see if Callie had left any telltale imprints in there, but one session with Boone was enough for the day. For a lifetime.

Not to mention the fact that I had more than enough negative images to keep me tossing and turning for who knows how long.

Boone had settled down . . . till we headed down the hall. Then the woofing and the wheezing started back up again, even louder than before.

At least the kitchen appeared to be hair-free. Gold Formica countertops and old brick walls screamed seventies, but the pine cabinets looked sturdy despite the grease that had darkened their finish. Painted, they'd be fine.

I brushed clean the seat of a Windsor chair at the breakfast table before sitting. "What long-range plans do you have for the house?"

Callie started pouring our drinks. "I was thinking of stripping and sealing the pine paneling, then rubbing it white. Or painting it white, if a wash is too busy. Same with the cabinets in here. And I'd like to do marble or granite countertops and floors."

Normally, I do my best not to offer unsolicited advice, but decorating seemed a safe topic, so I forged ahead with, "I love the idea of the white, but you might want to reconsider the granite, or the marble, which gets porous and holds germs. I know stone is popular, but it's not carefree. And if you drop anything breakable, it explodes into a jillion tiny pieces. Plus, stone or tile floors are really hard on your legs when you're cooking."

Linda gave my foot a brisk editorial nudge.

Callie picked up the tray of drinks and joined us. "What would you use instead?"

"I'd use solid-surface nylon on the countertops, white with a subtle variation in it, to keep things uniform and make the space look bigger. Or you could go with the granite look. It's very convincing. As for the floor . . ." I nodded toward the dining room beyond the breakfast nook. "Is there hardwood under the vinyl in here?"

She nodded. "Yep. Below two more layers of tile that probably have asbestos in them."

"Still, I'd bite the bullet and have them disposed of so you can get the hardwood sanded and redone in a light finish."

Some of the tension dissipated. Callie considered, visualizing, then said, "I hadn't thought of using wood for a kitchen floor."

"It's perfect," Linda confirmed. "Very chic. In a house where space is at a premium, the more uniform your floors, the better." She'd been a great decorator till she burned out and quit. "Do y'all plan to stay here, or do you want to turn the house and get something else?" she asked, being just as nosey as I was, ha ha.

Callie shook her head. "We'll stay. Wade bought it after the divorce, as is, and no other women have lived here with him, so there are no ghosts." She inflated slightly. "It's paid for. He doesn't owe anybody a red cent, bless his heart. With my teaching next fall, we'll be able to afford a yard service and some improvements."

Linda grinned. "I'll bet it'll feel pretty good to finally be making some decent money, Professor Bowman." She backpedaled. "Or will it be Professor Baker?"

Callie grinned right back. "Bowman. Definitely Bowman," she said with pride. "I can't wait."

She seemed so easy with Linda. I was jealous, but not resentful. Just sad.

We made stilted small talk about her job for a while longer. Then I cleared my throat to dispel the faint itchiness that preceded an allergy attack.

"Oh, Mama, I'm so sorry." Callie stood. "It's Boone, isn't it? Do you want me to get you a Benadryl?"

"Thanks, but I'd better not. I'm driving." I looked at the clock. "Oh, gracious. We've been here almost half an hour." I wanted to leave before I stuck my foot in my mouth again. "We'll let you get back to what you were doing." I rose, and Linda followed.

Callie got up and gave me a reassuring hug. "It's really good to see you. Could you just give me a little more notice next time? Say, an hour? I'd really appreciate it."

Only Sacred Tradition Eleven (No "I told you so's") kept Linda from saying it.

"I'll try, honey. I promise." Which was no promise. As Yoda said in *Star Wars*, "Do, or do not. There is no 'try.' "

We exited into the clean winter air and got into the car.

While Callie watched us back out of the driveway, I said through a strained smile. "I need éclairs. And Benadryl. And psychotherapy!"

As soon as Callie went back inside, I dropped the pretense. "Wash my eyes out with soap! Could you believe that place? It's a wonder she hasn't come down with asthma, or worse."

"She's fine," Linda soothed. "If Abby can survive where she lives, Callie can certainly survive in hers. She can always go to her room. It's wonderful."

"Wade ought to let her redecorate the house way she wants," I said, irrationally jumping into the turf issue on Callie's side. "He's lucky she didn't take one look and walk out for good." Not that I would have minded if she had.

This was turning into a very complicated business.

"I didn't get the impression that it was her taste he took issue with," Linda said. "Just throwing away his stuff. And face it, honey, lots of men are that way. For all we know, Brooks and John would be living just like Wade if they didn't have us."

"John, maybe, but not Brooks." I got back onto Howell Mill. "He's a surgeon. He's got that cleanliness thing working for him."

"I warned you, you'd regret dropping in."

"Tradition Eleven!" I snapped.

"Ooo-hoo-hoo. Somebody needs some serious flower therapy."

I sulked for three more blocks, then turned toward the afternoon sun onto Collier Road.

An hour later, I'd spent two hundred dollars on dozens of gorgeous silk apple blossoms, forsythia, delphiniums, foxgloves, and four verdigris containers to hold them.

"You were right about the flower therapy," I said to Linda at checkout. "I feel better." I looked at the total. "But John sure won't when he sees the bill."

"So, don't show it to him," she said, right on cue. (We'd been having this conversation in stores for more than three decades.)

John probably wouldn't even notice the flowers, but they would do me a world of good till the real things started coming out of my gardens.

Then I thought of Wade's train wreck of a house and shuddered.

"Aah-aah-aah!" Linda scolded, reading my non–poker face. "Whatsoever things are true, whatsoever things are noble, whatsoever things are lovely, think ye on these things."

I couldn't help smiling. "Ephesians four." I loved it when she quoted the New Testament back at me. "You almost got that letter-perfect."

"I'm Jewish. If I got it perfect, I'd start to worry." She began unloading her own brimming cart. "Tomorrow, we arrange. My house or yours?"

"Yours." She had a wonderful workroom at the back of her carport.

"It will be a good day."

I nodded. We'd done lots of mental health activities with her when Abby had moved in with Osama. Now it was my turn. "And the day after that?"

"We'll take it as it comes."

What would I do without my friends?

"You're on."

With luck, Callie would come to her senses before the wedding.

As soon as we were loaded up and on our way home, I mused aloud, "I wonder if the detectives have found anything about Wade."

Linda groaned. "You're hopeless."

"Guilty as charged," I said. "But people who live in glass houses . . ."

"Do yourself a favor," she told me, "and use me as a negative role model."

I tried, really I did, but it just didn't work. I had to have the scoop on Wade.

· 7 ·

It's a good thing God doesn't let us know what's going to happen.
If He did, we might never get out of bed.
—MY PATERNAL GREAT-GRANDMOTHER SIBLEY

The present. Second Tuesday in February. 11:00 A.M.
Swan Coach House Restaurant, Atlanta.

. . . .

TIME STARTS DOING odd things as you get older. On the one hand, it seemed like six months instead of six weeks since Callie had announced her New Year's Day shocker. But on the other hand, there it was, Valentine's already and time for our February luncheon, which gave me the sense that I was hurtling toward April's engagement party—where this would become a public reality—*way* too fast.

Meanwhile, I'd had Rachel over for supper three times. (She likes rare roast beef, fresh asparagus, baked potatoes, and berries for dessert. And lots of good red wine.) But instead of being grateful, she spent the entire time complaining about having to get a job. It hadn't taken John and me long to figure out that her idea of getting back on her feet didn't involve working.

Valentine's dawned cold and dreary to a pouring rain that made me want to hibernate, but John lifted my spirits considerably by waking me early with a breakfast tray of fresh coffee and warm blueberry muffins, garnished by a single, perfect pink tea rose and an endearingly mushy card. Then, after I'd finished the Jumble and my second cup, he'd invited me to join him in the shower for some squeaky-clean sex, which I'd been more than happy to do. Honestly, there's nothing like an orgasm (or three) to get you up and going on a dark winter's day.

After that, even the inevitable rainy-day traffic gridlock didn't squash my spirits. When I pulled into the space beside Linda's sensible Saturn at the Coach House parking lot, I was still feeling smug and sated.

"Hey," I called to her through the foggy windows.

When I looked for my umbrella, I realized I'd walked right past the crammed umbrella stand without taking one.

Rats.

I pulled my old faithful wool gabardine trench coat from the seat beside me and draped it over my red felt hat and purple Ultrasuede pantsuit, then braved the elements.

Linda got out with her ancient beige raincoat over her head, too. "I see I'm not the only absentminded one," she said as we splashed across the pavement toward the white marble terrace.

"I have a good excuse," I told her as we reached the sheltered entrance to the gift shop. "John brought me breakfast in bed, then got all frisky on me, and a good time was had by all." Careful not to splatter Linda, I shook the rain from my coat.

She scowled as she did the same. "No such luck at my place. Rachel still has her days and nights turned around, and ever since she's been on the other side of our bedroom wall, Brooks hasn't touched me."

"Poor baby, poor baby," I dutifully replied.

Only then did I notice she had on the ancient, pilly purple sweater and red knit slacks she only wore when she needed comforting.

We went inside to the luscious aromas of fresh coffee and cinnamon and hot bread. "You're a better soul than I for taking Rachel in," I told her. "I swear, I don't think we've made an inch of progress with her. She's too deep in victim mode to pick up on anything else."

Linda made a beeline toward the restaurant. "I keep trying to find something positive to compliment her about, but she's impossible."

I tried to think of something positive to say. "At least it's only temporary, till the condo is ready."

"Which won't be for another three weeks, at the earliest." Linda's nostrils flared. "The subcontractors are giving Teeny fits by not showing up."

"Poor baby, poor baby, poor baby!" I said with more conviction.

She sailed past the hostess's cheerful greeting without even registering it. "Rachel's so upset and needy, there's no telling when she'll be able to get herself together. So far, it appears her only skills are pampering herself and whining about every single material thing she's lost, complete with price tag."

I hurried to keep up with her as she strode toward our corner banquette.

Linda plopped down with an exasperated sigh into her regular seat. "I've got a bad feeling about this."

Maria appeared with warm rolls and muffins. "Welcome, ladies. Your red hats are most cheerful on this dark, rainy day."

"Thanks, Maria." Linda unfolded her napkin. "I'll have coffee today, please."

"Me, too," I ordered.

When she left us, Linda picked back up with, "Once a spoiled Upper West Side princess, always a spoiled Upper West Side princess, no matter what the financial realities might be." Visibly annoyed, she exhaled sharply, as if to vent her rising frustration. "Every time I try to get her to help with the laundry or supper, she goes on a crying jag to get out of it. I don't know how much longer I can handle it. She even had the nerve to fuss at me for keeping my dentist's appointment yesterday instead of keeping her company for the works at Spa Sydell."

"The works?" I said.

"No way was I going to pay a cancellation fee at the dentist's and go around with fuzzy teeth just so I can spend hundreds of dollars having my pores sucked and getting rubbed down with lotion." Practical Linda had little truck with such expensive pampering. "If I want somebody else to rub me down with lotion, I can get Brooks to do it for free."

After finally paying off Brooks's huge student loans, he and Linda prided themselves in living simply and saving for their retirement. But they certainly hadn't planned to have an indigent relative drop in from the far twigs of the family tree.

"Linda, Spa Sydell's expensive. How—?"

"Somebody sent her a condolence card with a check in it," Linda told me. "Did Rachel offer to pay me back for the things she charged? No. She blew it at a day spa. Oh, and get this . . ."

I leaned in, wondering what could top that.

"Brooks finally found her a good used car, a real little-old-lady car with only a few thousand miles on it that belonged to one of his patients' late mother. So he had it checked out, then drove it home to surprise Rachel, and guess what?"

"What?"

"We bring Rachel out and hand her the keys and tell her it's all hers, and she bursts into tears. Turns out, the woman doesn't know how to drive, and she's terrified to try."

"You are kidding me!" Driving was essential in Atlanta. I'd never even heard of anybody over eighteen who couldn't drive.

"No, I am not." Red in the neck, Linda swigged her ice water to cool herself down. "So now, we've got to get her driving lessons. And figure out some way to make her take them."

Maria came out of the kitchen with coffee. "Freshly made," she said as she filled our cups.

While she was doing that, two vaguely familiar middle-aged Tri Delt types glided into the restaurant and passed all the other empty tables in favor of the one right beside us, where they both sat facing us. They pretended not to look at us, but a few not-so-subtle smirks gave them away.

Their presence in the all-but-empty restaurant was so intrusive, they might as well have just plopped down in our laps.

Linda cocked an eyebrow, then became overly interested in her menu. "I'm gonna order something different today," she said, "even if I regret it."

One of the women cut her eyes toward me, but when she saw me looking, she swung back to her friend abruptly. Immediately Chicken

Little squawked, *Aha! What if Callie told her friends about Wade, and the word is out? Those women know. It's not even March, and you're already a sideshow.*

That's what obsessing about something you can't control will do to you.

A steady stream of diners began to take up the tables, and every one of them looked pointedly in our direction, but none so consistently as the girls beside us.

I leaned over and whispered low to Linda. "Am I just being paranoid, or are those women at the next table staring at us?"

"We have on red hats and purple outfits," she murmured back. "People always stare at us."

From the corner of my eye, I caught the women glancing our way again, then whispering to each other behind their hands.

I leaned even closer to Linda to make sure we couldn't be overheard. "Do you think they heard about Callie and Wade?"

"Oh, please. Listen to yourself," Linda bellowed, at which our nosy neighbors made a point of looking away. Seeing me flush with embarrassment, Linda dropped her voice to a more discreet tone. "They do look a little familiar, but we're not the only ones who eat here a lot. And they're not looking at us now. I think you are being paranoid. Get a grip."

If she wanted paranoid, I'd give her paranoid. "Aha," I teased. "So you're turning against me, too?"

"Very funny," she responded. Then she looked past me to the entryway. "Oh, good. There's Teeny." She smiled and waved. "All by herself. I wonder where Pru and Diane are." The three of them usually rode over together from Teeny's nearby headquarters.

Impeccable as always, Teeny had on a cute red rain hat with a deep purple belted raincoat, and carried a furled red compact umbrella. Two strangers followed not far behind her, only to sit with the eavesdroppers at the next table.

"Where are the others?" Linda asked Teeny as she sat.

"Diane's downstairs in the bathroom," Teeny answered. "She had something in a shopping bag she wanted to surprise us with."

Diane wasn't a surprise kind of person.

Not me. I love surprises. Except that last one of Callie's.

"Pru's not sick, is she?" I asked.

Teeny's pleasant expression changed to one of concern. "No. She got a phone call from Bubba"—Pru's Deadhead son who worked at a recording studio downtown—"just as we were leaving the office. Some kind of an emergency. I asked her if Bubba was okay, and she said he was fine, but she looked really stressed."

Linda and I exchanged pregnant looks. The last time Bubba had given Pru grief, she'd fallen off the wagon, hard. I couldn't help worrying that if the same thing happened again, we wouldn't be able to find her in time to save her the way we had last time.

"Should we go to her?" Linda asked, undoubtedly motivated by the same fear. "Give her support?"

Teeny poured herself some hot lemonade. "I called and offered, but she said she was fine." She let out a worried sigh. "So I guess we just have to wait."

Waiting. My very worst thing in the world. I trusted God, truly I did, but when it came to my family and best friends, I operated under the delusion that He needed my personal assistance to work His will.

"Oh," Teeny said. "Before I forget . . ." She leaned down and pulled a large manila envelope from her tote bag. My name was written on it in her elegant, precise hand. "Here's the report on you-know-who." She gave it to me.

The Universe zeroed in on the envelope, blotting out everything else.

I stared at it. Good news, or bad? And what would good news be? Bad news about Wade, to keep Callie from marrying him? But that would break her heart. "I'm afraid to look. What's it say?"

"I haven't seen it." Teeny laid her fine-boned hand on my forearm. "I did this for you, not me. And if I were you, I'd wait till you're in private to look at it. The walls have eyes here."

Mine shifted involuntarily to the group at the next table, but they were deep in their own conversation. Linda was right; I was being paranoid. Still, it wouldn't hurt to be careful.

"So." Teeny's expression softened with sympathy. "How are you two holding up?"

"Fine," I said with forced brightness, despite the fact that the investigator's report pulsed like Edgar Allan Poe's telltale heart beneath my hand. I wedged it onto my purse and looked up to see Diane arrive at the open doorway to the foyer and pause for dramatic effect.

Linda saw her and commented, "Y'all look. Diane's up there acting like Vanna White."

I didn't see any surprises so far. I recognized the slim, midnight purple jeans and red cashmere turtleneck she had on, and I'd already seen her lady-sized red cowboy hat and tooled red leather purse before, both of them recent gifts from Cameron the Cowboy, her ruggedly gorgeous forty-something "friend, not boyfriend" from Austin, Texas. (Her words, not mine.)

As she headed our way, the girls at the next table checked her out, their reactions ranging from envy to admiration to amusement to distaste, but that was nothing new.

"So where's the big surprise?" I asked as Diane glided closer.

"Beats me," Teeny said.

Then Diane rounded the next table and we all saw the surprise. Her jeans were tucked into an intricately stitched pair of tooled red boots that rose almost to the knee in front and sloped to a shaped calf in back, the toes just pointed enough to be flattering, and the tapered heels high enough to look great without being uncomfortable. Comfy and gorgeous—my favorite combination.

"Howdy, pardners," Diane said as she modeled them for us with a neat two-step.

Teeny leaned down for a better look. "Those are gorgeous. What a fabulous hybrid of a riding boot and a cowboy boot. Where did you get them?"

Diane colored, her smile a bit extra-broad. "Cameron sent them to me for Valentine's."

Ah, yes. Ever since she'd enlisted Cameron's help in the Vegas casino where we were trying to rescue Pru a year ago, Diane had denied that she and Cameron were an item. But if that were true, why did she go to Austin every weekend that he didn't come to Atlanta?

"They look like an exact fit," I said. "How could he pick them out so perfectly?"

Her coloring deepened further. "Cameron ordered them from the same place in Austin that did my custom black alligator ones. They're amazingly comfortable. The soles and heels are shock absorbent, so I can dance in them all night."

Boots or no boots, I'd have to take speed to dance all night.

Diane sat down and unfolded her napkin in her lap.

"That's a mighty expensive present from somebody who's not your boyfriend," Linda couldn't resist saying. "Is there something you'd like to tell us about you and Cameron?"

Diane straightened defensively, but her response was clear-eyed and direct. "Yes, there is something I'd like to tell you about Cameron: Thanks to the wells on his ranch, he can afford to be generous with his friends. Subject closed."

Definitely hit a nerve.

I wondered how much longer she could keep denying that they were more than friends, but there was no mystery why she did. Admitting she loved him would open a huge can of worms, because he was firmly rooted to his ranch, and she was just as firmly rooted to her life here, and never the twain shall meet.

Still, I had to admit, the idea of one of us getting frisky with a handsome younger hunk of a cowboy served as a happy confirmation of the survival of sex appeal after fifty.

Her situation was nothing like Callie's. Diane had no intention of marrying Cameron and asking him to adapt his life to accommodate hers. She just planned to enjoy the relationship while they were still having fun, then set him free.

She helped herself to the mini muffins. "Has anybody heard from Pru? I'm worried about her."

"Not since I called earlier," Teeny said.

"I think I'll just check on her, then." Diane hit speed dial, waited a while, then hung up. "She's not at her desk. I'll try her cell." She speed dialed Pru's cell, then waited again.

Just as she said, "Shoot. It routed me to her message," my cell piped up with "Ode to Joy" from the depths of my purse, and I jumped half a mile. Nobody but the Red Hat Club ever called me on the thing.

Three more choruses sang out before I located the red jeweled phone under the coupons, pocket calendar, sugarless cough drops, wallet, Sweet'N Lows, and checkbook in my purse. "Hello!"

"Hey. It's me." It was Pru, and she sounded upset. "Hang on a second."

"Where are you?"

"George?" Confused pause. "I thought I called Diane. I never can get this speed dial right, even when I'm *not* trying to drive."

A stab of alarm prompted me to blurt out, "Please tell me you're not driving." Pru couldn't walk and chew gum at the same time.

I heard the sound of brakes screeching and "Gaah!"

"Pru! Are you okay?"

She came back. "Whew. Almost bought it. I've got to get off this phone." Before I could question her further, she said, "I'll be there, but it'll take me a while. There's something seriously important I have to pick up on the way."

I couldn't get a read on her voice. "Pru, is everything okay? Are you—"

"I'm thinking twenty minutes, but it might take longer. Y'all go ahead and order. I have to hang up, or I'll have a wreck for sure, and if that happens, they'll pull my license for years. Gotta go. See you." The call went dead.

I stared at the cell phone as if it could tell me what I wanted to know, then looked up to find the others perched in anticipation. "She said she's on her way to pick up something important," I told them, "and she'll be here in twenty minutes or so. She wants us to go ahead and order."

"She called from the car?" Linda fretted aloud. "That woman should never even consider using a cell phone when she's driving. She's way too distractible."

Diane blanched. "Oh, y'all. She's only allowed to drive to and from work or on business." Thanks to DUIs in her past life. "If she has a wreck or gets a ticket, she'll really be in—"

"She is on business," Teeny said curtly. "On my orders. You're all witnesses to that effect."

Diane massaged her knuckles, something she only did when she was really worried. "Oh, I hope she's okay." Working together, the two of them had grown really close.

"No clue what she's picking up?" Teeny asked.

I shook my head. "Something important. That's all she said. Then she almost had a wreck, so I didn't think it would be a good idea to distract her with questions."

We all sat there, pondering.

Maria arrived with drinks and fresh bread for the others. Sensing our mood, she didn't make her usual friendly small talk. "Just let me know when you're ready to order, ladies," she murmured, stepping back.

Diane came to herself. "We're ready. I'll have the shrimp salad plate, but Pru won't be here for a while. You can take her order then."

Teeny got wild and ordered a chicken salad croissant instead of her usual, but Linda and I stuck to our Favorite Combination plates.

Worried about Pru, we all forgot about the joke I was supposed to tell.

"So, what's up with everybody?" Diane asked to fill the tense silence.

"Brooks found a great used car for Rachel," I said, leaving the rest for Linda to tell.

"Which," Linda said with emphasis, "she has no idea how to drive, and doesn't want to learn."

After a surprised pulse of silence, Teeny laughed aloud. "Typical."

Diane shook her head.

"Don't worry, sweetie," Teeny told Linda. "We'll make driving lessons part of her on-the-job training. Speaking of which . . ."

Linda flicked a hand in dismissal. "I wouldn't hold my breath about the job. I don't think she has any intention of going to work. Saturday morning, she got up with the chickens, then came in and announced we were taking her to Temple. After Brooks dropped us off at the front, she put on this 'poor pitiful me' helpless persona and hunted down every well-dressed, unescorted male she could find, then told them she was my cousin, new to the area, and she was so bereft, all alone in a new city with nobody to take care of her." Linda frowned. "So what are Brooks and I? Chopped liver?"

Teeny folded her lips inward in an effort not to laugh, her fine nostrils enlongating, but Diane tucked her chin in indignation. "After all
you and Brooks have done for her. And us, all those times we've tried
to befriend her. We don't count?"

"It gets worse," Linda fumed. "When we got to the Mourner's *Kaddish*, Rachel stands up and slathers on the grief thick as sour cream,
breaking into sobs every few lines and swaying like she's gonna faint.
If it wouldn't have made me look bad, I'd have clobbered her with my
prayer book!"

Linda's mouth flattened in disgust. "Brooks thought it was pretty
funny, but I thought it was blasphemous. Then afterward, we had to
drag her away from the men flocked around her. She handed out our
unlisted number on little pieces of paper like they were business
cards. Shameless. Absolutely shameless."

"So that's how it is," Teeny mused aloud. "She's trolling for another rich husband."

"Bingo," Linda said. "But I refuse to participate if she's gonna lie
like that right in front of God, the Torah, and the congregation. She's
already pestering me to take her to Ahavath Achim this Saturday, but
I told her I wouldn't."

But this could work! "I'll take her," I volunteered.

The others peered at me in mild surprise.

I shrugged. "If she wants to marry a rich old man, I'm all for it.
She'll be out of Linda's hair a lot sooner than if she tries to work her
way up from an entry-level job."

Teeny and Diane raised their brows and nodded in agreement.

"She has a point," Diane said to Linda.

I remembered what Callie had said about not having time to
waste, and Wade wasn't even sixty. "If he's old, he probably won't
beat around the bush," I reasoned. "So I'll gladly take her to every
well-heeled congregation in town if it helps her find what she's looking for." I pictured Scarlett stealing her sister's beau in *Gone with the
Wind*. "My guess is, she won't need long to land some poor, lonely
old schmuck."

"*Rich*, lonely old schmuck," Teeny corrected.

Linda rolled her eyes. "Okay. Take her then, but it's your funeral."

I couldn't let that one lie, unmentioned. "No, it's not," I quipped. "It's *his* funeral, poor old guy. Once he's married Rachel, it probably won't come soon enough to suit him."

Teeny groaned, but she never got the jokes, anyway.

"Tell her to call me this afternoon," I said to Linda. "I'll find out when services are."

"Enough about Rachel," Diane said to Linda. "Any news from your newlyweds?" Now that Abby and Osama were married, we all knew Linda was hoping for a grandchild.

"Nothing so far," she answered. "But I did the dreidel again, and it landed on the same letter that it did at Hanukkah, the one I designated to mean that Abby would have a baby soon."

Diane smiled. "I hope you asked it *how* soon."

Linda shrugged. "Soon is soon enough for me."

"I thought you said you weren't superstitious," I teased.

"I'm not," she responded with dignified aplomb. "Except when I hear what I want to hear."

Our food arrived just as all three of them turned to me for a progress report.

Diane fixed me with a pointed stare. "So, what's up with you?"

"I'm starving," I said, and launched into my lunch.

We were well into the meal when Linda looked past us and said, "Oh, thank goodness. There's Pru."

As we all turned to see, Diane's mouth fell slightly open. "Who is that?"

"She didn't pick up some*thing*," I said in my official Red Hat Club capacity as Stater of the Obvious. "She picked up some*body*."

Minus her red hat, Pru gently led a waif-thin little girl of about three or four with huge eyes, long black hair, and a fierce expression far beyond her tender years. The sleeves of her too-short coat barely came to her wrists.

The atmosphere in the room sharpened with curiosity as people made note of the cute little ragamuffin.

Halfway to our table, Pru offered to pick the little girl up, but the child shook her head and marched along as if she were bravely heading for some inevitable punishment.

"Oh, y'all," I breathed.

When they got to the table, Pru lifted the child into her arms so she could see us all. "These are my friends," she said softly. "They're really sweet, and they love little girls like you, so you don't have to be afraid of them."

The little girl shot us a wary glance, then leaned back against Pru. "Why are they dressed like that?" she asked with a worried look.

Diane grinned. "Everybody's a critic."

"They're dressed that way for fun," Pru responded, but something about the little girl's world-weary expression made me think she didn't know much about fun. She had the look of shelter kids whose childhoods had been stolen by hardship and cruel reality.

"They're all very nice friends," Pru assured the child. "After you get to know them, you'll like them, too. Now let's have some yummy food. Okay?"

The child nodded gravely.

Cuddling the little girl in her lap, Pru eased into her regular spot beside the kitchen door at the end of the banquette. "Y'all, this is my granddaughter, Peach Fouché. Her name is Peach because her daddy is from Georgia. And since her daddy is my son, I'm her grandmama. Isn't that wonderful?"

Whoa! Bubba had a daughter?

To a woman, our smiles froze in surprise.

A thousand questions raced through my mind—not the least of which was, how could they be sure this was really Bubba's child?—but there would be time for answers later.

"Peach's mama is very sick," Pru went on quietly. "She and Bubba fell in love at a Grateful Dead concert in California six years ago, but they lost track of each other after a few days and have been trying to find each other ever since."

We all knew Bubba hadn't been looking for anybody, but Pru's eyes begged us to go along with the fiction.

Six years. Subtract nine months, and that meant Peach must be five or six, but she seemed so small and frail for her age.

Chicken Little immediately equated the Deadhead connection with a random existence of drugs and abuse. What kind of hard life had Peach had with her mother? And what kind of sickness claimed her mother now? AIDS? Hepatitis C?

Peach carefully unfolded her cloth napkin and said to nobody in particular, "Mama prayed to the Blessed Virgin to help us find my daddy, and the Virgin told her in a dream that we would." She shot a shy glance up at Pru. "She told Mama about you, too, that you would have wavy brown hair and a nose that ended like a cherry." She pointed to the subtle indentation in the rounded tip of Pru's long nose. "And sad, soft eyes, and you would love me a lot."

I broke out in goosebumps. She'd just described Pru perfectly. How could she have known?

Maybe Bubba told her, my Sensible Self offered. But that was six years ago, when Pru was still a lost soul. I seriously doubted Bubba would discuss his mother the addict with his most recent concert conquest.

Pru smiled at Peach. "Yep. I'm Peach's grandmama. Isn't that wonderful?" She gave the little girl a gentle squeeze.

Peach slid off Pru's lap onto the banquette, but remained close against her side, with Pru's left arm around her waist. "I had another grandmama, but she died when I was three, so she's in heaven. Mama and I light candles at church to say hello." She tucked the napkin into the neck of her T-shirt. "My daddy's name is Bubba," Peach said, her manner matter-of-fact. "I finally met him today. He's a sound engineer." Big words for such a little girl! "He promised to take me to the studio after Mama gets better."

Teeny had gotten Bubba the job at a recording company downtown, and Bubba had blossomed, finally in his element. He'd actually showed signs of settling down, but he was still nobody's idea of a reliable father figure.

"We're so glad you found us," Pru told Peach, then redirected her attention to us. "Now Peach can stay with me while her mama tries to get well at the hospital." Peach's tiny features clouded at the mention of the hospital. "Bubba's taking her mama there right now," Pru explained, "so Peach came with me." She bent to look with wonder into the little girl's face. "I have a beautiful granddaughter named Peach. That's the very best surprise I've ever had."

I smiled at Peach. "Your mama must be very brave to keep looking for so long, Peach. Can you tell us her name?"

Peach nodded, but made eye contact only briefly. "Teresa Veronica Elena de la Guernica. But everybody calls her just plain Elena. Except my other grandmama, before she died. She called Mama by all her names when she was mad, just like Mama does me." She corrected herself. "Angry. Dogs are mad, people are angry."

Her mother's name was quite a mouthful, and decidedly aristocratic. "That's a very beautiful name."

"Yes." Peach scanned the table with mild curiosity, her gaze moving from object to object. "I have all of those same names, plus Fouché at the end, for my daddy. Peach is my love name."

Maria appeared from the kitchen with fresh mini muffins and butter. She laid them in front of Pru and crouched to eye level. "Ah, *que linda*," she said softly. "*Hola, mija.*"

Distant inklings of Spanish 101 from eighth grade translated: How beautiful. Hello, my daughter.

"*Hola, señora*," Peach responded easily, warming instantly to Maria. "*Como esta usted?*" She said it with a slight lisp, but she hadn't lisped when speaking English.

"*Muy bien, gracias*," Maria replied.

"Maria, this is my granddaughter, Peach," Pru said.

"She speaks Castillian," Maria informed us. "A very noble accent."

"Her mama was born in Spain and came here when she was about Peach's age," Pru told us. "She met my son Bubba at a Grateful Dead concert in California six years ago. Peach is five."

Maria smiled at the little girl. "Would you like a booster seat?"

Peach leaned closer against Pru and shook her head.

"We're fine like this," Pru said.

Maria nodded. "We have wonderful food here," she said to Peach. "I will bring you some. Would you like to start with some lemonade?"

Peach brightened, the first spark of animation in her expression. "Yes, please." Smiling, she looked up to Pru. "A good source of Vitamin C."

"Would you like it cold," Maria asked, "or warm, in a cup?"

"Warm, in a cup," Peach said as calmly as if she'd been offered the choice a hundred times before.

"What do you like to eat, Peach?" Pru questioned. "Your very favorite?"

"Toaster Tarts," Peach answered without hesitation, brightening further. "I had them at my friend Blakely's, but we don't have them at home 'cause they're not good nutrition." The promise of lemonade and food had definitely loosened her up. "They sure tasted good, though." Her stilted, adult speech seemed completely out of place coming from that tiny body. "We usually just have boring eggs and a piece of whole wheat toast and some tomatoes for breakfast. I know how to make those. And spinach. Spinach is easy. You just wash it and microwave it with a little water for three minutes, but don't forget to put the lid on."

Nutrition? Cooking, at five? I didn't even know how to set the table at that age.

Peach must have sensed our reactions, because she came to her mother's defense with, "Mama's usually too sick to cook when she gets home from work, so I do it." At the reference to her mother's illness, her hint of sunshine dimmed.

"We've got something even better than Toaster Tarts," Maria confided. "We call it frozen fruit salad, and it's like ice cream, only healthier. I'll bring you some with some fresh fruit, too, and our special little-girl chicken salad in crispy little hearts. Very nutritious. If you don't like it, we'll try something else till we find what you do like. Is that okay?"

Peach nodded, clearly wary.

"Great." Pru smiled her gratitude. "I'll have a chicken salad croissant."

As Maria left, Pru gave Peach another brief hug. "After lunch," she told us, "Peach and I are going shopping for all new clothes."

A brilliant smile transformed Peach into the little girl she was. "To Kohl's. And *Target*," she said with a reverence ordinarily reserved for far loftier emporiums. "Real stores, not the Salvation Army or the Goodwill. I get new shoes, too. Two whole pairs. One for special and one for play. And nobody else had them first."

On the spot, we melted beneath our red hats.

"Can I come, too?" I blurted out, wanting to get her slippers and fancy shoes and play high heels, too. And her own little red hat.

Pru laughed. "What do you think, Peach? Should we let Georgia come?"

Peach eyed me askance. "Are we gonna have to buy her anything out of my clothes budget? 'Cause if we are, I'd rather not."

The others hooted, but Peach seemed to understand they weren't laughing at her.

"Oh, no," I hastened. "I was thinking of buying some things for you, if that's okay." While she weighed that against her initial reservations, I went on. "It's been such a long time since I've had a chance to shop for little-girl things. My little girl is twenty-seven now, and she's getting married this summer." How easily I'd said it!

"My mama is twenty-three, but she might not make it to twenty-four," Peach said calmly. She picked up a poppy-seed mini muffin, the only ones left, and gravely inspected it. "She has leukemia. Not the easy kind. The hard kind, like my other grandmama died of." She took a tiny bite of muffin, clearly enjoying the taste. "But Mama promised that she won't go to heaven without telling me first." She sampled another taste, just as tiny, as if to make the muffin last. "If she has to go, she said she'll try really hard to let me be there so I will know the angels took her."

We all sat stunned. My throat thickened so, I could barely swallow. Linda, wide eyes welling, shot me an agonized look.

But Pru remained rock steady. "I can see that your mother is a very, very special person who loves you very much."

Peach nodded, her eyes safely anchored on the tiny bites of muffin as she plainly spoke the truths of her young life. "She does. She tells me all the time. And she's very proud of me." She turned to Pru. "She taught me to read when I was three, in English and in Spanish. Now I can read everything. The dictionary and the funnies are my favorites."

So much for Chicken Little's theories about abuse and drug addiction. Peach exhibited none of the defensiveness or secrecy about her mother that most abused kids do. And as far as I knew, addicts don't usually teach nutrition or English or reading.

This kid had to be a genius, and she sure didn't get it from Bubba!

She started to reach for another muffin, but froze halfway. "Is it okay for me to eat these?" she asked Pru, then whispered, "Are they extra?"

"Go ahead. They're free, all you want, with your food," Pru said without reacting. "You can have anything you want to eat today. We're celebrating that you're my granddaughter."

"Oh, good." Peach took another and resumed her conversation. "I know all my numbers, too, and I can add and subtract three columns. More, really, 'cause once you get the carryovers, you can do lots of columns, but I get pretty tired after three. Plus, I know all about making change with money. That's very important, 'cause people might try to cheat me since I'm so little."

Diane, eyes welling, covered her mouth with her napkin.

Maria arrived with food and hot lemonade. She poured the little girl's cup, then we all watched her take the first sip. Peach lit up like a hundred-watt bulb. "That is exceptional. Exceptional."

She retucked her napkin into the neck of her T-shirt, then shifted to her knees and came close to the table to pick up a fork with poise.

While Maria discreetly cleared our plates, we witnessed Peach's first bite of chicken salad, which she liked; frozen fruit salad, which she loved; cheese straws, which she thought were a bit too spicy; and shrimp salad, which she didn't like at all but managed to get down without comment, eyes watering as her face spoke for her. The crispy heart-shaped pastry shells turned out to be her favorite part of the meal.

"Those are called tim-*bahls*," I told her.

She corralled the last piece with her spoon. "Timbales." She looked up at me with keen intelligence. "What language is that?"

"French," I answered. "I think."

"I'm going to learn French, too," Peach informed us. "As soon as I'm old enough to go to elementary." She turned to Pru. "I went to Montessori at the college where Mama works. It's in Sacramento. Mama answered the phones there and went to classes. Till she got too sick and we had to find my daddy." She used her fork to push aside the purple orchid garnish on her plate to make sure it wasn't hiding anything. "Mama's going to be a teacher. Unless she has to go to heaven." With perfect manners, she carefully laid her knife and fork on the diagonal across her plate as she spoke. "I don't want her to go, but Mama says life is God's to give and take. And *her* mama is already up there waiting for her."

My soul and body! Just when I was about to lose it (and the others, too, from the looks of them), Peach turned in Pru's lap and asked her, "My daddy's kinda fat, isn't he? Has he always been fat like that?"

Pru chuckled. "Ever since he was a teenager. He eats too much junk food, but that's my fault. I wasn't a very good mother back then. I was sick myself, but not the same kind of sickness your mama has." All those terrible years Pru had lost to drugs and alcohol resonated in her simple confession, but she didn't dwell on it. "But I'm better now. And I promise you, I'll take very good care of you." She spoke with a depth of conviction none of us had ever heard before.

"I'm glad you got well." Smiling like a sad little angel, Peach cupped Pru's cheek in her hand. "Don't worry. I can teach my daddy all about nutrition. You, too, if you want. Then you both can get skinnier."

That finally did Pru in. "Good," she said, her voice thick with emotion. "Your daddy and I both need to learn about nutrition."

Maria arrived with the Swan Coach House's signature dessert—a meringue swan filled with light chocolate mousse. "Here's a special dessert for a special little girl."

Peach leaned close and inhaled the aroma, inspecting every inch of wing and neck and graceful head as we eagerly waited for her to taste the delicious treat. But she refused to eat it, turning to Pru to whisper, "It's so pretty, and it smells so good. Can I please take it home?"

"Absolutely," Pru whispered back.

My soul, my soul! Only concern for Peach kept me from bawling. It would hardly do the child any good if I went to pieces.

Pru looked to us in wonder. "You get up every morning, and you think you know how your life is going to be, and then your phone rings, and because of a terrible tragedy like leukemia, this amazing blessing comes into your life, and nothing will ever be the same again."

Linda bent closer to Peach. "We're so glad you came to our meeting. I hope you can come again."

"Speaking of meeting," Diane said, "who's got the joke this month?"

"Uh, maybe we should skip that," Teeny chided. "In case you hadn't noticed, we are G-rated, here."

Peach let out a loud sigh. "I'll say. Mama won't even let us have a TV. She says there's too much grown-up stuff on it."

I chuckled. "It's my turn to tell the joke, and it's G-rated."

"Okay, then," Pru said. "Let's hear it."

I pulled out the e-mail copy of the joke for one last refresher, then settled to tell it. "A bunch of guys are getting dressed in the locker room at the country club, and—"

"Whoa!" Linda said, her brows heading for her red hat. "That doesn't sound G-rated."

I retained my dignity. "Well it is. And kindly do not interrupt the joke. You'll ruin it."

Chastised, they listened.

"A bunch of guys are getting dressed in the locker room at the country club," I repeated. "And a cell phone on the bench rings, so a guy picks it up and answers. 'Hello?'

" 'Honey?' a woman's voice says. 'It's me.'

" 'Sugar,' the guy answers.

" 'Are you still playing golf?' she asks.

" 'No. We're done. What's up?'

" 'I'm over here at Tiffany's, and they have this gorgeous bracelet on sale, seventy-five percent off, and it's so fabulous. Can I buy it?'

" 'How much is it?' the guy asks.

" 'Four thousand, down from sixteen, and the stones are flawless.'

" 'Sounds like a great deal,' the guy says. 'And if anybody knows jewelry, it's you. Go ahead and get it.'

" 'You are so good to me.' The woman pauses. 'Oh, and I took the car to the Mercedes dealership for service this morning, and it needs a new transmission. Can you believe it? Three hundred miles out of warranty, and it goes. But the salesman was really sweet, and they have great prices right now. The big model would only be forty-eight thousand with ours as trade-in. Is it okay if I get one?' "

"Dollars?" Peach exclaimed. "For a car?"

I nodded. "Yep." Then I went on. "The guy thinks for a minute, then says, 'Okay, but for that price, I want it loaded.'

"The woman squeals. Then she says, 'And I wasn't going to bring this up, but you know that house you were looking at last year? The Neil Reid one, right off of Habersham, with the pool house and four-car garage and fabulous landscaping? They've marked it down tremendously. Only eight hundred thousand, firm. We have twice that much in the Schwab money market alone. Is it okay if I make an offer?'

" 'You're sure it's the one I liked?' he says.

" 'The very one.'

" 'Okay," he says. "But offer seven hundred fifty thousand first, and see if they'll counter.'

" 'You are the best!' the woman says. 'I love you! 'Bye.'

"The man hangs up, grinning, then raises the phone high and asks the other guys in the locker room, "Does anybody know whose phone this is?"

After a pulse of silence, we all started laughing.

All of us but Peach, who turned an intense expression to Pru. "Do people really have that much money, or is that just part of the joke?"

The stark contrast between her reality and the privileged world we knew instantly snuffed out our laughter.

Pru shot a brief glance at Teeny. "Some people really do."

Maria chose just that moment to arrive with the checks. Before she could distribute them, Teeny intercepted her, pressing a credit card into her hand. "Today's on me, in honor of Peach."

Maria nodded. Pru asked her to box the swan for Peach, and she took it away with the checks.

Teeny leaned toward Peach. "Some of those people who have lots of money like to share it with people like you and your mama. So I promise that whatever y'all need, there will be money for it. We'll get your mama the very best doctors and treatment. And you'll never have to worry about money again."

Skeptical, Peach looked from Teeny to Pru and whispered, "Is that part of the joke?"

Pru inhaled with a catch. "No. It's the very ever truth. That's my friend Teeny, and she's very generous, and very rich, and she loves to help people like you and me."

Peach inspected Teeny as if she were some alien species, then took a long, deep breath. "Thank you, Teeny. My mama needs really good doctors."

Pru slid out of the booth and took Peach's hand. "Come on, sugar. Let's go shopping."

Linda rose and asked, "Can I come, too?" At Peach's skeptical expression, she explained, "I'm hoping for a grandbaby some day, but it sure would be fun to buy some little-girl things now."

Peach shook her head in amazement and asked Pru, "Do they always want to tag along when you go shopping?"

Pru laughed. "Pretty much."

The little girl exhaled. "Well, okay then." She looked to us. "Just this once."

Teeny touched Pru's arm. "What hospital?"

"Emory."

"I'm on my way." Teeny got up, which didn't take her very far. Then she paused. "Rats. We were going to plan the parties for Callie at lunch. I completely forgot to bring it up."

Considering all that had happened, I couldn't blame her.

"Don't worry," Diane told her. "I'll call the others and talk to Callie. We'll put our heads together and get back to Georgia when we know the whos, whats, and wheres."

Could it really be that painless?

In light of Peach's problems, I had a better sense of perspective about mine with Callie and thanked God for my daughter's good health. "Thanks. I'd appreciate that."

I picked up my purse and saw the folded manila envelope that held the detective report, but this time, the bottom didn't drop out of my stomach. I decided to wait till later before I opened it, with Linda there to render moral support and her ever-practical advice.

On our way out, Maria handed Teeny her receipt and credit card, then presented Peach with a lovely little bakery box tied with a bow. "I put in an extra swan, so you have one to save in the freezer and one to eat," she said to Peach. "Free of charge, to celebrate your very first luncheon at the Swan Coach House. Your grandmama has been coming here since she was a teenager. You must ask her to bring you back again soon, okay?"

Peach looked at Pru, then whispered to Maria behind a cupped hand. "If we can afford it."

Maria nodded sagely and left us.

We all went outside and saw that it had stopped raining, but the air was raw. Peach huddled close to Pru, undoubtedly missing the warmth of California.

The valet brought up Pru's compact car first. She took out a dollar and extended it to Peach. "Would you like to tip the nice valet for getting our car?"

Peach's serious expression brightened a little. She nodded, accepting the dollar, then made a great show of handing it over to the valet. "Thank you for bringing our car."

"It's my pleasure, little lady." Grinning as he bowed, the valet opened the back door to reveal a child's booster car seat. He extended his hands to lift her. "Allow me?"

"No, thank you. I can do it by myself. I'm five years and three months old." She climbed into the car, then Pru strapped her in. Pru halted before heading for the driver's seat. "Meet y'all at Kohl's Perimeter. Children's department."

"Okay." We waved her off.

Teeny's blue MINI Cooper pulled up. " 'Bye, y'all," she said to us. "I'm off to Emory soon as I drop Diane at the office. Have fun shopping."

I turned to Linda. "Let's ride together. I'll bring you back to your car when we're finished." I unlocked the doors with my clicker. "Can you believe Bubba has a little girl?"

She nodded. "Isn't it wonderful for Pru? And terrible for Peach's mama? Poor girl. Judging from Peach, Elena must be a really good mother."

I got behind the wheel. As Linda sat beside me, Chicken Little took possession of my mouth. "God only knows what kind of father Bubba will make."

"Well, that's the point, isn't it?" Linda said, fastening her seat belt. "God does know, and He allowed this."

I turned north on Andrews and headed for Perimeter Mall. Since nobody else was listening, I dared to ask, "Do you think Bubba's really the father?"

"Do you think it matters?" Linda responded evenly. "You saw Pru. That precious little girl has found herself a grandmother. And a passel of great-godmothers. She's ours, regardless. And Pru has a true purpose in life again."

Chicken Little projected all sorts of complications. "But couldn't this be hard for Pru? She's doing so well with her sobriety, focusing on herself. I worry that—"

"Don't," she said, emphatic. "You saw her. This is a chance to show the love and responsibility she couldn't with Bubba. And Peach needs her. She and her mama need us all."

No arguing with that.

I took a deep leveling breath. "You wake up in the morning and think you know what's going to happen . . ."

· 8 ·

Don't set your sights too high, honey.
The best man in the world is still a man.
— MY PATERNAL GREAT-GRANDMOTHER PEYTON

The present. Wednesday, February 15. 11:00 A.M. Muscogee Drive, Atlanta.
. . . .

𝒯HE DAY AFTER our February luncheon and shopping trip with
Peach (where a good time was had by all), I got John off to
work, then completed my morning routine—a quick mile around the
neighborhood, bath, makeup, and daily Bible study—then invited
Linda over to hold my hand when I read the detective's report.

While I was waiting for her, I picked up the envelope. Whatever
was inside wasn't very thick, but did that mean anything, really?

As usual, I prepared myself for the worst by projecting every fear,
no matter how unlikely, to its wildest degree. *Subject is a convicted
pedophile . . .*

Even I knew that was absurd.

Subject is a chronic gambler . . .

That might be possible. Who knew how many scratch-offs Wade
did a day?

A church friend had just found out her married son was gambling away fifty dollars a day on scratch-offs. His five-year-old son had busted him by bragging how much fun it was to do them on the way to kindergarten. You never can tell.

I spun the report between two fingers. Even if Wade was clean as a whistle, I still didn't want Callie to marry a man old enough to be her father.

The doorbell almost made me jump out of my skin. "Coming!" Letting the report drop to the table, I hurried to let Linda in. "Thanks for coming. I really need moral support." I hugged her and took her coat. "How are things on the home front?"

"Wretched," she said as we headed for the kitchen. "Rachel sleeps till two, then doesn't lift a finger to help. Acts like she's at a spa. Did she call you last night?"

"Nope."

"Trust me, she will." She plopped into a chair in the breakfast nook. "I try to be compassionate, but I swear, I'm already fantasizing ways to get rid of her, including murder."

I thought of what Mama had said about mentally murdering my sister's ex, and chuckled. "Go right ahead and fantasize. It's therapeutic." I handed Linda a cup of chocolate-flavored coffee with one cream and two Sweet'N Lows, just the way she liked it.

"Thanks. You don't know the half of it." She took a sip, then nodded her satisfaction. "I really appreciate your taking her to services Saturday."

"You're welcome." I sat across from her with my cup—black, with two Sweet'N Lows. "It could be worse. It could be your mother-in-law who moved in."

Linda cocked her head, her silver hair aglow in the lamplight. "Actually, Rachel might be worse. At least Mother Bondurandt cleans up after herself—and me—when she's with us. She complains at the top of her lungs and criticizes my housekeeping the whole time, but she does it. And she cooks. Badly, but she cooks."

Poor Linda. "Why don't I come over and teach Rachel some basic housekeeping, like using the washing machine? You can go out while I do it."

"Bless you." Linda smiled like her usually happy self. "Assuming she's willing to learn, which is a big assumption."

The detective's report lay on the table between us, the eight-hundred-pound gorilla in the room, but I stalled a little longer, asking about Abby and making small talk. But when I offered Linda a second cup, she gave me one of those "down to business" looks and said, "Why don't you just hand me that envelope? I'll gladly shred it without reading it."

I glared at her, flat-mouthed. "I know you don't approve of this, but I didn't ask you over to talk me out of it. We both know I have to see what's in there. What I do about it, we can decide later."

"So you still won't listen to reason?" She looked at me with a lofty expression. "And you wonder why Callie's the same way."

Ouch! I drew back, defensive. "Linda! Tradition Five." (Mind your own business.)

"Okay," she capitulated. "Maybe that was a bit harsh, but I really do think you'll be sorry you ever had this done."

"If there's something awful in there"—besides what I already knew about Wade's past—"I'd never forgive myself for *not* opening it." I tore off the top and pulled out the bound report, which had no identifying marks on the cover.

Time to cross the Rubicon. I opened it and scanned the first page. "The summary says they did tax, financial, public record, personal, and Internet investigations, plus one month of continuous surveillance."

"A month, continuous?" Linda let out a low whistle. "You can bet Teeny laid out some big bucks for that."

"Thank you so much for reminding me of that," I snipped back.

For all her objections to my reading the report, Linda's eyes sparked with curiosity. "What were the results?"

"It gives a secure Web site and a PIN where I can check the detailed surveillance log and copies of his credit reports, deeds, birth certificate, marriage license, divorce decree, mortgages and satisfactions." Hmmm. "Man, the stuff people can get on you in this day and age. It's creepy."

"So, what does it say?" Linda never had been one to beat around the bush.

I scanned through the basic vital statistics: Born Wade Archibald—*Archibald!*—Bowman on March 22, 1946, in Birmingham, Alabama. "Ohmygosh! His middle name is Archibald!"

"You are kiddin'."

"Nope. Says so right there, Wade Archibald Bowman." I scanned the sparse biography till an unexpected item stopped me. "Oh. His big brother died from polio in 1950. How sad. Maybe that's why he never mentioned it." Shortly after that, the family moved from Birmingham to Beaverbrook, just off Collier Road in Atlanta. "Maybe that's why his parents came here in '51."

I scanned the next personal notation. Joined Peachtree Presbyterian Church in 1954. Attended E. Rivers Elementary, North Fulton High School. His transcripts were all there. I turned the pages. "Almost all A's. National Merit Scholar, Class Valedictorian, 1964. Attended Georgia Tech on full academic scholarship, Dean's List his first four terms, then barely scraping by till he flunked out. Private in the U.S. Army for two years, with a general discharge. Served in Vietnam. Two Purple Hearts. Unemployed for three years after that. Then he started working at the florist's."

After he'd completed rehab, something they didn't mention—a major oversight that made me question the accuracy of the rest of the report. But then again, the place John had taken Wade was a shoestring rescue ministry, not a regular rehab facility. Who knew what kind of records they kept on the men there, if any?

I moved on with, "He bought out the shop from the owners in 1980."

"So that's when he finally settled down," Linda said.

For a while, anyway. I went back to the report. "Married Madelyn Jean Oakes, June 10, 1981, at Cathedral of St. Philip. Lived in the Coronet Villas apartments till his parents moved back to Birmingham in 1985 and he bought their house." Nothing there I didn't already know. "Children Wade Robert, April 1, 1982; Brandon James, July 2, 1983; and Laura Elizabeth, October 15, 1989."

"Laura's the one who doesn't like Callie," Linda remembered aloud.

"She's openly against the marriage." Weird, how that made me feel defensive for Callie, even though I was against the marriage, too.

I began to paraphrase what I was reading. "Madelyn filed for divorce in April of 1994. Wade owed three hundred a month for each of his kids. He could have stopped when they reached eighteen, but he didn't. Just had the money put into individual accounts in their names."

Generous. And savvy.

I looked over that section again. There was no mention of rehab following the separation. "Linda, there's not a word here about the six months he spent in rehab after Madelyn left him." Worrisome.

She frowned, then came up with an explanation as wild as any Chicken Little had ever generated. "Maybe the detective's an alcoholic, too, and doesn't want to bust him."

This was serious. "If they leave out something that important, it makes me think they might have left out something else major."

She shrugged. "Could be."

I reviewed the page. "And no mention of alimony."

"No surprise there," Linda said. "Madelyn was the one who left him. Back then, infidelity used to matter." She straightened her plump self in righteous indignation. "Rotten, what she did, covering her ass with those kids by blaming him."

Talk about baggage . . .

"Moving right along," I said. "It says here that he cohabited with Brandi Nicole Frasier from October of 1985 till July of 1986."

That caught Linda's interest. "I thought they were married!"

"Me, too." I ransacked what was left of my memory. "I swear, John told me they were married."

Linda paused. "Maybe Wade just said so, to save face," she reasoned.

I had another, more disturbing idea. "Or maybe this stellar detective agency of Teeny's didn't do their homework."

I'd expected resolution from the report, but instead of clearing things up, the document just raised more questions. Frustrated, I moved on to the financials.

I scanned the exhaustive information, appalled by the intimate details spread before me. His complete credit history. His line of credit for the business, always paid back within a few months. Even the amounts in his retirement funds and bank accounts! He wasn't rich, but he was well-off, and clearly financially responsible. "No late payments anywhere," I told Linda.

"*No* late payments?" she demanded. "Not even a few thirty-day ones? That can't be right."

"None. Says so right here." I began to feel like a Peeping Tom. "His credit scores are seven-ninety, eight-ten, and eight hundred," I relayed. Out of a possible eight-fifty. "Wish ours were that good."

Linda dismissed my comment with, "Pooh. You and John are fine, aren't you?"

"Yep, but we won't finish paying off the equity line for three more years."

Linda eyed the report. "Okay. So Wade's solid as a rock in the financial department. That's good news, right?"

Unwilling to concede a positive, I ignored the question and read the next heading instead. "Criminal record." He'd been arrested for numerous misdemeanors back in the late sixties, but since then was only convicted of speeding, two DUIs, and a public drunkenness, all shortly after Madelyn left him.

"Convicted for misdemeanor marijuana possession, 1971. Did two hundred hours community service, plus two years' probation."

Linda dismissed that revelation with a chuff. "Well, surely you don't hold a little pot against the man. I mean, it was the seventies." (Which were Atlanta's sixties; we're always at least a decade behind the rest of the country.) "Who didn't smoke a joint or two?"

"Ahem. Think back, my dear," I reminded her. "I certainly never did."

"Oh, excuuuuse me," she retorted in her best Steve Martin form, "I guess those Mary Jane brownies you ate that time we were in Athens didn't count."

She would bring that up. I'd conveniently erased it from my memory. "I only did that once. I didn't like feeling like I was two feet from my body," I defended. "And anyway, it was brownies. I never *smoked* marijuana."

"Ah, yes. With you, always the letter of the law." She chuckled. "Anything else?"

Nothing of any consequence that I could see. "He ran a stop sign three years ago. That's it."

"See there?" She peered at me in challenge. "Feel any better about him?"

What I felt was embarrassed at having invaded his privacy so thoroughly.

"There's a whole section about his business stuff," I deflected, "but the bottom line is, he earns an amazing gross and quite a respectable net. Heaven help the guy if he ever gets sick, though. He only has two long-term employees for backup."

"Welcome to the world of the self-employed," Linda said. "Retirement is not an option."

Was Wade planning to live off Callie when he decided to slow down? I didn't like the thought of that.

I turned the page. "At last. The surveillance section." I scanned the summary and shook my head. "Based on this, it's amazing the man ever has time to take Callie out, much less play golf or tennis with John. He's up at four every weekday to go buy his flowers at the wholesalers down by the airport. On the way back to the shop, he drives through the Burger King at Peachtree Battle for coffee and a sausage biscuit, then he unloads the flowers and works at the shop till ten, when his assistant arrives and opens for business. Wade makes most of the deliveries himself, all of which appear to be brief and on the up-and-up. No sign of schmoozing with bored housewives." I read the next. "Fridays and Saturdays, he has weddings and parties to set up, then he has to take all the flowers and candles down afterwards."

Made me tired, just reading it. "He doesn't work Sundays."

Linda whistled. "That's gotta cost him a lot of expensive Jewish weddings."

I hadn't thought about that.

Glancing through the next section, I told Linda, "Good grief. He's active on six heavy-duty committees at Peachtree Presbyterian, and chairman of three. When does the man sleep?"

Admirable, but exhausting.

Yet wonderful as Wade seemed to be, there were still those omissions. I scolded myself for being so negative and admitted, "Looks like what John told me is right: He's a stand-up guy."

"So, there you are," Linda said, as if the matter were resolved. "I ask again: Feeling better?"

"Yes. And no." I sighed. "Yes, he seems a really decent, hard-working man. But they left out both his stints in rehab—and who knows if there are more I don't know about? And he's still old enough to be Callie's father. So no."

She looked at me in sympathy. "The biggest favor you can do for yourself and Callie is let go of this, get with the program, and get through this wedding."

That was rich. "If you figure out how I'm supposed to let go of something that has *me* by the throat," I said, only half-joking, "you be sure and let me know."

Linda looked at her watch, her personal signal that we'd said what needed to be said and it was time to move on. She rose. "Do you want Callie angry with you for opposing her, or happy because you supported her, even when it went against your better judgment?" She sized up my miserable expression as she placed her empty cup on the counter. "You know these things," she stated without judgment.

I stood to walk out with her. "When I imagined Callie's wedding, the groom was never pushing Social Security. With a grown family. I dreamed of grandchildren, not a son-in-law old enough to have them himself."

"Honey." Linda gave me a hug, then drew back to pinch my cheek the way *Bubbie* used to pinch hers. "If Wade's health holds up, there's no reason why they shouldn't—"

"He'd be eighty when their first graduates from high school! That sounds like a reason he shouldn't, to me."

Linda shook her head in sympathy. "Poor baby, poor baby, poor baby."

About time. " 'Poor baby' just about sums it up."

She sighed. "None of us knows what's going to happen tomorrow, much less in eighteen years. Look at Elena, so young, fighting for her life, yet with such courage and grace. Try to see the big picture." There she went again, being logical.

Remembering Callie's headstrong stubbornness at two, I quoted her. "I *not!*"

Linda laughed, but didn't retreat. "Oh, yes you will. It's the only way to keep Callie in your life, and you know it."

Grudgingly, I conceded, "I promise, I'll behave with Callie, even though my heart's not in it." I meant it at the time—assuming Wade didn't do anything really awful between then and the wedding.

"Even better, enjoy all the great parties we're gonna throw. You can cry with Callie later if things don't work out. For now, enjoy."

I let out a sharp sigh of resignation as we reached the door. "Thanks, honey. You're the best friend ever. You speak the truth in love, even when I don't want to hear it." I gave her a hug. "Want me to come over now and give Rachel a laundry lesson?"

Linda shook her head. "Thanks, not today. But soon. I won't let you forget."

She headed out into the cold, gray morning. Alone again, I picked up the detective's report and considered shredding it. I wasn't sorry I'd had Wade investigated. I just wanted more answers. Maybe I'd call the agency about the omissions. For the time being, I tucked the binder into an unmarked folder and put it safely at the back of the two-drawer file cabinet in our tiny study, where no one would find it.

Hours and a pot of homemade vegetable soup later, I remembered I needed to firm up my plans for Saturday with Rachel, so I dialed Linda's number.

Rachel answered with a sullen, "Bondurandts."

"Hi, Rachel. It's Georgia Baker."

"Oh. I'm glad you called." For the first time, she sounded genuinely glad to talk to me. "Linda says you're taking me to services this Saturday."

"Sure. Would you like to have lunch after? What's your very favorite food?"

"Chocolate cake," she fired back, "but don't get me near one. I have to watch my figure. Which is more than I can say for Linda."

What nerve! Insulting Linda that way, after all she'd done for

Rachel. I had to grind my molars to keep from giving that nasty little ingrate down the river.

Blithely unaware of her own rudeness and ingratitude, Rachel added insult to injury with, "Pick me up at eight forty-five. I like to get there early, so I can meet the old men. And wear something . . . frumpy, like you usually do. You know, something blah that'll blend right in without attracting attention. No bright colors," she added, emphatic. "And no black. The black's mine."

What a royal bitch! As always when my temper threatened to get the best of me, I retreated into duchess mode with an icy, "I'll be sure to wear something conservative."

"Great. Eight forty-five, then, sharp," she ordered. "Don't be late. And whatever you do, don't talk to anybody once we get there. I'll do all the talking."

Un-be-fricken-lievable!

She paused. "What kind of car do you drive?"

"A silver Chrysler," I answered. "Why?"

"What year?" Rachel demanded.

"It's three years old. What difference does that make?"

"I suppose that will have to do." The next sound was a click, then dead air.

Stunned by her rudeness, I glared at the "call ended" message that flashed on the screen of my phone. Not a single please or thank-you, just orders. And insults for Linda.

Scorched, I went to the pantry for some sweet sabotage. I'd show that haughty little lap-dog in the manger. I'd take over one of my irresistible devil's food cakes with seven-minute icing that very day. Then we'd see who watched her figure.

Heaven help me on Saturday at the synagogue. How I'd get through it, I didn't know. I only knew I was doing it for Linda, so I'd hold my tongue and help Rachel stalk a new husband. As if she'd really find one so soon, but you've gotta start somewhere. And the sooner we started, the sooner we'd get Rachel out of Linda's house. *That*, I could do something about.

· 9 ·

Wade's First Wedding

"Another One Bites the Dust"
—QUEEN

The past. Saturday, June 13, 1981. 6:15 P.M. Muscogee Drive, Atlanta.

LEAVE IT TO Mean Madelyn, the one who'd finally hooked Wade (or should I say, hook, line, and sinkered him?) to drag him and his friends through an eight o'clock formal wedding. White tie and tails were expensive to rent, and so alien to John that from the moment he'd put his on, he squirmed like it was full of bugs. True to form, Madelyn had insisted on the kind of white ties you actually have to tie. Heaven forbid they hook together in the back.

"Oh, my God," Madelyn had said when we were at one of the showers that I, as the best man's wife, was obligated to attend. "Can you believe it?" she'd blared, "Wade actually asked me if we couldn't have hook-on bow ties. I mean, how wretchedly tacky is that?" She'd recoiled in mock horror. "I had to sit down and explain to the man what 'first class' means." Then she'd tapped my arm with her long scarlet nails. "But don't worry. I'm going to polish that diamond in the rough right up. Just you watch."

I managed not to shudder on Wade's behalf. They weren't even married, and she was already running him down behind his back. "And what did Wade say to your little lecture?" I asked with as little sarcasm as I could manage.

The bride-to-be was too narcissistic to pick up on it. "He laughed," she said, "and told me this was the only wedding I was ever going to have, so I should have it just the way I want."

Poor Wade. You'd think, at thirty-four, that he'd know better. But thanks to a full-scale campaign worthy of Cleopatra by Mean Madelyn (a name John and I only used in private), he remained stubbornly, blissfully blind to her demanding nature.

The poor schmuck was so smitten, he bought the whole gooey, icky-poo act she poured on whenever they were together. She'd coaxed him into paying for not only the rehearsal dinner, but also all the flowers and the entire reception.

Frankly, I would be glad when the wedding that night was over so I could quit compulsively dreaming up ways to save Wade from himself—schemes so wild that if John knew I had them, it would permanently topple the pedestal he put me on.

"Here." I squared John's shoulders in front of me and took hold of the bow tie he'd been fumbling with. "Let me try."

John peered up at our bedroom ceiling to give me room to work on his tie, his tanned neck flushed with frustration from not being able to do it himself.

My first effort wasn't any better than his, so I untied it and started over. "Was that your mama on the phone while I was in the bathroom?"

"Yep."

John's mama was fabulous with the kids and insisted I let her have them at least one day a week, so they adored her and so did I, but this was the first time Callie would be away from me overnight. A nudge of separation anxiety prompted me to ask, "How are things going so far?"

"They're doing great, as usual," John reported. "Callie inhaled ten ounces of formula, burped long and loud on the first pat, then promptly went down." Like me, my roly-poly baby girl loved to eat and sleep.

Three months after having her, I was still wearing eight extra pounds of baby weight, plus the five I'd never lost from Jack.

"Jack and Mama were in her kitchen." John craned his neck against the starched collar. "They're making chocolate chip cookies." A sure way to wreck the kitchen but win the heart of a three-year-old.

It was such a luxury, not having to worry about the kids when they were with Elise. Weddings never start on time, so heaven only knew when we'd finally get to the reception, much less get home. As part of the wedding party, we were obliged to stay till the bitter end.

I focused on the tie. I'd read the "destructions," as little Jack called them, and knew what I had to do, but getting everything straight and even was harder than it looked. Especially on a moving target. "Honey, please hold still. We're supposed to be at the church in fifteen minutes." It wasn't far, but this was still rush hour.

Why Mean Madelyn wanted the wedding party there ninety minutes early was beyond me. She'd probably insisted just because she could. Boy, was Wade ever in for it.

John stilled, and I started retying, unable to hold back with, "I can't believe Wade's going through with this. How could he be so blind? Nobody can stand the woman. She'll use him up and spit him out."

"Wade's a free agent and a grown-up," John reminded me as he had whenever I'd brought this up. Only this time, he waxed eloquent (for John) with, "This is his mistake to make. Just like it was Teeny's mistake to make when she married Reid. And Pru's when she married Tyson. You and your girl gang knew those were train wrecks waiting to happen, but you put on your bridesmaid's dresses and smiled through it, then hung in there to pick up the pieces."

He craned his neck again, but this time, I was putting a final pull on the tie to secure a very nice-looking bow that left just enough room to be comfortable. "So I'm following your excellent example," he said as he looked at my handiwork in the mirror, "and putting on this blasted monkey suit and standing up beside my best friend with a smile while he marries a very selfish woman."

As usual when he did speak up, he made a darn good point. I had allowed my best friends to make their own mistakes. I should extend the same courtesy to John's best friend.

Either way, the wedding would happen regardless of what I thought.

Then John finished with a bright, "Of course, we can all hope he'll get lucky and she won't live long."

"John Baker!" Grinning, I gave his shoulder a swat. Nobody was more of a straight-arrow than my husband, but just when I thought I had him pegged, he'd throw out a remark like that to surprise me and make me laugh.

Still, I couldn't let the subject go—a characteristic that rose from my compulsion to mother anything and anybody within a mile of me, whether they liked it or not. "I'm just worried about Wade's sobriety." There. I'd finally said it. "He's been so great since you went with him to rehab. The more I know Madelyn, the more I think she's the Antichrist in crinolines. What if she drives him to drink?"

John shrugged into his tails, looking very dapper, indeed. "Nobody can make anybody drink if they don't want to. If Wade falls off the wagon, it's because he chose to take that one drink that leads to destruction." He put his arms around me. "Alcoholism is a disease of recidivism. People fall off the wagon. If he does, I'll call his sponsor, then take him to AA to pick up a white chip and start over. That's all I can do."

I looked into his clear-eyed gaze and felt tremendous respect and admiration for the man I'd married. He deserved so much more from a wife, but God willing, he'd never know that loyalty and affection were all I could ever give him. Not that he had it bad. I liked him immensely and made a comfortable home for our family. I even managed to act a passion I did not feel in bed, never letting on that I felt no fireworks and never had.

Life was good for all of us. I had gotten what I wanted by deliberately marrying a man I wasn't in love with: a decent, caring, attractive husband who couldn't break my heart. John was fun, a great husband and father, and best of all, steady and secure. That was more than I deserved.

Feeling a surge of gratitude, I hugged him, hard, and settled into the safety of his arms. "Did I ever tell you that you're the best man in the whole, wide world?"

"All the time. And keep it up." He pushed me back far enough to see the gratitude in my eyes, then smiled with a bright, steady flame of love that hadn't diminished since he'd fallen for me seven years before. He kissed me softly on the lips, then touched his forehead to mine. "I wish Wade could be as lucky in love as I am."

I covered a pang of guilt with a smile and picked up my evening clutch. "Come on. Let's get this over with so we can come home and sleep for whatever night is left without having to keep one ear open for the baby."

Fifteen minutes later, John dropped me off at the front of St. Philip's then parked the car and headed for the groom's lair. Meanwhile, I went into the main entrance.

Wade's flowers were always fabulous, but this time, he'd overdone himself. I entered through a latticed bower packed with every kind of white flower imaginable, then proceeded down the vestibule and through a festooned doorway to the main sanctuary, where the pews were decorated with white orchids and gardenias and fat white roses and lots of other gorgeous flowers I didn't recognize.

But the most exhilarating sight in the huge, lofty stone church was Teeny and Diane already there in the family pew on Wade's side, where I was supposed to sit. Bless their hearts, they'd come early to keep me company.

Abandoning my childhood lessons on reverence altogether, I waved and blurted out, "Teeny! Diane!" into the echoing silence.

Oops. Sorry, Lord. I've been a Baptist so long, I excused, *I've forgotten how to behave in an Episcopal church.*

Throwing one end of my white organza shawl up over my shoulder for modesty, I hurried to join the girls.

"Y'all are too sweet for being here so early," I told them. "Left alone in here, I probably would have fallen asleep and started snoring."

Teeny—Catholic to the core—laughed at the mental image, but Diane glanced around to make sure nobody else was there, then whispered, "Can you believe Wade's actually going through with this?" The question was obviously rhetorical, because she kept right on going with, "Maybe we should do the man a favor and gunnysack him and take him to Teeny's lake house."

When we considered that rhetorical, too, she ducked closer and insisted, "No, I'm serious, y'all. If ever somebody needed saving from themselves, it's Wade. He'd thank us in the end. Men can be so stupid about who they marry."

Teeny bristled in her classic, size-four satin dinner suit. "And women aren't?" She ought to know. She whispered back to Diane with uncharacteristic bossiness, "We're not gunnysacking anybody. We're going to sit here and behave ourselves and thank the good Lord that Reid and Harold"—her and Diane's husbands—"refused to come, so we can relax at the reception and have fun with Linda and Brooks and George and John."

Diane's dark brows shot up with delight as she made a pursed frown. "Well, ex-cuuuuuse me."

Teeny colored with embarrassment. Normally she was allergic to conflict. I'd only seen her this feisty one time before—four years ago when Reid had beaten her in a drunken rage for the first and last time.

Teeny had handled the crisis with wit and grit by threatening her rich, ruthless father-in-law with public exposure on TV and in the press, complete with photos of her injuries and a sworn eyewitness statement from their nanny. Addicted to his image as the god developer of the New South, Reid's daddy had regarded Teeny with a new respect and brought his son into line. Now safely separated and in her own home, Teeny lived a quiet life centered around her two little boys, allowing Reid to visit them only when he was reasonably sober and could behave.

But I recognized that brave front she had on. Had he tried to hurt her again? "It's Reid again, isn't it?" I asked her.

Teeny jerked her head the same way John had jerked his in that stiff collar. She swiveled to face us and leaned close so as not to be overheard in the excellent acoustics of the empty stone cathedral. "He turned up this afternoon so plastered that even his mistress of the month probably wouldn't have him." This was dire. Teeny never, and I mean never, talked about Reid's infidelities, no matter how open and indiscreet he was. "By the grace of God, the boys were with my mother. Reid rammed his truck through the service gate, then drove around from the back of the house." She rubbed a chill from her upper arms. "This time, though, he didn't try to hit me," she said with obvious revulsion. "He tried to do worse. Said I was his wife in the eyes of Mother Church and the law, and I had no right to deny him anything. That he paid for my house and servants, and he could come whenever he wanted and do whatever he wanted."

Diane looked at her, agape. "Teens, you didn't tell me!" She turned to me, shaking her head in disbelief. "Not one single word about any of this, all the way from my house. How did you know?"

"Just something in her expression." I grasped Teeny's hand and found it icy. Dear heaven, if he'd forced himself on her, I, personally, would drop him into the Chattahoochee with a concrete block tied to his ankles. "What did he do to you?"

"Down, girl." Teeny exhaled heavily. "He didn't do anything but scream at me and tear off my blouse. Big Dalton, not Reid, pays for our security, and as soon as the guards saw Reid's truck halfway up the front stairs with the door open, they booked it to the house. They know he's not allowed near us when he's drunk.

"Alvaline showed them where we were, and they came in pretending to be really glad to see Reid. Clapped him on the back and shook his hands, telling him they had missed him, so I could escape. I was so grateful, I didn't even care that they saw me in my bra."

Our keeper of secrets, Teeny probably wouldn't have told us at all if I hadn't paid attention enough to figure things out.

She straightened with characteristic grace and inner dignity. "So. All's well that ends well. That's enough about that."

"Has it ended?" I asked with a worried frown.

She nodded briskly. "One of Big Dalton's fencing contractors is there now with a crew, on double pay, replacing the back gate with the kind they use for embassies. Tomorrow, they're replacing the front one." She settled primly in the pew, back to her usual self. "Once those are installed, Reid'll need a locomotive to get through."

How she managed to keep such extreme measures from making her feel like a prisoner in her own home was beyond me, but Teeny always had been able to compartmentalize the bad things in her marriage.

Maybe Wade would be able to do the same thing with Madelyn.

As if she'd read my mind, Teeny added in her normal speaking voice, "Maybe Madelyn will give Wade some wonderful children to love. Reid did that for me, and because of them, I thank God every day that I married him."

We heard approaching footsteps and turned to see Linda and Brooks entering the church. At a trim, fit five foot one and five foot nine, they looked like America's perfect couple, which they were.

Linda scooted into the pew first, leaving the aisle seat for Brooks, who leaned past her and whispered to me, "They build these places like this strictly to intimidate Jews, don't they?"

I grinned. "Can't think of another reason." I waggled my eyebrows and said in a stage whisper, "It gets worse. They're going to have communion. Lots of talk about the shed blood and broken body of Christ. I hope you brought your ashes and sackcloth."

It sure was nice in the current ridiculous extremes of political correctness to have friends who didn't take themselves, or me, too seriously.

Brooks shot me a smug look. "Maybe I'll just take communion. How would that be?"

Linda swatted him with the forest green satin bag that matched her long skirt. "Brooks, cut that out. Somebody might think you're serious."

We all knew better and so did she, but a few people were starting to filter into the pews on the bride's side. Probably bridesmaids' escorts and groomsmen's wives.

Of all twenty-eight attendants—fourteen bridesmaids and as many groomsmen—Madelyn had only let Wade pick two: John as Best Man and Wade's AA sponsor (a connection I wasn't supposed to know, but did) as groomsman. The rest were Madelyn's friends and family. The guest list was probably just as lopsided.

Sure enough, by the time the ceremony started (twenty minutes late) her side outnumbered Wade's three-to-one.

The service was way too grand and way too long. Brooks and Linda sat out communion, of course, but after they'd waited through fifteen minutes of the overlong photo session that followed the ceremony,

I insisted they go on to the club to stake us out a table. "Y'all go, too," I told Teeny and Diane. "Keep them company till we get there. And make sure they don't run out of champagne."

After they left, I went to the ladies' room to relieve my aching, engorged breasts, which took at least ten minutes apiece with the little manual pump I'd brought. Then I headed back to the sanctuary.

By the time John was finally finished, my entire fanny had gone to sleep, and I was seriously considering stretching out in the pew to do the same with the rest of me. Still sleep-deprived from getting up with Callie, I was fading fast.

"Let's go, honey," he said, extending his hands for mine. "Time to party." He pulled me up, and we headed for the car.

John chuckled when I told him my butt was numb. "Think you'll be able to dance by the time we get to the reception?"

"I don't know." I took his arm and walked beside him toward the door. "But I'll sure be able to eat. And have a glass of champagne." A little of the bubbly in my milk wouldn't hurt the baby. Heck, maybe she'd sleep longer—not that I planned to make a habit of it.

"Let's hear it for eating and drinking."

The reception was even grander than the ceremony and, like the ceremony, took twice as long as it should have. But I did have fun dancing with John—until my high heels started feeling like torture instruments. It was two A.M. before we finally got home. Too tired for our usual bedtime routine, we each took a quick turn in the bathroom, then shucked down to our underwear and crawled into bed.

Sacked out facing me on his side, John lifted the sheet and motioned me over. "Spoon."

I scooted into the shelter of his lanky body, the safest place in the world.

"I give them a year," I said as I reached for the arms of Morpheus.

"Five," John said, then promptly fell asleep.

We were both wrong. They had three kids and lasted twelve before an ugly divorce left Wade in the gutter. Again.

· 10 ·

The most popular labor-saving device today
is still a husband with money.
—JOEY ADAMS

The present. Third Saturday in February. 8:45 A.M.
Margaret Mitchell Drive, Atlanta.

. . . .

𝒯HE NEXT SATURDAY morning I pulled into Linda's driveway right on time and sat there debating whether to wait quietly for Rachel, or tap the horn to let her know I was there, or get out and knock at the kitchen door, instead. On the off chance that Brooks and Linda were still asleep, I decided I'd go to the door. But I scarcely had one foot to the ground when Rachel bustled out of the front door, slamming it so hard behind her it echoed off the neat little houses across the street.

So much for sleeping in.

Not wearing an overcoat despite the cold, with her big black hat in hand, Rachel minced her way over in perilously high heels, then got into the back seat and slammed that door, too.

I bristled. Remembering Teeny's admonition not to criticize, though, I maintained my cool. "Whoa, sweetie," I said to her in the rearview mirror. "Last time I looked, I wasn't a chauffeur." I leaned over and opened the front passenger door. "You ride up front with me, or you don't ride."

Rachel actually looked embarrassed. "Sorry. Force of habit." She exited, closed the back door with more consideration, then got in beside me. "I've got a lot of things to get used to."

Just as I was about to soften toward her, she scanned my navy blue boiled-wool cardigan jacket, white cotton mock turtleneck, real pearls, gray wool skirt, and navy flats. "Perfect," she said, as cheerful as I'd ever seen her. "You look like a court recorder." Whatever *that* meant.

A light dawned in Rachel's spectacular deep-violet eyes. "Oh, I know . . . if anybody asks who you are, tell them you're my assistant. No names. Just my assistant." She settled back. "Perfect. Now step on it."

I resisted the urge to respond with Southern bitch. Almost. "We have a word down here that civilized people use whenever they ask somebody to do something. That word is *please*."

Rachel rolled her gorgeous eyes, making a face as she said a sarcastic, "Step on it, *please*." Turning toward the window, she muttered, "So fake. Down here, they hate you, but smile and say please. At least in New York, you know where people stand."

My temperature rose. "I've met a lot of kind, polite people in Manhattan. Maybe you simply failed to notice them all these years." I cranked the motor. "Nasty doesn't work here. Ever. It's a question of consideration. Decent people try to be nice to each other, even if we're having a bad day. It makes life a lot easier for everybody."

Like a sullen teenager, she turned back to me. "Can we just go, *please?*"

I pointed to her seat belt. "You'll have to buckle up, first, *please*. It's a law, here."

Exasperated, she jerked the belt across her and latched it. "Okay, okay." When I pulled out onto Margaret Mitchell, she relented a little. "I'm glad you were on time. If this synagogue is anything like the one we belonged to in New York, nobody but the rabbi and the old men will be there till the Torah service at ten thirty or so."

Back up Jack! "Ten thirty? They said nine! And nobody mentioned two services."

"Chill," Rachel said. "It's the widowers I'm interested in, and they come early."

It had been a long time since I'd attended Ahaveth Achim with my high school friend, Lenel Schrochi, so I looked forward to going back there, but not for three and a half hours straight!

I might have been a Southern Baptist for the past twenty years, but my fanny was reared Episcopalian. It went to sleep after ninety minutes, tops. "How long does the Torah service last?"

Rachel flipped down the visor mirror to check her hot pink lipstick. "Usually till twelve, twelve thirty. Who knows? I've never been to this synagogue before." She flipped it back and peered ahead.

Three and a half hours of trying to blend in and fake it while everybody around me was praying and singing Hebrew? I hardly remembered ten words from helping Lenel prepare for her bat mitzvah when we were thirteen. "I sure hope the pews are padded," I told Rachel.

"Me, too," she said without looking at me.

When we turned onto West Wesley for the short trip to Northside Drive, I stole a second look at what she was wearing.

Her suit—like the one she'd had on when she crashed our luncheon—was black, expensive, and perfectly tailored to her tiny waist, nonexistent hips, and impressive bust line. And her white satin blouse lay artfully unbuttoned almost to the bottom of her cleavage. Her only jewelry was her wedding band and a pair of gold hoop earrings.

"Shouldn't you take off your wedding ring?" I asked.

"Not yet." She continued looking at the big houses we passed. "Too soon. Trust me. They'll know I'm a widow."

As I am so often compelled to do, I stated the obvious. "You're definitely dressed to kill."

She actually let loose with a bubbly chuckle. "Hopefully not until the honeymoon."

"You are bad, woman," I joked with a grin.

She sobered. "But you're not." Her features open, she peered at me. "Is everybody down here as . . . *Goody Two-shoes* as you and Linda? 'Cause if they are, there's no way I'm ever gonna fit in."

"If you'll try being pleasant, you'll fit in," I assured her. My Inner Puritan couldn't resist a mini-lecture. "Remember, this is the South. We take hospitality and good manners seriously. If you do, too, you'll get along great."

Insecurity flashed across her face before she turned to stare out the window, her voice catching as she confided, "I miss New York. I miss my penthouse and my friends and my maid and my driver." Tears and pain thickened her whisper. "I even miss Karl, may he burn in hell."

"Your husband?" Nobody had ever mentioned his name.

She nodded and pulled a gorgeous cutwork handkerchief from her little quilted Chanel bag, then carefully dabbed her eyes.

I put myself in her place and wondered what it would be like to end up alone, foisted onto people I barely knew in a place as alien to me as this was to her, with none of the familiar comforts that had defined my life. Selfish though she was, I couldn't help feeling sorry for her. "Rachel, I'm so sorry all this happened to you. We all are. We'll all do our best to help you get through it, I promise."

She shot me a wary glance. "Why should you care? My friends in New York didn't even care enough to help me." She looked away again. "If you can't afford to play their way, it's 'Isn't it a shame about Rachel?,' and you're out of the game."

"We care because we love Linda. You're her cousin. Cousins count down here, so we'll do our best to love you." I could see she wanted to believe me, but still maintained a self-protective distance.

Just two more blocks. "The synagogue is at the bottom of the hill," I pointed out. "On the right, just past the light." It wasn't yet eight fifty when we turned onto Peachtree Battle to see that the main parking lot on the corner was still locked and empty, with cones blocking the front drive.

"Here we are."

Rachel eyed the cones with a frown. "Are you sure you got the time right?"

"Nine o'clock. I double-checked." It wasn't quite nine, but I saw a car turn into the far driveway. "Let's follow him."

We did, then made another right into a smaller lot with several cars in it. "Do you want me to park in a visitor's space?" I asked Rachel.

"Absolutely." She hesitated briefly. "Listen, I'm sorry about the assistant thing."

"You're forgiven," I said and tried to mean it. "I stick my foot into my mouth all the time, too."

Rachel looked almost shy. "Is it okay if I introduce you as my friend?"

Progress! I smiled and nodded. "Sure. But if we're going to be friends, you'll have to stop making cracks about my boring clothes."

She smiled, looking ten years younger. "I'll try." Still, Rachel being Rachel, she added, "But don't tell anybody you're not Jewish. I don't want to distract anybody from my grief." After retrieving her hat from the back seat, she made sure nobody was close enough to overhear, then leaned nearer to murmur, "I need results, and fast, so stay close, in case I need to faint."

Three and a half hours of Hebrew with a fake-fainting widow. Oy!

"I'll stay close," I said, "but you're about as fragile as a steel girder."

"Thank you," she responded, then put on her hat and sunglasses, abruptly transforming into the bereft, devoted widow. "Why don't you come ovah here to help me out?" After half a beat, she tacked on a sugar-coated, "Please," worthy of a belle.

I rolled my eyes, but did as she asked. Just as I rounded the hood, an older man in a yarmulke got out of a Jaguar a few cars over and extended a friendly (and curious), *"Shabbat shalom."* (Sabbath peace.)

"Shabbat shalom."

When I opened Rachel's door and started to help her out, he detoured our way. "Is everything all right?"

Playing along, I confided, "She's recently widowed and new to the area. It's been quite a strain."

Rachel stood in tiny perfection, taking my arm. *"Shabbat shalom,"* she murmured to the man, who avidly scanned her top to toe.

A widower? I stole a glance at his ring finger.

Rats. Married.

But then again, Rachel was still wearing her wedding ring.

Eager to help, he walked just ahead of us to get the door. "We're glad you came to visit us today. May you find comfort here."

We cut the corner of a dormant Holocaust memorial garden and entered a long hallway, glassed on the right to let in the light from the garden. Ahead, a neatly bearded man in a suit stood by a narrow table containing bulletins, prayer shawls for the men, and lace circlets with bobby pins for the more conservative women who still practiced symbolic head-covering.

"Shabbat shalom," the waiting man said, his expression revealing concern for Rachel. "I'm Rabbi Neil Shandling. Please let me know if I can be of any assistance."

"Shabbat shalom," I responded, patting Rachel's hand in the crook of my arm.

Rachel brought her handkerchief to her lips and nodded, then clasped it to her breast, modestly covering her cleavage in the process. Playing it to the hilt, she murmured sadly, "This is the first time I've been to services since my husband died suddenly and I was forced to leave my home in Manhattan."

"May God give you comfort," he said. "If you wish, please feel free to stay and talk after services."

Rachel extended a limp hand for him to shake. "Thank you so much. It's still very difficult."

"Our congregation has a strong commitment to our widows," the rabbi told her. "I hope you'll feel free to join us." He handed us each a bulletin. "We have several young widows in your general age group. I'd be delighted to introduce them to you after services, if you'd like."

Rachel cocked her head in genuine surprise, but she obviously had no need to meet the competition. "That's very thoughtful of you, but that won't be necessary."

"I hate to cut this short, but it's time for me to start," he said. "May I escort you both inside?"

"Thank you." Rachel tried to take his arm, but he deftly avoided having a strange woman glom on to him.

A careful rabbi, as well as kind. "It's just this way." He motioned to the double doors.

Screened by the brim of her big black hat, Rachel shot me an impatient "hurry up and help me" look.

So much for introducing me as her friend. I picked up a lace circlet and bobby-pinned it onto the crown of my head.

She halted and turned back to me. "Oh, please forgive me, Georgia." She motioned in my direction. "Rabbi, this is my new friend Georgia, who kindly offered to bring me to services." She leaned in as close as her hat allowed to confide to him, "I don't drive, you see. Very awkward, down here."

"Yes, it must be." He looked back to me. "That was most generous of you to bring her today, Georgia. You are most welcome here." He addressed Rachel as he led us into the main sanctuary. "If you ever need transportation to any of our services or activities, we'll be delighted to provide it for you. Simply call or e-mail our offices Monday through Thursday to make arrangements."

Just inside, he said, "I'll look for you afterwards," then hurried down the left center aisle toward the *bimah*—the raised platform across the front of the sanctuary. Cold sunshine lit his way from seven tall, stylized stained-glass windows on each side of the sanctuary that rose high above the side balconies.

The main sanctuary was much as I remembered from my friends' bar and bat mitzvahs. I handed Rachel an annotated Torah from the rolling rack by the door, then took one for myself. The prayer books were already in the pews. "Where do you want to sit?"

She shrewdly scanned the area, then headed for the aisle seats on the back row nearest us. "Last row, aisle. You go in first. I might need room."

To faint, no doubt.

I headed into the pew first, glad to see that they were comfortably padded. Looking around at all the empty seats, I noted that Rachel's prediction had proved accurate. With the exception of two middle-aged men in suits and yarmulkes, the only other people in the congregation were old men in their custom yarmulkes and blue-striped prayer shawls.

Once seated, I scanned the room for the rabbi and saw him emerge on the *bimah* from a concealed staircase at the end. He crossed behind an enormous, stylized, electrically lit menorah to the left of the platform, then greeted a woman in dark clothes, a prayer shawl, and a yarmulke—the only person seated in one of the many thronelike, heavy wooden chairs that flanked the Ark of the Torah on the raised platfrom.

A woman rabbi? If she was, things had changed here more than met the eye.

The Ark's two tall gilded, carved doors were closed into a high arch over the space that held the scrolls of the Law and the Prophets. Above and to the right hung a stylized golden star with a small light that served as a reminder of God's presence with His people.

The rabbi stepped to one of two podiums on either side of the Ark and spoke into the microphone. "We welcome you all to the morning services of Ahaveth Achim." He pronounced it Ah-*hah*-vah Ah-*cheem*, with a grating sound in the *ch.* "May we stand?" Then he started to recite the opening prayers in Hebrew.

Rachel bowed her head, sunglasses still in place, but I took the opportunity to steal a glance at the familiar memorial plaques on the far-left back and side walls. Beside each name whose death was to be memorialized that week glowed a small amber light.

I wasn't the only one who wasn't concentrating on their prayers. While they recited, every one of the old men scattered to our right stole an eyeful of Rachel, and I sensed a subtle stir among them.

Oh, please, let one of them be rich as Solomon and looking for love, I prayed most unworthily.

Then my Inner Puritan scolded me back to worship, so I opened the prayer book—first, the usual way, which instantly branded me as an imposter to anyone who might have been watching. Embarrassment flooded my chest and face as I flipped to the back and started there, as Hebrew prayer books do.

By the time I found my place, they were doing the *birkot ha-sachar.*

A tall man arrived on the *bimah,* kissed his prayer shawl, put it on, then went to the second podium and took his place. The cantor?

Sure enough, on the next prayer, he started singing in a strong, clear voice. Thanks to his good diction, I was able to sing along just a fraction of a second behind him, which startled Rachel so much she forgot to look bereft and stared at me in surprise.

I made a face, and she slipped back into persona.

No way would I confess that I had only a general knowledge of what I was singing.

The praying and sitting and standing and singing were reminiscent of Episcopal service, only in Hebrew, so I began to settle into the rhythm of the service.

From the English translations sprinkled throughout the prayer book, I was reminded that Jewish ritual focused on the power, the presence, the provision, and the permanence of God's love for His people, something Christians and Jews could celebrate together.

For a while, I was lost in the ancient cadences, awed by the fact that I was repeating the same prayers that had been lifted up for almost five thousand years.

Then it came time for the Mourner's *Kaddish*, and Rachel gave me a subtle poke. "Help me stand up," she whispered as the rabbi invited those who were mourning to participate, so I did.

Along with the two middle-aged men and one of the old ones, Rachel bobbed subtly as she recited the sibilant Hebrew rhythms that offered connection with the grief of millennia. Only when she reached the end did she falter and sway. I caught her and eased her back down into the pew, but not before several sharp-eyed old men lurched briefly in her direction, then kept their places when they saw I had everything under control.

As the service progressed, people started dribbling in on no particular schedule. They greeted friends quietly on the way to their seats, then chatted softly with their neighbors even as the prayers were being recited. Little by little, the members of the synagogue's clergy and board began to fill the chairs on the *bimah.*

Only then did it register that there were little brass name plaques all along the backs of the pews.

Sure enough, we were sitting in the Kaufmanns' seats.

I ducked under Rachel's hat to whisper, "What happens if the Kaufmanns come in and want their seats?"

She flopped her hand my way and said entirely too loudly, "Relax. They won't."

Sometime before eleven (I deliberately wasn't paying attention to my watch) when the pews had begun to fill, the rabbi announced the beginning of the Torah service. I did a quick head count and came up with three hundred, give or take a few.

Obviously, this synagogue didn't take a break between services.

After some of the earlier prayers were repeated, there was another Mourner's *Kaddish,* so Rachel laid it on thick yet again, only this time she didn't faint. She bent her head and trembled as if she were weeping as she recited the prayer, but not a drop escaped from behind her sunglasses.

This time, she attracted the attention of a little old man I hadn't seen before who'd sat at the far-right end of the pew in front of us. His tanned, muscular body tensed with acute concentration as he stared at her. Despite the good shape he was in, he looked too old even for Rachel, and he had on a wedding ring, so I focused on the prayers.

Then the Torah was brought out from the Ark, its colorful covers removed, and a young boy read from Leviticus. After a brief word from the female rabbi (?), a young girl read from Ezra, whereupon Rabbi Shandling said a few words about that passage, then we sang and prayed some more.

Then the scrolls were covered and paraded around the outside aisles, where the congregants touched their prayer shawls or books to the cover, then kissed them before returning to their seats.

I hoped that meant we were done.

Rachel took full advantage of the chance to draw attention to herself and left the pew to touch her prayer book, too—duly noted by every grown male in the vicinity, and even a few of the teenaged boys.

What was it about her? Did she put out some mysterious pheromone that canceled out how self-absorbed and annoying she really was?

On her way back to their seats, one of the round little old ladies gave her skinny little old husband a healthy swat for ogling Rachel, which made me smile.

Sorry, Lord, I prayed. *She's only interested in the widowers, I promise.*

My rear end was aching, but we had more singing and praying to do, yet. I truly believe that worship is a privilege and a joy, but despite the ample padding provided by my fanny and the foam cushion, my bones had worked their way through to the hard wooden pew beneath.

Finally, well after twelve thirty, we received a blessing and adjourned.

It was all I could do to keep from limping as I helped Rachel toward the aisle.

We hadn't even made it to the carpet when that cute little old guy who'd been peering at her flew down the vacant pew in front of us and stepped into the aisle, blocking our way. His blue eyes sparkling with life, he took her hand and easily sank to one knee before her, declaring, "I'm in love. Will you marry me?" which earned a genuine chuckle from Rachel.

"You're wearing a wedding ring," she noted dryly.

"So are you," he shot back without missing a beat. "Mine's in memory of my blessed wife Rachel, may God rest her soul."

Whoa! His late wife was Rachel? How spooky was that?

"Mine's for my late husband Karl," Rachel told him, clarifying her eligibility.

A gaggle of the old men collected nearby, trying not to look like they were eavesdropping, but not fooling anybody.

The little old widower kept those piercing blue eyes on Rachel. "Now will you marry me?"

"I'd have to see your financials first," she retorted in come-hither tones, completely forgetting to play the grief card.

"I'm richer than Donald Trump, but a whole lot better man," Rachel's instant suitor challenged. He motioned to the Greek chorus just behind us. "Ask anybody in town."

They nodded, some begrudgingly, some eagerly.

Unleashing two killer dimples, the old guy pinned Rachel with a sparkling grin comprised of what looked like his own teeth. "But money isn't any fun without somebody to share it with."

Bringing out the big guns, Rachel took off her sunglasses and turned those amazing violet eyes on him full force. The old guy almost lost his balance and fell over. She worked her long lashes better than Princess Di ever had. "I'd need references," she cooed. "All your ex-wives."

"Sorry." Rapt, he made a sad face and shook his head without breaking his gaze. "Haven't got any ex-wives. There was only my Rachel, God rest her soul. We were married for fifty-one years before the cancer took her." Tears welled briefly. "The greatest blessing in my life." He let out a sigh worthy of a smitten sixteen-year-old. "Till now."

One of the little old guys interjected, "He treated her like a queen. Ask any of the women here. They'll tell you. Just ask them."

Rachel blinked at her pursuer in earnest. "Don't worry. I will."

As always when God answers my prayers immediately just the way I asked, I second-guessed what was happening. Surely this guy couldn't be for real.

I mean, I know all of us had prayed that Rachel would find a husband, but this was way too convenient.

The man stood, his head just a fraction taller than Rachel's five feet plus heels. Despite his age and diminutive size, there was definitely something compelling about him. And some serious chemistry radiating Rachel's way.

She cocked her head in genuine interest, but kept on with her pithy questions. "Children?"

"Not yet." He waggled his eyebrows. "But I'd love some, and I don't need any prescriptions to do it. How many would you like?"

Rachel actually blushed. "We can settle that in the prenuptial. I'd want to know that the children and I would be provided for."

"Ah, my fair princess," he said with mock soberness. "I'm afraid I must put my foot down about the prenuptial."

Rachel's guard went up like the blast shield on an aircraft carrier. "Really."

He looked her square in the eye. "No prenuptials. No conditions. Married is married, and what's mine will be yours."

Whoa! If he really was that rich . . . Georgia was a community-property state by adjudication, if not by statute.

Rachel lit up as if he'd just sprouted wings and a halo.

The little old man drove his argument home. "I love to dance and to travel—first class, of course—and I love romantic dinners in fine restaurants, and plays, and the symphony. How about you?"

Now it was Rachel's turn to be mesmerized. "All of the above." She cocked her head. "Can we have an apartment in New York?"

He nodded. "Already got one on the Upper East Side, overlooking the park."

Joy and amazement on her face, she breathed, "Then I accept." Reason caught back up with her. "Assuming you're telling me the truth."

"He's telling the truth," the Greek chorus chimed in.

"Rachel," I scolded. "You just met this man. You know nothing about him. At least check him out with the rabbi before you make any commitments."

He cocked his head in awe. "Your name is Rachel? It's a sign."

Rachel dismissed me with a brief glare. "I prayed for a husband," she told me, "and here he is. Now bug off."

The little old widower shot me a merry grin and a genial, "Yeah, bug off," delighting Rachel.

"Pick me up tomorrow night at seven." Gazing at him dreamily, Rachel reached into her purse, then handed him one of the cards she'd had Linda print out for her. "Here's my cousin's number and address. We'll double-date with her and her husband. If you check out, we can be married."

"Rachel," I urged, "You don't even know this man's name."

She extended her hand to him. "I'm Rachel Goldman Glass. I don't have any exes or children, either."

Instead of shaking it, he bowed and kissed it ever so lightly, then straightened. "Solomon Reuben Rosenwasser, at your service, perfumier extraordinaire. You can call me Sol."

Rich as Solomon, quite literally!

Rachel's mouth fell open. "As in Rosenwasser perfume?" One of the most expensive and acclaimed labels in the world.

He nodded.

Rachel warmed to him even more. "I love your stuff."

"And I love you," he declared with youthful ardor.

She shook her head in amazement. "You don't even know me."

"Doesn't matter," he averred. "All these years alone, I've been praying and waiting for you, and here you are. I am going to make you *so* happy." Crazy as it seemed, something about him told me he would.

If this guy was for real, there was no justice. I had jillions of wonderful friends who'd been praying for decent husbands for years, and Rotten Rachel nails a billionaire in just a few weeks! The Red Hat Club wasn't going to believe this.

Suddenly remembering what she was about, Rachel put her sunglasses back on and lifted her chin with pride. "Till tomorrow." Her suitor stepped back, and she strode past him, her head held high, while the remaining old men exploded into a clatter of conjecture and admonition.

Sol just grinned. "Till tomorrow."

When I caught up with Rachel in the hallway, I started to raise objections, but she cut me off. "Shhh. Nothing till we're in the car."

Once we were belted in and on our way back to Linda's, I let loose. "This is crazy. What if this guy is some kind of nut? You don't even know how old he is."

Rachel was unimpressed. "It doesn't matter. I have friends in Manhattan who know people who can find out anything about anybody, and in a hurry. By the time he picks us up tomorrow night, I'll know whether he's telling the truth, plus a whole lot more."

"Trust me, a detective's report won't tell you anything about the kind of person he is behind closed doors." I should know.

"I already know what kind of person he is," she shot back. "He's a live wire, not afraid to take a risk, and he's funny and fun. And sexy." She shook her head in awe. "I'm still getting over the fact that a man old enough to be my great-grandfather is sexy."

"Grandfather," I corrected. "Or father."

"Whatever," she answered lightly, transformed into somebody totally different from the rude, desperate, self-absorbed woman who'd crashed our luncheon in January.

Still, this made no sense. Having brought her there, I felt responsible. "Just be careful. Half the alcoholics and cocaine addicts I know are charming as hell when you first meet them." I thought of Teeny's ex-husband Reid. "Not to mention the abusers."

Rachel shot me an irritated look. "Linda told me you're the one who's always praying about things and expecting God to answer. What's the matter? You criticizing God for doing it too fast, or what? You, of all people, should be thanking Him for this man. I am."

When she saw that I was still unconvinced, she added, "God loves widows. I prayed. You prayed. Sol prayed. God delivered. End of story." She let out a satisfied sigh and gazed beyond the passing houses with a smile. "I think I'm really going to like it here. When we're not traveling, or in our penthouse on the Upper *East* Side."

I could sense God laughing.

Okay, so maybe He *had* answered our prayers. Assuming this guy wasn't some kind of nut. I sent up an arrow of thanks, then braced myself to hear Rachel tell Brooks and Linda.

No way would I miss the looks on their faces when they heard *this* one.

· 11 ·

It's like the Beatles said: When something's meant to be, "let it be."
— MY PATERNAL GRANDMOTHER PEYTON

. . . .

*W*HEN RACHEL TOLD Brooks and Linda what had happened, their mouths dropped open, then they exploded with hugs and cries of *"Mazel tov!"*

"George, this is a true miracle," Linda told me. "Sol Rosenwasser is one of the most beloved philanthropists in this city, not to mention one of the warmest, wittiest, most sought-after dinner guests. I swear, that man doesn't age. I should be in such good shape."

"And his first wife was named Rachel," Rachel pointed out. "How perfect is that? I won't even have to worry about being called the wrong name. This is fate, I tell you. Fate."

"Sure looks like it." Linda shook her head in awe. "Every Jewish widow in town has been after him for years, but no go. Then Rachel walks in, and bam! He proposes. It has to be the hand of God."

Maybe it was the fact that I'd been instrumental in bringing Sol and Rachel together, but I felt responsible for what might happen.

"Maybe," I cautioned, "but what do you know about him, really? What he's like in private? I mean, the Mafia builds shrines and cathedrals all over the place." I frowned, remembering how far from his public persona Teeny's husband had been. "And we both know what Reid and his rotten father have donated to the arts in this town. That doesn't make them decent people."

"Yeah," Linda admitted, "but anybody who knows them knows what they're really like."

"I told you," Rachel repeated, "I'll have Sol checked out. And mark my words: Before you can say '*Mazel tov,*' I'll be the new Mrs. Sol Rosenwasser. Rachel the second."

Married and finally out of Linda and Brooks's hair . . . and their bank account.

Brooks exhaled with equal measures of relief and amazement, then shrugged. "I've never heard a bad word about the man."

Linda nodded. "I swear, I think he's golden."

True to their prediction, Linda called the next afternoon to let me know that Rachel's New York bloodhounds had promptly reported back (on a Sunday!) that Sol checked out, clean as a whistle for all of his eighty-two years. A model citizen since he'd moved his family's business to Atlanta to escape the Nazi occupation of France during WWII, he'd liquidated his holdings for two billion plus when his wife had fallen ill nine years before so he could devote all his attention to her.

In the years since her death, he'd kept himself busy traveling and building orphanages in the Arab sectors of Jerusalem and clinics in Africa, but he still had money to burn, and we all knew Rachel was more than eager to light quite a bonfire.

Sunday night—make that *very* early Monday morning—my phone rang at one. Bracing myself for an emergency, I snatched up the receiver as John reared up with a fuzzy, "Wha—?"

"Hello?"

"Sorry to call so late, George," Linda's voice said, "but I swear, if I didn't have Brooks, I'd marry Sol Rosenwasser myself."

Relieved, I turned to my husband. "It's okay, honey. It's just Linda with a Rachel report." I urged him to lie back down.

"Mmm." John was asleep the minute his head hit the pillow.

"You scared me," I fussed to Linda, easing back down myself.

"Sorry, but I couldn't wait to tell you what a miracle this is. You're not gonna believe it, but Rachel is head over heels, with our blessing, and so is Sol." She was so excited, she barely left any spaces between her words. "Sol took us over to his house near Ahaveth Achim—the same one he's lived in since 1963, a very modest mansion, considering his money—and we had the most amazing meal prepared by his personal French chef. Then, over brandy, he kept us all in stitches telling stories from his childhood. He must have been quite a handful."

I struggled to stay focused as she went on.

"We had so much fun, we forgot the time completely till Brooks looked at his watch and gave me a big poke. Georgia, this truly is a match made in heaven. Rachel's a different person around him. He's so affectionate and so accepting that her hard little heart has melted completely, and his vision is contagious. Who knew?"

"Amazing." It came out groggy, and I started to drift.

"He gave her the sweetest kiss at the door before he went back inside. Rachel turned around and collapsed sobbing with joy into my arms, swearing she was in love and praying that he should live and be well for a long, long time." She paused. "Have you gone to sleep on me?"

"No," I lied, rousing.

"What are you doing tomorrow morning? We're going to breakfast, then shopping for her wedding dress. Want to come?"

Rachel, getting up for breakfast? Now, *that* was a miracle.

"Can't. I've got wedding stuff with Callie." Now that Rachel was squared away, all my maternal instincts had zeroed back in on my daughter with a vengeance. "And no way am I telling her about Sol and Rachel. It'll only encourage her. Her situation is completely different." I steadfastly refused to believe God had a lesson for me in the September-December merger he'd worked for Sol and Rachel. "Wade is neither a billionaire nor a beloved philanthropist."

"You've got a point," she said. "I'll let you get back to sleep, then. Call me after you and Callie get together, and tell me how it went."

"Okay." I hung up and nestled back into my synthetic-down pillows.

My last thought before sleep was, *Not that I'm greedy, Lord, but I could use a miracle in Callie's situation, too. And it wouldn't hurt a thing if it was as instant as Rachel's, thank you very much.*

But God, having the best sense of humor and irony in creation, answered otherwise. As I said: There is no justice.

The present. March 7, 9:37 A.M. The Flying Biscuit Restaurant, McLendon Avenue, Candler Park, Atlanta.

CALLIE HAD PICKED the Flying Biscuit (neutral ground, safely out of Buckhead), for our coffee klatch, so I drove to Candler Park in a surprising lack of traffic and entered the sunny little restaurant more than twenty minutes early. As always, the mouth-watering aromas of coffee and fresh biscuits and bacon and ham suffused the space. I passed through the narrow main room for the quieter confines of the muraled Sunflower Room and sat at a window table, surrounded by cheerfully primitive painted mountains and fields of sunflowers.

"Mornin'," the waitress said as she arrived with coffeepot and cup in hand. "What can I git ya?"

"Coffee, black, and iced water, no lemon." As she poured my coffee, I took out my *AJC (Atlanta Journal-Constitution)* and happily occupied myself with the jumble.

Thirty minutes later, the jumble was solved, the crossword puzzle finished—I cheated—and I waited for my daughter with growing anxiety.

She's dead on the side of the road! Chicken Little squawked, but I ignored her.

The real question was, would I be able to hold my peace about Wade when Callie got there?

Until he'd come into the picture, things had always been so simple between Callie and me. Even when she was immersed in college life and her studies, she'd always made time for the occasional mother-daughter movie or outing, when we'd laughed and shared like friends. No touchiness or off-limits subjects. I had cherished her candor and maturity, and never took for granted how on track and sensible she'd always been.

Now our relationship felt like a minefield. How could I be open with her when Callie got defensive about anything I said about Wade or their engagement that might be construed as negative?

I missed what we'd had and wanted it back.

That's the trouble with living a charmed life: you expect it to keep on going forever, and when it doesn't . . .

Keep the lines of communication open, I told myself.

Use a light touch.

No third degrees . . . about anything: dog hair, the house, Wade's old junk, fornication. Especially not fornication. Been there, done that myself in high school, so I couldn't throw stones.

I caught the waitress's eye and lifted my cup for a refill. My third. At this rate, I'd be so zizzed by the time Callie finally arrived, I'd be blathering ninety miles to nothing, so I mimed "decaf" as she started toward me with the pot of high-test. She nodded and swapped the pot out for the decaf.

"I was just about to cut you off myself," the waitress said as she re-filled my cup, every bit the quintessential diner waitress—Flo, but with a bad perm instead of a beehive and dark roots in her dyed-red hair. "You was gittin' kinda glassy-eyed and fidgety."

"I am a little edgy," I confessed. "My only daughter's getting married, and I'm still getting used to the idea." I should have stopped there. I meant to stop there, but diner waitresses are the Southern Baptist equivalent of bartenders and always seemed a safe place to vent.

Not hairdressers. I knew better than to tell anything to those. You might as well put it on UPI.

"He's a lot older than she is," I confided. "A *lot*."

She cocked a pose. "Is he rich? Old is good if he's rich." Shades of Rachel.

Honesty compelled me to say, "He's comfortable, but not rich. And he's my husband's best friend."

"Mmmm-*mmmm*." She shook her head in commiseration. "Not so good."

"Yeah." I sighed. "But you can't tell kids anything."

"I hear *that*, honey." She tucked a stray lock of overpermed hair behind her ear.

Already repenting my indiscretion, I added, "But please don't say anything about that when she comes." I clutched my decaf. "She wouldn't like my talking about her when she's not here." Or ever.

"Well, I hope your daughter's fella works out better than my youngest's did," the waitress said. "She married an older guy, and after she turned thirty, he ran off with a teenager." She sniffed in derision. "Good thing they never had kids." She leaned in close. "She cain't have 'em on account of some sorry-ass boy in high school gave her a disease that messed up her female parts. Didn't even know she had it till too late."

I listened, appalled and fascinated that she would share something so intimate with a total stranger. Then I realized I'd done the same thing, to a lesser degree, so maybe she was just reciprocating to be polite.

"Now my older girl," she went on, one-upping me, "when her husband kept cheatin' on her, she dumped his fat ass. The only bad thing is, she brung her two kids home to my house, and I don't need to tell ya how *that's* workin' out. Don't get me wrong, they's good kids, but I been puttin' in for extra shifts here ever since, just to get me some peace and quiet."

I responded with our universal Southern, all-purpose reply that applies to any difficulties, however large or small. "Bless your heart."

I looked past her to see Callie breeze in from the cold, sunny day outside. Her red quilted jacket and white scarf set off her shining brown hair and big brown eyes. She looked so beautiful, so fresh.

Heads turned, as they always did.

I stood and waved, catching her attention. "Hey, there, gorgeous," I said as I gave her a hug. "You look wonderful." We sat. "What have you been up to?"

Surely, that was safe.

She plunked into the opposite chair at the little table, all smiles. "Working on the house. I got all the rooms polished and dusted. I just have to go through one more pile of papers with Wade, so I can organize what's left, and I'm done. Done, done, done." She flagged our waitress. "I'll have hot tea with lemon, and . . ." She turned to me. "Did you order yet?"

"Not yet. Just lots of coffee."

"This your daughter?" the waitress asked, raising red flags.

I felt my smile congeal. "Mmm-hmm." *Please don't say anything.*

"She is gorgeous." She turned to Callie. "Honey, you could have just about any man in this old world."

Callie laughed. "Well, luckily, I already found a great one." She picked up a menu and dismissed the waitress with a pleasant, "Thanks. We'll order when you bring my tea."

As soon as we were alone, she looked to me and frowned in concern. "What's up with you? You've got that glassy expression you always get when you're stewing about something."

I hate being so transparent. "Just too much coffee," I half-truthed. "There wasn't any traffic, so I got here early and lost track of how many cups of regular I had while I waited. I'll level out when I get some protein in me."

This is why I'm such a poor liar. I always get bogged down in way too much detail.

Our waitress came back with Callie's tea, and we both ordered eggs over medium, grits, biscuits, and bacon, crisp. Happily, the server left us without further comment.

I brought up the reason Callie and I had gotten together. "Did you and your godmothers work out all the showers and parties?"

She brightened. "Every last one. And guess what?"

I retrieved my two-year pocket calendar from my oversized bag and prepared to write. "What?"

"Teeny insisted on giving the engagement party, since Wade's parents are both dead. Isn't that fabulous? At the PDC." (That's the Piedmont Driving Club, for the uninitiated among you, one of Old Atlanta's last bastions of exclusivity.) "She said we could invite all Wade's friends, and all of yours and Daddy's, and all of mine. Isn't that wonderful?"

Wonderful?

I did my best to keep smiling. I had hoped for something intimate, more on a need-to-know basis. A bash like this would probably end up in the Peach Buzz column of the paper, and the entire city would know my daughter was marrying her father's best friend. "Did y'all settle on a date for that?" I asked in what sounded to me like a reasonable tone of voice.

Callie's eyes narrowed. "There you go again with that glazed expression. What's wrong?"

I couldn't control my inner thoughts, but I was determined not to let on how embarrassed I felt about all this. My own mother had already warned Callie of everything I would have, and Callie hadn't budged, so there was really no point to sharing my reservations.

I knew it was petty of me to care so much what other people thought about my daughter, but I did, and I couldn't help it. "Nothing's wrong," I said. "That's so generous of Teeny, but it doesn't surprise me. She's always thought of you and Abby as the daughters she never had."

Pen poised, I asked, "And what's that date for the engagement party?"

"Friday, April seventh. The club was available, and even though that's short notice, Teeny says she can have the invitations ready to mail in plenty of time. So we decided to kick all the festivities off in April, then space the showers out at reasonable intervals."

I marked the date. "Okay, what's next?"

"Diane's giving me the lingerie shower at 103 West on April fifteenth. Noon. That's a Saturday."

I wrote it down, but couldn't resist saying, "I hope, for my sake and your godmothers', that you girls will skip the stripper just this once." It had been the custom of Callie's girlfriends to hire a male stripper for their lingerie showers. But Callie was by far the most uptight of the bunch, so I was hoping she'd be able to talk them out of it.

"Mama, I can try," she said without conviction. "They know I think it's sexist and sleazy, but if they do it, they do it."

I patted her arm. "Just try. If they go ahead anyway, it won't be the end of the world."

"Linda's giving a kitchen shower on May thirteenth, at her place at two."

"A civilized hour. Bravo." I entered "Kitchen Shower, 2:00" in teensy letters on May thirteenth.

"And Pru is doing the tool shower at the clubhouse of her apartments on the twentieth of May. That's at five. We're cooking out." Callie grinned. "Pru said a girl needs her own power tools. She's giving me a sweet little cordless 5⅜-inch circular saw just like hers. I can't wait."

I filled in, "Tools. 5:00 Pru's clbhs."

"And, last but not least," Callie said, "Teeny insisted on giving me a linen shower on June third, at her place."

"But she's already doing the engagement party," I said, hoping that maybe we could get her to settle for the shower alone. John and I could do a small engagement party at Ansley Club.

"I know, but she insisted. And you know Teeny," Callie said. "Once she makes up her mind about something, that's it."

How well I knew, indeed. I entered the information.

"Okay, then. Looks like we're all set."

There is definitely something to be said for having friends to handle the details. All I had to do was select appropriate gifts and show up.

Much as I hated it, there was a ninety percent chance that this wedding was going to happen. And based on the detective's report, I had no concrete evidence to stop it. Just an overwhelming sense that it was going to be a huge mistake.

But as it always did whenever I thought of the report, a twinge of warning went off deep inside of me. I decided it was just my conscience, because if Callie ever found out I'd gone behind her back and had Wade investigated, she'd be furious.

Putting my calendar away, I spotted the floral gift bag in my purse. "Oh, I have a little surprise for you." I took out my perfect present. "Not for you, exactly, but I hope you and Wade will like it." I'd come up with the perfect atonement for dropping in on her. I handed it over, the contents wrapped in hot pink tissue paper.

"Oh, boy. I love surprises." Callie pulled out the tissue and unwrapped the extra-large leather dog collar with BOONE and the florist shop's phone number engraved on a brass insert. I'd bought it at Pet

World, then taken it to the jeweler's and paid double to have it inscribed while I waited, so I could bring it with me.

Callie's expression reminded me of the one she'd had when she was four and I made her taste scalloped potatoes—very mixed.

"Oh." Definitely not the desired reaction. She pinched her lower lip, a sure signal that she didn't exactly know what to say. She laid the collar at the edge of the table as if it might bite her.

The waitress brought our breakfasts, which smelled wonderful. "Y'all need anything else?" she asked.

"No. Thanks." I shifted my attention back to Callie.

"Mama, that is such a thoughtful gift. Really. So sweet. Especially since Boone scared you so bad. I'm really touched."

"Then why are you frowning, honey?" I asked as I buttered my biscuit.

She winced. "Boone died not long after you came over. I meant to tell you, but . . ."

That "but" spoke volumes. As usual, Chicken Little immediately projected the worst. Biscuit poised, I ventured, "How long after I came over?"

She picked up the pepper and overseasoned her eggs. "A few hours."

My stomach plummeted. "Oh, no. Please tell me it wasn't because he got so upset when I dropped by."

"Of course not. Don't be silly," Callie hastened to reassure me, but she was no better at lying to me than I was at lying to her. "I'm sure it was just a coincidence. You saw how old and sick he was."

Gad! I had literally scared Wade's dog to death!

Guilt conjured up a martyr's crown that weighed half a ton. "How is Wade taking it?"

Callie shifted in her seat. "He's better than he was at first. Eighteen years is a long time. He's still got some grieving to do, poor guy."

Compelled to right the wrong I'd done, I recklessly offered, "Can I buy him another dog? A really cute golden retriever puppy? Would that help?"

Who said that? Surely not me.

Callie's hands shot forward, palms out, "Oh, God, no!" She

backpedaled immediately with, "I mean, thank you, that's sweet, but I think a puppy would just about finish us off at this point."

All the more reason to get one.

"So, what did you do with Boone? After he . . . ," I asked.

Dog killer!

"When Wade got home from work, I left for a while so his kids could come over and say good-bye. After they left, we set up a lantern and buried him in the back yard."

Something in her expression . . .

"Wade's kids blame you, don't they?" I realized aloud.

Callie's smile showed just a hint of the hurt she must feel. "They blame me for a lot of things I had nothing to do with. Because I'm convenient, I guess. A safe target. Madelyn has told them the divorce was Wade's fault all along, and they have a lot of anger about that. Even so, he thinks it would only hurt them worse if he told them the truth about Madelyn. Then they'd have to choose who to believe. But he's done his best to be a present and responsible father to them. So we both ignore it when the kids get snide."

The question in my mind—the real and important one—escaped out my mouth even as I thought it. "That's very noble, sweetheart. But are you absolutely positive Madelyn's the one who's lying?"

"Mama!" Callie looked at me aghast. "How can you ask such a thing? I thought you were Wade's friend."

"I am. But I'm your mother first, and as such, I have to ask. How can you be sure?"

I might as well have asked her how she knew Wade was male. "He told me all about what happened," she whispered tightly, "how Madelyn dumped him for a rich surgeon, and I believe him. He was devastated. In case you have forgotten, he had a heart attack over it."

"No, he didn't," I retorted. "He got drunk and passed out and scared you half to death."

Callie inflated with outrage. "How can you say such a thing? I was there. I remember! I saw you give him CPR. I saw the ambulance take him."

"Memory lies, Callie," I told her. "Maybe Wade's lied about Madelyn, too."

"I cannot believe this," she said, her perfect complexion mottled with anger.

As long as I was being honest, I decided I might as well be hung for a sheep as a lamb. "What about that girl he lived with afterwards? What did he have to say about her?"

Callie flushed, her words low and clipped. "She was months after the fact. And Wade only let her move in with him because he was so lonely without his children." She pushed her plate away untouched. "When that girl found out how hard he worked, she got bored and left him, too. It's a miracle the man has any confidence left."

"Honey, the last thing in this world I want to do is upset you, but your future is at stake. As your mother, I want you to know the truth now, before you burn any bridges."

My daughter glared dagger eyes at me. "Consider them burned." I had never seen her so angry with anyone. "Nothing you could tell me about Wade will change my mind," she said in deadly earnest. "No, I cannot prove that he's telling the truth. I just know. But regardless of what happened back then, he is a wonderful man now, and I love him. And we are going to be married. So if you and I are going to have a relationship, I suggest you respect my decisions and never bring this subject up again. I mean it, Mama. This is a deal breaker. I'll never speak to you again!"

Just like that. Never mind the twenty-seven years I'd loved and encouraged and provided for her. Never mind that I only had her best interests at heart. Just shut up, or I'll never speak to you again. Something inside me snapped loose. I lowered my tone so as not to make a scene. "Once your engagement is made public, half of Buckhead will think you're just another middle-aged man's trophy bride. Just another chickie-boom. The other half will smirk behind your back and take bets on how long it will be before you realize what marrying a man past sixty is like, and divorce him." The better part of me was horrified to hear what I was saying, but three months of pent-up frustration had set my tongue afire of hell. "Yet you expect your father and me to smile and go along with this and keep our concerns for your future to ourselves."

"I *expect* you to trust my judgment and support me in my decision," she shot back.

Stubborn, stubborn, stubborn.

"Put yourself in our shoes, Callista. How would you feel if your beautiful, brilliant daughter had just completed her education and was finally ready to spread her wings and fly, when, after only four months of dating, she impulsively decides to tie herself to a person who's already been there, done that, and has the scars to prove it?

"And is an alcoholic. An alcoholic, Callie. Wet or dry, that comes with the package, and there are no guarantees. So does a jealous stepdaughter, a heinous ex-wife, and two stepsons who will tolerate the marriage, at best. That baggage is real. Marriage is complicated enough without all that to deal with. Wouldn't you want your daughter to wait, to sample life on her own, to meet men her own age and see what they were like?"

Callie's voice shook with indignation when she said, "Do you really think I haven't met plenty of men my own age already? Tech and Georgia State aren't convents, Mama. I've met plenty of young men, students and teachers alike. And plenty of them have been interested. The problem is, none of them has been interesting. Some are smoother than others, but under the surface, they've all had a vastly overblown sense of entitlement, besides being juvenile and egocentric. And every relationship they pursue has only one objective—long-range or short—and that's sex. I don't think much of the men in my generation, Mama. Wade's different. I know all about the bad things he's done in the past, but he got beyond them and learned from them and became a better man—a real man I love with all my heart."

"I know you love him now," I tried to reason, "but I've told you before and I'll tell you again, you have no idea what the long years with Wade will be like. Sure, he seems gallant and indestructible, but that's been in the heat of courtship. Life for the long run will be early bedtimes, special diets, doctor visits, AA meetings, and long hours of hard work. You'll have to watch those ten o'clock shows you love in the living room alone. And you'll probably have to go to faculty parties on your own a lot, too."

Callie continued to glare at me, stone-faced, her arms crossed tightly over her chest.

"And what happens when he's seventy?" I challenged. "That's only eleven years away. Are you willing to give up the most exciting part of your life just so you can be with Wade at the end of his? Have you considered Parkinson's and Alzheimer's and prostate cancer and Depends, maybe even a nursing home, within the next fifteen years?"

"Why should I?" Callie snapped back, beyond caring who overheard us. "Do you think about all those things with Daddy? Would you give up the next ten or twenty years with him, just to spare yourself what *might* happen to him?"

"That's apples and oranges! We had our good years. I want you to have yours." I knew I should stop, but anguish prodded me to speak the real and important issue. "Wade's already raised his family. Is that another sacrifice you're willing to make? Will you give up the chance to have children of your own? Or will you have them anyway, knowing that they'll probably lose their father when they need him most?" I reached for her. "I'm your mother, honey. Am I wrong to want you to have a family of your own and a generation to enjoy it with the man you marry?"

"Not that it's any of your business, Mama, but Wade and I have talked over all those things," she railed back at me. "As for life with Wade, the early nights and times alone come with the package, as you pointed out. So does a huge physical attraction. But life with him is no sacrifice. He's my best friend, an island of sanity, my refuge, just like Daddy is for you. I need Wade more than he will ever need me. And every day we have together is precious, precisely because of his age. I don't want to lose those precious days by waiting, and I won't. So I'm giving you a choice, Mama. If you want to be a part of my life, accept this. No more lectures, no more ridiculous projections. No more judgments. I've known how you feel about this from the moment I told you about Wade, and you went pale and rigid and grabbed Daddy's arm." Her voice broke, thick with emotion. "But I trusted you to love me enough to put your own reservations aside and be there for me, not try to tear down the best and truest thing in my life."

The chasm between us loomed huge and unbridgeable.

Do over, do over, do over!

But she was my daughter, not my best friend, and not obligated to give me a fresh start. "Sweetheart, I love you more than my life. I don't want this to come between us."

"You're the one putting it between us, not me." She stood. "Mama, I'd rather be hurt for believing the best of people than safe for believing the worst. I learned that from you." Then she asked me her own real and important question, one that scored a bull's-eye on my heart. "Why is it you can believe the best of everybody but the man I love?"

Ow, ow, ow. I stared at her across my cold fried eggs and bacon. "That's a fair question," I said. "I wish I had an answer."

She picked up her purse. "Think about it." She dropped a twenty on the table. "Breakfast is on me this time. I got a part-time tutoring job till school starts next fall."

"That's great, honey." I couldn't let her leave like this. "Callie, I—"

Callie shook her head. "I need not to talk to you for a while. Don't call me, and don't come to see me." She stomped away.

I could hardly stand to watch her leave. After she was gone, the waitress came over with more decaf. "Fresh pot," she said. "Need a top-up?"

"No thanks. I just need a check."

Callie was right: I was the one putting this between us. But that didn't erase the truth of my concerns. She believed in Wade and wanted to be with him, no matter what.

"Didn't go well, huh?" the waitress stated flatly as she sorted through the orders in her apron pocket.

"That's a massive understatement." It wasn't even eleven yet, and I'd ruined everything. Again. The diner compulsion to confide seized me again. "I killed my future son-in-law's dog."

Obviously an animal lover, the waitress recoiled in horror. "Lady, that is *cold*." She slapped the check onto the table.

"Not on purpose," I clarified. "All I did was drop in at their place, and the dog snuck up on me, so I screamed, and he was really old, and he got so upset and barked so much that he croaked right after I left."

"No wonder your daughter took off in a huff," she said with a skeptical eye. "I'd be mad, too. Droppin' in like that. And killin' that old dog."

"Honey, you don't know the half of it." The check was for $14.35. I handed her the twenty. "Keep the change."

Her face lit up. "Y'all come back, hear?" she called after me as I left. "I want to know how everything turns out."

So did I.

· 12 ·

Wade's Divorce

"My Whole World Ended (The Moment You Left Me)"
— DAVID RUFFIN

The past. Thursday, May 10, 1990. 2:45 P.M. Muscogee Drive, Atlanta.

OHN WAS AWAY on a seminar in San Francisco (lucky duck) when the phone rang that fateful afternoon in May. I was putting a couple of fryers in Italian dressing to marinate for the grill, so by the time I got my hands washed, the answering machine had finished John's crisp message on the machine.

After the beep, my ten-year-old daughter's terrified voice exploded through the speaker into the sunny kitchen, curdling my blood. "Mama! Mama!" she shrieked. "You have to be there! Pick up! You promised you'd always be home while I was helping Wade!"

Propelled by a blast of maternal adrenaline, I bolted across the kitchen for the receiver. Seconds slowed to eons.

I never should have let her talk me into letting her help Wade at the flower shop after school, no matter how hard she'd begged me! No matter what a respectable, devoted family man Wade had been for the past twelve years. No matter how much Callie loved working with the flowers and looked forward to the money she made.

"Mama! Mama!" The words tore out of her and pierced my heart.

I snatched up the receiver and shouted to be heard over my daughter's rattling panic. "Callie! I'm here! What's happening?"

"I think he's dead." Words no mother ever wants to hear. She broke down in sobs.

Dear God. Had there been a robbery? I'd always worried that there might be a robbery. What if the robbers were still lurking around? "Who's dead? Wade?"

The fear in my voice deepened hers. Only rapid, choking gasps and sobs came over the phone.

Heart pounding, I forced my voice to calm. "Take a deep breath, honey. Slow down." I took my own advice even as I gave it. "Tell me exactly what's happening." When she continued to sob, I tried to jolt her back to reason with a stern, "Callie! Answer me this minute! Are you okay? Did anybody hurt you?"

The poor child was totally unglued and just cried harder.

Of all times for the car phone to be gone. I could have used it to call 911, but John had taken it with him to the conference so we could reach him if we had an emergency. "Callie," I pleaded, "please say something. Let me know you're okay."

"I'm okay!" she lashed out.

Thank God.

"It's Wade!" she told me. "He's on the floor, and there's blood coming from the back of his head. He's not breathing!"

She loved the man like a second father. "A lot of blood or a little?" I asked with a calm I did not feel.

"A little," she managed.

In a knee-jerk reaction, I blurted out, "Where's Bea?" Wade's faithful, chubby longtime assistant. Callie was never supposed to stay if Bea wasn't there! Ironclad. No Bea, and Callie was supposed to go right back to school and call me to come get her. No exceptions, for everybody's sake.

Picking up the recrimination in my tone, Callie got defensive. "I don't know where she is." She started to cry again. "I came in and hollered, but nobody answered, then I saw Wade's leg sticking out from behind the counter . . ."

"Honey, listen to Mama now," I coaxed her, my mouth dry as overdone turkey despite my relief that she was okay. "Hang up and call 911, and tell them you need an ambulance and the police. I'll be there in three minutes. Three minutes."

Dear lord, she was only a little girl. And Wade—was he really dead? "Now tell me back, sweetie. What are you going to do when you hang up?"

"Call"—teary gasp—"nine"—teary gasp—"one"—gasp—"one."

"That's good. I'm on my way. Call 911."

I hung up, scribbled a note for Jack, then bolted for the car, my mind clamoring with a hundred horrible possibilities. I must have driven like a maniac, but all I remember is my frustration when I got to E. Rivers Elementary, just across Peachtree from Wade's. Buses still blocked the right lane and parents clogged the line at the light after picking up their kids.

I almost went out of my skin while I inched toward Peachtree. "Come on!" I hollered at the cars in front of me, honking my horn and flashing my flashers as I crept toward the intersection. Didn't people know they were supposed to pull into the intersection for a left turn when their lane had a green light?

The green light switched briefly to orange, then turned red, leaving me stuck to stare across four lanes to Wade's shop in Peachtree Battle Shopping Center. So close.

I sent up an arrow prayer: *Please, God, let me get to my child. And let Wade be alive. Please.*

Suddenly, miraculous as the parting of the Red Sea, there were no cars coming on Peachtree either way. None. So I sped across against the light (almost losing my muffler at the gutter on the other side), then careened the wrong way down a parking aisle that offered the only clear path to the shop, honking my horn in warning. As usual for that time of day, there were no empty spaces near the stores, so when I got to Wade's, I threw the car into park before I was fully stopped (definitely not a good thing to do, from the awful noise it made), and jumped out, leaving the motor still running, blocking four parked cars and the entire lane.

"Callie!" I yelled as I burst through the shop door and ran inside. Overhead, the incongruously cheery tinkle of the spring-mounted bell echoed across the cool, perfumed silence that suddenly reminded me of a funeral home.

"Mama!" Callie's head shot up behind the counter, her terrified expression melting with relief as she clutched the phone. "My mother's here," she told the emergency operator. "I'm hanging up now."

She raced to cling to me. "The ambulance is coming. Oh, Mama. Poor Wade. He must have had a heart attack or something."

My maternal heart could only think first of what a horrible ordeal this was for my daughter. Callie adored Wade. He was always joking with her but treated her with real respect when it came to her talent with flowers, which had made his own little girl jealous on more than a few occasions. I had worried that Callie was developing a crush, but John said I was being paranoid and insisted she was as safe with his old friend as she was with us.

I stroked her hair and took a steadying breath. Time to find out if Wade was beyond help. I'd never actually done CPR before, and I was stone-cold scared of finding him dead. "Let me see if there's anything I can do to help. You wait here and keep an eye out for the ambulance and the police." I sat Callie down in the white wicker chair near the register, then braced myself to round the counter.

Heart pounding, I stepped toward the coolers to find my husband's best friend sprawled on his back amid the scents of a thousand blossoms, a small pool of blood oozing from his head. He sure didn't seem to be breathing, and his skin looked waxy.

Please, Lord, don't let him be dead. He has a wife and family, and he's been such a model citizen since he got married. Not that Mean Madelyn was anybody's idea of a homebody, but Wade was a fabulous father. He came home every day and made supper for the family, then put the kids to bed and went back to work. *Please don't take their daddy from his kids.*

When I knelt to give him CPR, even the smell of all those flowers couldn't cover up the truth that assailed my nostrils. The stench of booze reeked from his skin and his slack mouth. I lurched back reflexively, flashing on the way he'd mauled me that first time John had brought him over to our house on College Circle.

But this time, he didn't come to and get grabby.

Still wary, I winced at the fumes as I placed my ear against his mouth.

Sure enough, a faint waft of air came and went from his lungs. I poked around looking for his carotid pulse and eventually found it, strong and steady.

Only then did I allow myself to get angry.

Drunk! He probably cracked his head when he passed out.

Scaring my baby half to death, when he was simply garden-variety plastered!

John's faint voice echoed, nonjudgmental, behind my indignation: *Alcoholism is a disease of recidivism.*

A disease whose consequences Wade had visited on our daughter!

My Sensible Self interrupted. *He's barely breathing, and he definitely doesn't look good. Better start CPR.*

She was right, as usual, but that didn't mean I had to like it. I let out a groan. If he tried to stick his tongue into my mouth the way he had that first time, I'd slap his face off.

A fearful "Mama?" came from Callie.

"It's okay," I assured her. "He's breathing, just barely, but he's breathing. And his pulse is strong. I'm going to try CPR." I pinched his nose, gently tilted his head back, getting blood on my hand, and began to blow air into his chest. Then chest compressions: one, two, three, four, five, six, seven, eight. Then breathe.

I heard a siren approaching in the distance and prayed it was ours. The sooner I could turn Wild Man Wade over to the pros, the sooner I could take Callie home and put this behind us. No way was she ever coming back here.

The siren got louder. "Mama, can I go out to show them where we are?"

"Wait till they get closer," I said between breaths, feeling dizzy when I sat up.

Pace yourself, my CPR instructor's voice came back from memory. *You won't do anybody any good if you pass out yourself from blowing too hard.*

Oh yeah? my Rebellious Inner Child retorted. *Maybe I'm just getting drunk from the fumes.*

I heard Callie jump to her feet. "I can see their lights turning off Peachtree! They're here!" She ran for the door and exited, setting off the bell. "Here!" I heard her shouting from the sidewalk as the door closed. "We're here!"

I resumed breathing for Wade at a gentler pace. Only a few minutes more, and I could take Callie home. As soon as I got her settled, I was calling John and letting him know just how "safe" his old friend was.

The paramedics arrived with a flurry of activity. Still no sign of the police. "We can take it from here, ma'am," the one in charge told me. "We'll have him at Northside emergency in no time." Piedmont was a lot closer, but not as well equipped for serious problems.

I leaned back, monumentally relieved. Only then did I feel my knees aching on the hard concrete.

"Here. Let me help you up," the other EMT offered. "Take it slow. You might be a little light-headed." He helped me to stand, then went back to work on Wade, putting on a neck brace while his partner started an IV and radioed back and forth on his walkie-talkie to the emergency room.

I dialed Wade's home, but nobody picked up. After his jolly greeting said, "Hi! You've reached the Bowman family. Leave your number at the beep," I obliged with, "Madelyn, it's Georgia. Wade's being taken to Northside emergency. Please get there as soon as you can."

Clinging to my side, Callie watched the paramedics work, her brown eyes big as zinnias. "Is he going to be okay?" she asked, clearly afraid of the answer. Wade had been unconscious for the entire time she'd been there, and no telling how long before.

"He seems stable," the paramedic reassured her. "We'll do everything we can for him." He noted Wade's wedding ring, then mine. "Ma'am, your husband took a nasty knock when his head hit the concrete—"

"He's not my husband," I corrected tersely.

"He's our friend, Wade Bowman," Callie explained, as much of a stickler for accuracy as her scientist father. "Daddy's best friend," she further clarified.

"I just tried to call his wife," I told the paramedic, "but there was no answer, so I left a message. He has no other family. It's Wade Bowman on Peachtree Hills Avenue."

He nodded, noting the information on a pad in his kit. "Thanks. Do you know the phone number?"

I did but suddenly couldn't recall it. "Sorry. It's in the book." I frowned at Wade's continuing pallor. "Can you tell what's wrong with him?" I asked. "How bad it is?"

The guy hesitated. I wasn't a relative. But in deference to Callie's concern, he said, "His pupils aren't reacting equally, which indicates pressure in the brain. He may have had a stroke, then fallen. We won't know till we get him to the hospital." Sensing my unasked question, he added, "In addition to that, he shows evidence of . . ." He stopped to shoot a self-conscious glance at Callie, then resumed with "*substance* poisoning. Blood tests will show how severe, but based on my experience, it's a good thing you helped him breathe. People that deeply intoxicated can easily die of respiratory arrest."

"Thank you," I told him. "I needed to know for sure."

I moved Callie to arm's length and squatted so I could talk to her at her level. "Come on, honey. Wade's in good hands, now. They'll take care of him. Let's get you home."

"No, Mama, no." She grabbed my forearms, a harsh gleam of panic back in her expression. "We can't just leave him alone. He needs somebody there with him till we can get ahold of his family. You always say nobody should ever be in the hospital alone till they can look after themselves. They need somebody to protect them from mistakes."

True, but . . . "We'd just be in the way, honey. And the doctors wouldn't even be able to tell us anything, because we're not family," I gently explained. "I know they'll find Madelyn and the kids soon." Unless Mean Madelyn had taken the children on another of her expensive junkets to Florida, leaving Wade to stay home and work

seventy-hour weeks to pay for it. "They're probably at soccer practice or just running an errand."

"But they're not here now," Callie insisted, "and we don't know
when they'll be back." A statement that turned out to be prophetic.
She started crying again and turned to the paramedics, who were
strapping Wade into the stretcher. "Daddy said Wade was God's answer to his prayers for a brother when he was little, so I could call
him Uncle Wade." Seeing her so desperate, I teared up, too. "Doesn't
that count?"

They looked at her in sympathy. "Go with your mama, sweetie,
like she says," the one who'd talked to us told her. "I promise, I'll
make sure to tell the doctors to be extra, extra careful with your
daddy's best friend, here."

Callie clung to me, wailing. This last affront had pushed her beyond her precociousness to the end of her wits. "We can't leave him!
What if they make a mistake? We can't leave him alone there!"

The truth was, John would have said the same thing. And under
any other circumstances, I probably would have, too. My Inner Puritan stuck her bony finger in my face and shook it. *Do the right thing.*
He needs somebody to protect him till they find Madelyn.

I gathered my daughter close. "Okay, baby. Okay. I'll call Linda or
Teeny to come stay with you and Jack. As soon as she gets there, I'll
go to the hospital."

Even though the one Wade needed protection from was himself.

"Oh, thank you, Mama," Callie cried. "Thank you." I saw the
wheels turning in that junior Bigbrain of hers. "But please, can't I go,
too? Jack's fine by himself. He's in high school. He knows to lock all
the doors and not let anybody in. That way, we could go right now,
with the ambulance."

This time, I wasn't budging. "Nope. Home you go. Like you said,
we don't know how long it will be till they find Wade's family, and
you have tests tomorrow. You need your rest."

"It's only algebra," she said. "Bo-ring. I could make a hundred in
my sleep."

True, but I wasn't budging. "I'm taking you home, and that's that.

We'll just have to trust the Lord to look after Wade till I can get there. I think God's up to the job, don't you?"

She nodded reluctantly.

I called Linda. While the phone rang on her end, I peered toward the parking lot and asked the paramedics, "Is my car still out front? A brown Chrysler minivan?" I didn't see it.

Callie produced the keys from her pocket. "I forgot to tell you. While I was waving for the ambulance, a nice lady moved it into a space for us."

I said a grateful arrow prayer, glad it hadn't been towed or stolen. That would have just topped this day right off.

Linda answered and, as usual, was more than happy to help. "Maybe Abby can be a positive distraction." The girls had been playpen pals and got along famously.

It was rush hour by the time they made it to the house, so I didn't get to the hospital till almost five thirty. As soon as I found out what was going on, I called home with a status report for Linda to relay to Callie, then Diane and Teeny.

Social services called the police and asked them put out an APB on Madelyn Bowman's Mercedes, but she and the kids were nowhere to be found. It didn't occur to me that something might have happened to them till hours later.

Frankly, anybody might drink if he was married to the likes of Mean Madelyn, but I stopped short of true sympathy. Wade had known Callie was coming to the shop. He shouldn't have put her in the middle of this, regardless. Still, I couldn't be as mad at him as I wanted to be, because he'd hurt himself so much when he fell.

Diane showed up at the hospital on her way to a Billy Joel concert with Harold, bearing my favorite roast beef sandwich with mustard, mayo, and pickle on white from Henri's Bakery, plus an éclair, bless her heart. She apologized profusely for not being able to stay, and said Teeny's boys had chicken pox, so I was on my own.

I absolved her completely and sent her on her way. Then I fortified myself with saturated fats and chocolate while I sat in the uncomfortable plastic chair to keep vigil over Wade.

When hour after hour passed with no response to the dozen hideously expensive, "Call me at Northside Emergency!" roaming messages I left on our car phone, all my frustration and anger deflected to John for not checking the phone.

By ten P.M., worry began to creep into my irritation. Was he okay?

Well, if he was, I fumed, he was in big trouble for being incommunicado for so long! That was the whole point of his taking the car phone: so we could reach him in an emergency. Absentminded scientist or not, he should have kept in touch.

I was eavesdropping through the cubicle curtain as the head of emergency discussed the bad news on Wade's last CAT scan with the neurosurgeon when the receptionist paged me to admissions for a phone call.

John! Loaded for bear, I passed the doctors on my way. "Don't do anything till I get back," I told them, as if I had a say in the matter. Then I qualified, "Unless it's urgent."

The receptionist saw me coming. "Mrs. Baker?" When I nodded, she pointed to an unmanned admissions desk. "You can take the call over there. Line three."

I sat down in the (thank heaven) padded chair and punched three. "John?"

"God, what's happened?" he asked in bald panic. "Are you okay? Is it Callie? Jack? Mama?"

I kicked myself for not telling him it was Wade in the message. His logical scientist's mind had assumed something awful had happened to me or the family. Instead of fussing, I issued a heartfelt apology. "Oh, honey, I'm so sorry. I should have told you. I guess I overdid the messages, but I was so frustrated. We're all okay." If you could call Callie okay after what she'd been through. "It's Wade. He got falldown drunk at the shop and fell down onto the concrete, cracking his skull and giving himself a subdural hematoma."

John groaned with a mixture of relief and concern, followed by a heavy exhale.

I'd tell him about the surgery in a minute, but first, I had to get my outrage off my chest. "Callie found him lying there, John, bleeding and cold. You couldn't even tell he was breathing. She thought he was dead and called me, hysterical. I calmed her down enough to call 911, then I left Jack a note and flew over there in the car."

Anger thickened my voice as I relived everything in the telling. "Our daughter was so traumatized, I don't know what this will do to her. I wanted to take her home and just hold her till she fell asleep, but she insisted I go to the hospital to watch over Wade till they could find his wife. When I tried to beg off, Callie got hysterical again, and I realized she needed me to be here more than she needed me to be with her. So I enlisted Linda to babysit, and here I am. For how long, I don't know. So far, there's no sign of Madelyn or the kids, and Wade is still unconscious."

"Thank God you're there in spite of what he did," John said. "Nobody unconscious, not even a drunk, should be in the hospital without someone to watch over them."

How many times were my own words going to come back to me this day?

John's voice softened. "You always were the best person I ever knew."

He wouldn't think so if he could have read my mind.

"Damn," he spat out. "Of all times for me to be three thousand miles away . . . and leave the car phone in my room. That's the whole reason I brought it with me, so you could reach me in an emergency."

Hearing him voice my own accusations, I realized how petty I'd been to blame him for being his absentminded Bigbrain self. Instantly, I did what I should have in the first place and forgave him completely. "John, you didn't do it on purpose. You had that big presentation on your mind. Don't you dare beat yourself up over this. It's not your fault."

My Inner Puritan shifted the bony finger of judgment. *It's Wade's fault!* So much for forgiveness.

"So," I asked, "how did the presentation go?"

"Famously, for what it's worth," he dismissed. "So what's going on with Wade?"

"The doctors have been monitoring the bleed," I told him. "At first it was minor, but the last CAT scan showed that it's grown, so they're probably prepping him for surgery right now. I ought to get back."

But I couldn't bring myself to cut the steadying connection with John, so I kept on talking. "The doctors have been really good. I'm not a relative, but since I'm the only one here, they've spoken up loud enough so I can eavesdrop on everything through the curtain."

"If they're prepping Wade for surgery, you probably ought to go back," John said, mirroring my own reluctance. "Honey, I'm so sorry you and Callie got sucked into this. Something really horrendous must have happened to cause him to fall off the wagon."

Madelyn? I wondered in a flicker of premonition. "Madelyn's car is gone, but they haven't looked in the house." Chicken Little spit out several daunting possibilities that my mind refused to address out of loyalty to John's friendship with Wade. "Maybe the police could find some clue there to where Madelyn is." Or something worse.

"It's all gonna be okay, honey," John promised. It had taken ten years to train his super-logical Bigbrain to say that no matter what, but by then, he could do it with believable conviction. "I'm catching the next plane out of here."

"But it's so late. Wait till morning. Get some rest."

"It's only seven here, and I'm coming home. Delta has plenty of red-eye nonstops to Atlanta. I'll get on one, even if I have to hijack it. See you in a few hours."

Music to my ears. " 'Bye. Be safe. I love you." The sooner we hung up, the sooner he'd be here to put his arms around me.

"I love you, too," he said with a softness that made it more than a cursory farewell.

When the call ended, I dialed nine for an outside line and called the house. "Hey," I said to Linda when she answered. "How are things?" It was a great comfort to know she never tried to sugarcoat the truth. If she said Callie was okay, I could count on it.

"The girls are out cold," she said. "Jack's still writing a paper in his room. Why can't my daughter be as responsible with her schoolwork as your kids?"

I knew the question was rhetorical. "I hope Callie isn't having bad dreams."

"When I turn in," Linda said, "I'll move Abby to the sleeping bag and take the other twin, just in case."

"What would I do without you?" With her there, I didn't have to worry.

"You'll never have to find out, sweetie. What's up with you?"

"John finally called," I told her. "He's catching the next nonstop flight home. Wade's brain bleed has increased, so they're going to have to operate to prevent damage. They say he'll probably be okay, barring complications. Still no sign of Madelyn."

I really needed to wrap this up and get back to the ER. "Listen, Linda, I hate to keep you up any later"—she rose at five every morning—"but there's a spare key to Wade's house in the key locker over the washing machine. It's marked. Do me a favor and give it to the police if they come over for it. I'm going to ask them to look in Wade's house for something that might tell them where Madelyn might be."

"Great idea. Consider it done. Why don't you come home and get a little rest after they take Wade to surgery?"

"No way could I close my eyes," I said. "I'll stick around and wait for John. He's coming straight here."

None of my best friends and I ever tried to argue each other out of a responsible decision, so she accepted what I'd said. "Okay. I'll call back after they pick up the key. Where will you be?"

"In the neurosurgical waiting room, I guess. Or the one for ICU, once they're finished with the operation."

"Don't worry," she said with her usual quiet confidence, "I'll find you."

"Thanks."

The line went dead, and I left to resume watching over Wade till they took him upstairs to open his brain. I could make it till John got there. Then I could collapse, but for the moment, I had to be kind to someone who had traumatized my child.

I tell you, living out my "born again" Baptist faith was no picnic sometimes.

Wade did fine through the four-hour surgery, and John arrived just in time to see him taken up to intensive care, where the police were in the waiting room with news that they'd gone to Wade's and discovered a note from Madelyn taped to his golf clubs—one of the few things she hadn't taken with her. She wrote that she'd found a man who appreciated her and could give her and the children the finer things in life, so she was leaving him and keeping the kids. I was able to be a lot more forgiving when I realized that Wade's behavior was probably an indirect suicide attempt.

We didn't tell Callie any of that. We just told her Wade made it through the operation and would have a long, long recuperation, so she couldn't go back to the shop.

And she didn't. At least, not until Wade had long since recovered his sobriety and outgrown his chickie-boom rebound. By then, Callie had her working papers and cajoled John into letting her arrange flowers again after school.

Can we say, big mistake?

If I had known then what I know now . . .

13

Lies between lovers are like stones in your shoe.
Even a little one can cripple your progress.
—LINDA'S *BUBBIE*

The present. Second Tuesday in March. 7:15 A.M. Muscogee Drive, Atlanta.

· ·

*B*REAKFAST!" I CALLED as I placed John's buttered whole wheat toast beside the scrambled eggs and bacon on his plate, then set it opposite mine on the table in the breakfast nook. No toast for me. I poured us both cups of mocha supreme flavored coffee, my big splurge now that I'd resolved to lose the ten pounds I'd gained feeding my fears for Callie with sugar and chocolate. I hadn't heard a peep from her in a week, and the rift between us weighed heavy on my heart.

John breezed in and gave me a peck, then took his seat. "Now, that's a breakfast." He surveyed the food with a satisfied smile, as if he hadn't eaten the same thing almost every day for more than a third of a century. (Bigbrains take great comfort in routine.) "Good job, woman."

Ah. He only got primitive when he was in a good mood. "You Tarzan, me Jane." Maybe for just that day, I could avoid the raw subject of Callie and Wade. I hadn't heard a word out of her since our blowup.

I stirred two artificial sweeteners into my coffee, then inhaled the aroma. "You seem awfully happy today," I commented. "What's up?"

He finished a healthy bite of eggs, then smiled his irresistible little-boy-proud smile. "After lab and my lecture, we're having the last grant application meeting for our electromagnetic propulsion research, hallelujah, amen. I can hardly wait to see that sucker signed, sealed, and sent off. Frank's hand-delivering it to Washington. Then we'll all sit back and wait."

"You know they'll give you the grant. I'm so proud of you." No wonder John could let go of worrying about Callie. His Bigbrain was full of things like harnessing electromagnetic energy to drive pollution-free cars and space shuttles.

"It's only a start, but we have some very promising directions to go in." He continued to eat with gusto.

I was jealous. "Maybe I ought to get a job," I said impulsively. "Something to keep my mind off things."

His cup halted halfway to his mouth, and John's happy candor shifted to guarded assessment. He searched my expression before saying, "If that's what you want, go for it. I've never doubted for one minute that you could do anything you set your mind to, and do it well. But Linda will go into withdrawal." He made an effort to brighten. "Of course, you might have trouble getting a four-hour lunch break for your Red Hat Club meetings."

"I could always go to work for Teeny," I mused aloud, knowing perfectly well that I wouldn't. But it felt good to toy with the idea. "She likes my clothes designs. Maybe I could do something with that."

John frowned. "So, is that the plan with y'all?" he asked with uncharacteristic pique. "Everybody goes to work for Teeny?" He stabbed at the strawberry jam. "Maybe I should apply for a grant from her, too."

Whoa! What was *that* all about? "Where is John Baker, and what have you done to him?" I countered. "He was just here a minute ago rejoicing about his grant application."

John sighed, his focus on his plate. "Sorry. Before all this Callie business, I never once resented your relationship with your friends.

But lately you seem . . . away—closer to them than you do to me, and I don't like it."

Unprecedented, such talk from my ever-patient, always-level husband.

Alarm bells went off, accompanied by "bad girl!" messages. I'd thought I'd gotten away with keeping mum about the detectives and my big fight with Callie, but he had sensed the subtle change in me.

"John, I . . ." What could I say? Unburdening my conscience might make me feel better, but it sure wouldn't do him any good. "I love you more than ever," I declared. "This distance has nothing to do with that." What I wouldn't give to be able to let go and accept things the way he had. "I wish I could get past this, just lay it down the way you have, but I can't. It's stuck in there, spinning, spinning, spinning, and I don't know how to shut it off. I'm frantic for Callie." I stopped, afraid I might blurt everything out. "I have to get through this somehow. It's not fair to obsess all over you, so the girls are my sounding board. That's all it is."

"I know." He looked to me from the far side of this new divide with longing. "I just miss you. The happy, busy, sexy you."

"I miss her, too," I confessed. "And she misses you."

He surprised me further by globalizing the conversation, something unusual for a scientist who was all about specifics. "Does anybody have a clue when they get married?" he asked. "Did Diane? Did Linda? Or Teeny or Pru? Did *you*?"

"Of course I did," I answered without hesitation. "Marrying you was the best thing I ever did, and you have never let me down. Not once. We just see this one thing differently." I cocked my head, a thread of fear wending its way into my heart. "Did you know what you were getting into with me?" That I wouldn't be able to love him the way he deserved for so many years?

He sighed again, then got up and circled me from behind in the solid comfort of his arms. His head beside mine, he said with bacony coffee breath, "No."

I froze and didn't breathe till he finished with, "I had no idea how wonderful it would be having your warmth and your joy and your loving kindness in my life." He squeezed. "And your passion." Even though it had come so late. "All my hopes were so much smaller than what you have given me."

No poet ever said it better. I dissolved.

What had I ever done to deserve such a man?

I rose and turned into his arms, holding on for dear life. "Are you trying to get me back into bed?" I joked, too full to speak what I was feeling.

Sex was one place where we felt no distance, even now.

"Ha!" He glanced at the clock. "Now there's a perfect ending for a great breakfast."

I reached around him to close the mini blinds. Then I unbuckled his belt, nudging him toward the vintage breakfast chair I'd just vacated. "Why don't we just do a little experiment to see how much weight and motion this sturdy little chair can take? If it works, we could apply for a grant."

He sat in it, facing me. "And if it doesn't?" he asked, seductively lifting my robe and gown.

Desire erased all thought of anything but who we were and what we were up to. I straddled him. "We'll buy stronger furniture."

The chair held up just fine.

That same day. 10:40 A.M. Swan Coach House, Atlanta.

BUOYED BY OUR kitchen caper and anxious for the company of my friends, I got to the Coach House ten minutes earlier than usual. Once I convinced the gift shop lady to let me come out of the cold, blustery sunshine and into the decidedly chilly restaurant, I took my place in our regular banquette, hoping the heat would come up soon.

Maria appeared from the kitchen with a pot of hot diet lemonade. "Welcome, Mrs. Baker." She poured the steaming treat into my ice-cold cup. "I'm sorry we're still so cool here. They just turned up the heat for the dining area."

The lemonade warmed me all the way down. "Bless your heart," I said with a swell of affection for this woman who had looked after me and my best friends so well for so long. I realized with shame that

I didn't even know if she was married or had any children. "Maria, are you married?"

Her smile broadened and her soft Spanish accent warmed. "*Sí.* Twenty-three years with my Juan. We have three girls and two boys, all as American as apple pie." Five kids! "That's why I love this job so much," she confided. "I get home early enough to help them with their homework." Maria winked and leaned in closer. "I had to leave school when I was twelve, so I am learning with them, and I love it. But don't tell my kids. I do not want them to think it is okay to quit school."

All this time, and none of us had ever thought to ask. Class guilt shamed me further. "Thank you for sharing that with me."

She nodded. "I would stay and talk with you, but I must get ready to open."

More guilt. I was making her job harder. "Oh, please. Don't let me keep you." Watching her go, I settled back to enjoy my lemonade.

Eleven rolled around, then another fifteen minutes passed as people started drifting in, during which I drank the whole pot of lemonade and ate three mini muffins without even thinking about calories.

Oh, well. I should have known better than to start a diet on a Tuesday, anyway—especially Red Hat Club Tuesday. Any idiot knows that diets have to start on Mondays.

I called Linda's cell phone, but got a new message. "Sorry. I can't work the call waiting on this contraption without hanging up on everybody, so please leave a message. I may get it, or I may not. Call me back if I don't call you. I hate these contraptions."

It made me laugh.

Little by little, the tables began to fill.

I hoped Linda was okay, and hadn't been driven to suicide by Rachel. Sol's schedule was so jam-packed that Rachel still had plenty of time to kill, even though her fast-forward courtship was coming along famously.

More of the lunch bunch arrived, but there was no sign of my cronies till ten minutes later, when I was glad to see Diane and Teeny head my way from the lobby. Seemed it was a tardy day for everybody but me. I waved, feeling like we'd been separated for months.

Diane had forgone her usual red hat for a red velvet headband with her old-faithful dark purple gabardine coat. Teeny was elegant as always in a red camel hair jacket over matching slacks and a gorgeous purple satin blouse. And Pru had on a psychedelic-print purple Nehru jacket with matching bell-bottoms—probably original issue.

Twenty paces behind them, who should walk in but Rachel, unescorted and uninvited, and dressed in her Black Widow best.

Rats. No way could we talk freely with her there.

I only had a few seconds to warn the others as they sat. "Don't look now," I murmured, "but Rachel is right behind you."

Teeny swiveled to see her and said through a fixed smile, "Well, damn." An unprecedented use of profanity.

Pru, bless her heart, broke into a big smile and waved to Rachel in welcome.

"I hope Linda didn't have car trouble," Diane worried aloud.

"I think she's on the car phone with somebody," I said. "It was hard to tell from her new message."

Rachel minced her way up to our table on her four-inch stilettos. "Where's Linda?" she asked as she sat, clearly annoyed. "She left twenty minutes before my cab came. I wanted to surprise her."

"Well, you surprised us," I said, none too gently.

"Did you try to call her?" Rachel demanded.

"Yes. Her new message is a stitch. I asked her to call us, but I haven't heard anything back."

"I hope she's not dead on the side of the road," Teeny said.

Rachel blanched. "Do you really think she might be? I mean, judging from the maniac drivers in this place, it wouldn't surprise me, but—"

Soft-hearted Pru explained, "It's okay, Rachel. We always say that whenever any of us is late, because our grandmothers always said it. For us, it's sort of a joke."

Over the years, we've cobbled together our own little language of movie quotes, lines from songs, and inside references from our pasts. It occurred to me that Rachel might feel the way I had trying to use my ancient high school French in Paris: I managed to understand most of the individual words people spoke, but I knew I was missing way too much of the real meaning.

Rachel frowned. "A very little joke, if you ask me." She glanced skyward, waggling prayerful hands back and forth, dry-spitting exactly the way Linda did. "*Tui, tui, tui.* She should live and be well."

In that instant, they might have been the same person, which was way too spooky for me. And apparently for the others, too. They sat staring at Rachel with widened eyes.

Diane ended the brief silence with, "Now, on to trivialities." She stood and took off her coat with a dramatic sweep, revealing a striking red leather strip belt looped through a star-shaped hole in a big gold buckle in the shape of Texas that lay across her taut tummy. A very taut tummy, so much so that it diverted my attention from her belt buckle.

"You've been working out!" I accused good-naturedly. "It's still winter. We're supposed to be keeping our insulation."

Diane actually blushed as she took her seat, something so alien from her usual quick rejoinders that all three of us honed in on her with sharpened interest.

I leaned closer to make out the details on the buckle. "That's fabulous." Artfully executed steers grazed on either side of an arched gateway with the name of Cameron's ranch, the flying C. Typically Texan: big, proud, and anything but subtle. "Cameron the Cowboy done good with this one."

Rachel inspected it with an appraising eye. "Very nice. Fourteen or eighteen carat?"

Diane's color deepened. "Fourteen, if you must know. Eighteen's too soft for a piece this size."

Rachel waggled her brows. "What did you have to do to get it?"

As Diane inhaled to launch into a stick-that-in-your-pipe-and-smoke-it speech worthy of *Designing Women*, peacemaker Teeny jumped in with, "Wow, Diane. What is this, the twelve months of Christmas, Texas style?"

"Something like that," Diane said, still glaring at Rachel, who remained clueless as to how insulting her question had been. At a warning glance from me, Diane exhaled heavily. Suddenly self-conscious, she covered the belt with her napkin and scooted closer to the table.

"If you're embarrassed about it," Pru kidded, "why did you wear it?"

"It seemed like a good idea at the time." There was something unspoken in her eyes that signaled me to back off, so I did. Everybody else but Rachel did the same.

"So, who's the fella?" she asked with a mercenary gleam in her eye.

Since Rachel had never even heard of Tradition Five (MYOB), Teeny once more steered the conversation back to safer ground with, "It's not like Linda to be so late. First January, now March."

"I'll check on her again." Pru whipped out her new cell phone (only she had heeded Teeny's request for us to upgrade), flipped it open, then brought it close to her mouth and said emphatically, "Linda, cell."

Seeing our amazement, she explained, "Bubba helped me program my upgrade to take voice commands. Yours'll do it, too."

The very idea of zero-tech Pru uttering words like *program, upgrade,* and *voice commands* shifted our paradigm for the Universe.

Her attention reverted to the phone. "Hey there, Miss Linda. Where are you?"

She pivoted toward the doorway, and we followed her line of sight to see Linda's old-faithful red Fendi purse wave from behind a clutch of sculpted, personal-trainer types waiting to be seated.

Pru did her imitation of Gilda Radner's Emily Litella. "Never mind." She flipped the phone shut with a dimpled smile.

When Linda emerged from the crowd, I let out a ladylike little wolf whistle. "Whoa. Check out that pantsuit." The clean-lined ensemble made the most of her petite, barrel-bodied physique. "Very nice." As was her attractive red cashmere hat with a turned-up brim.

Diane preened. "I finally talked Linda into letting me dress her."

Love had softened Rachel a bit, but Rachel being Rachel, she let out a most unladylike snort. "Why bother, big as she is?"

We all turned to her, aghast.

Diane had had enough. Her neck mottled by indignation, she growled out, "Why, you little—"

I headed off a serious set-to with an overzealous "You look mahvelous" to Linda. She did, as much because of the radiance on her face as from her flattering outfit. Something happy was definitely up. She didn't even register Rachel's presence, much less her insult. Instead, she responded to my compliment with our standard imitation of Goldie Hawn's fey rendition of "Thank you *so* much" from *Butterflies Are Free*.

"You look like the cat that ate the caviar," I said as Linda took her place. "What's up?"

Ignoring my question, she asked, "Who has the joke?"

"You do," Teeny and Diane and Pru and I said in unison.

Linda chuckled. "I have the joke." Grinning, she clapped her palm over the soft brim of her red cashmere hat. "Gracious. I rehearsed the thing halfway over here. Wait a second. It'll come to me."

After only a few seconds, her smile broadened. "Nope. Gone as the last piece of rare roast beef at a bar mitzvah." She spread her napkin. "Oh, well. I'll think of it later."

"So," Diane said, cutting to the chase as always, "what's got you so happy you forgot the joke you rehearsed half the way over here?"

Linda practically smiled her face off and held up a dreidel. "The dreidel was right! I'm going to be a grandmother, God willing!" She dry spit three times. "*Tui, tui, tui,* we should all live and be well."

We all erupted into congratulations. First Teeny, then Pru, and now Linda had entered that blessed, golden circle of grandmotherhood— assuming all went well with the pregnancy. I said a brief arrow prayer to that effect. At last, Abby had given her mother something to rejoice about with her whole heart.

Rachel seemed suddenly withdrawn and silent, but the Red Hats' questions overlapped. "When?" "When did you find out?" "Are they excited?" and "Do they know what it is?"

Linda basked in her moment. "They're very excited, but not half as excited as I am. It's due the end of July. And no, they don't know if it's a boy or a girl yet, but they want to. They're having a 3-D sonogram tomorrow."

"Oh," I said, "those are fabulous. You can really see what the baby looks like."

"When did they tell you?" Pru repeated. "We want all the details."

Linda kissed the dreidel and laid it on the tablecloth. "That's why I was late. Abby and Osama had just gotten out of the OB's. I had to pull over, I was so beside myself."

"Which OB are they going to?" I asked.

"Dr. Richardson." The same one we all used, bless his good old-fashioned heart. "She missed four periods before she got around to buying a pregnancy test last week." Linda beamed. "Hard to believe, but you know Abby—the doctor's daughter wants nothing to do with them. She didn't have any morning sickness or anything, and she's so scatterbrained, she probably didn't notice she'd skipped her periods till the third one. The drugstore test was positive, but she wanted to make sure before they told me." She preened and repeated. "I was the very first one they called."

"Of course you were," Diane said. "Who else? Certainly not Mama-sama."

I glared at her. Nothing like throwing a wet burqa on Linda's happy moment. Osama's mother (Mama-sama, of course) had come over for one last-ditch effort before his wedding to talk him out of marrying Abby and renouncing his faith and his family, his tribe and his nation. In two weeks as Abby's guest, she'd spoken only Farsi to her son, ignoring Abby completely except for a few nasty insults in crisp English.

Teeny piped up a little too brightly with, "Our little Abby, expecting. I can still remember holding her in my arms, all pink and precious. And now she's going to have a baby of her own." Then her smile suddenly collapsed. "Oh, gosh." She leaned forward and whispered urgently to Linda, "Does Osama smoke pot around her? Couldn't that have an effect on the baby?"

Rachel's eyebrows shot up as she regarded Linda with renewed sharpness. "Pot?" she bellowed. "Your son-in-law smokes pot? Oh my God!"

Heads turned halfway across the room at the interruption.

Talk about a gaffe!

"Rachel," Linda said tersely. "If you yell, I'm taking you home."

Rachel pouted. "Sorry. No more yelling, I sweah."

But even that wasn't enough to dampen Linda's spirits. "To answer your question, no, thank God, Osama never smokes around Abby," she said to Teeny. "She's always insisted that he do his toking elsewhere. But just to be sure, after I congratulated Abby, I asked to speak to Osama, and I told him in no uncertain terms that I'd narc on him personally if he smoked *anything* within a city block of that baby, born or unborn."

"You go, girl," Diane said.

Linda clasped her hands before her face in glee. "I can't wait to start buying baby stuff." And this was just the place to start. The gift shop had gorgeous baby clothes.

Her excitement was contagious. Teeny reached across the table and squeezed her wrist. "Grandchildren are the most fun ever. You are gonna love it."

"What did Brooks say when you told him?" I asked Linda.

Her face fell. "Gawd. I promised Abby I'd tell him right away, but I was so excited and so anxious to get here and tell y'all that I completely forgot."

"Uh-oh," Diane said. "Time's awastin'."

"Well, you can't do it from here," I advised. "If he hears this herd-of-birds background, he'll know where you are, and he'll know you've told us first. Very not good." I rose. Usually we retreated to the ladies' room for privacy, but there was no cell phone signal down there. "To the art gallery!" It was quiet in there.

The five of us headed for the exhibit space on the other side of the gift shop with Rachel in tow, then ran off the lone browser by crowding around her way too close. Once she was gone, Diane posted herself at one entrance while Pru patrolled the other to make sure Linda wasn't disturbed as she dialed Brooks's super-private cell number.

Rachel looked at the watercolors on display. "How quaint," she said with disdain, the same comment she'd used when Diane had taken her to the High Museum downtown.

Linda tapped her foot as the cell phone rang and rang. "He always answers my ring unless he's in surgery. Maybe he had an emergency."

Mondays, Wednesdays, and Thursdays were Brooks's regular surgeries, but he did get an occasional patient with unexpected complications or injuries.

Linda's expression cleared. "Hey," she said into the phone. "Can you talk? It's important." Still smiling. "Oh, good." She paused for dramatic effect. "The kids just called me." She crossed her fingers and lied, "No, I haven't gone into my meeting yet. I wanted to talk to you first." Another pause. "Guess what? You're gonna be a granddaddy, God willing!"

Brooks let out a whoop so loud, Linda jerked the phone away from her ear. We all heard his barrage of excited questions that followed. Linda put the phone back to listen. "Whoa, whoa, honey. I can't answer if you keep firing questions at me. One at a time." She listened. "It's due July twelfth, and they won't know what it is till they get the 3-D sonogram tomorrow. But they do want to find out, which is great, because I want to know what color baby clothes to buy."

After a pause, her joy shifted abruptly to annoyance. "No, they didn't say a word about that, and I certainly wasn't about to ask them." Another pause, with eyes rolling. "No, I don't think it's a good idea to get it cleared up now. They probably don't even know, themselves." Pause. "Brooks, I am asking you not to bring this up. Not till it's born, at the earliest."

It wasn't hard to figure out what she was talking about. Brooks wanted to know if his first grandchild would be brought up Jewish, Moslem, or Rastafarian. Or nothing.

"Honey, you are singin' to the choir here," Linda went on. "Of course, I want it to be brought up Jewish, but that's their decision, not ours. Could we please focus on the wonderfulness of this for now? Our only daughter is going to have a baby. A *legitimate* one. Can't we just be happy about that?"

Her expression eased somewhat. "Okay. You're forgiven . . . as long as it doesn't happen again. But I meant what I said about leaving them alone about this. I will not have you gettin' them all riled up."

The more aggravated Linda became, the thicker her Southern accent got.

Abruptly, her expression went slack. "What?" Tears welled in her eyes, but clearly not from sadness. "Well, sure. Absolutely. When?" Clearly touched, she started crying silently in earnest. "No, that's wonderful."

I handed her a clean hankie from the pocket of my blazer. (Tissues make me sneeze, so I always carry one—a comforting anachronism that is worth the washing and ironing.)

She dabbed away the overflow, nodding. "Yes, I'm crying." The next pause was punctuated by a soft, adoring smile. "Have I told you how great you are?" She sighed like a smitten teenager. "Okay. See you tonight. I love you. Bring champagne. We'll celebrate."

Those last two words resonated exciting possibilities.

Seeing that kind of devotion after all these years made the rest of us well up, too, and my empathy was sharpened by my own third course at breakfast.

Rachel took everything in with a strained smile, clearly feeling the isolation of her own situation, and I truly felt sorry for her. The worst part of living a selfish life is, you're left with just yourself, and that had to be awfully lonely. Even though Rachel was six years younger than Linda, she'd probably missed her chance to have children of her own.

Linda closed her phone with a satisfied click.

"So, what's so wonderful?" Diane asked. "Besides the baby?"

"Brooks is finally taking me to Ireland." Something he'd been promising to do since his residency, but never managed with his busy surgical schedule. Linda misted up again. "We'd been planning to leave May nineteenth for a couple of weeks at the beach, but now it's Ireland instead! He said once the baby's here, we won't want to leave, so we're finally going. First class, all the way. Castles, a personal chauffeur, gourmet meals, the works. Just the two of us. And we'll be back in plenty of time for the wedding." She said it as if she still couldn't quite believe it. "We are really going to Ireland." Dabbing at fresh tears, she dry-spit three times to keep from tempting fate. "*Tui, tui, tui.* God willing, and we should live and be well."

I hugged her, hard. "You sounded just like your *bubbie* when you said that." And Rachel.

Linda perked up, taking the comparison for the compliment it was. "I'd rather look like her." Like Mama, Linda's mother wore a size ten and had the energy of a thirty-year-old, something she got from her mother.

Resolute, Linda turned in the gallery and motioned us back toward the restaurant. "I'm gonna be a *bubbie*." She laughed. "Come on. I am famished. Lunch is on me, in honor of the occasion."

"Why, thank you, ma'am," Teeny accepted graciously.

Lagging back with Rachel, I took her arm and said, "Come on. You're gonna have a new baby cousin. Let's go celebrate."

She looked at me with a quivering smile and nodded, suddenly seeming very small and very fragile.

On the way back to our table, we detoured by the baby gifts and oohed and aahed over all the cute things, but reserved any purchases till we found out if it was going to be a boy or a girl.

Maria was waiting for our order when we sat. We all ordered our usuals, but Rachel took forever perusing the menu. "I forgot to ask last time," she said to Maria. "Is your food kosher?"

"No ma'am," Maria said. "I'm sorry, it's not."

As if it mattered, anyway. Rachel had told me herself that she hadn't kept kosher since she married.

"Okay, then. I'll have the Favorite Combination, but substitute another chicken salad for the shrimp." No pleases, no thank-yous, just commands. Boy, did this woman have a lot to learn.

With our orders in, Teeny proposed that we all go in together to throw a honkin' huge baby shower for Abby at the PDC on Teeny's membership.

"Speaking of showers," Linda said to me, "were the dates and everything okay with you for the ones we planned for Callie?"

"They were fine." I said. "All I ask is that somebody provides me with some serious tranquilizers before the lingerie shower."

Diane spoke the words as she wrote in tiny letters "Valium for GA" on the shower date of her pocket calendar. Then she looked to me with reassurance. "I've already spoken to Callie's bridesmaids, and they swore they weren't getting a male stripper this time."

I'd believe that when I saw it. I pointed a finger in warning toward them all. "And if any of you gives her split-crotch panties, or anything of that ilk, I will never speak to you again. I cannot handle the idea of Wade and . . ."

Had I just said *ilk*?

When Linda raised her hand in the Girl Scout salute, the others did the same. "No split-crotch panties," she swore.

"Or anything of that *ilk*," Pru teased. Her subtle emphasis on the word was a good-natured prod at my tendency to lapse into cross-word puzzle words when stressed.

Diane's evil grin was worthy of Jack Nicholson. "We won't need to bother with the nasty underwear. Callie's girlfriends will take care of all that, I'm sure."

I groaned but maintained my composure. "I wonder if plastic surgeons can do permanent smile implants," I said through a forced grin. "I could always have it reversed afterward."

"I'll check into it for you," Teeny offered.

"Thanks." After three months of alternating drastic projections, embarrassment, and denial, these plans made Callie's wedding all too real.

Like Linda said: It could be worse. Wade was sober, healthy, productive, and smitten.

Maria arrived with our lunches, but just as we were about to dig in, Linda piped up with, "I remember!"

Forks poised, we stared at her, blank.

"Remember what?" Diane asked, as clueless as we were.

Linda chortled. "My joke. This is a good one."

Wishfully eyeing my chicken salad, I lowered my silverware. "Let's hear it."

"Two women were standing before St. Peter at the pearly gate," she began. "He said to the first one, 'We're taking a little survey this month. Would you please tell me how you died?'

" 'It was awful!' the first woman said. 'I got so furious at my husband, I had a heart attack and croaked.'

"St. Peter nodded. 'Goodness. And how did that happen?'

"The woman sighed. 'I came home from work early because I knew my husband was having an affair, and sure enough, there he was in the bed, naked, wild-eyed, and guilty-looking. So I started searching the house. I knew he had a woman in there somewhere. I tore through every closet, every room, looked under every bed, but nothing.' "

Linda leaned forward. " 'I knew his bimbo was hiding somewhere. The harder I looked, the more upset I got, until finally I had a heart attack. My husband gave me CPR for forty-five minutes till the paramedics got there, then went with me to the hospital, but I died three hours later.' " Linda leaned back.

This sounded all too familiar, but I held back till she had finished.

" 'Mercy,' St. Peter said, then asked the next woman, 'And how did you die?'

" 'I froze to death,' the other woman said, then turned to the first one. 'And if you'd only looked in the freezer, we'd both still be alive.' "

Linda waited, grinning, for our reactions.

We looked at each other, knowing that everybody but Linda (and Rachel) had wised up.

"What?" Linda said. "Why aren't y'all laughing? Don't you get it?"

Pru and Diane and I got very busy eating our lunches, but Teeny, usually our clueless one, leaned forward. "Oh, sweetie, we get it. It's a really good joke. We thought so last fall, when Georgia told the same one, only with men instead of women."

"And hers was longer." Pru rolled her eyes. "*Lots* longer."

I bristled. "Not *that* long." The others were suppressing smiles.

Rachel observed with what I can only describe as a twinge of jealousy.

Linda got defensive. "Well, it's not the same at all. I mean, George's joke was about a refrigerator, and some guy doing yoga, and this is about a freezer and . . ." The light went on. "Oh my gosh. It is the same joke, isn't it?" She laughed, and we joined her. "Oh . . . my . . . gosh. This is the first time ever, isn't it? Nobody's ever repeated the same joke before."

"Not that I can remember," I told her. "But my memory's not worth a flip anymore, either." Vitamins and hormone replacement had helped me, but Linda's breast cancer ruled out hormone therapy for her.

"Losing some memory wouldn't be bad at all if we could choose what to forget," I mused. "You know, like when you're lying in bed at night and stuff you can't do anything about keeps spinning, spinning,

spinning in your mind, and you can't get to sleep. How great would it be to hit the delete button and forget it?"

I could tell the others knew I was talking about Callie and Wade.

Diane nodded. "I'd like to erase the mental image of that bimbo in Cobb County riding my ex in their love nest." Catching him had been her idea, but an image like that is indelible.

"I'd erase the memory of how much I love chocolate éclairs," Linda said. "Make that pastries of all types. And ice cream. Flush it out of my mind once and for all."

At the mention of chocolate, Rachel shot Linda a look of reproach, but kept her mouth shut. Maybe she was improving, after all.

Pru's features softened. "I've forgotten more than enough. I need to remember everything, to help me stay sober," she said with absolute sincerity.

How I wished I could forget about Wade and Callie, even for a few hours, but I couldn't. Chicken Little wouldn't let me.

At the thought of my inner doomsayer, she let out a maniacal cackle of satisfaction, which I countered by practicing my smile of graceful resignation.

Might as well. This was Linda's day. I didn't want to rain on her parade. "Well, considering the circumstances, I'm amazed you remembered it at all. I'd forget my own name if I found out Callie or Jack was going to make me a grandmother."

"Your day will come," Linda reassured.

I wished I could believe that. Jack was such a nomad workaholic, he hadn't had time for even a girlfriend. And Callie . . .

We settled to our food and were almost done when I saw an over-dressed, over-made-up Rachel clone blow into the lobby with all the frigid force of the March wind that came with her. She had on what looked like a genuine Chanel suit in black, with stilettos that probably cost more than my car, and yards of pearls. I couldn't help looking from her to Rachel. Except for Rachel's huge black hat, they were almost identical.

The woman charged to the doorway, stopped to scan the tables, saw us, then minced a beeline toward our corner.

"Oh my gosh," Linda said. "Isn't that Wade's ex, Madelyn Vandercleef, heading this way?"

Buckhead matrons can smell a confrontation a mile away, so by osmosis, every native in the place stopped what she was doing to watch with glee.

Teeny squinted at her. "Whoever she is, check out those bazooms. Not nearly as convincing as mine. It looks like she's got softballs stuffed into that silk blouse." She shook her head.

"I don't think it's Madelyn," Diane said, then dropped to a whisper. "Madelyn had a really big butt for her size." Aside from this woman's high and hard bustline, she was built like a twelve-year-old boy.

"Lipo," Rachel said with authority. She flopped a hand in the air. "Trust me, I know."

We'd all had a nip here and a suck there, but thanks to amazing surgeons, the effects were subtle, unlike the woman bearing down on us, who looked anything but natural. As she got closer, her overzealous facelift became obvious.

"The last time I saw Madelyn," Teeny said, sweetly as you please, "she wasn't Chinese."

We responded with a chorus of "Ooo, hoo, hoo"s.

"I'm afraid it is Madelyn," I said with growing apprehension. "I never forget a face, even when it's had a nose job."

Normally, we're not nearly so catty, but this woman was obviously up to no good. She had a brittle gleam in her eye and a hard set to her mouth, and it didn't take a rocket scientist to figure out why she was here.

I was in for it, as Callie's mother.

"Something tells me this is not going to be pretty," I murmured as she drew close.

"Don't worry, sugar," Linda said. "We've got your back."

Madelyn halted to scan our little gathering, her expression haughty. "Well," she said loudly enough for anyone within ten feet to hear, "I thought Laurie was exaggerating when she told me how I could find y'all, but it appears she wasn't. Those tacky getups scream for attention."

Manicured talons shifted her bead-encrusted designer bag under her elbow. "I'm sure y'all remember me. I'm Madelyn Vandercleef." She zeroed in on me. "You're Georgia Baker, aren't you?"

I would have denied it, but the hostile look in her eye erased any hope of escape. I nodded.

"Wade Bowman is the father of my children," she said in strident tones that carried in spite of tablecloths and padded walls. "One of whom is still an impressionable teenager who's been subjected to the flagrant immorality of that daughter of yours."

No preliminaries, just a shot to the jugular. My daughter was corrupting hers.

The better part of me reacted with, *How dare this woman drag out our dirty laundry in public?* The rest of me slid under the table and prayed to disappear.

As always when I'm blindsided, though, I went into neutral, which is probably just as well. It wouldn't do to slap her and risk messing up that nose job, especially with so many witnesses.

Diane intervened with a piercing stare. "Gee, I'm not sure I *do* remember you," she said. "As I recall, Maddie was a much quieter, more polite person." She used the nickname Madelyn had always hated in high school.

"With a much bigger nose," Linda added.

"And an A cup," Teeny said in precise, ladylike tones.

"And a much bigger butt," Pru added with a dimpled smile.

Madelyn flushed, eyes narrowed and her lips compressed, but she wasn't about to be intimidated.

Though I appreciated my friends' solidarity, this was no time for target practice. Nostrils flaring, I shot them a warning glance, then quietly addressed my assailant. "Why don't you sit down and lower your voice?" I offered, to the others' chagrin. "So we can quietly discuss whatever brings you here, like ladies."

"Whatever brings me here? Are you just clueless," she snapped loudly, "or as insensitive to *my* daughter's morals as you are to your own daughter's?"

Them was fightin' words, but I was determined not to let her steal my dignity. Agonizingly conscious of the attention from the tables around us, I put on my duchess persona. "I don't think it's a good idea to continue this conversation in public," I said softly but firmly. I meant to take the high road, really I did, but when somebody goes after my kids, I can't answer for the results. I heard my voice clip out, "I'll be happy to talk to you discreetly, but the other people here didn't come to witness a live episode of *Jerry Springer*, so I suggest we do this another time, in another place. If you insist on making a spectacle of yourself and my daughter's private business, you are not welcome, and I must ask you to leave."

Madelyn's expression lit with an unholy light. The battle had been truly joined.

Teeny's blue eyes went huge, and Pru, Linda, and Diane exchanged major uh-oh looks. Rachel, on the other hand, seemed to be enjoying the whole scene immensely.

Maria, pitcher in one hand and coffeepot in the other, froze.

Me and my big mouth. I should have gotten out while the getting was good. Madelyn would probably have followed me, but at least we wouldn't be doing this in front of a hundred people.

Madelyn just got louder. "I hardly call it private when your unmarried daughter moves in with my children's father," she all but shouted, "a man old enough to be *her* father, in case you hadn't noticed."

Even the tourists and the waitstaff clammed up to listen at that one.

Rachel laughed and said to me, "I hope he's rich."

"He's not," Madelyn snapped, causing Rachel to grimace and back off.

My whole neck went hot as a curling iron. What was Madelyn hoping to accomplish? Did she really think that by publicly embarrassing me, she could influence Callie?

Blessedly, the hostess provided a distraction by coming to the doorway and rapping on a glass with a knife to get everyone's attention. "Excuse me, please, ladies," she called out, "but there's a black Mercedes parked in one of our handicapped spaces by mistake. Could the owner please move her car? The valets will be happy to—"

Madelyn pointed a maroon talon at her. "I am not finished here," she blared. "That car has medical plates, and if you so much as touch it, I will sue your ass off."

The hostess recoiled, appalled, even as the rest of the diners focused with disapproving fascination on Madelyn.

Was the woman really that obnoxious, or was she on something?

Between Rachel's outbursts and this one, our Red Hat Club might very well get banished.

Maria's concerned expression shifted to one that would have had a lightbulb over it in the comics. Pulling a cell phone from the pocket of her uniform, she retreated toward the kitchen.

Clearly not giving a rat's patoot what anybody thought of her, Madelyn rounded on me and resumed the floor show with, "You tell that daughter of yours that she'd better pack up and clear out of that house, or she'll live to regret it. I will not have *my* daughter subjected to that kind of immorality when she goes to visit her father."

Every time she said *that daughter of yours*, it felt like a hard finger poke in the chest.

Linda—as another mother whose daughter had moved in with an inappropriate man—fluffed up like a robin in the snow. "There must be something wrong with my ears," she said to Madelyn in deadly sarcasm. "Am I actually hearing you throw stones at *anybody*? You, who dumped Wade—a decent, faithful, hard-working husband, dedicated father to your children—for medical plates, a house on Habersham, and a new Mercedes every two years?"

Madelyn didn't flinch. "Faithful husband, my ass. Did it ever occur to you that I might have had damn-good reason to look elsewhere for comfort? Wade's the worst kind of hypocrite. I wonder how his church friends would feel if they knew about all his women—the ones who get a quickie, and I do mean quickie, with the roses for their dinner parties. He's got dozens of them all over Buckhead, even now."

My chest solidified with dread. Dear heaven, what if that was true? But the detectives had said there was no indication of monkey business going on with his deliveries.

And wouldn't I have heard something about it before this? Surely . . .

Madelyn read my reaction. "If you don't believe me, ask yourself why the most successful florist in town insists on making so many of the high-end deliveries himself."

An immaculately dressed baby boomer sitting next to Madelyn raised her hand and asked, "Excuse me, but could you please tell me the name of that florist?"

Oh, lord. Audience participation!

Laughter erupted within earshot, then spread all the way across the room in the wake of a buzz of repetition.

"Flower Bower," Madelyn shot back.

Madelyn put me back into her sights. "I'll say one thing for Wade, he was always discreet, which is more than I can say for that daughter of yours."

"Excuse me," Diane challenged, "but considering the way you're acting, I hardly think you're qualified to even use the word *discreet*."

"Butt out," Madelyn said without taking her glare from me.

I met her gaze with a cold one of my own, my voice lowered. "You act as if my daughter were the only one responsible for her moving in. Why don't you take this up with Wade?"

"I tried," she shot back, "but he won't talk to me, which comes as no surprise. He never would face his mistakes." She leaned in. "Another little tidbit: Did he tell that daughter of yours that he has a bum ticker?"

John had never said anything about Wade's having heart problems.

Madelyn regarded me with a sly smile. "Or is that daughter of yours just in this for the insurance?"

That bitch! I shot to my feet, but Teeny came between us before I got physical. "Madelyn, this conversation is absolutely inappropriate, on every level imaginable," she said. "You are disturbing the peace of a public place. Please leave, or I *will* ask the management to help you do so."

Seeing Madelyn redden further, the duchess in me took over to forestall disaster. I sidestepped Teeny to meet Madelyn's glare with a steely one of my own. "My daughter is a grown woman," I stated calmly. "Her decisions are her own. I love and respect her, even when we disagree about those decisions." Heart racing, I managed to maintain an icy calm I did not feel. "If you have anything to discuss with my daughter, I suggest you contact her directly, preferably by mail, so there can be no misunderstanding." And plenty of proof.

So far, so good.

Then my Evil Twin added, "I'm sure you know the address. It's the one on the voluntary child-support checks Wade still sends every month, even though that daughter of yours dropped out of school and is well over eighteen."

Hand to heaven, I don't know where that came from, but the unspoken "woo-hoo-hoo" in the room was deafening.

Madelyn sneered at me. "What Wade does or does not do for *our* children is none of *your* G.D. business. He owes Laurie that support, and more. Though I can see how those payments would annoy his unemployed lover."

Before I could defend my daughter, Linda did it for me. "Callie is not unemployed."

I flinched when Linda said her name, even though that particular bit of information was no mystery to anybody who knew me in the room.

"She has a doctorate in theoretical mathematics," Linda went on, "and a contract to teach at Oglethorpe next fall. She is a brilliant and respected professional."

My motherly instincts wanted to shout, "Put that in your pipe and smoke it!" but that wouldn't have helped a thing. This was going nowhere but downhill. I had to put an end to it, pronto. If worst came to worst, we could all adjourn to the bathroom, which we probably should have done in the first place.

I tried to ease past Madelyn, but she would have none of it.

"Don't you even think about leaving. I have more to say."

My temper spiked again, but I managed to keep it under control. "Maddie," I said, "Callie's a grown woman, a free agent. Coming after me, here, makes no sense whatsoever. If she and Wade do end up getting married, I would hope the two of you can work out something civilized, for your children's sake, if nothing else."

Madelyn smoothed her pearls, undaunted. "I have no reason to work anything out with that daughter of yours. If she goes through with marrying him, she can't act surprised when Wade robs the cradle with somebody else."

The hostess approached from just behind her and stopped, wary. "Excuse me, ma'am. I don't know where it came from," she told Madelyn, "we certainly didn't call anybody, but a wrecker is towing your car away." She winced and drew back.

"What?" Madelyn's complexion went dusky with outrage. "Well, don't just stand there like a bimbo! Stop them!"

She started after the hostess, then pivoted for one parting salvo. "And Wade cheats on his taxes. The payroll ones, too."

At last, she left.

I sank back into my seat, sick to my stomach. I would have been relieved to have her gone, but I knew all of Buckhead would be talking about this within the hour.

Smarting, I noted all the women who had dialed their cell phones, and the ones huddled in conversations with occasional guilty glances our way.

My voice quavered as I breathed out, "That was the most embarrassing experience of my life." I wanted to burst into tears, but I wouldn't give Madelyn the satisfaction, so I settled for moaning, "Do you think any of that was true? What am I supposed to do now?"

"Another surveillance," Teeny said briskly, "and a much more thorough investigation."

She was right, of course. This couldn't be ignored. "Thanks. I'd appreciate that."

"Why does Madelyn care if Wade marries Callie?" Pru asked.

"That's the point, isn't it?" Diane said. "It's no skin off her nose. She bagged her own big game when she married Sonny Vandercleef. She's set."

Rachel avidly took this all in.

"Maybe she's just spiteful and doesn't want Wade to be happy," Pru offered.

"I wish I could believe that," I admitted, not really knowing what I believed or what I wanted to be true. The only thing I was sure of was that I didn't want Callie's heart to be broken—then or later. And I didn't want her to bear the brunt of public speculation. "Madelyn's a lot of things, but she's never been irrational."

"I don't care what her motive is," Linda groused. "She was completely out of line to embarrass you that way. Callie's too smart to be fooled that way, anyhow. Mark my words: All that stuff about Wade is just hoo-ha." She arched an eyebrow. "I could just shoot Madelyn for raining on my parade. I'm going to be a grandmother, and thanks to that witch, y'all all look like the dog just died."

"Don't mention dogs dying," I said, "or you'll finish me off."

Linda threw up her hands. "I give up."

When Maria arrived to top up our drinks, Diane immediately zeroed in on her smug expression as she refilled my tea. "You're looking mighty pleased with yourself, Miss Maria. What's up?"

Maria glanced left, then right before leaning in close to confide in her soft Hispanic accent, "Did I ever mention that my nephew has a wrecker service in Chamblee? He does a lot of work in Buckhead." She refilled Teeny's glass. "Sometimes I fix him a box lunch, and he comes by to pick it up." Her expression went earnest. "I pay for it, of course."

After an instant of shocked comprehension, we all erupted in gleeful gratitude. "Maria, you are a genius!" I jumped up and gave her a sidelong hug, careful of the pitcher she held. "You saved me from getting into a knock-down, drag-out cat fight," I whispered.

She responded with shy awkwardness. "But this must be our secret," she whispered back. "The lady said she would sue—"

"That was no lady, and nobody's suing anybody," Diane reassured her. "She was illegally parked and properly notified that she should move her car. She has no case."

"But don't worry," I promised. "We'll be discreet."

I'd never use that word again without remembering what had just happened.

I unzipped the compartment on the side of my purse and took out my State Trooper hundred-dollar bill. "Please don't be offended," I said as I pressed it into her hand. "But you have done me a great service today, and I'd like you to have this."

She stole a peek at it, then closed her eyes briefly with an expression of gratitude and relief. "I am honored to accept. It is much needed." She smiled again. "Now, I must see to my other tables."

Just when things were heading back to normal, Diane stood, spoon in hand, and rapped loudly on her water glass, sending a shudder of "What now?" tension through the room before she made a resounding declaration. "Ladies, I propose a toast," she announced with a proud smile. "To Linda Murray, who, God willing, will be a grandmother in July. *Mazel tov.*"

Tension evaporated as glasses lifted in tribute all around us. A collective *"Mazel tov!"* was followed by brief applause.

Grandmotherhood is the great equalizer.

We raised ours and joined the tribute. That, at least, I could celebrate without reservation. I beamed at Linda. "You're gonna be a fabulous grandmama. I just know it."

She lifted her glass to me. "And you're gonna be a fabulous mother-in-law. I just know it."

"Thanks." Assuming there was a wedding, which had suddenly become a big if.

14

You can take your troubles with you when you go to work in a garden, but
you can't bring them back. Somehow, they always end up buried there.
— LINDA'S *BUBBIE*

The present. Saturday, April 1. 9:45 A.M. Muscogee Drive, Atlanta.

. . . .

*W*ITH CALLIE'S ENGAGEMENT party looming less than a week
away, I needed some serious attitude adjustment, and thanks
to Linda, I had plenty of garden therapy to accomplish it. The day
before—despite the fact that Easter (the safe date for planting in Atlanta) wasn't until the middle of the month this year—a warm, long-
range forecast from the weatherman had prompted her to drag me up
to the wholesale nursery in Alpharetta to buy our showy red dragon
leaf begonias. No picky tea roses or all-white gardens or leggy peren-
nials for me. Despite the shade that would cover my flower beds
when the trees leafed out, I like my flowers bright and hardy and pro-
lific, even though that means replacing them every year.

Now, on this sunny morning, I looked forward to getting my
gloves into the loamy soil and beginning something beautiful that
didn't have anything to do with my daughter's totally inappropriate
choice for a husband.

So I started the month of April wearing old clothes, brand-new flowered garden gloves, and no makeup, on my knees in the cool soil of my back-yard flower bed. The corkscrew augur on my cordless drill gave me a sense of power as I whipped out the planting holes and added half a handful of time-release fertilizer into each one. Once the plants were snuggled in and mulched, then watered with StartUp, they would grow lush and spectacular. Until they did, their neat rows gave me a sense of order and control.

With Beethoven's Fifth playing on Second-Cup Concert from my vintage portable radio, I savored the morning sun on my back and lost myself within minutes in the soothing ritual of planting. So, half an hour later, I never heard a thing before I was jumped from behind and snatched to my feet as a black satin bag covered my head. The drawstring on the bag tightened only enough to keep me from seeing my assailants.

It was just like those nightmares where somebody ambushes you, and you can't move or even scream. I froze in shock as my attackers taped my wrists together.

Duct tape! Duct tape means death!

What the hell? This was Atlanta, not Baghdad! But it was happening, and happening to me!

Chicken Little had an aneurysm on the spot and expired without a single dying doomsay.

Adrenaline finally kicked in, and I screamed bloody murder and started fighting for my life, butting one of them with my head and landing a healthy kick on another.

"Ow! Quit that!" Diane's voice entreated, "or the neighbors will think you're really being kidnapped. It's only us!"

Relief, confusion, and fading panic warred for control of my mind. I stopped fighting and tried to gain my balance on the mossy grass. "Are you crazy?" I hollered through the black bag. My fight-or-flight response shifted from terror to fury. "I could have had a heart attack! Untape me this minute!"

"I told you we shouldn't have snuck up on her like that," Linda's voice chided the others.

"She's okay," Diane said. "You're okay, aren't you?"

"No thanks to y'all," I bit out, furious. "What in blue blazes would possess y'all to gunnysack me? Get this thing off my head!"

"We can't take it off yet." Pru's response was apologetic. "Really, it's going to be great. Just relax."

"Relax?" Obviously, they'd gone crazy. "My best friends just put a bag over my head and duct-taped my hands, and you want me to relax?"

Not responding, they took my elbows and guided me across the yard to the accompanying rustle of what sounded like lots of slick fabric. All I could see was the inside of the bag, faintly illuminated by a few stray shards of light that leaked in from beneath my chin. I felt the grass turn to asphalt beneath my feet as they hustled me up the driveway toward the street.

"Oh, shoot!" Linda fussed. "She got dirt on my dress!"

Linda never wore dresses. She always wore suits or separates.

"No biggie. It's just a little mulch," Diane reassured her. I heard swatting. "There. Brushed right off."

"This is exactly why I didn't want to put these on till after," Linda snitted.

What did she mean, *these*?

I felt a whack on my muddy knees as Diane said, "Let's get her cleaned up before we put her in the front seat." More hands brushed and tidied. They hoisted me up into the car, which I immediately identified as Brooks's SUV by the lingering tangy scent of yesterday's begonia purchases. Tugging off my yard sneakers, Diane said, "Leave those by the front door. She can get them later."

"Stop talking about me in the third person," I complained. "I'm right here, and I can hear just fine through this damned bag, which I insist you remove immediately."

"Just relax," they all said in unison as I was buckled up.

"Whose brilliant idea was it to tie me up and put a bag over my head?" I asked. "I need to have a word with her!"

To my surprise, Pru responded with a giggle and, "It was my idea, and I have *two* words for *you*: Las Vegas."

She would bring that up. That was where we'd staged Pru's spectacular intervention worthy of *Mission: Impossible,* then sedated her and spirited her away to rehab.

"That was different," I argued. "That was for your own good."

Pru's response was sunny as ever. "And this is for yours. So calm down."

"Honest, George," Linda said from the driver's seat. "I promise, you're gonna love it."

Considering the lame stunt they'd just pulled, I wasn't convinced, but my friends had never lied to me yet.

Well, they'd lied (especially Teeny)—we were human, after all— but never to my detriment, so I decided to go along.

Speaking of Teeny, I hadn't heard her. "Where's Teeny?"

No response.

We rode for a few minutes with numerous brief stops and turns, then turned up a fairly steep hill, engine straining, and came to a halt. Diane got out and helped me into what sounded like a loosely enclosed space. Next she carefully led me a few yards, then up a step and through a door.

The minute we crossed the threshold, I recognized the familiar scent of Linda's house: the lingering aromas of the homemade breakfasts she made for Brooks every workday of the world at five A.M., only now, there was a provocative overtone of chocolate and fruit and roses.

"Okay," Linda said after the door closed behind me. "We're going to change your clothes. You are *way* underdressed for this particular occasion."

"Wait just a minute," Pru said. "Let me make sure the coast is clear." She hurried through the swinging door to Linda's dining room, then returned almost immediately. "Okay. Teeny's got the guys back in the sunroom. Strip away."

Guys? Strip? "Now wait a minute . . ." I wrenched free of whoever was holding my arm. "Who are the guys in the sunroom?"

A few stifled chuckles were the only response.

I heard a truncated snort from across the room as Diane and Pru laughed nearby. "These guys are hired help," Diane explained. "We just don't want them wandering in while we're undressing you."

Brisk hands jerked down my elastic-waist denim jeans.

"Y'all!" Only when I felt cool air on my legs did I remember that I'd worn the granny pants with the hole in the fanny. Thank goodness, my yard shirt (one of John's old button-downs) was long enough to conceal the fact.

"Step out, please," Pru directed.

In spite of my embarrassment, I did as she asked. Like all "good" Southern girls, I almost always do as I'm asked when the request is polite, even when it's unreasonable.

"We're gonna untie you and take the bag off, but not until we get your sacred word of honor that you won't peek," Diane said. "I mean, not even a tiny, blurry slit, George. We went to a lot of trouble for your benefit to do this, and if you look, you'll ruin the whole thing. Swear."

"Far be it from me to ruin your fun," I retorted, "even though y'all scared ten years off my life in the process." I paused to let them squirm just a little, then relented. "Okay. I swear not to peek." Then I felt compelled to qualify, "Unless something painful or immoral transpires, in which case, all bets are off."

"I solemnly swear," Diane said, "nothing painful or immoral will transpire."

"Except for this," Linda said as she cut the tape, then tore it off in one blinding, fuzz-rending motion.

"Ow!" I massaged my wrists, but didn't look.

"Better quick than slow," Linda said. Off came the bag.

My closed lids went red from the light as I took a long, cool breath of unrestricted air. "Whew. That feels better. But any more pain, and I'm looking."

"Okay. Now stand still. I swear, you'll thank us in the end."

Within minutes, they'd stripped me to my underwear, sponged me clean, redressed me in what felt like a prom getup, and handed me over to an unidentified male with a lisp who made up my face, then put me into a very tight wig.

All the while, not one little peek, which is a miracle, considering my overactive curiosity.

"Ow," I complained when he stuck my scalp with a hairpin.

"Sorry, sweetie," he told me without a shred of sympathy. "No pain, no gain."

I felt the wig and detected an updo with a well sprayed clump of curls at the crown.

Linda's return was marked by a gasp. "It's amazing," she said. "I wouldn't fool anybody, but Georgia . . . Frederico, you are a genius, just like Amy Weinstein said."

Frederico? He sure didn't sound foreign.

"That's why you called me," he gloated out. "And, I must say, I think this whole idea is brilliant, I can't wait to tell my other clients about—"

"What?" Linda interrupted. "You swore yourself to secrecy! One word to anybody about this, and I'll tell every woman in Buckhead you ruined my hair! I mean it."

"Oops," he said. "Flog me with a soggy smock. Almost let the cat out of the bag."

"You'd better not." Linda took my hand. "Come on, Georgia. One more short walk, then we'll let you see. But when I tell you to open your eyes, you need to look forward and smile, okay?"

"Whatever you say." No big mystery there. We were going to have our picture made.

Linda led me through the dining room, redolent with the scents of chocolate and fresh fruit, and on into the living room, where the red glow behind my lids brightened intensely under the heat and glare of lights. I sensed the others gathered around me as Linda placed me carefully in a chair, then put what felt like a nosegay into my hands. "Okay, everybody, get ready."

Diane said, "Remember, George. Straight ahead, and smile. Open your eyes!"

I did, and was blinded by an array of scrimmed photographer's lights so bright I could barely make out somebody snapping away from behind his tripod.

Flashes went off in rapid fire. "That's it," a man's voice said. "Think happy. Think carefree. Having the time of our lives. Just a few more, all looking at me. Fabulous. And that's it." The lights faded.

"Thank you so much, ladies. I've set up the DVD recorder to tape y'all as you sit." He headed for the kitchen.

Still seeing spots, I looked down and discovered I wasn't in a formal.

"Aaagghhhh!" I was in my wedding dress, a column of white organza over satin that fell from an Empire waist, with alençon lace at the hem and a bateau neckline, and short, puffy sleeves.

The others laughed with delight at my surprise.

"No way. I'm twenty pounds heavier than I was on my wedding day, but the dress fits." I turned to the others, who had on their wedding dresses, too—except for Pru, who wore a dead ringer for the funky psychedelic bell-bottom pantsuit she'd had on at her elopement in Ringgold.

Seated beside me, Teeny wore her classic gown as beautifully as she had when she'd married Reid. On my other side, Linda was brunette again, looking like her college self, only rounder, in a wider version of her wedding dress. But even her extra weight didn't erase the unmistakable presence of the lovely bride she'd once been.

When she saw me studying her dress, she turned so I could see the clever insert in the back. "Teeny had her seamstress make these so we could zip up. She had to guess on yours, but it looks like she got it perfect."

Pru leaned in from where she was standing, behind and to the right. "I got my outfit new. Can you believe seventies is back in?"

"Lord, no," I said. "It should have stayed buried. But on you, it looks good."

Diane leaned in from behind my left. "You look just like you did at your wedding."

"So do you," I said. "This is so great."

"It's your reluctant mother-of-the-bride shower," Teeny said with wicked delight. "And you ain't seen nothin' yet."

I felt as if time had turned itself inside out, and we were all girls again. "Honey, y'all can bag me and tape me anytime, as long as the surprise is as good as this one," I gushed. "You are all so beautiful."

"So are you," the others said in unison.

Diane pushed me to arm's length and eyed me up and down. "It's spooky how much you look like you did the day you married John. Except you're not whacked out on Valium."

I'd been so nervous at the rehearsal that Brooks, who had just started dating Linda, had brought me some mild sedatives at the rehearsal dinner, with instructions that I take half a pill at bedtime and a whole one when I got up. I did, and I was so looped at the hairdresser's the next morning that I didn't even protest when she got my updo wrong. Even worse, I barely remember my wedding.

I looked at Diane, still slim in her classic Princess Grace gown, and saw the girl she was in that college chapel so many years ago. "You look the same, too."

Only then did I turn to see my reflection in the mirrored wall by the front door. Diane was right. It was spooky. From across the room, I did look the same, right down to my wrong hairdo. I felt as if I were looking across the decades instead of the house, to that blessed, reluctant day a third of a century ago.

Shows what a little distance and middle-aged eyes can accomplish.

Even my bouquet was just like the one I'd carried.

My hand went to the curve of my cheek. Judging from my reflection, Frederico had managed to erase the years and recreate my youthful glow. "Man. I don't know what kind of makeup that guy Frederico uses, but I want to buy some."

"Sold!" he said from the kitchen, where he was obviously eavesdropping.

In the dining room, a lavish spread of all our favorite foods and a bowl of lemon-mint iced tea punch were arrayed around a small wedding cake decorated like the one at my Spartan reception.

"Georgia, we need to get a few photos of you alone," Teeny said. "We all did ours before they picked you up. I wanted to have one done for John. He smuggled your wedding dress to us."

John had found my wedding dress in the attic? "*My* John, who can't find the suit he wore the day before in his closet?" Amazing.

"I had to help him." Teeny laughed. "It took forty-five minutes with him on the cordless phone while he searched your attic, but he finally located the box. Good thing you had it labeled."

The photographer appeared and did my portraits, then we all dived into the refreshments while Teeny helped him gather up his stuff and leave. "I'll bring the proofs to your office on Monday," he told her on his way out.

Frederico followed in his wake, pressing a card into my hand as he passed by, with a suggestive, "I'd love to do you again, anytime. Call me."

Linda motioned me toward the sofa. "Time for the fun stuff. Sit in the middle, and we'll get started."

I crossed to the white leather sofa and plopped down between Diane and Pru, facing a pile of wrapped presents and aging wedding albums on the glass coffee table.

"I can't believe we actually pulled this off," Pru said. "It was all I could do to keep the video camera focused while this gang of brides snuck up on you in the yard and threw a bag over your head. I've never seen anything so hilarious in my life."

"We decided to wear the dresses to the pickup," Diane explained, "in case anybody saw us and called the police. I mean, how seriously would you take it if somebody reported a bunch of brides kidnapping a housewife out of her backyard?"

"Very Monty Python," Linda said.

"But how did you know I wouldn't catch you sneaking up on me?" I asked.

"We know you." Linda gloated. "It wasn't by accident that I took you to get those begonias and suggested you put them in this morning."

I'd been had.

Teeny settled cross-legged in the space between my feet and the coffee table, her tulle skirts ballooning around her. "Okay, everybody. Move in close." She leaned forward to pass me a heavy purple package the size of a shoe box, with a red bow. "Open Linda's first."

Diane handed me a pair of scissors with mother-of-pearl inlaid handles. "It's okay for the mother of the bride to cut the ribbons at her shower."

"Absolutely." Linda grinned. "May she have a grandchild for every cut."

Not likely, considering Wade's age.

I took my time unwrapping the gift so I could savor the anticipation. It was a shoebox, but a lot heavier than shoes. I lifted the lid to find an IV bag of sterile saline, a disposable syringe, an ampoule of some drug I didn't recognize, and a prescription bottle with thirty pills of the same drug, refillable three times.

"It's a great new antianxiety drug that doesn't make you sleepy or cause memory loss," Linda explained. "The IV version is only if you have a serious meltdown."

I would have laughed if I hadn't thought I might really need it. But the others looked so earnest, I couldn't help chuckling.

Linda beamed. "Only a true friend will give you drugs. Legitimate ones, that is." She pointed to the box. "There's a gift certificate in there, too."

I lifted the IV bag to find an envelope. Inside was a brightly colored certificate that entitled me to a six-hour shift with a private-duty registered nurse. "That's in case you need the IV. Or get the flu or the stomach bug at the last minute. Brooks says fluids work wonders."

When I looked more closely at the pills, she added, "He said to start off with half a pill at bedtime and see how it does for you."

I turned to her, flat-mouthed. "I appreciate the thought, but the last time he told me to start with half a pill and it would be just fine, I hardly remembered anything from the hairdresser's to the honeymoon."

She looked at me askance. "Well, he still feels really bad about that, but this stuff is different. It doesn't cause memory loss."

I dropped the bottle back into the box, "Come to think of it, maybe for this wedding, a bit of amnesia might come in handy."

Teeny tucked her chin. "I thought you said you were reconciled."

"I'm working on that. Seriously. But I haven't read the second detective's report yet. Even if it's clean, that doesn't mean things are going to be easy." I perused the remaining gifts. "What more do we have for the reluctant mother of the bride?"

The next present Teeny handed me was in a flowered little gift bag with pink tissue paper. "That one's from me," Diane said.

Inside, I found a small black velvet bag with something heavy inside, but when I tried to open it, I saw it was sewn shut.

"It's not supposed to open," Diane explained. "Squeeze it. There's a button."

I felt it and pushed. Hilarious, infectious laughter erupted from the bag. You couldn't hear it without joining in, and we all did. When it finally quit, we wiped our eyes and fanned ourselves. "Whew. That's fabulous. I'm taking it with me everywhere till the wedding's over."

Teeny handed me a narrow package.

"That one's from me," Pru said proudly.

I unwrapped it to find a pair of hot pink, heart-shaped, rose-colored glasses. "I might have known. They're fabulous."

"I tried to find them in readers," she said. "But they only come plain."

I put them on and posed. "Oooo. Things look really odd."

Pru let out her burbling giggle. "*You* look pretty odd in those glasses."

"Who cares?" I primped. "They're absolutely perfect. Thank you so much."

The next gift Teeny handed me was wrapped in silver paper, about the size and weight of a phone book, with an elaborate silver bow. I read the tag. "To Georgia. Love, Diane."

Carefully, I opened the neatly tucked ends. "My, my, my. Now this is interesting." I pulled off the wrapping to reveal a box of candy. "Forrest Gump Chocolates. Ha!"

If ever I was in the mood for a guilty indulgence, it was now. Delighted, I opened them to find three layers of identical shiny dark chocolate candies. "Ooo. Yummy." I popped one into my mouth and started to chew, but by the second chew, my eyes watered and I groped for a cocktail napkin to spit it into. "Bleah," I said after I'd gotten rid of it. I took a swig of iced tea to wash away the taste. "Coconut." And the whole box looked identical. I turned to Diane. "Honey, you know I hate coconut."

"Oh, they're not all coconut," she said with a grin. "They're assorted. They all just look the same, 'cause"—the others joined in with glee in true Forrest Gump form—"'life is lahk a box of chocolates; you never know what you're gonna git.'"

"Even Wade for a son-in-law," she finished, giving me a hug as we all dissolved into laughter. "I thought it was appropriate, under the circumstances."

"Kamakazi candy. Only you."

One more present left, the size of a boutique tissue box.

"This one's from me," Teeny said as she handed it over, deadpan. "Something serious."

"Compared to tranquilizers and laughing boxes and rose-colored glasses?" I knew better than to be fooled by those big, innocent baby blues.

I unwrapped a cheap corrugated cardboard box stenciled with Chinese writing and inventory numbers. I cut the tape and opened it to find a foam block inside.

A figurine?

I pulled it out and opened the foam to discover a soft plastic set of realistic pink lips and white teeth in a ladylike grin, with a little plastic gizmo with two soft "wings" that extended back into the mouth of the wearer, so I could bite down to hold it in place.

Teeny couldn't control her glee. "Try them on, then bite down."

I glanced at the "Made in China" stamp on the box.

She read my mind. "They're safe. We had them tested. And I sterilized them myself. Go ahead."

They fit fairly comfortably—a lot better than the wax lips we'd sported as kids. It took a second to get used to the feel of the gizmo on my tongue and the plastic between my molars, but I bit down as instructed.

A proper voice that sounded suspiciously like Diane's gushed forth with "Well, isn't that lovely?"

The others rolled with laughter.

Linda raced toward her room. "I'm gettin' a mirror. You have *got* to see this!"

"Bite down again," Teeny urged.

"I'm so happy for you," the voice cooed. Definitely Diane's.

Linda arrived with the mirror and I took one look and started laughing, too. The effect was somewhere between Miss America and the Joker from *Batman*. "Where did ooo geh dis?" I asked from behind the perpetual smile.

Teeny giggled. "One of my subsidiaries found a similar product and contracted with the Chinese manufacturer to license them for sale in the U.S. with our own sayings." She retrieved a shopping bag from beside the sofa and started handing out boxes to the others. "These are prototypes. I didn't think it would be a big deal to have them use lithium batteries—I wanted them to be rechargeable and last a long time on a charge—but that meant they had to adapt cell phone circuitry for the voice playbacks, so they barely got here in time."

Awed, I asked, "You did this in two weeks?"

Teeny shrugged. "Three, actually. I got the idea when I was thinking about this shower. Diane and I came up with the sayings, and Bubba recorded her at the sound studio. The factory had most of the technical changes worked out by the time we overnighted them the recordings. And voilà."

I looked to Diane. "I thought 'at was ooo," I garbled out from behind my smile. All this, just for me. I took off the lips to inspect them. "These are gonna sell like hotcakes."

"I know," Teeny said. "We've projected the price at twenty-nine ninety-nine, plus shipping, Internet sales only. But if we get a strong response, we may be able to cut the price significantly. It's the lithium batteries and the recharger that run up the cost." She was proud of herself, and justifiably so. "I've already planned the ads for next year's bridal magazines. And we're doing another model for stressed office workers, in men's and women's."

"And a husbands' and wives'," Diane said. "We want all of y'all to help us brainstorm the sayings." She looked to me. "But not till after the wedding."

Teeny signaled the others, who turned away, hands to mouths, then looked back with uniform plastic smiles in place, sporting assorted shades of lipstick. She pointed to Linda, whose smile said, "Isn't that precious?"

Linda pointed to Pru. "Lucky, lucky you."

I replaced mine and waited to be called on.

Teeny went next, a repeat of "Well, isn't that lovely?"

We kept going around, getting more hilarious with every one, even the repeats, till all seven sayings had been aired. My personal favorite was, "Perfect. Absolutely perfect."

Linda's was "I'm sure it will all work out beautifully." But Pru voted for "I'm *so* pleased, I can't stop smiling."

Cheeks aching from laughter and jaws sore from holding my synthetic smile in place, I took mine out, but couldn't stop grinning. "That is hilarious. Can I use it at the engagement party?"

All five of them furrowed. "I think it would be better," Teeny suggested, "if you saved them for the lingerie shower."

She had a point.

"I'll bring along a couple of spares, just in case we get a glitch," Teeny offered. "They are prototypes, after all."

I leaned back and surveyed the presents in the lap of my wedding dress. "This is the best surprise y'all have ever come up with."

I'd woken up that morning straining under the weight of my fears for Callie, and now I was going home relaxed, buoyed by the wisdom and humor of these precious friends. How could I adequately express my gratitude?

I couldn't. But the wonderful thing was, I didn't need to. They knew.

"Thanks, y'all," I said anyway. "You're the best."

Diane grinned. "No way were we going to let you go through all this without fortification. Especially the lingerie shower."

"Bring it on," I boasted. "I am ready."

We spent the next thirty minutes going through our wedding photos and reminiscing. I realized the others had a reason for doing it, but I enjoyed it, anyway.

We did Pru's little collection of snapshots last. I put down the hilarious shot of Tyson and Pru saying their vows across my draped, swollen, iced-down fanny in the doctor's office in Ringgold. (After being stuck on I-75 for two hours by a big wreck, I'd taken to the woods to relieve myself and gotten bitten by a copperhead.) "Okay. I get it. We didn't know any better than our kids do how our marriages would work out."

They exchanged pregnant glances.

"That ought to make me feel better about Callie, but it doesn't,"

I told them. "I know what Wade's capable of, and it scares me to death."

Diane arched an eyebrow. "What he *was* capable of. None of us is the same person we were back then. Like Callie said, try to give him the benefit of the doubt."

I sighed. "Maybe I will. After I see the second detective's report."

"You know she's going to marry him, regardless," Teeny said.

My daughter had her mind made up, just as I had when I'd married John. And Teeny hers when she'd married Reid. And Diane, when she'd hitched her wagon to Harold's star and ended up getting taken for a ride. And Pru, though her prince charming Tyson had turned out to be a total roach who'd led her down the primrose path.

None of us would have listened. And, the truth was, even under the best of circumstances, marriage was still a crap shoot.

"Okay, okay, I get it," I said. "Unless Mean Madelyn's accusations about Wade prove true." Then, all bets were off. Even if Callie hated me for it, I'd have to tell her. "But if they're not true, I'll do my best to give Callie my blessing."

The others signaled their approval with a round of prim opera applause.

Things definitely could be worse. Callie could have eloped like Pru had, gotten married without me there. Now, *that* would be a tragedy.

At least I'd be there to watch her take her vows, just as I would be there if it didn't work out.

Like it or not, what was, was, as Pru so aptly put it. In six days, all of Atlanta would know that Callie and Wade were engaged.

Ironic, that Rachel had found exactly what she was looking for in a man in less than two weeks; Diane had Cameron the Cowboy, the perfect man for her, but refused to marry him; and my Callie had a very imperfect man, and insisted on marrying him. As I said: There is no justice.

Good thing I had those talking lips to see me through the next couple of months.

· 15 ·

. . . .

*F*OUR DAYS LATER, my famous spaghetti sauce was sim-
mering away, and the vermicelli neared a perfect al dente
when the phone rang. Spoon in hand, I grabbed the receiver, then
hurried back to the pot to make sure I didn't overcook the pasta.
"Hello?"

Linda's voice demanded, "Turn on the TV! Channel eleven, the national news. Hurry!"

A chill of dread ran through me. Expecting some major disaster, I
switched on the set to see a helicopter shot of a private yacht in a tropical bay surrounded by smaller boats, some of them moving, some of
them moored alongside.

The news anchor announced, "Reliable sources have revealed that
perfume billionaire Sol Rosenwasser was married this evening
aboard his yacht, the *Rachel,* in Miami bay. The bride is reputed to be
one Rachel Goldman Glass, widow of prominent Manhattan plastic

surgeon, Karl Glass, who died only four months ago." The camera zoomed in on Rachel dancing with Sol on the wide Stern deck.

"She didn't even invite us!" Linda fumed through the receiver.

The newsman went on. "At fifty-three, the new Mrs. Rosenwasser is more than thirty years her husband's junior, giving rise to speculation as to her motives in the marriage, but a source close to Rosenwasser declares that the two met at Rosenwasser's synagogue in Atlanta."

The camera shifted to a close-up of the earnest little guy from Sol's Greek chorus. "It was love at first sight when Sol saw her standing there at services. He went straight to her and proposed. I was there. She laughed at first, then they talked, and she accepted! I'm telling you, it's a true love match."

"Yeah," Linda quipped. "Her love for his money."

"Oh, come on," I said as the camera panned back. "I think she's really fallen for him."

The screen shifted to stills of the Clintons, Jimmy and Rosalynn Carter, a man in judicial robes who looked vaguely familiar, and another man I'd never seen in front of an Israeli flag. The newscaster went on. "Witnesses have identified past presidents Clinton and Carter, Supreme Court Justice Roberts, Israeli Ambassador Sallai Meridor, and Nelson Mandela as witnesses to the surprise nuptials. A spokesman for Mr. Rosenwasser said the newlyweds will spend their honeymoon touring Mr. Rosenwasser's orphanages and clinics in Africa and the Middle East."

"Ooo-hoo-hoo," I said to Linda. "I'll bet she didn't plan on anything like that for a honeymoon."

"Serves her right, for not even calling to tell me," she retorted.

The anchor concluded, "After this message, we'll return with breaking news about North Korea's nuclear program."

I turned off the TV.

"Can you believe that?" Linda said. "I thought they were still shopping for her trousseau." Sol had said he didn't want to see her wearing black ever again, so he'd taken her to New York, where she'd gone hog-wild on his nickel. "I can't believe she didn't even tell me she wasn't coming back."

"I'm sure they didn't want anybody to find out. Judging from that flotilla of paparazzi, is it any wonder?" Why was I defending Rachel?

I caught myself and promptly issued Linda her due. "Poor baby, poor baby, poor baby. She's an ingrate. A dog in the manger."

"Once a scorpion, always a scorpion," Linda quoted, appeased. "She didn't even bother to take her clothes. Or her luggage. What in this good green earth am I supposed to do with them?"

"Use the luggage, and give the clothes to Teeny," I proposed. "If she can't wear them, she'll know somebody who can." I thought of her once-indigent employees at Shapely and smiled at the prospect of their inheriting Rachel's elegant widow's weeds.

I smelled something pasty. "Oh, hell! The vermicelli!"

I leapt to the stove and found the pasta fused to a sodden lump. "Rats. It looks like a giant matzoh ball, and I don't have any more on hand."

"Sorry," Linda said. "Want me to bring you some?"

John came up from the garage. "Oh, boy. Spaghetti! I'm starved."

"Yes, bring some angel hair or vermicelli," I told Linda, "enough for all four of us. Y'all can stay for supper."

John nodded in approval.

"Yum," Linda replied. They both loved my spaghetti, which had everything in it but the kitchen sink. "We'll bring the wine. See you in a few minutes."

John brightened as I hung up, enfolding me for a sweet kiss. "What happened to the vermicelli?"

"Linda called and told me to turn on the TV, and there was Sol's yacht on the national news. He and Rachel got married on it this evening in Miami, complete with paparazzi, two past presidents, the Israeli ambassador, and a Supreme Court Justice as witnesses. *And* Nelson Mandela. By the time the story was over, the vermicelli had boiled to glue."

"Sol and Rachel married? Good." He gave me a squeeze. "Let's just hope it lasts. Wouldn't want her turning up on Brooks and Linda's doorstep again." He let me go, then grabbed a tomato wedge from the salad on his way toward our room. "I'm gonna grab a quick shower. Back in a jiff."

Alone in the kitchen, I shook my head. Leave it to Rachel to snub us all, and after everything we'd done to befriend her.

We all commiserated over dinner.

Three hours later, Brooks and Linda had been gone for about five minutes—long enough for us to get into our pajamas and into bed, when the doorbell rang.

"I'll get it," John said, throwing his tattered white beach robe over his skivvies. "They must have forgotten something."

After the front door opened, I heard low voices that didn't sound like Linda or Brooks.

John came back into the room holding a heavy cream-colored envelope with only our names inscribed in a strong hand, and another blank one, both sealed with wax. "It wasn't Brooks. It was a courier. In a suit!"

He handed me the envelopes, then dropped his robe and climbed back into bed. "Why don't you open them?"

A courier? "Well, I'm a little scared to. Good news never comes in the middle of the night."

"Jack was born in the middle of the night," he said. "I'd call that good news." He handed me my reading glasses. "Go ahead."

I broke the seal and opened the gilt-lined envelope to find a correspondence card with Sol Rosenwasser's name in small letters across the top.

I read aloud:

Dear Georgia and John,
I've always been a man who believes in rewarding kindness when
I can. The help and friendship you and your friends extended to
my Rachel can never be repaid, but please accept this small token
of our gratitude. We are honored to call you friends.

> *Sincerely,*
> *Sol Rosenwasser*

"Sounds promising." John flopped beside me, his head deep in the pillow. "Better cut to the chase. I'm about to conk."

I pulled a printed card from the other envelope that showed a spectacular setting for elegant, secluded tropical villas with private beaches and pools. "Please be our guests for two weeks at your convenience in the Queen's Villa at Royal Beaches Enclave and Spa, Maui, Hawaii!" My voice and heartbeat got louder with every word. "All spa amenities, first-class airfare, gratuities, transfers, and expenses provided!

"John! Sol's sending us to Maui, first class! Just you and me!" Fatigue forgotten, I leapt to my feet and started jumping on the bed. "We're going to Hawaii!" I singsonged. "We're goin' to Hawaii! We're goin' to Hawaii!"

"Aaagh!" John rolled up to tackle me before I could do any real damage.

Breathless and grinning, I hugged him to me, hard, reveling in the feel of his body against mine. "We're goin' to Hawaii."

He rolled up to lean over me with a smile. "There's the girl that I've been missing." He stroked the hair away from my forehead. "I'll have to thank Sol for finding her for me."

Looking up at him, I giggled like a kid. "I think she lives in Hawaii. First class."

"Nah." The affection in his eyes began to smolder. "I think she's been here all along." Just as he bent to kiss me, the phone rang. He kept right on going, but punched the answer button on the cordless receiver and put it to my ear. Don't tell anybody, but John has this one little kink: He loves to ravage me while I'm on the phone.

"Georgia!" Linda's voice exploded. "A courier just came to our house with a letter from Sol. He's paying for our entire trip to Ireland. The whole thing! First class."

"Mmmmm."

John released my lips and shifted his lower.

"He's sending us to Maui," I managed to gasp out, closing my eyes in pleasure. I left the receiver against my ear, but I didn't pay attention to another word that Linda said.

Maybe there was justice, after all. We were going to Maui. But for the moment, I was busy climbing the stairway to paradise.

· 16 ·

The Dreaded Engagement Party

Life happens anyway.
— ANONYMOUS

The present. Friday, April 7. 6:45 P.M. Fourteenth Street, Atlanta.

ORMALLY, JUST SEEING John in his tux was enough to make me want to rip it off him, but not on the night of Callie's engagement party. As we drove toward Piedmont Park and the Driving Club, my handsome husband reached over and covered my cold, lap-clenched hands with his big warm one. "It's going to be okay. You're going to be fine."

"I'm not so sure about that." A dip in the jet stream had sent the temperature almost to freezing, and even my mink jacket hadn't been enough to bring the blood back into my fingers. Heaven help my begonias. "Between Callie and Wade, they know everybody in town. Teeny's secretary sent out two hundred invitations, and she only got ten regrets. I have an awful feeling that this party is gonna end up being the social sideshow du jour."

"Nah." John let go of my hand with a parting pat. "How many

times have I heard you complain that people don't bother to RSVP anymore? Only half the people you invite to things ever come."

I wish. "Her secretary got a hundred and sixty acceptances."

"Oh." He tucked his chin and regrouped. "So they're all coming. But honey, the people here tonight are our friends, and Wade's and Callie's. Trust me, they're here to have a good time, not embarrass anybody. It'll be fine."

Men just don't get the social fine points. John was blissfully oblivious about the veiled pity and subtle smugness I was about to face. But regardless of how this all panned out, tonight was Callie's night, and I was determined to keep my misgivings to myself.

"Just don't go off with the guys and leave me alone, okay?" I pleaded. Usually at these things, the men and the women divided pretty early to visit with each other, but tonight, I needed John's anchoring presence beside me.

"Just call me Elmer," he said. As in the glue. Nerd humor.

We reached the Driving Club's unobtrusive driveway, and John turned in.

I closed my eyes and said yet another arrow prayer for the ability to convince my daughter and the guests that I was happy about all this. When I opened them, we were rounding the turn to the porte-cochère, where Linda, Pru, Teeny, and Diane stood waiting with Callie, all of them shivering in party clothes the colors of spring.

I've never been gladder to see my friends.

No little black dresses for the dreaded engagement party—not since Diane had pointed out that under the circumstances, black might send some ironic signals we didn't intend. So we'd opted for a spring palette.

Linda had on iris. Diane wore soft blue. Teeny looked like a duchess in a yellow Chanel dinner suit with black trim. And Pru's lavender outfit looked fresh and flattering.

But Callie stole the show. Her emerald green, softly layered silk dress matched the stones flanking her engagement solitaire. The vibrant color set off her dark eyes and hair and made her skin look like ivory. I saw her from a fresh perspective as the beautiful woman she'd become, well and fully grown, and my mother's heart almost melted. But facing her after our fight wasn't going to be easy.

John let out a low whistle. "Whoa. Get a look at that daughter of ours. They sure didn't make lady mathematicians like *that* when I was in school." He waggled his eyebrows at me. "I had to find you in the English department."

Precious man. He didn't say much, but when he did, it was almost always perfect.

Before I could think of an appropriately seductive comeback, Linda beat the valet to my door and pulled it open. After a cursory, "Hi, John," she briskly motioned me out. "Let's get this show on the road. We're all freezing out here in these party duds."

John responded with a dry, "Don't mind me. Y'all just go ahead."

Conscious of the elegant surroundings, I locked my knees and ankles together before demurely swinging them out of the car. "Y'all didn't have to wait out here," I said as I rose.

Linda scrubbed her arms. "What are friends for? Now head for the heat. Pronto."

Greeting the others on the way inside, I went straight for Callie. I wanted to put my arm around her, but a sharp glance kept me from doing it. "Hey there, my beautiful girl."

"Hey, Mama."

I sensed the tension beneath her thin veneer of politeness. She knew as well as I did that we were all under the microscope tonight, but this was the path she'd chosen.

"Honey, you look like a queen," I offered in an effort to thaw things out between us.

"Thanks. So do you," she said stiffly. "Pink is definitely your color."

We entered the club to find Brooks waiting and the distant sound of "Candle in the Wind" from the direction of the ballroom.

"Gracious," Brooks said, eyeing the lot of us. "Y'all look so pretty, it's hard to figure out who's the bride."

Diane laughed, turning to Linda. "Did you pay him to say that?"

John came in behind us just as Brooks gave me a hug. "May I check your coat for you?"

"Sure." I shrugged out of it, then he headed for the cloakroom while John went over to hug Callie.

"Hey there, sprout." John caught Callie in his arms and started dancing her toward the music. "Remember when you used to do this with your feet on top of mine?"

Callie laughed, matching his steps with a natural grace neither John nor I had given her. "It's one of my favorite memories."

He nodded with approval. "You've definitely improved since then."

"So have you," she said with a sparkle in her eye that she hadn't had for me.

Linda pulled open the ballroom door so they could dance right on in, followed by our pastel parade.

The ballroom looked like a magical bower of spring. A gorgeous display of branches laden with cherry blossoms rose from dozens of tall glass cylinders. And artfully artless low arrangements of spring blossoms decorated a comfortable perimeter of round, candlelit tables dressed in moss green damask.

Once inside, Callie took mercy on her daddy and let him off the hook just in time to meet up with Brooks, who handed him my claim check.

"How come I'm always on the shift that has to come fifteen minutes early?" Brooks asked my breathless husband.

John shrugged. "Look at it this way: You always get first crack at the food. And the bar."

"Speaking of which," Brooks said to Linda, "what can I get you to start?"

She answered what she always did: "White wine."

"How about you?" John asked.

No booze for me. "Tonic and lime." Not great for the breath, but definitely good for the wits, which I would need if I had any hope of getting through the evening without putting my foot in my mouth.

John touched my waist. "I'll get your tonic and be right back."

"Thanks, Elmer." He'd better be.

John grinned his irresistible big-little-boy smile and headed after Brooks.

Since I hadn't had time to eat before we came, I made straight for the buffet line. No ho-hum selections there. The food encompassed everything from appetizing low-carb treats to total decadence by the bite. I took a plate and went for the ones with the most protein. "Teeny, the food looks fabulous."

"Be sure to try the baby Cornish pasties and the little gingerbread-raspberry bowls," she said, pleased. "The chef worked out the recipes just for me."

I popped in a Cornish pasty. "Mmmm!" Within a minute, I'd polished off half a dozen, then started on the rest of my selections. Once I'd wolfed down a sufficient amount to keep my blood sugar from tanking, I crossed the room to talk to Callie.

She still held back, but there was more warmth in her voice as she said, "Isn't it perfect, Mama? The cherry blossoms came from Maryland. And Wade and I wanted the table arrangements to look really natural, like something from a garden, but low, so everybody could see each other." She scanned the results with pride. "Didn't he do a fabulous job? I swear, watching him work is like watching a great artist sculpt," she gushed. "You have no idea how much thought and preparation goes into what he does. I learn something new every day."

Speak of the devil. Wade walked in wearing a perfectly fitted classic tux. He immediately honed in on Callie and made straight for us, his face lit up like a smitten teenager.

This was it. In spite of my good resolutions, my smile congealed and my insides went tight. Luckily, Callie had eyes only for him and let go of me before she felt my reaction.

I decided to open with something safe. "The flowers are magnificent, Wade," I said as he approached us. "Great job."

To my surprise, he bypassed Callie to give me a polite hug.

Not that I'd expected him to hang all over her. Callie had always been the touchy-feely type, but not so, Wade—a fact for which I was grateful on that particular night. At least he wouldn't embarrass us by holding on to Callie's fanny in public the way so many of the men our age did with their baby wives.

I wasn't sure whether it was consideration for John and me, or Wade's natural reservation about public displays of affection, but when he stepped back, he didn't put his arm around Callie, though it was obvious she wanted him to. "I'm glad you like the decorations," he said as she took his hand, "but Callie had as much to do with them as I did. She's got quite a talent for floral design, and some wonderfully fresh ideas."

She blushed and looked moon-eyed at him. "Everything I know, he taught me."

Who was this goofy, coy overgrown adolescent, and what had she done with the confident woman who had met me at the car?

Personally, I don't think hormones and intelligence are mutually exclusive, but this particular instance might have been an exception.

And where was John? He'd promised not to leave me to fend for myself. I scanned the room and found him with his back to us—my drink dutifully in hand—avoiding the inevitable by sampling his way through the buffet alongside Brooks.

So much for Elmer.

"John, honey," I called in a voice that sounded tense even to me, "here's Wade."

A slight hesitation and shift of muscle betrayed his reluctance to face the music, then he turned and bravely abandoned the dependable realm of food for the emotional minefield of facing Wade and Callie as a couple.

"Hey," he said to Wade, handing me my drink.

"Hey, yourself," Wade answered with an awkwardness they'd never shown before. He peered at John's plate. "What's good?"

"Everything."

Wade nodded. The four of us stood there at sixes and sevens for long moments till Teeny joined us. "People are starting to arrive," she said. "Would y'all rather we greet them formally at the door, or just mingle?"

As far as I was concerned, mingling presented the potential for too many awkward moments, like introducing yourself to people you don't know, then introducing yourself all over again. And again. It's that third one that really gets on their nerves and makes me look like I'm either swacked or senile. Plus, with all the background noise at parties, I have a lot of trouble filtering voices, much less names, especially when there's a band. So I much preferred catching folks just outside in the hallway, where I could hear and Teeny could deftly prod them to identify themselves.

John must have thought the same thing, because we both said "formally" at the same time Wade and Callie said "mingle."

The four of us exchanged a nervous chuckle.

Teeny smoothed the moment with, "Why don't we start out saying hello to people just outside the doorway as they come in, so we can all hear them, then mingle after everyone's arrived?"

As the hostess's request, it was a polite decree.

"Sure." Callie leaned closer to Wade. "That'll be fine, won't it, honey?"

"Teeny," he said, "I am so overwhelmed by your generosity in throwing this party that we will gladly do it any way you want."

She patted his arm. "I'm just doing what your parents would have wanted to if they were here." Graciously said, as usual.

We all headed for the hallway. "There's no need to be rigid about the order in which we receive people," Teeny said to Callie and Wade. "Why don't y'all let George and John stand by me, so folks can linger with you two at the end if they want to."

"You've got it," Wade said.

Thirty minutes later, we had greeted a steady stream of Wade and Callie's friends without incident. Our friends were a different matter. As I'd feared, I hit some kinks with a few of the wives who'd socialized with us and Wade. They treated me with exaggerated concern, as if Callie had been diagnosed with some terminal disease, instead of marrying somebody in our set. But even then, only one woman— the wife of another Tech department head—crossed the line.

John and her husband immediately started talking shop, but I knew I was in for trouble when she tucked her little handbag under her upper arm and made a beeline for me with both hands extended. "And there's our Georgiaaaaa." Eyes welling, she clutched both my hands to her breast, leaning in to say a clearly audible, "We know how hard this must be for you and John, but I must say, you're both holding up awfully well . . . under the circumstances. You're in our prayers, sweetie."

From the corner of my eye, I saw Callie go rigid.

Did this idiot person think my daughter was deaf and blind?

Channeling my Inner Duchess, I squeezed the woman's hands right back, looked her square in the eye, and told her the truth. "Wade has been John's closest friend for more than thirty years. He's a fine man, and Callie adores him." Okay, so the fine-man part was more of a hope than a definite, pending the detective's report, but it might be true. I finished with, "I know you'll join us in wishing the two of them every good and gracious thing." Now, *that* was truer than true.

Clearly unused to being confronted, the woman balked, but I refused to look away or release her hands till she broke eye contact first.

I won.

Ruffled, she grudgingly conceded, "Well, of course we all wish them well." She tugged at her husband's arm. "Come on, Walter," she ordered with a definite note of sarcasm, "let's say hello to this *fine man* Callie's marryin'."

Callie shot me a pointed look of pride and gratitude before smothering the passive-aggressive little witch with kindness.

I could take all the potshots at Wade that I wanted to—in private—but nobody was going to embarrass my daughter in public and get away with it.

After that, things went smoothly till Wade spotted a lone straggler our age coming into the building. Teeny was just greeting the last couple in line, who introduced themselves as fellow teachers at Oglethorpe with Callie.

"Oh, good." Wade turned to Callie. "Here comes Alan Dailey. Great guy. He runs Cherry Blossom up in Sandy Springs."

Callie nodded. "Oh, yeah. They beat us out for that huge debutante party. I hear he's good."

"He is. We've been rivals since college, first at golf, and now in business."

Mention college golf, and John's nose goes up like Smokey sniffing an illegal campfire. He asked Wade, "Is that the Alan Dailey who shot five under par for State to beat us in sixty-seven?" The man can't match his socks, but he can remember every single golf tournament he ever played in.

"One and the same," Wade said, "but we're friendly rivals now."

The guy stopped and glanced toward the bathroom. Probably waiting for his wife.

Callie didn't wait for the Oglethorpe people to get to her. She leaned past me to shake the woman's hand. "Jane! I'm so glad y'all could make it. Mama, this is Jane Evans and her husband Richard. She's with the math department at Oglethorpe and helped me get the job. And Richard wrote the definitive textbook on twentieth-century American lit and has tenure in the English department."

"That's quite an accomplishment," I said to him, then focused on Jane. "Callie's so excited about teaching with y'all."

"She could have gone almost anywhere she wanted," Jane said, "but lucky for us, she wanted to stay small and local."

After they met Wade, Callie barraged the two professors with questions about school, leaving Wade free to poke John and whisper, "We ought to get Alan to play a morning foursome. When does Jack have to—" Wade froze, his eyes locked past John.

Both of us followed his line of sight to see a spectacular blonde wearing an equally spectacular engagement ring join his old pal.

Definitely not the wife of her escort's youth. Way too overtly dressed in a skintight neoprene little black dress cut down to there, she was a poster child for chickie-booms if ever there was one.

Wade pivoted back to the Evanses so fast, it looked like somebody had swacked his head with a driver, but it didn't take a psychic to see that his mind was still on the blonde. "Tell me," he asked the couple, "what's it like with both of you working on the same faculty?"

Trying not to be obvious, I scoped out the sex kitten as she and Wade's old rival approached. The man was relaxed, but the girl moved like a panther on the prowl. When Teeny greeted them, the girl caught Wade glancing her way and narrowed her eyes at him, pointedly raising her engagement ring into view.

As always, the body told the story, and hers was screaming heavy-duty history.

Meanwhile, Callie was blissfully oblivious, laughing at a funny anecdote Jane was telling.

While Callie was winding up her conversation with the married professors, Wade's friend moved from Teeny to John and me. "Hi, I'm

Alan Dailey, a fellow florist and longtime friend of Wade's. Please allow me to introduce my fiancée Beth Sutton."

Wade wasn't looking at her, but Beth sure was looking at him.

"Glad y'all could come," John said, his face void of recognition. "This is my wife, Georgia Baker," he repeated for the jillionth time that night. "We're Callie's parents."

Without even looking at us, the girl brazenly sized Callie up and down. "Ah, yes," she said. "Callie." She extended a limp, manicured hand my way that good manners compelled me to take.

I let go as soon as was decent.

Callie finished with the others, then turned her attention our way. "Hi, I'm Callie," she said to the blonde, clearly oblivious to the undercurrent between her and Wade. She smiled warmly at Alan. "Wade's told me so many nice things about you, Alan."

The girl took Callie's hand in both her own, her solitaire prominently on top. "I've been so curious to meet you, Callie."

I smelled trouble, with a capital T. Of all times for there to be nobody left in the receiving line to hurry things along.

"My claim to fame," Alan told Callie, "was hitting the best golf game of my life to beat your future husband when we were in college, but time has evened up our games. Now Wade beats me as often as I beat him."

Callie laughed. "I'm a firm believer that every man needs to be beaten regularly." Clever, clever, but she still hadn't picked up on the girl's predatory vibes.

Only when Alan addressed Wade did Callie realize something was going on. Alan shook Wade's hand. "Wade. You remember Beth, of course."

Social code for "You two were once an item."

Red alert!

That meant Callie wasn't Wade's second young girlfriend (counting the brief fling after his divorce). She was at least his third. That made it a pattern, and a very disturbing one.

Heat rose from my chest to my neck.

Madelyn's warning echoed in my mind. How many more cradles had he robbed?

Consideration for Callie's feelings was the only thing that kept me from doing a stompin' devil dance on the spot.

Beth dropped Callie's hand as if it were soiled. "He'd better remember me," she said to Callie. "*My* claim to fame is being engaged to the two handsomest straight florists in Atlanta." She slid her finger behind Wade's lapel and slowly drew it downward. "Wasn't I, Wade?"

Engaged to her! And clearly, Wade hadn't told Callie, who colored up as she shot a hurt glare at him.

"Oh dear." Beth laid a talon theatrically to her lower lip. "Did I let the cat out of the bag?" She angled a sly look up at Wade, earning a frown from her escort.

More than a little ruddy himself, Wade gave a brief spasmodic twist against his collar as his arm circled Callie's waist. "That was a long time ago."

Beth nodded, gloating. "Two whole years. Seems like another lifetime."

I could have drop-kicked Wade Bowman on the spot for leaving Callie open to this kind of embarrassment. He should have told her!

I wasn't alone. John looked like he was ready for a come-to-Jesus meeting with his best friend. "This is the first I've heard of any of this," he grated out, low, to me.

Fortunately, Callie had inherited both my expertise in social innuendo and her father's flat-footed practicality, so she could take care of herself. Her flash of hurt shifted immediately to patronizing concern for Beth. "Of course you didn't let the cat out of the bag. Wade and I don't keep any secrets from each other. He told me absolutely everything of any significance about his past." Quite the actress, she gazed at him with absolute trust before reverting to Beth. "I'm so glad to see that you were finally able to put your heartbreak behind you and give love another chance."

Wade's face tilted slightly in amazement as he witnessed my brilliant daughter's powers of deduction.

Flat-mouthed, Beth focused sullen fury at Callie, whose expression remained innocent.

"Congratulations, Alan," Callie said warmly. "You're getting a great girl, here." She beamed. "Isn't it wonderful that we've all moved on, and you and Wade can still be pals?" She turned back to Beth, who had gone stone-faced. "You must be so excited, Beth. I know I am. Our big day's June seventeenth. When's yours?"

Now it was Beth's turn to redden, and Alan's to freeze.

Teeny's expression brightened with glee, but John frowned in confusion.

Wasn't it Dr. Laura who said a woman with a ring and a date is engaged, but a woman with a ring and no date is just a mistress with a ring?

That would teach Wade's snotty cast-off to dis my little girl in public!

Alan beat a strategic retreat. "Come on, honey," he said, steering his *mistress with a ring* toward the food. "We've monopolized these good folks long enough." He waved to Wade. "Call me next week. We'll do nine after market one morning."

Callie waited till they were well out of sight before she said to Wade through a fixed grin, "Wade and I don't keep any secrets from each other. He told me all about his past."

Not that I didn't want to hear what came next, but for once, I knew when it was politic to leave. I grabbed John's arm. "Time to mingle, now." But he balked, glaring at Wade.

John didn't anger easily, but when he did, it was chilling.

Teeny sized up the situation and intervened. "I was just going to suggest we mingle, myself," she said. "I think most everybody's here by now." She circled Callie's waist, her small Chanel-clad sleeve beneath Wade's. "Wade, honey, may I please steal your lovely bride for a few minutes? I'll have her back soon."

Smart move, separating them till Callie calmed down enough to realize this wasn't the time or place to go into what had just happened. Callie would listen to her godmother, and I was too angry to speak without saying something Callie would resent.

But if Teeny had Callie out of the way . . .

"Perfect," I said, taking Wade's arm. "We'll keep him company while y'all are gone."

"Just for a while," Callie said, "then I want him back."

Not till I got through with him.

I'd have taken him outside, but it was too cold, so I headed for an empty table at the far end of the ballroom from Callie—and the band. Clearly, not for mingling.

John made no effort to keep up appearances. Glowering, he told his old friend, "We need to talk. Now."

Wade regarded him with a mixture of defensiveness and concern. "I hardly think this is the time or the place."

"Oh," I interjected, "this is definitely the time and place, because if you don't come up with an acceptable explanation for what just happened, there may not be an announcement."

Wade colored. "I'd say that was up to Callie."

Cissie Youngblood picked just that moment to swoop in and do that fake Euro-kissy thing, her jeweled evening bag lifted in one hand and a flute of champagne in the other. "Georgia, sweetie. I had no idea Callie got her doctorate! In theoretical mathematics, no less." She gave John's ribs a playful poke with her bag. "The acorn didn't fall far from the tree, did it?" She took a sip of champagne. "I know you both must be sooo proud."

Cissie could sniff out the tiniest whiff of conflict at a perfume convention, which had kept her the root of the Buckhead grapevine for more than twenty years. So I had no intention of giving her any ammunition. "Thanks, sweetie. Callie worked so hard for that. Did you know she's teaching at Oglethorpe, starting next fall?" Wade made a subtle move toward escape, but I tightened my grip on his arm. "Wade is just as proud of her as we are, aren't you?"

"Absolutely."

I leaned in confidentially to Cissie. "Such a sweet man. And he absolutely adores Callie. We're all *so* pleased about this."

Cissie's expression said she wasn't buying that for a second. "What about you, John?" she asked him. "Are you *so* pleased that your best friend plans to marry your daughter?"

The nerve!

John surprised us all with his trademark boyish grin. "Absolutely. But I'd be even more pleased if you'd dance with me." He aimed a purposeful look at Wade. "Will y'all excuse us? We can continue our discussion when I get back."

Bless his heart. If ever a diversion was called for, it was now.

"Whew," Wade said. "I owe John. That woman has been trouble from day one."

Still holding fast to Wade's arm, I resumed our progress toward the table in the corner. "He did that for Callie, not for you. He's very angry with you, and so am I."

A cute little cocktail waitress intercepted us. "What may I bring y'all to drink?"

"The lady will have a tonic and lime," Wade said. "As for me, I think hemlock might be in order."

The waitress's brows drew together, but she kept smiling. "I'm sorry sir, but I'm afraid we don't have that brand."

"And *the lady* will have a flute of champagne," I snapped. "Make that two."

"I'll have tonic and lime," Wade told her.

"Now," I said when she left. "Where were we? Oh yes. Very, very upset."

Wade didn't waste time making apologies or excuses. "If I were in your shoes, I would be, too. What do you want me to do about that?"

Now that most of the room was behind us, I dropped my cheerful veneer. "Tell me how many girls young enough to be your daughter you've been involved with, and why I shouldn't be alarmed by that?" I didn't need to tell him I was Callie's mother and had a right to know. "Why did you hide your engagement to that little witch even from John?"

Reaching the table, I sat in the chair with my back to the party and drew Wade down into the one beside it. "Once, I could understand. Twice is concerning. Three times establishes a pattern, Wade, and not a healthy one."

"George, there is no pattern." He met my skepticism with sincerity. "As for the rest, please don't take offense, but this is between me and Callie."

Wrong! Maybe I did need to remind him. "You and I have been friends for three decades. I stood by you in your divorce. John is your best friend. And Callie is our daughter. We trusted you with both our children, and we were grateful they had a safe place to work. But this thing with Callie . . . Put yourself in our place." I had to make him see. "What if I died, and you sent Laurie to work with John, and lo and behold, she comes home and announces she's marrying him? What would you do then?"

Wade grinned. "I'd gunnysack him to save him from himself. I love my daughter, but she'd run through every cent he had and never give him anything but grief and chaos."

"That's not what I meant, and you know it," I said, flustered. Where was John when I needed him? Beyond Wade, I spotted my husband working toward us with a short glass of amber liquor in one hand and a tonic and lime for me in the other, constantly waylaid by friends. Then Diane intercepted him and delivered him straight to us.

She leaned in and whispered to me, "Teeny has Callie occupied. The rest of us will set up a perimeter so y'all won't be interrupted, but if you don't start mingling before long, people will talk."

"Thanks." What would I do without my friends?

John handed me the tonic just as the waitress arrived with my two flutes of champagne and Wade's tonic. After she gave us our drinks, I took a long, slow sip of bubbly.

John took a slug of whiskey, then sat on the other side of Wade. "I have never pried into your private life, Wade," he ground out, "but I want to know why you hid your engagement to that girl from me and Georgia, and how many other girls Callie's age you've been involved with. Talk straight to me. Our friendship is riding on this."

Great minds with but a single thought.

I could see that John's ultimatum didn't sit well with Wade, but he remained calm. "There were no other girls. And there's no pattern." Wade looked to me. "After the divorce, I was hurt and angry and so lonely without my children, I thought of killing myself, especially knowing how Madelyn lied to turn them against me.

"I met Kathy at a bar. She liked to rescue people, so she rescued me. The sex was casual for her and purely therapeutic for me. We both knew the relationship would never go anywhere, but it kept me from putting a gun to my head or falling off the wagon for good. And I was able to help her work out some of her problems. When she found somebody her own age, I was glad. By then, I was able to handle things."

It had the ring of truth, and I saw no signs of duplicity as he spoke. "And Beth?" I challenged.

Wade made sure nobody was within earshot before he answered. "I make it a policy never to say anything negative about anybody I've dated. In this case, I'll make an exception, but only for you, and it can't go any further. That means Callie, too. You have my word, I'll tell her everything, but what I say to y'all has to stay between the three of us at this table. Agreed?"

John and I looked at each other, then nodded in unison. "Agreed."

Wade leaned in and dropped his voice. "Beth got fixated on me when I did a lot of the flowers for her debut class. She has plenty of her own money and didn't want to come out, but her parents blackmailed her into doing it. She never told me what they had on her, but it must have been something choice.

"So at first, I was her revenge, suitably unsuitable. But when she found out I wasn't interested, she really went after me. Beth will do anything to get what she wants, and I was the first thing she ever wanted that she couldn't have. She got so relentless, threatening all kinds of things if I didn't go out with her, that I finally agreed to a few dates, hoping she'd get tired of me, but it had the opposite effect."

He sighed. "I was the first man who hadn't jumped into bed with her, genuflecting before he did. Instead, I tried to talk to her, figure out why she was so screwed up. I counseled her spiritually, hoping she could know the love of Christ and start there, but she was too caught up in the temporal to care about the eternal. Instead, she got it into her head that I was some knight in shining armor."

He glanced out the windows to the azaleas beyond. "I finally pulled the plug when she dragged me to Tiffany's to look at bracelets and ended up having them show her diamond solitaires. I told her we were just friends, not even really dating, but she bought one with her trust fund money anyway and told her family we were engaged."

John's eyes narrowed. "You expect us to believe that? She pursued you? Bought her own engagement ring and concocted the whole thing?"

Wade shook his head. "It's the truth. When I saw how delusional she was, I met with her parents and told them what had happened.

You can't imagine how relieved they were that I wasn't a gold digger. They said they'd take care of it, and they did. I can only guess that they used whatever they had against her to keep her in line."

He sighed, losing focus. "She and Alan are a lot better suited. He likes money and mindless sex and will have no problem living off his wife. But it still makes me sad to think of Beth. She has so much materially, but she's desperate and lonely and doesn't have a clue about what really matters." One eyebrow arched. "An awful lot like my Laurie. How I wish I could have made a difference there."

This whole thing was getting so Freudian, I felt seasick.

What in the world were John and I supposed to do with that tall tale about Beth? Yet Wade had told it with absolute sincerity, and as far as I knew, Wade was honest to a fault.

Instead of clarifying things, our heart-to-heart had just raised more questions.

Even I was at a loss for words.

And Callie, what would she think when he told her?

How I wished I hadn't promised not to talk to her about this.

All three of us almost jumped out of our skins when a cheerful voice behind us piped up with, "Sorry to take so long getting back to y'all, but the bars are jammed." The waitress stopped beside me. "Can I bring anybody a refill?"

Obviously not the brightest bulb in the pack. Wade had two untouched tonics in front of him, I had both flutes, and John had only taken one drink from his whiskey.

"We're fine," Wade told her.

John eyed my champagne askance. "Babe, it's not even eight thirty."

"How well I know." It only felt like midnight. I took another long, slow sip, savoring the bubbles and the crisp taste on my tongue, which promptly started to go numb around the edges.

John stood and moved around to pull back my chair. "Let's get you some food."

I picked up both flutes and rose. "Sounds like a plan."

Wade stood, too. "That's it?"

John paused. "You've never lied to me before. On the strength of that, I'll believe what you told us. But if you hurt or deceive my daughter, Wade, you answer to me."

He met John's gaze without wavering. "I will not hurt or deceive her."

"You already did," I said quietly. "I saw the look on her face when Beth said y'all had been engaged."

What else was Wade hiding?

John gave me a squeeze and called off the hostilities with, "Come on, Mama. We've got some eating and dancing to do, then an announcement to make."

In spite of everything, he was really going to sanction Wade and Callie's marriage.

"Thanks," Wade told him. "You won't regret it. I swear."

Callie caught up with us when we got to the buffet. She made a great show of teasing Wade about hiding in the corner with us, then leaned over to me and whispered, "Satisfied?"

I whispered back, "Ask yourself the same question after he talks to you, then come see me."

Ten minutes later, I saw them talking as they glided through a slow dance on the floor. Only a mother's eye would have read the progression of Callie's subtle reactions to Wade's confession, but the dance ended in a long, soulful eye lock, then a kiss of atonement.

"She bought it," I said to John. She must have, because she never mentioned it to me again.

John put his arms around me from behind. "So did I. It's settled, then."

Wouldn't life be simple if that were the case?

I drank my second glass of tepid champagne in two gulps, but was still dead sober when time came for us to announce the engagement. John's memorized speech was short, sweet, and eloquent.

Everybody clapped.

Callie was radiant.

Wade was proud and happy.

All of Callie's godmothers applauded vigorously.

The band struck up with "She Loves You."

And I smiled like a mule eating briars, then drank two more champagnes.

To everyone's amazement, including mine, I remained sober till I finally crawled into bed and passed out, my last conscious thought a question: What other skeletons was Wade Bowman hiding in his closet, and would the detectives find them?

I didn't have to wait long to find out.

Tuesday, just before lunch, my doorbell rang. I wasn't expecting anybody, but maybe it was a package. No truck in the driveway, but I spotted Teeny through the sidelight. Odd that she hadn't called. I opened the door and was answered with a perplexed frown. "Hi. What's up?"

"Maybe nothing. Maybe something." Teeny came inside and waited till I closed the door behind her to pull a large manila envelope from her attaché-style shoulder bag. "Does the name Nora Green mean anything to you?"

I thought for a moment. "Not off the top of my head, but you know how awful I am about names. Should it?"

Teeny pulled out a color printout of a grainy photo of an average-looking woman and showed it to me. "How about this? Does it ring any bells?"

I was a lot better at faces than names, but the photo didn't look familiar, either. "Sorry. She's pretty nondescript, though. I might have seen her and never noticed." I proffered the image back to her, but she motioned for me to keep it.

"Show it to John," Teeny instructed. "His photographic memory will come in handy. Just ask him if he's ever seen her before. If he says no, then mention the name. Let me know what he says."

"What's with all the cloak and dagger?" I slid the photo back into the envelope. "Is she involved with Wade in some way?"

"That's what we're trying to find out." Teeny leveled a warning gaze at me. "I know it's useless to ask, but please don't go jumping to conclusions. This could be completely on the up-and-up."

"Or not," I shot back.

She started for the door. "George, honey, obsessing over this will just make you miserable. And the rest of us. Try to set it aside till we have the facts. That's all I'm asking."

"I'll try. I promise." The trouble was, I was already doing it. I waved as she got into her car, then pulled out.

The second I was alone, two huge, drastic questions overwhelmed my thoughts: Who was Nora Green, and what did she have to do with Wade?

Maybe John would know.

· 17 ·

The Dreaded Lingerie Shower

Never underestimate an old woman. She's still a woman.
—LINDA'S *BUBBIE*

. . . .

I SHOWED JOHN the photo as soon as he got home.

He didn't recognize the woman. Not only that, he didn't even ask why I wanted to know. Just looked at the photo, processed it for about a minute, then handed it back with, "Sorry. Never seen her before." The name didn't jog anything either. "Nope. Never heard of her, either." And that was that.

As if I'd never asked, he drew me to him for a quick kiss, then a hearty, "What's for dinner?" Clearly, he didn't give a rat's patoot who Nora Green was or why I'd asked.

Would that I had earth-shaking matters of physics to occupy my idle mind, the way he did.

"Homemade chicken pot pie," I answered, doing my best to cover my frustration.

"Yum." He kissed me again, this time with feeling, almost as if a little romance was a consolation prize. "Will it keep?"

"Long enough," I answered, more than willing for the distraction. He knew me all too well.

The present. Saturday, April 15. 10:58 A.M. Muscogee Drive, Atlanta.

THE MORE I dread going somewhere, the earlier I get ready. Who knows why? So on the morning of Callie's lingerie shower/luncheon, I had been dressed and "sittin' on the bed with my pocketbook in hand," as my granny used to say, for half an hour while John was finishing the paper at the breakfast table. I still had a quarter of an hour left to wait when he finally came upstairs and headed for the bathroom.

He walked past without looking up from his sudoku puzzle, then closed the door and turned on the shower.

Men are lucky. When they go to a shower, all they have to do is strip and enjoy the hot water.

For "girls" of the bathtub generation like me, showers mean parties, which—for us Buckhead baby boomers—meant control-top pantyhose, makeup, high heels, facing those extra pounds we've gained since we last saw everybody, and choosing the perfect gift.

Now that ordinary lingerie departments look like buying clubs for streetwalkers, choosing Callie's present was a challenge. The last thing I wanted was to evoke any risqué images of her and Wild Man Wade.

Gag me with a steam shovel, as Pru would say.

So I'd played it safe and bought a hooded, white terrycloth beach robe like the ones John and I had worn—in a dozen incarnations—since we'd gotten a pair as a wedding gift. It was the unsexiest thing I could find that I knew Callie would like. She'd been borrowing ours since she was a little girl.

If I could have counted on all the other gifts being as tame, I wouldn't have worried about the next four hours. But I knew better. Callie was the last of her friends to marry, and their tradition of raunchy gags and male strippers was a rite of passage that gave no quarter to the hapless mothers and grandmothers present.

Speaking of grandmothers . . .

If things got out of hand, I'd be the one, not Callie and her friends, who heard about it from Mama for the rest of her earthly days.

The bird clock in the kitchen sounded a loud chirp, chirp, chirp, *wonk, wonk,* the call of the white-breasted nuthatch that announced eleven o'clock.

I'd need to leave in ten or fifteen minutes to make it to 103 West by eleven thirty and help Diane with the last-minute preparations.

I looked into the mirror to make sure my most confidence-boosting outfit was in order: slimming black slacks, a white satin camisole, my faithful clear pink blazer, and 36-inch pearls with matching earrings. And my favorite antique gold Spanish cross that I wore every day. The look was timeless and dignified—perfect for the mother of the bride.

I closed my eyes for an arrow prayer, one of a jillion in the past few months. This one was specific. *Please, Lord, if they've hired a stripper, give him a flat tire on the way.* Just to be safe, I added, *And a dead alternator.*

All I sensed was a wry divine smile, which was hardly reassuring, but God definitely has a sense of humor, so I braced myself for the worst.

It wasn't God who flashed the image of Callie's opening a pair of edible panties at the shower, which vividly morphed into Wade's happily diving for dessert.

"Aaagggh!" I covered my eyes and willed myself to think of cute puppies and kittens.

"George?" John came out of our bathroom, his lanky self rosy and warm and damply disheveled in his threadbare beach robe. "Are you okay?" So much for beach robes not being sexy.

"Sorry. I didn't mean to scare you." I tried my best to appear nonchalant, but my reflection in the dresser mirror looked like I was soldiering through a high colonic. "I'm fine. Really."

He surveyed me with approval. "Well, you certainly look fine. Woof." He moseyed up behind me and sniffed the back of my neck, sending a frisson of electricity across my skin. "Mmm. You smell good," he said with more than my Chanel No. 5 in mind. His terry cloth–covered arms drew me back against him, bringing me into contact with definite confirmation of the compliment.

Why is it men have such an unerring instinct for amorous bad timing? Under normal circumstances, I might have jumped his bones for a quickie, but on this day of our daughter's lingerie shower, sex was the last thing I wanted to think about. Ours. Wade and Callie's. Anybody's.

I gave his arm a dismissive pat. "Sorry, but I'm trying to psych myself up for this party, and that's not helping. You know what kind of nonsense Callie's friends have pulled at their lingerie showers. If one of them gives her a pair of edible underpants that your pal Wade is gonna—"

John's reaction was more severe than mine had been. "Aaaaggh!" The fearless flagpole went instantly limp, and he jumped back as if I'd just broken out in boils. "Do not finish that sentence. Damn!"

Oops. "Welcome to my world."

"Did you have to be so graphic?" He paced, arms akimbo, his expression haunted. "I was having enough trouble with this as it was. Damn." More pacing. "I'm a man. We're visual. Now every time I look at my best friend, I'll see him . . ." He shuddered, then rubbed his eyes as if to erase the image I had raised.

"Oh, honey, I'm so sorry. I wasn't thinking." About him, anyway. I gave myself a good, swift mental kick in the pants. I'd been so caught up in my own worries that it was easy to lose sight of how hard this was on him, too. "Can I call a do over?" I hugged him, but it was his turn to stand there rigid as a hat rack.

After a few seconds, he eased, but only a little, and gingerly returned my embrace. "Sorry. I overreacted." Then he stepped free of me. "It's one thing for Callie to marry a man my age, but it's another thing entirely for her to marry a guy I got drunk with and watched carouse all through college. A guy who bragged about all his sexual escapades and fantasies and the stupid stuff he did. My mind knows that's not the Wade he is today, but I keep flashing on the stuff he did and said back then."

"Oh, honey." John was a physicist, a Bigbrain, far more comfortable with the intellectual world of facts and figures and proofs than airing his feelings. This was the first time he'd opened up since Callie had told us about Wade, and I was so glad he had, but I had no idea how to respond. "He's your best friend," I offered. "If anybody knows what kind of man he is, it would be you."

"Yeah, well . . ." John pulled his underwear out of the drawer, slammed it shut, then stepped into his boxers. "You'd think. But the trouble is, for all the years we've been friends, I don't really know that much about him beyond golf or tennis or social situations."

Whoa! Major insight for a guy thing. Judging from his tormented expression, though, such introspection didn't come easy.

He shucked the robe and drew a white tee over his still-taut torso. "I mean, he seems really decent. He's not a lush or a mooch. Never bets too much, and always pays with a smile when he loses. He's always on time, and he never stood me up for anything."

Ah, what a simple criteria men have for their relationships.

John put on his socks, then his jeans (the pair that showed off his great butt), still trying to convince us both that Wade was worthy of our daughter. "He says all the right stuff and acts like a gentleman, even on his fourth shot in a sand trap. He's principled in his business. He's active in his church. But . . ." His expression twisted.

Ah, yes. The other kind of "great but."

John heaved a sigh. "It feels totally disloyal even to think this, but ever since Callie announced she was planning to marry him, I've been wondering what kind of person he is underneath. And after that Beth girl came out of the woodwork, I'm wondering even more. I know I said I believed him about that. I wanted to. But Wade's explanation is just so implausible . . ." He jerked a plaid flannel shirt out of the closet with such force that the metal hanger bent into a diamond. "What if he's lying? What if all that nice guy stuff is only skin deep?"

I swallowed, hard. If John wasn't sure of his best friend . . .

I seriously considered telling him about the investigation, but worried how he would take it.

He stepped into his loafers. "Sorry," he said, looking half his age and twice as adorable as a man had a right to look, despite his worried expression. "I promised myself I wouldn't bother you with all this, but it just came out."

"I'm so glad you did." I went over and hugged him, my head against his chest. "Callie's our daughter. We should talk about this to each other. It's the only safe place to do it."

I had my Red Hat Club, but John's only sounding board was Wade, who was now off-limits.

"She's made up her mind," he argued, his voice a deep rumble in my ear. "What good will talking do?" Ever the scientist, tied to results.

I drew him a little tighter and decided to come clean, but knew better than to poison John's relationship with his friend by repeating Madelyn's accusations. "I have a confession to make. I'm having him checked out by a private detective. The initial results gave him a clean slate, but just to be sure, they're looking further."

He stilled, and I held my breath. Then his body relaxed.

"Good," he said with conviction. Major relief! "But how much is that costing? Who did you hire? Are they reliable?"

Considering how defensive John had been when I'd mentioned going to work for Teeny, I braced myself for a negative reaction. "It's not costing us anything. Teeny's paying for it, for Callie's sake, not ours. She's using the firm that does her corporate security. The detectives are very thorough, and very discreet. Wade will never know unless we tell him."

Again, my husband surprised me. After a brief pause, he patted my back. "I'm glad. Maybe now I can sleep at night without dreaming Dr. Jekyll and Mr. Hyde nightmares about Wade."

No recriminations about not telling him, or being underhanded. Just relief.

Nightmares . . . Poor guy. When I suffer, it's never in silence, but John had been stewing on this all alone out of misguided concern for me.

"I've asked Teeny to have them check Wade's story about Beth Sutton, too," I added.

"Good." He gave the top of my head a peck as he let me go. "Have fun at the shower. But if it gets raunchy, I don't want to know. The edible panties image went way over my decency threshold, as it is. I'm having a hard enough time looking Wade in the eye, already."

"Did I mention Mama is coming to the shower?"

He laughed. "Only about a dozen times." He cocked his head with a smile. "You'll be fine. You're a master at convincing people you're happy when you're not."

And what did he mean by that? Chicken Little immediately wondered if he'd known I was only pretending to love him all those years, but John's happy, lucent expression contradicted that suspicion.

"Where you off to?" I asked as he headed out.

"To the lab, to wash my mind out with physics."

What I wouldn't give for some brain-stain remover of my own. "Let's go to Fratelli di Napoli tonight," I called after him. "Kick back over a platter of chicken piccata with a nice bottle of wine. Then we can go to a funny movie, or come home and watch one of those comedy DVDs I bought." Twenty hours of vintage standup routines by famous comedians—serious therapy.

John hollered across the living room, "It's a date. I vote for the video."

"Great. I should be home by four." I picked up Callie's gift and headed after him.

Lord, just get me through this one shower without embarrassing Callie or hurting her feelings, I arrow-prayed. *And I'll be fine for all the others. I promise. Amen.*

I added a hasty postscript. *But don't forget about giving the stripper a flat tire.*

A scant twelve minutes later, I walked into the upstairs dining room at 103 West and found Diane adding her decorations to the last two tables set up behind a wide, U-shaped seating arrangement. She'd already softened the restaurant's standard white skirts with genteelly worn cutwork cloths and lengths of antique alençon lace, overlaid at various angles.

"Hey, there!" she called to me. "Come help me with this. I have something to tell you."

I headed over, worried. But as usual, my fears proved worse than reality.

"We'll put the unopened gifts here." She handed me one end of a cutwork cloth. "I've been talking to Callie's pals," she said, "and they have sworn on a stack of Bibles that they're not getting a stripper."

I wanted to believe her, but . . . "Are you sure they weren't just saying that?"

"They really sounded sincere." She eyed the angle, then motioned me to shift the cloth before we laid it down. "And they mentioned what a straight-arrow Callie is, so I think they're on the up-and-up." She unfolded a large square of gorgeous ecru lace and handed me a corner. "Let's center this on the diagonal."

"I sure hope they weren't kidding," I fretted. "I cannot answer for how my mother will react if some Chippendale gets down to the buff."

"Well, I guess they could have been putting one over on me to keep it a surprise," Diane said, "but I don't think so." She motioned to the last table. "Let's get that last one for the presents after they've been opened, then we can start setting everything up."

We were just about done when Pru and Teeny arrived together and headed our way. Teeny greeted us with, "Put us to work."

Pru had on a flattering tiered white voile dress with a pleated bodice and ruffled cuffs covered in pale embroidery.

"What a darling dress!" I said.

She laughed. "Original issue, honey. I found it in my brother's attic last week. Vintage seventies." She pulled the scant fullness of the skirt to the side. "I fill up a heck of a lot more of it than I did, then. But, hey, I can wear it."

Peach was definitely a gift from God to Pru. I hadn't seen her so happy and positive since she met Tyson.

Speaking of happy and positive, Linda arrived ready for business. "Look at y'all goofin' off, and the tables aren't even finished. Get to work."

"Here." Diane handed her a box filled with pairs of rolled antique napkins in engraved silver rings, each set with a numbered sticker, and a numbered seating arrangement. "Y'all can put out the favors. The rings are monogrammed, so match them to the seating key." Organized, as usual. "Oh, and I put a Jesus seat at that end of our table." (A Bible Belt colloquialism for an extra place setting, just in case—so the Lord will have a seat when he returns.)

Scanning the chart, I saw that Diane had put Callie to her right, then me, then Mama. "Uh-oh." I pointed. "Diane, honey, please let me move Mama to the other side of you." The last thing I wanted was to have Mama next to me if a stripper showed up. "Teeny, you won't mind being on smelling salts duty, will you?"

She shook her head. "Not a bit."

I made cocker spaniel eyes at Diane. "Please?"

She leveled a mock scowl at me. "Chicken." After hesitating a bit just to torture me, she relented. "Okay. She and Linda can swap."

Double bonus.

Diane went back to the favors. "Cross the napkins at the top of each setting like this." She demonstrated. "While y'all are doing that, I'll go tell the staff they can set out the silverware. Then we can put out the flowers and the extra doodahs."

She bent forward to whisper. "I snuck in two gallons of my roasted butter pecans." We all brightened, diets be damned. "There's a box of pretty little bowls for them over there. I don't want anybody gettin' snockered on mimosas before we eat."

Pru laughed, long past being sensitive about her sobriety. "I'll try to keep the teetotalers from eating them all up."

"Speak for yourself," I said.

By noon, everything was in place, finished to perfection by Wade's low, verdigris containers filled with artistically messy arrangements of white tulips, spirea clusters, narcissus, and full-blooming white roses. And none of the staff said a word about the contraband pecans, which I couldn't wait to dive into.

A visibly pregnant Abby was the first guest to arrive, looking re-markably subdued for her counterculture self in moss green layers that showed off her baby bulge.

"Aaaagh!" Callie hurried to embrace her. "Look at you! Are you excited?"

"Very." Abby beamed and produced a remarkably detailed sono-gram of a curled infant that left no doubt as to the sex. "Osama thinks he looks like me."

We all clamored for a look, and I was catapulted back to Abby's birth. "Ohmygosh!" The wonders of modern science. "His mouth and chin are exactly like yours when you were born."

"That's what Mama said." Abby smiled with pride. "But I'm hoping he'll have his daddy's big brown eyes." She peered at the printout. "Of course, you can't tell much here, because the eyes are still pretty half-baked."

Half-baked? Eeyew.

On that note, Linda handed Abby Brooks's super-duper, no-flash-needed digital camera. "Thanks for taking the pictures today, honey." Diane was the only decent shot among us, and since she was busy being hostess, Abby had offered to step in. Linda couldn't resist instructing, "Do some shots of the decorations first. Then after we're all seated, try to make sure you get everybody in at least one photo. And be sure you get one of Callie with each gift." Her voice dropped. "But if you-know-who turns up, only take a few, right at the first. Nothing embarrassing."

No naked stripper for the shower album, thank goodness.

Abby aimed a wicked grin at Callie and winked. "Oh, sure, Mama. You bet."

"It's five past noon," Diane announced. "Come on, Callie. Let's go greet our guests. The rest of you, sit down and relax. You earned it."

I took her at her word and found my place at the head table.

Mama was one of the first to arrive, but after a wave to me, she stayed out front with Callie.

So I settled down to munch buttered pecans and divert my worries playing "Who is that?" with Linda as Callie's girlfriends, past and present, trickled in and found their places.

Even though there was champagne in Linda's mimosa and none in mine, she still recognized a lot more people than I did, and Callie was my daughter.

Gradually, most of the twenty-three who had accepted the invitations found their places, and the hum of female voices escalated to an animated roar punctuated by squeals of reunion.

When all but a few seats were filled, Diane took her place beside me. Then we all settled down, serenaded by a string quartet of female student musicians Diane had heard at Oglethorpe. In the tide of conversations, the waiters began serving shrimp cocktails.

By twelve thirty, the last guest arrived.

Diane rose and lifted her glass. "I propose a toast," she said in ringing tones. "To our precious Callie, one of the sweetest, smartest, most admirable young women I've ever had the privilege to know. And I'm not saying that because she's my goddaughter. She's a true pearl, and Wade is blessed, indeed, to get her."

"Hear, hear!"

Callie blushed as we all stood and lifted our glasses—mine and Pru's filled with plain punch—and drank to my daughter, then took our seats.

Diane gave Callie's shoulders a hug, then announced, "Since several of you have to work on Saturday, we're going to do things a little differently today and open presents while we're eating." Polite applause erupted from those in real estate and retail sales. "So let's see what lovelies you've brought for Callie's trousseau."

An old-fashioned word for an old-fashioned girl.

But several of Callie's pals let loose with evil little giggles, which did not bode well.

Teeny helped Diane hand over her heavy present first.

"Whoa," Callie said as she accepted it. "This thing is heavy as a box of rocks."

Linda dutifully recorded the comment, which would later fill in the blanks of a humorous wedding-night script—a game we'd played at our own showers, and still enjoyed.

Callie tore off the elegant wrapping, and sure enough, the cardboard container underneath showed a hot-rock spa.

"It's all the rage on the West Coast," Diane explained. "They're ancient river stones with different crystalline structures. When you heat them and put them on your acupressure points, they give off different wavelengths to relax you."

"Oh, lord, Diane," Linda said as she wrote down the gift and the giver. "Tell me you haven't gone New Age on us."

"It's not New Age," Diane protested. "It's a spa thing. Very scientific."

Not exactly lingerie, either, but it beat crotchless panties.

I passed the big white bow down to Pru, who threaded it through a paper plate to be used as a bouquet at the wedding rehearsal—another custom that linked our own weddings to our daughters'.

After the box of rocks, the next few gifts were perfectly lovely: several demure nightgowns, a pair of white satin slippers, some sets of matching bras and panties. (Knowing Callie disliked wearing thongs, Diane had included a discreet "No thongs, please" in tiny script at the bottom of the printed invitations.)

We enjoyed our way through the delicious chicken salad plate (made from my recipe!), and I gradually let my guard down.

Things were going swimmingly till a leathery little old man in an odd-fitting sailor suit and jaunty white sailor's cap appeared in the doorway, a heavy shopping bag in his hand. "Is this the Callie Baker shower?" he hollered like somebody who was half-deaf.

Which he probably was. The guy looked like a cross between Popeye and Methuselah. He had to be eighty if he was a day. And what was with that sailor suit? I couldn't put my finger on why it fit so strangely.

Abby laughed and started snapping away.

Distracted by the interruption, the cellist hit a sour note, and the music halted. Diane looked perplexed, then rose, the picture of graciousness, and motioned the quartet to resume playing. On her way to intercept the intruder, she murmured to Callie, "I'll take care of this. Just keep opening presents." Then she glided, double-time, to find out what was going on. Callie started unwrapping the next gift, but the real show was going on at the open doorway, and even she couldn't help watching.

Diane reached the little old man and murmured something into his ear.

He squinted and blared, "What? You're mumblin', darlin'. Cain't hear if you're mumblin'."

Diane frowned. "Yes," she said loudly. "This is Callie Baker's shower." She eyed the heavy shopping bag. "Do you have a delivery?"

"Do I ever!" he hollered cheerfully. Bag in hand, he strode past her with surprising speed. "This is the place, and I am the man!"

Diane hastened after him. "Hey, wait a minute!" She couldn't very well tackle him; he might break a hip. "Stop!"

Undaunted, the little guy charged into the center of the U formed by the tables, drew a boom box from the bag, and set it on the cut-work right in front of Cherry Thompson, then spread his arms. "Hello, ladies!" he hollered with a grin. "Are you in for a treat! I'm the Ancient Mariner. Name's Popeye!" He pointed to his squinting left eye. "But they don't call me Popeye because there's anything wrong with these baby blues." He opened the eye wide and executed a bump and grind. "Just wait till I get down to the nitty-gritty, and it's *your* pretty little eyes that will pop!"

Oh, no! I dared not look at Mama.

Callie's friends shrieked and exploded with laughter.

Her grad school roommate called to her over the ruckus. "Looks like you're gonna get a preview of your wedding night, Callie!"

Clearly surprised and more than a little perplexed, Callie laughed but showed no sign of embarrassment.

Linda leaned over and said beneath the ruckus, "Well, it beats a Chippendale, I guess."

That remained to be seen.

Diane hesitated, clearly torn, but when Callie—not wanting to be a spoilsport—waved her back to the front, she shrugged in resignation and headed for her seat.

Popeye hit the button on the boom box, and it blared out the pulsing music of "Wild Thing," sung by a chorus of enthusiastic geriatric voices, which was his cue to start his exotic dance. To my amazement, he moved with the agility of a twenty-something.

Well, almost. It was the almost that made it even better.

He executed every move with dead seriousness, interspersed with hilarious "takes" on the occasional hitch in his get-along and aged appearance.

Everybody, including Callie, had hysterics. The guy was so cute and ingenuous that even I couldn't keep from laughing.

There was still, however, the matter of Mama.

Spare yourself, my better judgment counseled. *Don't look at her.*

But I couldn't help myself. I pivoted, only to find her laughing even louder than Callie.

"Is this priceless, or what?" she called to Callie.

She was eating it up, wiping tears of laughter from her eyes!

By then, the room had squared off between Callie's friends' clamors for more, and the baby boomers' good-natured cries of "No! Not that!" and "Stop, stop!"

Callie put two fingers into her mouth the way her daddy had taught her and let out a huge wolf whistle.

Her friends hooted, hollered, and clapped to egg the Ancient Mariner on.

Gyrating to beat the band, he tossed off his sailor cap, which freed a halo of wispy white hair that he stroked like they were the curls of Adonis. Next, grasping his long sleeves one at a time, he ripped open the Velcro that secured the fabric, revealing the loose, overtanned skin that hung from his arms. He slung each of the sleeves between his legs and proceeded to polish his crotch, then sent them sailing toward Callie, who dodged just in time.

After striking a few bodybuilder poses with his barely there biceps, Popeye waggled his underarm dingle-dangle to the music, then tore off the rest of the sailor blouse to reveal his sunken chest with grizzled hair peeking from the scooped neck of a skin-tight blue tank top. The Lycra glorified every gaunt rib and imperfection.

My generation countered the girls' cheers with "Put it back on!"

The little guy had perfect timing, never laboring anything too long. At a crescendo in the music, Popeye tried to tear away his white bell-bottoms, but the Velcro won. Miming embarrassment, he freed a few inches at the bottom of the legs, then tried again . . . and again, and again, each time funnier. My face hurt from laughing by the time he succeeded and revealed wiry legs in matching blue bicycle shorts that looked spray-painted on.

I thought we were going to lose Linda. She got so tickled, she had a coughing fit.

Either our little old man was seriously packing, or he'd stuffed the front of the Speedo we could see outlined underneath.

Wash my eyes out with soap! The last thing I wanted to see was such a graphic glimpse into the future, assuming John and I should live so long.

Meanwhile, our gawking waitpersons had been joined in the

doorway by a huddle of other staffers who took it all in with broad grins on their faces.

I was okay till Popeye wriggled up right in front of Callie and got so graphic she went bright red and covered her face with her napkin, shrieking.

That was enough. "I think that's enough!" I hollered for real, but Callie's friends would hear none of that.

"Boo!" they yelled in my direction.

"Lighten up, Mrs. Baker," Callie's best friend Angie called with a grin.

Linda, properly perched in her chair, nudged me. "Yeah. Lighten up, Mrs. Baker," she said loudly over the music. She cocked her head toward Mama, who sparkled with life and humor. "Don't be such a stick in the mud. Take a note out of her book."

I pointed my polished acrylic nail at Linda. "I'll speak to you about that later."

Fortunately the stripper retreated and began the laborious job of pulling his tight tank top off over his head. "I know you ladies can relate to this," he shouted through the Lycra that covered his face. "It's a lot like support pantyhose."

Spurred by his polite apologies as his elbows struggled like a sack full of aardvarks underneath the fabric, I let go and laughed along with everybody else.

When Popeye finally got the tank top off, he twirled it above his head, then sent it sailing into Callie's lap. I dabbed at my runny mascara with my lace hankie, a stitch in my side.

Then the music switched to "Thriller" (with "Stripper" substituting for the title in a cracked, wavering senior citizen imitation of Michael Jackson over the full instrumental). On cue, Popeye hooked a thumb into the waist of his bicycle shorts and started miming the pop star's love affair with his own crotch.

Enough was enough. I crouched over to Callie and pleaded into her ear, "Honey, I swear, I think I'll expire on the spot if he gets down to that g-string. Really."

My daughter looked torn. "If you want me to stop him, I will," she said back into my ear, "but none of my friends ever stopped the stripper before."

I shot a silent plea to Diane, who read my expression and got up, retrieving the tank top from Callie's lap and the rest of the tearaway outfit from the floor behind her. "Thank you so much," she said loudly to Popeye as she moved swiftly down the side table. "But I'm afraid we'll have to cut this short." She hit the stop button on the boom box, and silence fell like a huge wet blanket.

Amid calls for more, jeers, and applause, Diane motioned for the quartet to resume, then took firm hold of Popeye's flabby upper arm. "We've all had a wonderful laugh, but we still have dessert and more gifts to open. Thank you so much for coming." She handed him his clothes.

Popeye took it in good stride. "It's your nickel." Neatly laying the components of his outfit across his arm, he scanned our gathering with a grin. "Who knew when I signed up for aerobic dancing at the old folks' home that I'd end up having this much fun?" he shouted. "And making good money, to boot. I've had to hire on a second fella to keep from disappointing anybody." He winked. "But he's not nearly as good-lookin' as I am."

"I'll show you to the men's room where you can dress," Diane said, trying to steer him out. No way was she having an almost naked man exit one of her parties in broad daylight, even if he was in his eighties.

When he reached for his boom box, Popeye leaned toward the seated guests with a wink. "I do private bookings, too," he said in a loud stage whisper. "There's a whole menu of extras," he went on, waggling his eyebrows. "Only eight dollars apiece. Ten percent discount for cash."

The table erupted afresh.

Diane's face all but imploded as she tried to keep from joining them. She hustled Popeye away, scattering the staff to their duties as she neared the door.

"Please leave as soon as you're dressed," we heard her shout through the men's room door to be sure he heard her.

Now that that was over, I began to relax. If there had to be a stripper, this was fine.

Diane returned to her seat and we all settled back down.

"I don't get it," Callie said. "The girls swore they weren't going to do anything like this. I mean, I really thought they were telling me the truth."

Mama said briskly, "Your friends didn't send the stripper." A hush fell on the room as we all pivoted to find her with a smug smile on her face. "I did."

Our mouths dropped open.

"Oh, don't act so shocked," Mama said to Callie. "I ran into Angie one day at the grocery store, and she told me they weren't going to have a stripper because you're such a straight-arrow. After I thought about it for a while, I decided maybe you needed to loosen up a little."

"Mama!" I scolded, hardly believing my ears.

Mama was anything but contrite. "All the other girls had strippers at their lingerie showers. Why should Callie be the only one who didn't? So, when I saw this guy at Mary Rose Ellison's eightieth birthday party, I knew he'd be perfect." Her expression went haughty. "Mary Rose almost had an aneurysm, but she's always been too uptight for her own good."

"Hah!" Callie jumped up and drew Mama to her feet. "My grandmother sent Popeye!"

Her friends beat on the tables and cheered. Mama gave her best Queen Elizabeth wave, then sat back down with an emphatic, "Enough of that, now. Let's get back to the loot."

We were all grinning as Callie opened several more gifts, all of them demure, elegant, and simple, just like my Callie.

But just when it looked like my fears had all been for naught, Teeny handed her a small pink gift bag. "No card. And who is this from?"

She waggled it, scanning her friends.

No answer.

Uh-oh.

She unfolded the pink tissue to find a prescription bottle. I leaned closer, but all I could make out on the label was "Sexall Drugs" with a 900 number. I whisked my reading glasses from my purse to read what I could of the inscription. All of it was way past raunchy.

Scanning the convincing facsimile of a real prescription label,

Callie blushed and struggled to make her grin convincing, but my maternal magnifying lens saw the strain around her eyes and mouth when she said, "Oh, my goodness. An X-rated prescription label for Viagra."

"That's *RX*-rated," her freshman roommate Stephanie corrected to the sound of laughter that had a definite edge to it.

Callie opened the bottle and shook out a few of the pills inside. "Goodness. Looks like real Viagra."

And how, pray tell, would she know that, I'd like to know!

Her friends had the same reaction, but a lot rowdier. "She recognizes them!" "I told you!" "Tried 'em out, then, Callie?" "What happened to our Goody Two-shoes?"

Callie went scarlet but managed to counter with, "And who had these lying around, I might ask?"

I wondered if her embarrassment was all for Wade, or if the subject had activated a guilty conscience. Not that it made any difference, really. She was an adult, and what she chose to do in that department was long past my input.

Her friend Jennifer looked surprised, then hastily explained, "Y'all, they're samples!" Now the laugh was on her. "Really. My sister's a nurse. She got them for me!"

"Good thing," a girl I didn't know well called over the laughter. "Wade's gonna need some for the honeymoon. The spirit may be willin' but the flesh is definitely over the hill."

Callie's flinch was subtle, but I caught it. "I'll be sure to notify a doctor if it lasts more than four hours," she retorted, "but not before we've enjoyed every minute of it!" She laughed along with the others, but I could tell she was really mortified underneath. The stripper was one thing; he'd entertained us at his own expense. But the man my tender-hearted Callie loved was the brunt of these jokes.

It hurt my heart to see her embarrassed that way.

Then I remembered my mother-of-the-bride talking smile. I bent over and took the lips from my purse, then slipped them on and sat back up. I waited till the others had started to notice them before I bit down to activate the recording. "Isn't that lovely?" came from behind the plastic teeth.

Every girl in the room had a fit, including a delighted Callie.

Interspersed with a healthier wave of laughter, I heard: "Where did you get that?" "Ohmygod! That is the most hysterical thing I have ever seen! I want one!" "That is *too* funny! Do it again."

I bit down again. "Lucky, lucky you!"

More laughter.

Callie shot me a grateful glance. Now, instead of razzing her, her friends were focused on what my lips would say next. I felt the chill between us begin to thaw.

I bit down twice more before palming the fake smile for later.

Wisely, Teeny handed over my gift next.

"To my darling daughter," Callie read. "Love, Mama." She unwrapped the slick white paper and opened the lid. When she pulled the robe from the box, I saw the same look of delight she'd had when she got her first two-wheeler. "Oh, it's just like yours and Daddy's! Finally, my very own. Thanks so much."

I realized it was a symbol of passage to her, but for the symbol to be complete, there needed to be two, just like John's and mine. "I have one for Wade, too," I lied, resolving to pick one up on the way home. "So y'all won't have to steal ours at the beach." The second two weeks of every August for the last twenty years, we'd rented the same beach house at Isle of Palms.

"Oh, we can't come to the beach," she tossed out, carefully folding the robe back into the box. "My new job starts the tenth."

No Callie bringing life and laughter? Even if Wade came with her and they "did it" on the other side of our bedroom wall . . .

I could hardly wrap my mind around how empty that big, beloved place would be with just John and me rattling around in it.

First, Jack had been too busy with his own work to come, now Callie.

The empty nest syndrome exploded like a wrecking ball to the heart.

As I said, I'm no poker face. I felt Linda's hand close on my elbow. "Smile, sweetie," she whispered. "We can cry over it later."

Her sympathy almost undid me, but I rallied. "Maybe next year," I said to Callie, "we can change the dates so y'all can come."

She laughed, blessedly oblivious to my reaction. "Great. But we can't all wear our robes at once. We'll look like a Klan meeting."

I managed a convincing chuckle. "Wouldn't want that."

I hid my feelings behind the fake smile as Teeny handed Callie another gift. Inside the box, she found a sexy negligee wrapped around a bottle of senior special multivitamins.

I stuck in my plastic smile and bit down. "How very perfect." Again, the laugh was on me.

The rest of the gifts went pretty much the same way. A few nice ones, interspersed by gags like a homemade "Happy Honeymoon" card that held a brochure for an AARP cruise, a long-term health care policy in Wade's name (that looked legitimate) with the first quarter's premium paid.

By the time the last gift (a case of BenGay) was opened, Callie's smile was wearing thin. As the waiters came around for the final refills of tea and coffee, she stood and tapped her water glass with her knife. "Thank you all for coming, and for your gifts. And for making this day special. And for being my friends. I'm so glad each and every one of you is here."

Even though they'd embarrassed her, her statement was sincere.

Proud of her generous spirit, I shot her a look of approval.

Diane signaled the end of the luncheon by adding her thanks to the guests, then announcing that the antique napkins and napkin rings were theirs to keep. As she left the head table to circulate, the guests stood, too, and started their leisurely exit.

After a quick trip to the loo, Callie and I joined Diane in the lobby to say good-bye to everybody, while Mama helped the rest of the Red Hat Club pack up the gifts and stack them on the banquette by the front door. As soon as the dining room was clear, they boxed up the decorations and got the flowers ready to take to the senior municipal housing over on Pharr Court.

There were only a few girls left when a waiter came by with a final round of mimosas, so I decided it would be safe to imbibe. Taking my place by the exit, I sipped my drink down with less-than-judicious thirst, so by the time Jennifer of the Viagra brought up the cow's tail, my lips were numb.

Shamefaced, Jennifer took Callie's hands. "Callie, I . . . well, I was just trying to be funny. I mean, none of us think Wade is really . . . impaired or anything. I was just . . ."

Callie maintained a soft smile, but didn't jump to make it any easier.

Her friend looked away. "Anyway, I'm sorry."

Callie hugged her. "I forgive you. But I love Wade, and it really bothers me to think any of this silliness might get back to him and hurt his feelings. He knows I'm going to get kidded about the difference in our ages, but he hates that for my sake. So could we just let today's fun be the end of it, and let it go at that? I'm really counting on all of you to help us out."

I listened with pride in her gentle diplomacy.

Jennifer looked relieved. "Consider it done. I'll talk to the others. We want you two to be happy."

"Then we're all on the same page." The air cleared, Callie walked her to the door.

When she returned, I put my arm around her. "You handled that perfectly. How did you get to be such a wonderful, compassionate . . . grown-up?"

She grinned. "I learned it from my mama. And my godmothers. Especially the part about forgiving. My friends and I don't call it do-over like y'all do, but it works for us, too. No grudge boxes allowed."

Callie gave me a squeeze, then pulled free. "I'll start loading up the presents." She grabbed an armful and headed out toward the car. Watching her go, I thanked the good Lord that I'd gotten through the shower without humiliating her or myself.

Mama put her arm around my shoulders as easily as if she'd done it all my life. "You did a wonderful job with that girl, honey. Bravo. You can be proud of her." She sighed. "I still wish I'd told you more often how proud I am of you. And your brothers and sisters."

"We knew," I said, my heart swelling to hear her say it. "I'm proud of you, too, you devious thing, you," I said with admiration, aware that the words were slightly slurred. "How many eighty-four-year-olds hire a stripper for their granddaughter's lingerie shower? And get their ears pierced for the first time, all by themselves?"

She chuckled. "I'm the only one I can think of." Never easy with sentiment, she stepped free. "Come on. Let's help the others finish cleaning up."

Not wanting to lose the faint buzz I felt, I noted a lone mimosa left on a tray at the bar. "One more mimosa, and I'm there."

Mama arched a brow. "You know it'll give you a headache."

Mothers will be mothers, after all.

And daughters will be daughters.

I picked it up and took a swig. "Maybe not this time."

I got hilarious for the next fifteen minutes as we loaded up Diane's and Callie's cars, then Mama had to leave my car in the parking lot and drive me home. I was sound asleep before we got out onto Paces Ferry.

"I told her not to have that second mimosa, but would she listen?" I heard her tell John as he unbuckled my seat belt. "The manager said it was okay to leave her car overnight, but y'all'll have to pick it up after church tomorrow."

Even half-asleep, I didn't miss the not-so-subtle motherly hint that I shouldn't miss church.

I didn't say anything. I was too sleepy.

"Thanks for bringing her home. Drive safe, now." John took me inside and put me straight to bed with "You little lush, you." Then he took off his clothes and crawled in with me, even though it was only four.

"Fratelli?" I murmured as I curled against him.

He chuckled. "Another time. How did the shower go?"

"Tell you later," I murmured on my way to oblivion.

His snoring woke me up at ten to a hideous taste in my mouth and a sledgehammer headache, but I never admitted it, not even to him.

Without waking him, I managed to sneak into the kitchen for four glasses of cold water and some graham crackers to protect my stomach, then I took a maximum dose of ibuprofen and crept back into bed.

I'd managed to get through the dreaded lingerie shower. Now I just had to get through the next two months.

But no more mimosas, and I meant it. Really.

· 18 ·

Folly and Innocence are so alike,
The difference, though essential, fails to strike.
— WILLIAM COWPER

The present. Second Tuesday in May. 10:40 A.M. Muscogee Drive, Atlanta.
....

*A*FTER YET ANOTHER late-night dinner party for Callie and
Wade—this one with John's boss and his wife—the phone
roused me from a dead sleep to a stab of strong sunlight and the vague
sense that something wasn't right. Squinting and disoriented, I groped
for the receiver, then retreated under the covers with it. "Hullo?"

"Mama?" Callie sounded surprised. "Are you okay?"

Hallelujah, she sounded just like her old self, warm and concerned.

"Sure," I said, even though I was worn out from all the parties and
late evenings. Huge yawn.

Phew! You know you have death-breath when you offend yourself.

I stuck my face out of the covers, turning away from the bright bits
of sun that sneaked through the blinds. "I'm just sleepy. Couldn't get
your daddy to stop talkin' shop with the dean after y'all left." Big
stretch. "We didn't get to bed till almost two."

"I had the opposite problem," Callie confided. "Wade started begging me to leave before they even served dessert." Little wonder, since he had to get up at 4:30 every morning to go to the flower market.

"Mmm." Man, did it feel good to be in bed. I'd put down roots into my pillowtop mattress.

"Do you want me to call back later?" Callie asked, something unsaid beneath the question. "I just wanted to ask you about Abby's bridesmaid's dress before you left for your luncheon."

Luncheon?

I froze in mid-stretch.

What luncheon?

A shot of adrenaline brought me bolt upright, my eyes on the clock. Nine forty. "This is Tuesday?" I gasped out, already knowing the answer. "Red Hat Tuesday?"

" 'Fraid so."

"Aaagh!" Of all times for the bleemin' alarm clock to flake out on me.

The world wouldn't end if I was late, but nobody bothered to tell my body. Heart pounding, I landed on my feet halfway to the end of the receiver's twenty-five-foot spiral cord, pulling the base off the bedside table in the process.

"Poor Mama." Callie's tone was apologetic. "All these parties have really worn you out, haven't they?"

"Fine. I'm fine," I lied. Passing the dresser mirror on the way to the potty, I saw my ugly stepsister reflected back at me, her hair stuck out at all angles, bags under her eyes, and "rack marks" from the sheets etched deep into her skin.

"Are you there?" Callie asked gingerly.

"Yes. I'm here," I snapped, not meaning to. I closed the bathroom door on the cord, stretching it to the limit when I sat.

"Well, there's no guessin' what you're doing," Callie said as I relieved myself.

Our vintage-tiled bathroom magnified every sound. "Sorry."

The flush sounded like a class five hurricane.

Shower. Hair. Makeup. Just the bare essentials.

No time to shave my legs. Forget the dress I'd planned to wear. Go with the pantsuit.

"What was it you wanted to ask me?" I asked as I grabbed my electric toothbrush.

Hurry, hurry, hurry.

"It can wait," she said, guarded. "Call me this afternoon when you get home."

"No, go ahead, if you don't mind having me brush my teeth in your ear." *Lots* of toothpaste.

After a brief pause she said, "Brush away." Another pause, then she launched with determined cheer into a touchy subject. "Abby's already gotten too big for the dress she got to wear in the ceremony. We've narrowed the replacements down to three, and I was wondering if you could help us decide which one would be best."

I stopped brushing, grateful that the toothpaste prevented me from firing back with, "Never mind the dress. Replace Abby." (Which I wouldn't have said, really, but it felt good to think it.)

Eight-months-pregnant bridesmaids. Please. Callie knew better, but she'd overruled me when I'd told her it wasn't in good taste. Instead of watching Callie, everybody in the church would be watching Abby and wondering if her water would break.

But tacky is in the eye of the beholder, and Emily Post was fast losing the battle with a generation whose idea of propriety had been shaped by totally tacky soap operas and even tackier talk shows.

Underneath, I knew Callie's asking me to help choose the dress was an attempt to smooth over our disagreement about Abby by bringing me into the process, but I was just stubborn enough not to go along. "Oh, sweetie, I appreciate it, but you two girls can decide without me just fine. I'm way too old-fashioned for Abby's taste, anyway."

"No, really, we both want your opinion."

Not.

What Callie really wanted was for us to see eye-to-eye the way we used to about everything that really mattered.

I wanted that, too. But much as it pained me to admit it, we probably never would. We'd reached the great divide, and its name was Wade.

"Yikes. It's almost ten till," I deflected as I headed back to the bedroom to hang up. "I need to hop into the shower. I'll get back to you this afternoon."

The words were hardly out of my mouth before the "Be Sweet" fairy bonked me on the bean with her Guilt Wand for refusing to play along with Callie, so I softened. "And honey, I'm so glad you called and waked me up. I might have slept through the whole morning."

"It wouldn't be a tragedy if you missed just this once," Callie said. "Aren't y'all gettin' sick of each other by now?"

"Only a little," I admitted.

Try *a lot*. Because I'd given jillions of parties and showers for Callie's various groups of friends, they (and their mothers) were reciprocating with a vengeance—and inviting all of Callie's legendary godmothers to everything. I tried to get the others to divvy up the parties between them and regret the rest, but they all came to everything anyway. So, for the first time since high school, we were wearing on each other.

Hurry, hurry. Late, late.

I ended the conversation the way I always did when Callie was little. "I love you to pieces, honey."

"I love you back more, my mama," she responded on cue, then we hung up.

Stripping as I went, I raced for the shower. Hair still damp, I got ready in a record twelve minutes, but didn't realize I'd forgotten my earrings and mascara till I was halfway to the Coach House.

I drove in such a snit that I barely noticed the rain-washed absence of pollen in the sunny spring morning. When I finally walked into the restaurant thirty minutes late, I was sure I'd be the last one there, but saw that Pru's seat was empty.

I hoped she wasn't sick. Or worse, that something had happened with Elena.

Teeny and Linda were dressed in deep purple spring splendor, but Diane was still in her Texas phase, wearing dusty purple denim and a red straw cowgirl hat with a clutch of roses at the crown.

She peered at me and cocked her head. "Are you okay? You look like you're coming down with something."

"Well, good morning to you, too," I snipped as I plopped into my seat. "I'm not sick, I just forgot my mascara. And my earrings. I feel naked."

"We were getting worried. You didn't answer your cell phone," Linda said, her expression seconding Diane's concern.

I hated being so late. Hated it, hated it, hated it. "My cell phone's at home on my dresser, charging. I was in such a hurry, I forgot it."

I noted the fatigue on their faces. "Y'all don't look so spry yourselves." It came out with more of an edge than I'd intended. To make up for it, I explained, "John wouldn't leave last night till after one, so I overslept. If Callie hadn't called me, I'd still be slack-jawed in bed."

"We would gladly have taken you home early with us," Linda said. They'd left at ten, pleading Brooks's dawn rounds. "The dean would have understood."

"Lord, Linda, people are talking about us enough, as it is," I grumbled. In our circles, couples left together. Always. "Who knows what they'd say if I left a party without John."

"Point taken," she admitted.

Now that they knew I was only suffering from mascara deficiency and fatigue, we fell into a dull silence that I broke with, "Where's Pru?"

"Coming. She was putting out a fire at work, but she'll be along, and Peach is coming with her."

"Oh, good." I could use a little-girl fix.

After another brief silence, Linda smacked herself on the forehead. "Where is my brain? Y'all, major news on the Rachel front."

We all perked up. "What?"

She pulled an encased silver disk from her purse. "She sent us this DVD of her and Sol touring his clinics. You won't believe it, but Rachel was acting like Lady Bountiful. No makeup. Simple T-shirt and jeans, hiking boots. Feeding sick children and talking to their mothers. Calmly waving the flies away from babies. I swear, she's done a one-eighty. And she's happy. You can see it in the way she fusses over Sol and waits on him."

"Waits on him?" Diane said. "I'll believe that when I see it."

Linda waggled the DVD. "You can. It's on here. But the best part was the letter that came with it." She leaned in and lowered her voice. "Seems the late Dr. Cocaine had a really teeny weenie, and before Sol, Rachel had never had an orgasm."

"Never?" Teeny asked, incredulous. "Poor baby. No wonder she was so disagreeable."

That explained a lot.

Linda nodded. "Turns out, Sol's hung like a horse and knows how to use it, so when he got ahold of her, Rachel thought she was dying, but she didn't care." She got so tickled her voice went higher and higher, and we laughed with her. "Now she's singing 'Ah, Sweet Mystery of Life' at least twice a day, and Sol doesn't need a prescription to keep her on key." She flapped her napkin. "Good thing Sol's got a medical mission on the yacht with them, just in case." She chuffed to settle herself down, but her voice thickened with laughter again when she added, "Brooks and I watched the DVD in bed last night, then I read him the letter. When I got to the part comparing sizes, he dove under his pillow and started singing 'The Star-Spangled Banner' into the mattress."

I could just see it, bless Brooks's proper little heart. Oh, would John get a kick out of this.

"Embarrassed him to death," she gasped out, dabbing at tears with her napkin. "The man operates on people's privates all the time, but God forbid he hear anything about orgasms or a remarried widow comparing her husbands' peerless pestles."

It took plenty of napkins and/or hankies to bring us back down to earth, but tumped-over tickle boxes were always therapeutic.

"Whew," Diane said. "That was some news. After that, my joke will be a letdown. Maybe we ought to skip it."

"No, no," Teeny and I said.

"You're not going to get out of it that easy," Linda told her.

"Okay." Diane remained reluctant. "Shouldn't I wait for Pru?"

"Nope," Teeny said. "Let's hear it."

"Okay." Diane composed herself, then began, "A man went for a hike in the woods and got hopelessly lost. After wandering around for three days with no food or water, he came to a deep river and saw a town in the distance on the other side, but the water was too swift and deep for him to cross. Exhausted and thirsty, he fell to his knees. 'Dear Lord,' he prayed, 'please make it possible for me to get across this river and find my way back to civilization.' "

She snapped open her fingers with a "Poof! God changed him into a woman. She got the map out of the backpack, hiked half a mile up the river, crossed the bridge, and made it to town in time for dinner."

Man-bashing, but funny. We all laughed, but she was right—it was an anticlimax after our giggle fest about Rachel.

Maria arrived with refills for our usual warm-weather collection of sweet and unsweet tea. "You ladies seem to be having a wonderful time, I hate to interrupt to take your orders, but I'll gladly do so if you're ready."

Diane rubbed her hands together. "Pru's coming later, but she told us to go on and order. I'll have the usual."

"Shrimp salad," Maria said as she wrote on her pad.

Teeny got wild and ordered soup and half a chicken salad sandwich, but Linda and I had our usual Favorite Combo.

"So," Linda said to Diane after Maria left. "You haven't said anything about getting another gift-of-the-month from Cameron." He usually had them delivered just before our meetings so she could show them off. "Did he forget this month?"

Diane blushed to the roots of her artfully colored brown hair. "I'd really rather not say."

The use of our standard evasive answer only piqued our curiosity. We all perked up a bit.

"Uh-oh. Out with it," I prodded.

"Yeah," Linda said. "What's the matter? Is it X-rated?"

Diane's blush mottled. "No. Well, only in a sense. It's nothing. Tradition Five. MYOB."

We never have been very good at that particular tradition.

"Okay. No problem," Teeny said. She flipped open her super-thin cell phone and pressed a button. "Cameron, cell," she said distinctly into the hidden mike.

"Teeny!" Diane snatched the phone, closing it before it finished dialing.

Linda flipped open her cell phone and said Cameron's name, too.

"Okay, okay," Diane relented. "I'll tell you, if you must know, but please keep it to yourselves."

Linda snapped her phone shut with a satisfied smile.

Diane leaned in so she wouldn't be overheard. "He's been teaching me how to fast draw and shoot at the ranch. And I'm getting really good at it. So he sent me a pair of six-guns, specially scaled to my size. With red leather holsters to match my boots."

"A pair of six-shooters?" Linda blared, drawing attention from nearby tables.

Diane slumped down under her red straw hat. "Thank you so much for your discretion."

I leaned forward, fascinated. "What's it like to draw and shoot that way? Is the gun heavy? Can you hit anything?"

"Yes, the guns are heavy, even the ones he had made for me. They have long barrels for accuracy. That's why it takes lots of practice to train your muscles just to get them out of the holsters. Learning to hit things takes a lot longer."

Diane never met a challenge she couldn't master, so I repeated my question. "Can you hit anything yet?"

"About half the time now." She made sure nobody but us was paying attention before going on. "Cameron said I'm the best student he's ever seen." She dropped her voice another notch in volume. "Y'all, you have no idea how empowering it is to shoot things. Nothing alive, of course," she hastened to qualify. "We shoot at empty soft drink cans filled with water so they won't blow off the fence. We set them up away from the animals, and take our time." Her eyes lost focus. "I mean, when you actually hit one of those cans . . ." She inhaled sharply through her nose. "Oh, my. It's positively erotic."

"Ooo-hoo-hoo," Teeny crowed, flicking the American Beauties on Diane's hat. "We're gonna have to start callin' you Guns and Roses."

Linda let out an evil chuckle. "And does Cameron help you with your guns?"

"Yes." Diane blushed. "At first, he stood close behind me and guided my movements, but now I can do it all by myself."

Linda waggled her eyebrows. "And how's he with *his* six-shooter?"

A sly smile curved Diane's perfectly made-up lips. "Hits the bull's eye every single time."

"Oooo," I said, my mind filling with possibilities for me and John. "Can I borrow the holsters, and your hat and boots? Just for a night. I'm thinking water guns, and—"

"No, you may not!" Diane straightened and said too loudly, "Get kinky with your husband in your own boots and holster."

Heads turned and eyebrows lifted all around us.

"Diane," I scolded, saying her name with three syllables.

Teeny groaned. "TMI." (Too much information.)

"Oh, come on, Diane, let me borrow them," I coaxed, enjoying the chance to goad her a little. "Where could I find the real things in Atlanta? And anyway, they'd be way too expensive. And the holster wouldn't be *red*. Please? Just one night."

"I knew I shouldn't have told y'all." Diane shook her head. "Why did I tell y'all?"

Teeny laughed. "Because we really would have asked Cameron."

"Does Tradition Five mean nothing anymore?" Diane complained.

"Oh, this is minor, and you know it." Linda straightened her napkin in her lap. "You would have told us sooner or later, anyway. So it was sooner. No biggie."

Maria brought our food. We started to eat, but conversation fell flat. Rachel's sexual awakening and Cameron's six-guns were tough acts to follow, and we'd pretty much exhausted everything else at all the parties we'd been to. So after we discussed the dearth of decent entertainment on TV (besides *Desperate Housewives, Grey's Anatomy, Boston Legal,* and *Medium),* we fell into an awkward silence.

Taking advantage of the lull, Ginny Mitchell—an ALTA (Atlanta Lawn Tennis Association) fanatic neighbor of mine—left her team table and came over, her expression one of exaggerated concern as she approached. "Hey, Georgia," she murmured, crouching beside my seat. "Don't y'all all look cute in your . . ."—her pause held a taint of condescension—"little outfits." She leaned closer. "Is everything okay? You were all laughing, then you suddenly seemed so down that we were worried something terrible might have happened, what with the wedding and everything." Subtle, telling emphasis on *wedding* and *everything.*

What nerve!

The others lasered her with looks that showed they were on to her gossip-hungry little game, but I didn't have it in me. "We're fine,

Ginny," I assured her, smarting under my smile. "We're all just suffering from spring fever and antihistamines."

"Oh, so it's just that," Ginny said, clearly unconvinced. She laid
her napkin to her chest. "We were just so concerned for you."

Spare me. "No need to interrupt your tennis talk on our account,"
I said with a saccharine smile. "We couldn't be happier. All of us."

She paused, clearly unconvinced. "You know, we've always admired the way y'all have stuck together through thick and thin, *especially* lately."

Her exaggerated kindergarten-confidential inflections got on my
last nerve.

"You've been through so much." Ginny's sidelong glance at Linda
wasn't an I'm-so-sorry-you-got-cancer look, but an I'm-so-glad-I-
don't-have-a-daughter-or-*son-in-law*-like-yours indictment. Linda bristled, but Ginny's eyes stayed wide with fake innocence. "I mean,
really . . . No matter *what* gosh-awful mess y'all get into, you help each
other through. That takes guts."

Guts? That tore it.

My Inner Duchess summoned up an icy smile. "It doesn't take
guts to be kind or loyal when you're truly friends." I looked her up
and down. "Though I have to admit, both of those qualities seem to
be getting rarer and rarer all around us."

Before that sank in, Teeny drew fire to herself with an innocent,
"Fortunately, we haven't had to soldier through anything lately, but we
all have to sometimes, don't we?" She batted her baby blues. "Speaking
of which, how's Tara holding up?" Tara being Ginny's daughter, whose
husband was systematically sleeping his way through every bored,
willing young matron in Buckhead.

Ginny shot to her feet, icy. "She's perfectly fine." She added a
pointed, "Just like y'all."

Touché!

Without another word, Ginny retreated to her table.

Smiling, Teeny waved to the tennis team and murmured through
her teeth, "I just love puttin' a bitch like that in her place. Could you
believe the chutzpa, comin' over here like that just so she could sneer
at our outfits, then expecting to get the scoop on bad news?"

I'd known that people were gossiping about Callie and Wade, but I hadn't been prepared for such an open foray. I could have killed Madelyn Vandercleef for making my private business so public that a backbiter like Ginnie Mitchell felt entitled to participate.

Diane craned her neck toward the entryway. "Oh, good. There's Pru." Her expression cleared. "Oh, look."

We all pivoted to see Pru and Peach arrive in matching hats, hers big and Peach's small.

Peach lit up when she saw us and scampered over. "Hey, Aunt Teeny." She hurled herself into a hug, bumping her hat askew and laughing as she set it straight.

Then she moved on to Diane. "Hey, again." She'd gotten really close to both of them, coming to work with Pru on holidays and after school. "Guess what? Father Chasen came to see Mama last night, and Mama and Daddy got married, right there in Mama's room, and I got to be the flower girl, just like I'm gonna be at Callie's wedding."

While the rest of us carried on over that, Pru sat still and uncharacteristically restrained.

"And guess what else?" Peach asked without pausing for an answer, "A very-ever judge came, too, and made it official that Daddy's my legal father. Nobody can ever take me away from him and Pru-mama." She patted Pru's cheek. "Pru-mama let me pick what I wanted to call her."

Linda nodded in approval. "Pru-mama sounds just perfect to me."

"I love it," Pru said, hugging her. She turned to Teeny. "Thanks so much for rushing the adoption through. I can't tell you how much that meant for Elena's peace of mind."

Teeny hadn't said a word about it, but that was typical of her, quietly making things happen in the background.

Peach shot me a radiant smile. "I love your outfit, Aunt Georgia. Do you like my hat? Pru-mama says it's okay for me to wear a red one, even if I'm not fifty yet."

"You look mah-velous," I said.

"I made a new rule," Pru said. "Red Hats are required at meetings if you're under thirteen or over fifty."

"I like that rule," Diane said. "I move we make it official."

"I second," Linda said. "All in favor?"

We all raised our hands.

Peach hopped over to wrap her arms around Linda's softness. "You're so sweet to hug, Aunt Linda. I bet Abby hugged you all the time when she was little like me."

Linda's answering smile was wistful. "Not often enough."

Peach skootched into the far end of the banquette next to her grandmother's place. "Can I get frozen fruit salad and chicken salad?" she asked as Pru slid in beside her. Then she made a face and dropped her voice. "But not any of that suh-rimp stuff. Yuk." She shuddered at the memory of her first—and last—taste.

"It's pronounced *shrimp*," Pru corrected calmly. "And one of our most serious rules here is that nobody has to eat anything she doesn't like."

Peach beamed. "I like that rule." She'd really blossomed since coming to live with Pru. Commandeering her grandmother's napkin, she spread it over her lap with great deliberation.

She had lost her gauntness in the past weeks, and her hair had a healthy luster, leaving her bright-eyed and confident despite her mother's illness.

Maria arrived with a lemonade and an extra setup for Peach. "*Hola*, my beautiful little señorita. What a charming hat; just like a grown-up lady," she said with exaggerated courtesy. "I took the liberty of bringing you a lemonade. Would you like to start with some mini muffins, perhaps?"

"Wellll . . ." Peach hesitated, eyes casting from one side of her lap to the other. Then she motioned Maria closer with a tiny finger, looking up through her long, dark lashes. "I like the little muffins," she said in a loud whisper that was a child's version of Pru's. "But do you have any without all the little bugs inside?"

Bugs?

Maria's mouth twitched a little, but her confidential response was reassuring. "Ah, *niña*, those are not bugs. They are the tiny seeds of the poppy, a very beautiful flower."

Relief washed across Peach's face. "Oh. We have poppies in California. Lots of them."

Linda frowned. "You ate the muffins the first time," she said to Peach, "even though you thought they had bugs?"

Peach's answer was cheerful. "I was *really* hungry, and they tasted good." She inspected a muffin at close range and frowned. "We had lots of poppies in California. Why do they put the seeds in the muffins instead of in the ground?" She scanned us. "Don't they want to have poppies in Georgia, too?"

"That's a very good question, Peach," Pru said. "Maybe when we get home, we can go online and look up how poppy seeds became a seasoning."

This, from Pru, who had never willingly looked up anything in her entire academic career.

Peach beamed. "Don't you just love the Internet?"

Linda shook her head. "Goodness, no. Scares me to death. I always get lost."

Peach shot her a look of encouragement. "Don't worry. I can teach you how. All you need is somebody to show you, and some practice."

Such a little grown-up.

Grateful for Peach's cheerful presence, we all settled down and enjoyed our lunches. Pru was just deciding on whether to order dessert when her purse erupted with the Grateful Dead. "Uh-oh. That's Bubba. Sorry, y'all, but I'd better get it," she said, retrieving her cell phone. "Y'all go on and order dessert," she said as she flipped it open, then turned aside with a finger in her ear so she could hear in the noisy room.

Diane looked at the menu as if she hadn't seen it a thousand times. "Let's see. How bad do I want to—" She noticed Pru's sudden stillness the same moment we all did.

We went quiet.

"I see," Pru said, the weight of ages in that single phrase. Eyes closed, she turned back toward us, the lines in her face down to bone. "So she's—" She nodded, bleak, yet resigned. "We'll be there as soon as we can."

Uh-oh. Elena must have taken a turn for the worse.

Pru's eyes welled with unshed tears. "Just hang in there, honey. We're coming."

A chill went down my spine. Had Elena died?

Poor Peach. Poor Bubba.

Pru hung up, eyes welling, and shook her head when Peach was looking the other way. "Come on, Peach, honey. We need to go to the hospital."

"But we didn't get to eat."

"I'll bring you later. Your mama really wants to see you." Rising, Pru extracted a stack of envelopes from her purse and laid them on the table. "Elena wanted you to have these." Past tense. "I'll call from the hospital. Please keep tomorrow morning open." She took Peach's hand. "Come on, Miss Red Hat Sunny Bunny. Let's go see your very-ever legal daddy and your mama."

Poor kid.

As if Peach sensed what might have happened but didn't want to face it, she didn't pepper her grandmother with her usual barrage of questions. "Okay. 'Bye, y'all."

Somber, we waved good-bye. "See you soon."

Maria appeared and took our dessert orders—heavy on the chocolate—then left us to peer in silence at the weak, but orderly handwriting that spelled out our names on the envelopes.

Diane opened hers first and started reading loud, "Dear Diane . . . Peach is so lucky to have you for a godmother. I want her to believe her dreams can come true. Since I cannot be there with her, please share your wonderful ability to organize and accomplish goals. I thank you for your unquestioning support, kindness, and practical help. Love, Elena." A slow tear escaped and ran down Diane's cheek.

I read mine next. "Dear Georgia . . . Thank you for your enthusiasm and optimism, and your intimate love of God. And your curiosity. Please help my daughter to see the beauty in the world our Creator has made, and to love learning about everything He has given us. Help her to appreciate the joy that books and teachers can bring to her, and the opportunities of an education. Thank you for your prayers and your strong faith, and for believing in me." My voice broke with emotion. "Love, Elena."

Linda wiped her eyes with a tissue, blew her nose, then read.

"Dear Linda . . . Thank you for your open arms and open heart. Please teach my little Peach to respect those of other faiths, races, and ideas. Your love and lack of judgment have been a model for both of us. Love, Elena."

We looked to Teeny, but she no longer held her letter. She'd read it; I saw her. "What happened to yours?"

Teeny colored. "I'd rather not read it aloud."

Diane plucked it from her purse. "Then I'll do it for you." She opened up the letter. "Dear Teeny . . . How can I begin to thank you, not just for all you have done financially to help me fight for my life, but for rushing through the adoption and arranging for our marriage. Not to mention your generous financial provision for Peach. I do not have the words to show the depth of gratitude Bubba and I both feel. I leave this world unwillingly, but confident that my precious child will be well loved and provided for. God has blessed us all so richly with your help and friendship.

"Please teach her how to keep a confidence, and the value of patient endurance in hardship. Peach and Bubba will need you and all of their godmothers to help them go on without me and reclaim their joy. I can go to God in peace, knowing that they will be surrounded with love and good advice. Love, Elena."

That did it. We all dabbed away at our runny mascara.

Diane folded the letter and handed it back to Teeny. "I hope when my time comes, I'll be able to face it with half her dignity and grace."

Maria handed out our desserts and topped up our drinks, but didn't intrude on our sadness with conversation.

We ate without a word and were almost done when Teeny's phone rang. She checked the screen with a frown. "It's Pru." She put the phone to her ear and answered softly. "Hey, honey."

A long sigh escaped her, telling us what we'd all feared. "I'm so grateful she was able to hold on till Peach got there." Pause. "Don't worry about work. Take all the time you need to help Peach, with pay. Is there anything we can do?" Her brows knit. "I see. Please give them our love. I'll tell the others." She paused again. "You're sure we can't bring any food?" Another weight-of-the-world sigh. "Okay then. See you in the morning."

She hung up and told us what we already knew. "Elena died just a few minutes after they got there, but she was able to make her final good-byes to Peach."

When the transplant had failed, we'd all known it was just a matter of time, but her death still came as a shock anyway. "How's Peach handling it?" I asked.

Teeny shook her head. "Hard. She fell apart. But maybe that's for the best. She's getting out all her anger and grief. She and Bubba will stay with Pru for at least the next few weeks." She straightened. "Elena didn't want to be embalmed, so the funeral's tomorrow morning at Arlington, at ten. She wanted us all to be pallbearers."

Seeing the bewildered look on my face, she hastened to reassure me. "We won't have to carry the coffin. They'll use that rolling caisson from the funeral home. We'll just walk beside it to the grave, then the undertakers will transfer it to the . . . whatever they call that thing that puts it into the ground."

Elena had been so wise to be so young, and now she was gone. I'd long since learned the futility of trying to reduce God's motives to human terms, but at times like these, I had to struggle to trust Him. Suddenly, my worries for Callie paled, and I said a prayer of heartfelt gratitude for her good health.

"Husbands?" Linda asked.

Teeny shook her head in denial. "Just us and Callie—people Peach knows. Elena wanted to make things as easy as possible for her."

Maria appeared with our checks. Seeing our ruined makeup and sad expressions, she hesitated, then ventured, "Please excuse me for being nosy, but has something happened?"

After all her years of discreetly serving us so well, I certainly didn't mind her asking.

Teeny nodded. "Peach's mama died just a few minutes ago, but she got to say her good-byes to Peach."

Maria hesitated again, then mustered up the courage to ask, "I know it is not proper to intrude, but may I come to the funeral? It's not my place, but Peach is such—"

"I think Peach would be glad to see you there," I said, making an executive decision. "You've always been so kind to her, and hearing your condolences in Spanish would probably be very comforting."

"Absolutely," Diane seconded.

"It's a graveside service tomorrow morning at ten," Teeny told her, "at Arlington Cemetery on Mount Vernon in Sandy Springs. If you'll give me your address and phone number, I'll pick you up and we can ride together. Would that be okay?"

Maria was clearly relieved by the offer. "Oh, thank you. That would be wonderful." She tore a blank sheet out of her order book and wrote down the information, then handed it to Teeny. "It's not far, just over on Buford Highway." She collected our payments. "I'll have these right back for you."

We waited in silence, each of us lost in her own thoughts about what had just happened.

When Maria brought back my credit card, I signed the slip and tipped her three times the cost of my lunch, in case she had to miss any work to go to the funeral.

It felt strange to get up and leave when we were done, maybe because we'd just shared something so profound.

We exchanged subdued hugs, then headed outside like so many sleepwalkers. "I'll see y'all tomorrow morning," I said when my car came up.

All the way home, I prayed for Peach and Bubba and Pru. Then I called Callie and told her the news.

"Oh, Mama," she said without her new reserve. "I'm so sorry. Of course I'll come. Let's ride together."

She wanted to be with me. I said another prayer of thanks. "I'm sorry, too, honey, and not just about Elena."

"I know, Mama. Me, too."

There's nothing like a death to put things into perspective. "I'm so glad you'll be there with me tomorrow. I love you."

"I love you, too."

Whatever happened with Wade, at least we could be close as we laid Elena to rest.

· 19 ·

*Everybody dies. God decides when, but it's up to us to
accept His decision with grace.*
—LINDA'S *BUBBIE*

. . . .

*T*HE NEXT MORNING dawned cool and fair, with a gentle breeze.
When I picked Callie up just after nine, she told me Wade had
stayed up late making a blanket of pink roses for Elena's coffin, his
gift of sympathy for Peach.

It was a very generous gesture, and I said so.

We spent the rest of the ride out to the cemetery talking about the
final arrangements for the wedding.

We found the Catholic section and parked behind Teeny's car just
as she and Maria were getting out of her convertible.

"Callie! Maria!" Peach ran across the graves to greet each of them
with a long hug. Maria bent and spoke at length in Spanish, her tone
gentle, and the weariness in Peach's face eased.

"*Gracias,*" Peach said when she finished. She took Maria's hand
and led her to the sunny spot where the grave was ready for Elena's
coffin, no tent to block the warming sun.

After exchanging greetings with the others and the priest, we headed for the hearse while Callie and Maria sat with Pru and Bubba and Peach. The undertaker did all the work, but we flanked the simple pine coffin and escorted it to the grave, then sat.

Peach must have cried herself out, because she soldiered through the brief Catholic internment rite without a whimper, even when Pru took her up to the coffin to collect a rose for remembrance after the priest concluded the ceremony.

Blinking back tears, Bubba stood and gathered Peach from his mother's arms. "What a beautiful rose, but not as beautiful as your mother. We'll keep it to remind us of how pretty she was." He turned toward the narrow road. "Time to go. Where would you like to have lunch, sweetie?"

With the resilience of children, Peach focused on the now and grabbed hold. "Can we go to Clown Pizza? All of us?"

Loud music, tons of toddlers, a kiddy arcade, and a balloon castle. But if that was what she wanted, that was what we'd do.

"Sure," Callie said to her. "I'll bet I can eat more pizza than you can."

" 'Course you can," Peach shot back, her hollow expression banished by a mischievous glint in her eye. "You're a grown-up. But I bet you can't eat more than my daddy."

Callie laughed. "I think you're right, but I'm willing to try."

"You're on," Bubba said, his own composure restored.

Diane nodded. "Actually, the pizza's pretty good there."

On our way back to our cars, Linda stopped Pru. "Do you want me to cancel the kitchen shower? This Saturday is so soon—"

Pru didn't hesitate. "No, please. Peach loves the showers. It'll be a good distraction for both of us."

I looked to her in concern. "Everyone would understand if you didn't want to do the tool shower. We could—"

"We'll do it," she said with quiet resolve.

Linda gave her a brief hug. "Just let us know if you change your mind."

Pru's expression was drawn, but resolute. "Thanks, but I won't change my mind."

Life goes on, and so would the wedding.

We all ate way too much pizza, but Peach had fun, and there's nothing like indigestion to make you know you're alive.

I tossed and turned all night, but it wasn't about Callie, for a change. Only a little was about the onions and anchovies I'd eaten. The rest was about poor Peach's having to grow up without her mother.

Even at my age, I couldn't imagine life without Mama. Until Callie had decided to marry Wade, I know she'd have said the same thing about me. Now, I wasn't so sure.

Curiosity is nothing but a bad mix of jealousy and not enough to do.
It'll always get you into trouble.
— MY GREAT-GRANDMAMA SIBLEY

The present. Monday, May 22. 9:12 A.M. Muscogee Drive, Atlanta.

. . . .

*D*ESPITE ITS PROXIMITY to Elena's death, Linda's kitchen shower came off fine. Callie got three times more great things than her little kitchen could hold. Jealous of all the wonderful gadgets, I offered to relieve her of whatever she didn't have room for, but no go.

The next Friday, right before Brooks and Linda braved international airport security for their flight to Ireland, we all got together—including Bubba and Peach—at the Barbecue Kitchen on Virginia Avenue for a little bon voyage meat-and-three luncheon.

Once the second-honeymooners were off, John and I resumed the round of dinners and cocktail parties Callie's friends and their parents owed her. I don't know exactly when it happened, but somewhere along the way, I started getting used to Wade and Callie as a couple, and so did John.

By the time Pru's tool shower rolled around day-before-yesterday,

I was actually looking forward to the wedding so we could go back to our normal lives.

That shower came off well, too, providing a great distraction for Peach, who helped plan the party and chose all the decorations. Wade and I both were jealous of the rolling toolbox and cool, woman-sized rechargeable power tools Callie got—so jealous that I went out the next day and bought myself a little circular saw just like hers. And a router. And an eighteen-volt heavy-duty cordless drill. With a lithium battery.

Now that it was Monday morning, John had headed for his morning lecture, leaving me to start my week in the breakfast nook, trying to balance my checkbook—a necessary but frustrating ordeal I'd put off long enough.

A warm little memory of Elena wrapped its arms around me, then evaporated.

Oh-blah-dee, oh-blah-dah, life goes on.

Back to the day-to-day, and my least favorite chore.

I had the bank's total within a hundred and forty-three dollars of mine (in their favor, of course) when the phone rang.

I picked up before caller ID came on. "Hello?"

"Hey," Teeny said, her curt greeting a cue that she was in executive mode. "How are you doing?"

I heard her shuffling papers in the background, so I kept my answer brief. "I'm good."

I was, except for a lingering pensiveness brought on by what had happened with Elena.

"Have lunch with me."

No amenities, no explanations. Something must be up.

"Sure. When?"

"Today?" she suggested.

"Works for me," I answered. "Where?"

This had turned into a totally guy conversation!

"Houston's at Colonial?" She covered the receiver and I heard a muffled, "When's that guy from New York coming in today?" The line cleared. "Is eleven thirty too early? I've gotta be back here by two."

"Great. See you then."

Two hours and some change later, I'd been waiting for about fifteen minutes in one of the quieter corners of Houston's when Teeny came in and joined me.

"Sorry I'm late." She laid her attaché-style leather purse on the table. "Things got crazy at the office."

"You're forgiven." I spread my napkin in my lap. "So, what's up?"

She opened her purse and drew out a fat, sealed 9 by 13-inch envelope. "The final report came in on Wade this morning." She handed it to me. "I figured you'd want to see it as soon as possible, what with the wedding being in only a few weeks."

I held it as if it were a letter bomb. "You're not going to believe it, but I swear, with everything that happened with Elena, I'd completely forgotten about this."

Or maybe I'd just blocked it out. But seeing that report woke everything back up again, with a vengeance.

Teeny extended her open hand with a wry expression. "In that case, why don't you hand it back over, and we'll both forget about it—permanently?"

My grip tightened reflexively on the envelope. "I thought you were all for finding out."

"I was, but I'm not so sure anymore," she said. "The more I've thought about this, the more it bothers me."

Taken aback, my mind hurled a mean little thought from its darkest recesses. "I know Linda is against this. Has she been talking to you about it behind my back?"

Teeny looked exasperated. "From Ireland? Anyway, she wouldn't do that, and you know it. Neither would I."

What was wrong with me? I didn't think that way. I'd never thought that way. "I'm sorry. That was totally out of line."

"You're forgiven," she said without hesitation, "but see what this stuff is doing already?"

As ye sow, so shall ye reap.

But the beast that was my compulsive need to know had been roused. I turned my attention to the envelope, noting how much fatter it was than the last one. Did that mean there was a lot more to read about inside? Since good news is no news, did that mean they'd found something bad? Was Nora Green another secret love of Wade's, past or present?

"I'm serious, Georgia," Teeny said in earnest. "Forget what I've spent. It's worth a hundred times that for you to do what's really best here—not just for Callie, but for yourself. Callie adores Wade. Let me shred this, burn it, whatever, then trust God to look after her."

If only it were that simple. "God doesn't come between us and our choices," I reminded her, "even when they're self-destructive. But I'm not God; I'm Callie's mother. I think she has a right to know if what Madelyn said was true. And who Nora Green is."

"And what if Madelyn was telling the truth, or Nora Green is involved with Wade?" Teeny said. "And you tell Callie, then she decides to marry him anyway?" She shook her head. "I knew Reid had problems, but I believed him when he said he'd changed."

"But what if Madelyn was lying," I countered, "making all that up out of twisted spite? And what if Wade was telling the truth about that Beth chickie-boom? And Nora Green is just a friend?" I straightened. "Shouldn't John and I know that?"

Teeny eyed me askance. "I thought you weren't going to tell John."

"I wasn't, but I changed my mind," I admitted, defensive. "He's been best friends with Wade for more than thirty years, but even he was having doubts. So I told him about this, and he was glad."

Her brows went up. "I don't know why that makes me feel better, but it does. A little." She leaned back in surrender. "It's your call, honey. I just don't want this to be something you'll end up regretting at leisure."

"It's a hasty marriage that ends up repenting at leisure," I reminded her. Not that Callie's was hasty, but it might well be repented. Better to know the truth now.

I pulled open the envelope and drew out two folders, one of them a copy of the previous report, which explained some of the thickness.

I set that aside, then opened the new one. Scanning past the preliminary section that explained the methods, areas, and duration of the investigation, I came to the medical section and started reading. Appalled, but not enough to stop reading, I narrated, "This has a list of Wade's doctors, hospitalizations, and prescriptions. How could they get all this confidential information?"

Teeny winced. "I don't know, and I don't want to," she said, then immediately followed with, "Oh, lord, I sound like White House staff."

I rescanned the entries. "Well, Madelyn was right about one thing. He has a cardiologist, and he takes beta-blockers."

Couldn't those make men impotent? Yet another wrinkle in this convoluted mess.

I'd begun this with all the best intentions, but now it seemed to have taken on a life of its own, sprouting dark tentacles left and right.

Teeny shifted uneasily. "I'm not really comfortable hearing this. Would you mind doing that later?"

I couldn't help myself, I had to know. "How about if I just read it silently?"

"Georgia, honey"—that was twice in one sitting she'd used my whole name. Major serious—"your silences speak volumes. That face of yours is the world's best mime. Please. I'd rather you waited. I'm asking, as a favor to me."

I couldn't refuse, not after she'd done this as a favor to me. So I reluctantly put both reports back into the envelope and stuck it behind my purse on the seat, then did my best to pretend it wasn't there.

Still, it remained like an invisible wall between us, making the rest of our lunch so stilted and awkward that I wondered if I'd permanently diminished our friendship by asking this of her.

When we finally headed out of the restaurant, I stopped at the curb, out of earshot from the waiting lunch crowd. "I'll think about not reading it. Seriously."

"Good." Teeny's big blue eyes pinned me where I stood. "I have another favor to ask you."

"Sure. What?"

"If you do decide to read it," she said, "please don't tell me about it. As your friend who loves you, I would hope that all this could stay between you and John and, if necessary, the parties in question, but that's not what I'm asking. I'm only asking not to be brought into it any further."

So this *was* a barrier and would continue to be one unless I decided to throw the thing away unread. That made my heart hurt, because I knew I couldn't.

"Mum's the word," I told her. "Just between John and me and, if necessary, the parties involved."

More secrets to keep.

Then a thought blurted itself out. "But what if everything's on the up-and-up? Wouldn't you want to know?"

Several people sitting on the low stone wall turned to look, so I stepped closer to Teeny and lowered my voice. "I mean, we all heard what Madelyn said. Half of Buckhead did. It only seems fair to let y'all know if she was lying."

Teeny shook her head. "You and your contingencies." She considered, then relented. "Okay. If everything's fine, by all means, tell me." She added a qualification of her own, "Assuming you read the report."

I gave her a good-natured nudge. "Was that a contingency?"

She grinned. "Yes. Wanna make somethin' of it?"

"No, ma'am."

We parted smiling.

On the strength of Teeny's advice, I decided not to do anything till John came home at four and we could talk it all over. At least then, we could reach a consensus.

Unless we couldn't agree.

Then what would I do?

Why, oh why, couldn't Callie have fallen in love with somebody less complicated?

. . . .

NEVER ONE TO make snap decisions, John absently stroked his lower lip as he looked at the envelope on the dining room table. (We always have our serious conferences there, but never over food.)

I knew he wasn't seeing it. That Bigbrain of his was turned inward, assessing risks, weighing costs, exploring contingencies.

I waited in silence, more than grateful to have his help in dealing with this decision.

Pretty soon, I had a vacant stare of my own going as I reviewed what I had to do in the coming week. After that, I started making a mental grocery list.

I don't know how long we sat there, but eventually, John came out of his trance with a deep breath. "I need to be the one to read it. And deal with Wade myself if there's anything damning in there." He stood, picking up the envelope. "It's not fair to put you or Callie in the middle of this, and Wade's been my friend for a long time. I owe him this much, at least."

Like everything John did—except marrying me—his solution made perfect sense. Yet I felt compelled to ask, "But John, is that fair to you?"

His kind face went grim. "If Wade's not on the level, there's nothing fair about any of this. But if he's the man I've always thought he was, he and Callie never have to know about this report."

"You'll tell me if there's nothing?" I asked. "The girls all heard Madelyn's accusations. I want to let them know if—"

"Sure." He gave my shoulder a squeeze with his free hand. "I'll tell you." Tucking the report under his arm, he made straight for the bourbon and poured three fingers (!) before retreating to the tiny study we'd converted from a screened porch.

John never drank whiskey unless we had company, but I could hardly blame him.

Feeling both relief and dire suspense, I watched him close the study door, then I got up. Cooking comfort food provided one of my favorite distractions, which accounted for most of the twenty extra pounds I was carrying.

"I'll start supper," I called. "How about shepherd's pie?" His favorite. It took a while, but wasn't complicated.

"Great," came through the door to the study.

As the butterpeas and potatoes were boiling, I chopped and sautéed a fat Vidalia onion, then took that out and added a pound of ground sirloin to the pan, browning it well. Then the meat went into the onions so I could make gravy from the cracklings in the skillet, all the while wondering what John was finding beyond the medical section.

After adding the onions and meat to the gravy, I poured the mixture into a greased casserole, then added a layer of well-drained butterpeas.

Glancing at the clock, I saw it had been almost thirty minutes. That seemed like a pretty long time. The report wasn't *that* thick.

I took out my frustration on the potatoes, mashing away at them with a little condensed milk, some salt, and a lot of butter. Then I topped off the casserole with them and turned on the broiler. Most people garnished the casserole with cheddar, but I liked it better plain, the way they served it in England.

Thirty-five minutes, he'd been in there.

Worried, I threw together a quick green salad, then popped the casserole into the oven to brown. That took another five minutes.

I shut off the broiler and set two places at the table. Another five minutes, and still not a sound from the study.

Forging ahead, I turned the chandelier on low, poured us each a nice Merlot, then called, "Dinner's ready. Do you want me to hold it?"

John's answer gave nothing away. "No. I'll be right out."

Hot pad. Casserole. Salads and dressing.

Still no John.

"Honey?"

At last he emerged, but he was neither frowning nor smiling. "Man, that looks great," he said without enthusiasm when he saw the table.

He crossed to help me with my chair. Bless his heart, he always helps me with my chair. And opens my car door, when I give him the chance. And walks between me and the street.

I peered at him till I sat, but he volunteered nothing.

"Bad news?" I couldn't help but ask.

He gave a sharp exhale as he helped push in my chair. "Maybe, maybe not."

For cryin' in a bucket! What was *that* supposed to mean?

I was ready for some answers!

John sat to my right and reached for my hands to say the blessing, just as he always did.

I took his in mine, my attitude anything but prayerful.

Maybe, maybe not?

"Heavenly Father," he prayed, "thank You for this food and the hands that prepared it. All we have comes from You. Help us to be good stewards, not only of the material things, but the circumstances you have allowed in our lives and those of our children. In Christ's name, amen."

I took his plate and served him on automatic pilot. "So you're not going to tell me."

"I'm not even sure if there's anything to tell." Savoring a bite of casserole, he showed the first animation of the evening. "Mmmm-mmm-mm-mm-mmm." It isn't called comfort food for nothing. "Callie'll have to go some to cook like that."

"Callie doesn't cook," I reminded him. "She nukes." The pie was good, even if I did say so myself, but that was the last thing on my mind.

No way was I going to ignore this particular elephant in the kitchen. "So, when will you know whether there's anything to tell?" The wedding was just weeks away. "*How* will you know if there's anything to tell?"

He raised his eyebrows, maddeningly calm about it. "Don't know." He savored another bite.

Unacceptable.

Maybe I should have let Teeny shred the thing, after all. This was going to drive me crazy.

"I'm gonna need a lot of sex to get through this one." I didn't realize I'd spoken the thought aloud till I saw John perk up with a delighted little smile. "And a lot of wine," I added—which for me was only two and a half glasses. I took a healthy slug of the Merlot. "Otherwise, I'm gonna end up wild-eyed and stiff as an ironing board all night."

John lifted his glass in a toast. "What's sauce for the goose is sauce for the gander." He drank deeply, too.

Then he took pity on me. "There is good news," he offered. "He's not drinking again or hooked on Internet porn or anything like that. As for Wade's explanation about Beth Sutton, Tiffany's must be harder to crack than Fort Knox. The detectives included all kinds of confidential info on Wade, but they couldn't come up with anything about the ring, one way or the other. In the rest of the report, for the most part, he works hard and goes to church and goes home and plays tennis and golf with me."

This was definitely not working out the way I'd planned, but that seemed to be happening with increasing frequency in my life. "What about the other part?"

"Concerning, but inconclusive." He reached over and cupped the side of my face. A gentle stroke of his thumb released a frisson of desire in me. "I don't want to confront Wade till I know it's necessary. He may never speak to me again."

I leaned into his touch, closing my eyes and thanking God for a husband like John. "Okay." I straightened, prescribing my favorite home remedy for stress. "Now hurry up and finish eating so we can go bang our brains out and get some decent sleep."

The prescription worked fine until my nightly appointment with the bathroom at three fifteen. The minute I stood, my head exploded with red wine's revenge, so I took three ibuprofens, did my necessary, then crawled back into bed to massage my temples. I tried to go to sleep after that, but every time I dozed off, I was ambushed by vague and distressing dreams that involved Callie and us and Wade, and being lost or hurt and unable to find help. Meanwhile, John was breathing deep in blissful unconsciousness.

The ibuprofen eventually started to work, taming the sharp pain that stabbed through my eye to a dull throb, but by four I realized I wasn't getting back to sleep.

Maybe some hot vanilla milk, Mama's favorite insomnia cure.

I didn't plan to look at the report when I got up and went downstairs. I just somehow ended up sitting in the comfortable little easy chair in the study as I drank my hot milk, staring past the rhododendrons to our sleeping neighborhood.

Then my eyes drifted down to the empty desktop.

Where had he put it?

In the drawer? the beast whispered.

Completely without my permission, my body reached for the

center drawer and slowly pulled it open, the hairs on my neck rising when the wood scraped softly.

I told myself not to do this, but I didn't listen. One by one, I checked the drawers, but didn't find it.

My eyes fell on the nylon backpack that served as John's briefcase. Sure enough, there was the report.

Past the Rubicon, I closed the door with exquisite care, then turned on the tiny lamp beside the chair.

Glasses.

I gingerly pulled a pair of readers from the pencil holder on the desk, then sat down and did what my instincts told me I shouldn't.

Jumping at every tiny ambient sound, I worked my way past page after page of mundane information, then more uneventful surveillance. Then I turned to a bombshell: an entry chronicling multiple recent trips to a hotel near the airport to meet with a forty-eight-year-old woman named Nora Green, a housewife from San Francisco.

My blood ran cold.

I read on: Outings to the Cyclorama and Stone Mountain, brunches, late lunches all over town. For a solid week, Wade must have spent every hour away from Callie with this woman.

How could John have thought this was a *maybe*?

I turned the page to find color printouts of more than two dozen snapshots of Wade with his arm around Nora Green, who looked a lot more attractive than she had in the photo Teeny had shown me. His hand on her elbow as they walked together. Bent together in deep conversation and laughter in restaurants. Wade, kissing her cheek good-bye at the entrance to the hotel on at least five occasions. No clinches, but a peck is still a kiss.

Reason reminded me that at least they weren't going up to her room together.

I looked at the photos again and saw that their bodies weren't close to each other when they kissed—just his hands on her upper arms and hers on his forearms. But they were in public, and Wade never had been one for PDA. (Public Display of Affection: a detention offense in high school.)

Dark tentacles of doubt sprouted by the hundreds.

The report said that the woman went home a week after she'd come, and Wade went back to his squeaky-clean existence.

After a thorough investigation, the agency had been unable to come up with any connection between Wade and this woman, and could find no record of further communication.

She'd hung up when they called outright to ask her, then blocked all further efforts to contact her.

The movie *Same Time Next Year* came to mind.

A hickory nut hit the roof and nearly gave me a heart attack. Heart hammering, I quickly read through the remaining two weeks of uneventful surveillance, then carefully replaced the report and my glasses exactly as I'd found them. Still tingling, I turned off the light and gingerly opened the door. I had tiptoed halfway across the living room when I remembered my mug.

Yaaah! I'd almost done it again: told on myself.

Back I tiptoed, reclaimed the cup, then took it to the kitchen sink. As water ran into the cup, I just stood there in the dim glow from my dormant appliances, overwhelmed by questions and conjecture.

The overhead light came on abruptly, scaring me half out of my wits. I whirled around to find John standing there in his boxers, one eye squinted shut, hair askew, and his hand still on the switch.

"I wondered where you were," he said.

Bless his heart, he always came looking when he woke to find me gone, and he always said that same thing.

Wondering if guilt was plastered all over my face, I headed toward him, arms extended. "I woke up with a headache and couldn't get back to sleep, so I made some vanilla milk."

He drew me in, turning off the light. "Come back to bed. I'll massage your temples. Then you can do mine." He took me back toward the bedroom. "The next time I decide to mix too much bourbon and too much wine, remind me of this."

"I will."

He tightened his arm around me. "Don't worry, honey. Everything will be all right." Regardless of reality, those magic words still had the power to soothe. He stifled a yawn. "I'll copy down the agency info and give them a call tomorrow to see if we can come up with anything more. I don't want to risk taking that report to work."

Thanks to the warm milk, I yawned and felt myself getting drowsy. "Thanks, sweetheart. What would I do without you?"

"Don't know and don't want to find out."

Back in our room, I stretched out on the bed, and he started to massage my temples with strong fingers, making it hurt so good.

"Don't worry, honey," he repeated softly. "Everything will be all right."

If only it could have been.

· 21 ·

You shouldn't brag about your happiness, or the evil spirits
will get jealous and steal it from you.
—LINDA'S *BUBBIE*

. . . .

*J*OHN CONTACTED THE detective agency the next day, but couldn't come up with anything more conclusive. Fortunately, there was a break in the wedding festivities, so I didn't have to see Callie for a week, during which Chicken Little had plenty of time to wear herself out. So, by the time we all had dinner with a devoted gay couple of Wade's florist friends, I was able to face my daughter with some semblance of grace.

The next morning, Diane picked me up for a drop-dead-absolutely-have-to-find-a-mother-of-the-bride-dress shopping trip. Maybe it was my reluctance about the wedding, but nothing I'd found so far—even custom order, which was out of the question by then—had been right. Twelve stores and two hundred miles later, we headed for my house with six possibles.

"Look," I said when we turned off Peachtree Battle. "Callie's here."

"Excellent." Diane nodded. "She can help pick out your dress."

"Diane, I swear, I'm not that crazy about any of them."

She glared at me, finally done in with my dithering. "George, in the past four months you've seen everything even remotely suitable within a hundred-mile radius," she repeated for the fifth time in as many hours. "And that's saying something, considering what a shopping town this is. Not to mention my volunteering to have my design staff whip up something lovely for you, but noooooo, you said you wouldn't know it till you saw it. Well, guess what, you've seen everything, and nothing's it. So you have to pick." Then she let fly with, "This wedding is going to happen whether you find a dress or not. It'll hurt Callie's feelings if you show up in one of your usual uniforms, and as her godmother, I refuse to let you do it. So you're gonna pick something. Today. And you're gonna act excited about it for Callie's benefit. Got it?"

"Okay! I'll pick one!" I relented. "But I reserve the right to sulk till we get to the door."

"No, you will not," she clipped out, looking down her nose at the hood. "You will get out of this car with a smile on your face. Callie might be watching."

I gave her a long raspberry, but did as she asked. Laden down with dresses as we headed for the front door, I said through a fixed grin, "Okay?"

Her answering smile was smug. "Very good. Keep it up."

I unlocked the door and we entered with a crumple of shopping bags. "Callie?" One slipped out of my hand and landed on the floor. "I'm so glad you're here," I called into the empty living room. "You can help me pick out my dress for the wedding."

Silence.

Something unexplainable drew my eyes to the study.

Callie was sitting in the chair, holding the open report in a death grip, pain and fury etched in her tear-stained expression.

"Oh, God! No!" The bottom dropped out of the Universe.

"I was looking for my birth certificate, for the license . . ." She faltered as she stood, then she lurched into the living room. "I cannot believe this."

My heart broke to see the aching disillusionment in her face.

"Oh, honey." I threw down the dresses and moved to comfort her, arms extended. "It may not be what you think. We're not sure—"

Callie recoiled, her anguish turned to a revulsion I had never seen in her. "Don't touch me!"

The front door closed softly behind me as Diane left us to this awful moment.

But what came next was more awful, still.

"How could you?" Callie accused. "And I know it was you! Don't even bother denying it. Daddy would never think of doing something this . . . underhanded." She shook the report at me like a bloody murder weapon. "This is beyond beyond, even for you!"

The truth slammed into my chest like a cannonball. "Honey, you don't understand," I scrambled, desperate. "Madelyn made all these allegations, and—"

"Madelyn?" I wouldn't have thought it possible, but she grew even angrier, her tortured features flushing. "That's your excuse, Madelyn?" Callie shook her head in disbelief. "Everybody in Atlanta knows she's a lying, mercenary bitch! She's done everything she could to try to poison Wade's kids against him, all because he tried to get custody after Sonny Vandercleef got her pregnant."

Pregnant!

"Honey, this is your future we're talking about! Can you blame us for wanting to be sure she was lying?" I pleaded. "Your father and I love you too much to let you make a terrible mistake. We only did this to make sure Wade was really the man we thought he—"

"I *know* who Wade is!" She hurled the report at me. "And don't you dare try to put any of this off on Daddy! Daddy knows who Wade is, too! If he ever doubted that, it was because you made him."

She hated me. My daughter hated me!

Desperate, I lashed back with, "Do you know Wade flunked out of Tech because of his drinking? Or that he came home from Vietnam so tormented and poisoned on booze and pot that the woman he loved put a continent between them without leaving a forwarding address? Those memories are as fresh to me now as if they'd just happened, and they're a part of who he is!"

"He told me all that," Callie shouted. "We have no secrets."

"Did he tell you about the time he got so drunk he sexually mauled Linda in public, so John had to have him locked up? Or that he's spent months and months drying out, twice on court order?"

"He's not like that anymore," she railed. "He's been in recovery for years."

I knew I should stop, but I couldn't. "He'd been in recovery for years that time when you found him in the shop after Madelyn left him! It wasn't a heart attack. He was drunk! Do you want to spend your life shadowed by the possibility of that happening again?"

Callie blanched. So he hadn't told her about that time. But she held on to her fury. "I believe in him! You just want to tear him down."

"Callie, darling," I pleaded. "Before your daddy, I loved a man once, as passionately as you love Wade. I wanted him more than anything. I couldn't see then how selfish he was inside, how wrong for me, even though everyone I knew warned me. When he disappeared, I thought my life was over. My heart broke into a jillion pieces. But then I met your daddy, the best man in the world. I'm your mother. I don't want you to have to settle for less than the best."

"There are no perfect men out there! Trust me, I've looked." Still clenching the report in her hand, Callie turned to stare out the window rather than look at me.

"Callie, most girls go through an older-man phase," I said, forcing my voice to calm. "They never stop to think what kind of baggage comes with a man like Wade. Your father and I just want what's best for you." The harder I tried to convince her, the more rigid she became, so I switched to, "This woman in the report—"

She spun on me with contempt etched into her features. "Forget that woman!" she shouted. "And I am no adolescent going through a phase. I'm a grown woman in love with Wade, warts and all. And don't you dare try to blame Daddy for any part of this. He told me in the beginning that I was old enough to make my own decisions, and he would always be there for me!"

She stepped closer in menace, shaking the report in my face. "This was you!" she shouted. "All that negative . . ." She struggled for the next word. ". . . *shit* you dream up in that sick imagination of yours! Well, this time, you've gone too far."

"Callista, I know this makes you angry," I tried to reason. "But I am your mother. Surely you can see that I only had your best interests at heart. Try to see this with some sense of perspective."

"Perspective?" Her eyes narrowed in contempt. "The only perspective you have is a twisted, suspicious one! Telling me to focus on the good in life, not to worry. What a hypocrite! You hate Wade because of his past mistakes, and you're just looking for an excuse to tear him down. Never mind what a friend he's been to you and Daddy for the last thirty years. Well, it doesn't matter what's in that damned report! I love him, and I'm going to marry him!"

So Wade was right, and I was the bad one for uncovering his faults. Just like Abby when Linda had showed her Osama's rap sheet. Miserable, I stood mute.

"The only breaking up that's going to happen is me and you," Callie railed. "I hate you for this!" She threw the report at me. "You're not my mother anymore! You're fired!" Hands fisted, she started toward the door.

This wasn't the Callie I knew. Never, in all my life, had I dreamed she would say such a thing to me.

"Callie, no!" Tears blurred my vision as I reached out to keep her from leaving. "You're upset. You don't mean that."

Flinching when I came near her, she glared at me, suddenly ice cold and clipped out. "I mean every single word. Nothing you can say will fix this, Mama." She stepped over a shopping bag to put more distance between us.

"Callie, I love you," I said through tears. "I'll do whatever you want to make this right. Anything, just—"

"Anything?" She halted beside the dresses Diana had draped across the wingback chair. "All right, then." Her expression went sly. "Stay away from us. Do not come to any more parties. Do not call me. Do not come see me." She kicked the shopping bags full-force, sending them flying. "Do *not* come to my wedding!"

"Callie! I have to be there. I'm your mother. Even if you're furious at me, I have to be there. Please, we can work this out. Please—"

"I told you, you're not my mother anymore. And you're not invited!

I mean it!" She stormed out, slamming the front door so hard, the glass cracked in one of its high row of panes.

I sank to the floor, sobbing. "Oh, God! Oh, God. Oh, God."

But God hadn't had anything to do with what I'd done. This was mine to own. I'd played right into the hands of the great accuser, and he'd just collected a terrible cost.

Too distraught even to call Linda, I cried there till I had no more tears, and all that was left was a deadly ache where my daughter's love and respect had been.

Then I stumbled to bed and crawled in, where I hid from what had happened in a deep sleep till I woke to find John sitting beside me, alarm on his face. "Honey, what's the matter? What happened?"

I didn't think I had any more tears, but I did. With a wrenching ache, I threw myself into his arms. "Oh, John, Callie found the report. She was devastated." He stilled. "I thought she was upset about Wade and that woman, but she turned on *me*. Blamed me, and she was right. You never would have done this. Now she hates me! She fired me as her mother and told me I couldn't come to any more parties." The next escalated to a wail worthy of *I Love Lucy*. "She said I can't even come to the wedding!"

John drew me tighter. "Oh, honey." He kissed my forehead. "She only lashed out at you because she's so in love with Wade. And probably terrified by those pictures. You're a safe target, that's all."

No recriminations. Just love and logic.

I did not deserve this man. I didn't deserve my daughter.

He rocked me gently. "I'll give her some time to cool off, then I'll take her somewhere and talk to her," he said. "Tell her this was as much my idea as it was yours."

"But it wasn't your idea," I argued. "They were already investigating when I told you. You never would have even considered anything like this, and Callie knows it. She hates me."

"Shh, shh, shh." He smoothed away the hair that had fallen in my eyes. "I'll help her understand that she doesn't have to side with you or Wade. This is bad, but she'll come around. She loves you."

How I wanted to believe that, but I couldn't. "John, you didn't see her face," I said, suddenly out of moxie. "She hates me for this. Truly, horribly hates me."

"Ah, sweetie," he consoled. "Poor baby, poor baby, poor baby."

Only three? "This is a five, John. I really screwed up."

He let out a dry chuckle. "Maybe a four, but not a five," he said gently. "Five is Callie sick or hurt . . . or worse."

He had a point. "A four, then," I said.

"Okay. Poor baby. That's your extra." He laid me back down onto the pillows. "Go back to sleep for now." He gave me a gentle kiss on the lips. "This will all work out, honey, I promise."

For the first time ever, I took no solace from those magic words.

"I don't think so," I told him. No matter how much John loved me and Callie both, he couldn't fix this. Fresh tears leaked from the corners of my eyes when I closed them.

"Go to sleep, honey," John soothed as he rose. "You'll feel better in the morning."

I knew I wouldn't. Like a diamond shattered at its fatal flaw, trust once broken could never be fully restored.

Callie would never again trust or respect me the way she had before my "sick imagination" had sown this poison between us.

And she would marry Wade without me, in spite of what he may have done.

Linda and Teeny were right. I should have shredded the report.

· 22 ·

Diamond Dust

The sole consolation about hitting bottom is that there's no way to go but up.
— ANONYMOUS

The present. The next Saturday. Muscogee Drive, Atlanta.

OUR DAYS LATER—during which I had condolence visits from Teeny and Pru and Diane (Linda was still in Ireland with Brooks), plus at least a dozen consoling phone calls, several of which were transcontinental—John took Callie to lunch to talk to her. I tried to keep myself distracted in the garden, but by the time three thirty had rolled around, I couldn't stand the suspense any longer. I pulled off my garden gloves and punched in the number to John's cell.

"Hey." His curt greeting was a cue that he was either busy, which could be okay, or he didn't want to talk to me, which meant things hadn't gone well.

"Hi," I said in subdued tones, fingers crossed. "How did it go?"

When he hesitated, I knew.

"Oh." Chicken Little had predicted as much.

"She just needs more time," John said. "She seemed fine at first, but every time I brought up the subject, she cut me off. Worse than a little kid with her fingers in her ears. Said this was just between the two of you, and she had no intention of discussing it with me, because she knew I'd tell you everything." He sighed. "I offered to keep our conversation in strict confidence—even from you—but she wouldn't budge."

"Oh." I'd have gone nuts wondering what they'd said, but he wouldn't have told me. When John makes a promise, he keeps it.

"Sorry, honey." His tone lifted. "I did find out she doesn't intend to tell Wade about the report." He paused to let that sink in. "All she told him was that y'all had a huge fight and were staying apart for a while."

A while? I tried to take some comfort in the temporary term, but found none.

John kept on talking. "Then she told me she'd never speak to either one of us again if we so much as breathed a word of this to him." Never mind that Wade might be cheating on her. "Or if a Red Hat did."

"They won't," I hastened to say. "We've already discussed that." Endlessly. "It wasn't easy, but I managed to talk them into staying hands off about this, even with Callie."

"Good." I heard him close a drawer, a sure cue that he was ready for this conversation to be over.

But I wasn't. Even now, I couldn't keep myself from projecting. "Won't Wade wonder when we don't show up at any more of the parties?" (John had stoutly refused to go without me.)

"He's a guy, honey," John said. "We rarely second-guess what y'all tell us."

After a weighted pause, he ventured, "Speaking of Wade . . . I told Callie that I wanted to talk to her as her father, which she was okay with . . . till I brought up the pictures in the report." Another pregnant pause. "Big mistake. She bowed up, clammed up, and walked out."

Oh, no. Now this was coming between them.

Tears welled up and overflowed. (I was developing a permanent ring on my fanny from the pity pot.) "Thanks for trying, honey."

"Don't worry, sugar, I'm not giving up," my precious husband said. "This was just the first try. We will work this out. It may not be before the wedding, but we'll work it out."

"John, let it lie," I said emphatically. "I do not want this to come between the two of you."

"Georgia Louise Peyton Baker," he said just as emphatically. "I am your husband and Callie's father, and I have no intention of allowing this to fester between the two of you. I know she's upset, but it's not like you took out a hit on Wade. You had somebody check up on him, with her best interests at heart. Callie needs to grow up, suck it up, and stop acting like a child. We are going to those parties, and our daughter will keep a civil tongue in her head, or I'll . . ." He hesitated in frustration.

A stab of totally inappropriate humor ambushed me with my first smile in days. "You'll what? Ground her?"

The tension in his voice eased. "I'll take her to the woodshed, even if I get arrested for it."

Lord, I loved this man. "I don't think Wade will let you."

"Then I'll take him, too."

My smile softened. "Did I ever tell you you're my knight in shining armor?"

"Damn straight," he huffed in masculine pride.

"Let's hold off on the parties for a little while, at least," I decided aloud. "Teeny's linen shower is coming up." Even though the others had promised to stay out of this, I wanted my friends around me when I faced Callie for the first time. "I'll go to that. I think things would work out best if it was just us girls when we first see each other."

John bestowed his highest compliment: "Now, *that's* logical." There was no mistaking his relief at having completed his foray into the treacherous realm of conflict and emotion. He confirmed my reasoning with approval. "She won't have to worry about what Wade might overhear, but with all those witnesses, she'll have to behave herself."

"Well, thanks for trying to talk some sense into Callie. I really appreciate it."

He sighed. "Sorry it didn't do any good."

I wasn't offended when I heard him open another drawer, signaling his return to the refuge of Bigbrain work after completing his dangerous mission. "G'bye, Sir Lancelot."

Expecting his usual distracted "Hmmm" as he hung up, I was pleasantly surprised to hear a heartfelt, "This *will* work out, honey."

Bless his heart. "I really hope so." I just didn't think so.

---

*Saturday, two weeks before the wedding. 12:30 P.M. Plaza Towers,
Peachtree Street, Buckhead.*

I DELIBERATELY WAITED till everybody else had had a chance to arrive before I took the elevator up to Teeny's dual-unit condo.

Heart pounding (had a lot of that lately), I transferred the wrapped set of Egyptian cotton sheets to my left hand and placed my right palm against the lighted plate beside the door. Teeny had all five of us programmed for unrestricted access. A beam of light scanned up and down, then the door opened with a click.

Just as I'd hoped, everybody was gathered in the dining area, chatting like magpies while they loaded up clever little tray-plates from the fabulous buffet Teeny's cook had laid out. Scanning the guests, I spotted Callie out on the balcony oohing and aahing as Peach showed off her adorable pair of floral overall knickers and matching pink straw hat with a band of flowers around the crown.

So far, so good.

Teeny caught sight of me and glided over. "Georgia," she said for public consumption. "So wonderful to see you." She put her arm around my waist and led me toward the buffet, murmuring from behind a fixed smile. "Nice and easy. It's gonna be okay."

I felt like Scarlett arriving at Melly's in her brazen red dress.

Obviously trying not to be obvious, Pru and Diane gravitated in our direction.

"Help yourself to food," Teeny said. "It's such a gorgeous day, I'm gonna eat outside. Why don't you join us when you're ready?"

Us, meaning her and Callie.

I suffered a sudden onset of cold feet and procrastinated by taking my own sweet time choosing from the buffet. I was delicately transferring the eighth jumbo shrimp to my little tray when Diane came up beside me. She peered at the heap of shrimp. "Hungry?"

"No," I said through a smile, glancing out to the balcony to make sure Callie was still safely occupied. "Scared."

"I don't blame you," she said briskly, "but you can do this."

That's what Linda had told me when she'd called from a castle in Ireland.

Diane picked up a dessert plate and tried to decide between the apricot flan, the chocolate éclairs, a huge bowl of berries and nectarines, and a tray of homemade strawberry shortcakes. "We're here for you, honey."

Pru moved close on my other side. "Absolutely."

All three of us focused on Callie at the same time. Teeny was sitting alone on a double bench on Callie's right, with Peach in a little chair to Callie's left. Half a dozen of Callie's church friends had claimed most of the chairs. Luckily, there was an empty seat in the shade near the door.

Diane gave me a gentle nudge. "Get out there and get it over with."

She was right. Putting this off wouldn't help a thing.

I sucked up my courage and stepped beyond the glass wall's concealing glare.

But before I could sit down, Teeny blew my cover with an overcheery, "Georgia! Come sit by me." She patted the space beside her.

Callie's attention jerked my way, the easy smile on her face congealing.

I wanted to look away, spare myself the thinly veiled contempt I saw in her eyes, but I couldn't.

Peach launched to her feet with a delighted, "Aunt Georgia!" She bounded over and wrapped her arms around my legs. "I'm so glad you're here. Now all but two of my good-godmothers are here."

Good-God mothers?

Pru spoke up behind me. "That's what she calls y'all, her good-godmothers."

Good God.

Peach didn't take offense when the other guests thought that was hilarious. She let me go and patted the space beside Teeny. "You sit right here, so I can see you." She scanned the crowded space. "I'll go get Aunt Diane, and we'll all be together." Away she raced.

"She is the cutest thing," one of the girls said to Pru.

Pru nodded. "Thanks. She's doing remarkably well, considering."

When the girl looked puzzled, Pru opened her mouth to explain, but Peach—dragging Diane out from the dining room—beat her to it. "My mother went to heaven," she announced, completely oblivious to the appalled silence of Callie's friends. "She didn't want to. She wanted to stay here with me," Peach said as she steered Diane toward an empty Chinese garden stool. "But Mama said we don't get to decide those things," she recited as if it were a litany. "So she gave me a daddy and a grandmama, and five whole good-godmothers to keep me company after she left."

Before the other guests could react, Teeny reached out and pulled Peach into her lap for a quick hug. "Yes she did. And you, my darling, my dear, are the wonderful present she gave us." She eased Peach off her lap. "Speaking of presents, did Callie tell you that you're our official present-unwrapper for this party?"

Focusing on her new pink sandals, Peach unself-consciously retracted her fists into the arms of her pink tee, then pushed them forward like bosoms. "Yes, she did." She turned to Pru, suddenly all business. "And she said it was okay to tear the paper, but if you ask me, that's a big waste."

Still the frugal little grown-up.

I looked with longing at my daughter and caught her in an unguarded glance my way. She quickly focused on Peach, but her expression had softened just a little.

Please, Lord, please, give my daughter the grace to forgive me just a little.

Callie busied herself talking to her friends, and I was grateful that she didn't feel compelled to escape my presence by going inside. She was civil, which was enough. At least for today.

She remained guardedly civil through the presents, even thanking me for the sheets. But there was no warmth there.

If anyone else sensed the estrangement, they didn't let on. Peach was entertaining enough to keep us all occupied with running chatter as she opened the towels and embroidered handkerchiefs and blankets and sheets. Teeny's dual-control electric blanket was a big hit with the little girl. "We had one of those, only it was a double. We didn't have any heat in California, but it sure could get cold sometimes."

And then, all too soon, the party was ready to break up. Grateful for how things had gone, I made every effort to keep a low profile. I was just about to slip out before the others when Callie broke off the conversation she was having to call after me. "Don't go yet," she ordered with a strident edge to her tone. "I need to talk to you."

It didn't take a genius to realize she wasn't planning to make up, but at least she was speaking to me, even though I probably wouldn't like what she had to say.

Fighting the urge to flee, I forced myself to linger till the only ones left were Callie, me, and Teeny, who closed the door on the last guest and made straight for my side.

"Teeny," Callie said, "would you please excuse us?"

Teeny put her arm around my daughter and stated a quiet, "No, I will not."

Callie bristled. "This is just between me and her. It won't take long."

Teeny smiled. "This is my house," she said affably. "If you want to speak to your mother in private, why don't you call her later?"

Bless her heart, promise or no, she was trying to run interference for me.

"No," I said. I couldn't bear seeing this come between them, too. "It's okay. I want to hear what she has to say."

Teeny's eyes begged me not to do this to myself, but I had to start somewhere with Callie. "I'm sure, Teeny. Please." If my daughter had something to say to me, I would take it. I braced myself for the worst.

Teeny shook her head, then made for the kitchen, gathering empty glasses along the way.

Callie waited till the swinging door settled to speak, and I was totally unprepared for what she said. "I've decided you can come to things," she begrudged, eyes averted. "But only because Wade

threatened to call off the wedding if I didn't make up with you."
Anger escaped from beneath her polite veneer. "He'd feel differently if he knew what you'd done, but he's a far more loyal friend to
you than you were to him." She took a leveling breath. "So I'm
telling you, you can come to things again. I won't like it, but I'll be
civil." She pinned me with a defiant glare. "But don't push it. And
don't think this means that anything has changed about the way I
feel. After the wedding, I want you to leave us alone. Is that clear?"

I nodded. "Crystal." Seeing her, hearing her, I saw myself scolding
our son Jack after he'd gotten his second DUI in college. Heard the
same anger and disappointment I'd felt when I'd lectured him, then
told him we were taking away his Jeep.

Only now that I was on the receiving end of such disappointment
and condemnation did I understand how very, very sorry he must
have felt.

"Thank you, honey," I told my daughter. "I appreciate this more
than I can say. And I won't push it. I promise."

"You promised you wouldn't come to the parties," she snapped.

"I lied." Finally reaching my threshold for dire remorse and guilt,
I felt a dawning sense of perspective stir inside me. "I was desperate.
For you, and your future. Callie, I'd give anything to undo what I did,
but you're still my daughter, and I still love you more than my life. I
can't believe you'd write me off over a disagreement—granted, it's a
big one—but surely it's not bad enough to erase the rest of our relationship." I tried to think of the worst crime imaginable. "Heck, I'd
still love you, even if you shot your daddy dead in the middle of the
living room."

Callie remained unmoved. "Easy for you to say. You know I
wouldn't." She put an end to our conversation with a frosty, "I'm
done. Please leave."

I tucked my purse strap over my shoulder. "Okay, then." Without
looking back, I headed out into the empty hallway and heard the
gentle swish as the door closed behind me.

On my way to the elevator, I forced myself to send up some serious
thank-you prayers. She hadn't made a scene. She'd promised to be

civil. Even though it was under duress, she'd said I could come to things, sparing us all embarrassing conjecture.

All in all, things had gone better than I ever would have expected. The only trouble was, she still hated me.

· 23 ·

It's a shame that good times don't last forever, but it's a blessing that the bad times don't last forever, either.
—LINDA'S *BUBBIE*

. . . .

*A*T THE SOLE remaining dinner party the next night, Wade made a great show of putting us at our ease, which obviously annoyed Callie. Still, she remained superficially pleasant. By the end of the evening, I'd gotten the hang of circulating out of Callie's way.

Starting on Monday of the Wedding Week, I searched the stores high and low for something distinctive and memorable to give Callie's attendants at the bridesmaids' luncheon on Friday, but came up with nothing. Tuesday, I even called Linda in Ireland and asked her to look over there, but she didn't come up with anything, either. Nor did any of my other Red Hats.

Goaded by perfectionism, I'd set my heart on finding something unique and personal and not just nice, but useful.

With the luncheon only three days away, I called Diane for the second time, hoping she'd had a fresh brainstorm. "I'm under the gun here. I barely convinced Callie to let me do this luncheon, and now I can't come up with anything memorable for her attendants."

"Get them cute necklaces," she repeated. "You know, those sorta chunky ones with the semi-precious stones."

"I tried, really and sincerely," I said, "but they all look like the Flintstones to me."

I heard her phone buzz, then Diane's secretary came on her intercom. "Sorry to interrupt you, but Mrs. Williams, Sr., on line three," she announced. "She says it's an emergency."

Diane's ex-mother-in-law. "Oh, lord," Diane moaned. "Is it okay if I put you on hold for a sec? Gotta see what that crazy witch is up to now."

We both knew it wouldn't be good. "I can call you back in—"

"No! You're my excuse to get rid of her."

"Okay. Happy to oblige."

The hold music was Enya, lilting mellow as always. Since Diane's conversations with her ex-mother-in-law were generally terse and monosyllabic, I expected her to be back in two songs, at the latest. But I was halfway through the second song on the album and just about to hang up when she finally clicked to my line, spitting nails.

"I'm sorry, but that woman needs to die," she bit out. I knew she didn't mean it. But I also knew Mrs. Williams, so on second thought, maybe she did. "You will not believe what she just did," Diane fumed. "She called to inform me that she wants me to give her back that Regency couch she gave me as a wedding gift. Not a word about it when we were dividing the property in the divorce. Now, all of a sudden, it's an emergency, and she just up and claims it!" Nobody got under Diane's skin like Mrs. Williams. "Can you believe the nerve? When I said no, she went ballistic and said it was a family heirloom, and since I was no longer family, she was entitled to get it back. Seems Harold has decided he wants it." Diane's ex—the coward, having his mother do his dirty work.

I forgot the rules (sympathy only when we're whining, no logic allowed) and tried to reason with her. "Honey, as Nancy Reagan said, just say no, and let her spin her wheels all she wants."

Diane's voice escalated. "She said she'd sue me for it! It's worth almost ten grand, so we're not just talking small claims court, here. She'd drag me into court with a perfectly frivolous suit. Force me to get a lawyer. I'm telling you, on a monster mother-in-law scale of one to ten, this woman is an eleven."

"So what else is new? Poor baby! Poor baby!"

"Only two?" Diane protested. "This is at least a three! Lawyers are involved, here."

"Okay," I hastened. "Poor baby, poor baby, poor baby. There."

"I swear," Diane said. "God should have done Ten Commandments for mothers-in-law. Or make it twelve. MILs as evil as mine need at least two extra commandments."

A light went on inside my brain. "Diane, you're brilliant! That's what I can do for the bridesmaids! And for Callie, too, to show her how sorry I am. I can do the Twelve Sacred Traditions for Magnificent Mothers-in-Law! It's perfect." I thought aloud, "My computer has a booklet publisher. And I can get one of those spiral-binder machines at the office supply, and do cute covers. I already have a laminator. Diane, you are a genius."

"If I'm such a genius, why couldn't I talk Harold's mama out of suing me?"

"Why not just give it to her? You don't even like that sofa."

"I know it, but I refuse to let her get away with this," she grumbled. "I'm only keeping the thing for Lee till his taste grows up."

Ah. She'd spoken the solution herself. "Sweetie, you *are* a genius. Look at what you just said."

She paused, then I could almost feel her smile. "Of course. Thank you, thank you, thank you! I'll send it to Lee in Germany. I don't care what it costs. That'll keep me out of court, and the sofa out of Harold's living room, the greedy scumbag."

"Win, win." I just love it when things work out that way.

"I owe you big time for this one, sweetie," she said.

"Okay, then," I said, "help me with this project. Mother Williams is a perfect negative example. Work off that, and see what sacred traditions you can come up with. I'll call the others and ask them, too." For the first time since the dreaded report, I was really excited. "This is gonna be great. And once I get the booklet done, I am going to obey every single tradition."

I sensed her smile again. "Or at least try," she qualified.

"No try. Do," I misquoted Yoda from *Star Wars.*

And I would, too. Regardless of what was going on with Wade, I would be a good mother-in-law—for Callie's sake.

"I've got an even better idea," Diane proposed. "Get the traditions all typed up, and e-mail them to me. I'll have the ad department do the booklets. You can come down and help decide on a stock art cover, then they'll bind them with the machines we use for our special catalogues."

"Perfect. Thanks." I hung up feeling much better about life. Now that I had a job to do, I was able to keep my mind out of the past, and the books came together even better than I'd hoped.

I woke up at six on the day before the wedding. It was already eighty-five degrees outside, reminding me of another hot June morning thirty-two years before. Grateful for our air-conditioning, I lay in the bed beside John and wondered what Callie would be thinking when she woke up. Would she be happy, or would our estrangement take the shine from her wedding celebrations?

I said a heartfelt prayer that it wouldn't. Then I got up and quietly went about getting ready for the bridesmaids' luncheon without disturbing John. He'd taken the day off to play golf with Wade in a final farewell to his bachelor state, but the only tee time they could get was a mad-dogs-and-Englishmen slot.

As soon as I was breakfasted and dressed, I went straight to the study to check on *The Twelve Sacred Traditions of Magnificent Mothers-in-Law* one more time. My best friends and I had come up with some great rules (many of which Linda and Teeny and I had already broken), adding just enough wry anecdotes to keep them from being too serious.

I looked at the cover yet again and congratulated myself. It was perfect: the Victorian title font was printed over a stock image of tightly packed pink rosebuds, with the date and all six of our names underneath.

We had definitely done good with that one.

I was admiring our handiwork when John surprised me from behind by wrapping his arms around me. He then proceeded to check out the curves under my pink crepe dress.

What was left of my female parts promptly did a flip, but the wrong-way romance gene had struck again. "John, you'll wrinkle me all up," I protested with less-than-convicting force.

"That's okay," he murmured, his voice dusky. He'd already brushed his teeth, leaving no doubt as to what he wanted. "I'll iron it for you."

John, an iron, and rayon crepe? I don't think so.

I turned around to face his morning-prickly jaw. "What do you think?" I showed him a bound copy.

He took it without looking at it and dropped it on the desk. "I read one last night," he said, then nipped at my earlobe. "They're great," he murmured, his hands knowing exactly where to stir me. "You ought to publish them. Make a fortune." His lips brushed down the side of my neck, sending a shiver of delight through me. Then he hefted me up onto the desk, causing an avalanche of books as he drew me hard against his formidable "Good morning, I want you."

Instinctively, my legs wrapped around him. I was ahead of schedule, after all. And sometimes there's a lot to be said for the occasional quick-and-dirty. I could use some endorphins before facing Callie again.

Weak woman that I am, I gave in, and thirty minutes later (not so quick after all, but yummy), I was ironing my dress in the kitchen while John happily munched his way through a huge bowl of Kix.

I'd already repaired my hair (which wasn't hard, because I was wearing a really nice, superlight straw picture hat that matched my pink dress). Everybody was wearing hats. We'd made it the luncheon's theme.

"I wonder what Callie's thinking today?" John mused with uncharacteristic pensiveness. "Do you think she's worrying about those pictures?"

"I'd worry about those pictures," I said. "But she hasn't wavered one iota." I sighed. "I guess the report just polarized her loyalties."

I finished the dress and hung it up to cool before I put it back on, then turned to look at him. "It's past time to give all that up, the worrying and the projecting. Callie and Wade are getting married tomorrow, and things will work out however they work out. We might as well enjoy the wedding and hope for the best." It felt so good to be able to say that and mean it.

John looked me over with pride. "As always, you end up where you ought to be. You're right. Time to start expecting all the best."

He went back to his Kix, and I put my dress back on.

When I started to leave, he rose. "I'll carry those books to the car for you." Ever my knight in shining armor.

He gave me a parting kiss through the open window of my car. "Have fun with your girl party."

Not likely, if Callie was still in her mega-snit, but I was still muzzy enough from lovemaking not to dither about it.

"Try not to bake yourselves senseless on the course," I shot back. "Callie's mad enough already. If you or Wade ends up with heatstroke, she'll really be ticked off."

"I'll wear my white hat," he promised, and I smiled, picturing him in the rumpled old thing. John in golf attire was so dorky, he was adorable.

The thought kept me smiling all the way to the Coach House. That, and the lingering afterglow.

After lugging the booklets past the regular lunch crowd, I took the little elevator up to the private dining rooms. Diane and Wade had outdone themselves with the flowers and decorations.

"Well, if it isn't the mother of the bride," Diane said.

"Oh, y'all," I told them, "this is perfect."

Diane was always scouring garage sales and thrift shops for design inspirations, so she'd accumulated a dozen ornate cathedral-length bridal trains that were now draped artistically across the pink tablecloths. "These are gorgeous, but won't they get ruined with us eating on them?"

"Honey, every one of 'em is Scotchgarded to smithereens. You could dump Drano on 'em, and it would just slide right off."

I turned my attention to the flowers. Wade had outdone himself with long, trailing bouquets of white peonies, simple daisies, baby's breath, and pale tea ivy for centerpieces. "The flowers are glorious. You are truly a master."

Wade beamed. "Thanks, Mom," he teased.

A tiny part of me cringed, but the better part of me reached into the bag I'd set in a chair and got out a little book. "I made one of these favors for you, *son*." I handed it to him. "If I ever get out of line, just call me and tell me what number I've broken. I hereby do solemnly swear, I will straighten right up." I should have shut up then, but my evil alter ego couldn't resist adding, "Unless you hurt my daughter. Then I will run you down in the street and back up three times, just to make sure Callie can collect the insurance."

Diane's eyes went huge with alarm, but Wade just laughed. "Spoken like a true mother lion." His humor shifted to convincing sincerity. "Don't worry. The only way I would ever hurt Callie is by dying." Little did we know how prophetic that statement would prove to be. "And I intend to fend that off as long as possible. Your daughter wouldn't accept my proposal till I swore to do everything I can to stay healthy. So I've gone organic, upped my exercise, and dropped the fat in my diet."

That was my Callie: She'd addressed the difference in their ages with a very sensible contingency.

Wade checked his watch. "Wups. Gotta go play my last round as a single man." He laid down the book, then lightly grasped my upper arms and leaned over to give me a polite peck on the cheek, just as he'd leaned toward that Nora Green woman in the photographs. And just like her, I reflexively grasped his elbows.

"It's okay," he said, his hazel eyes telegraphing commitment. He let go and picked up the book. "I swear on my life, I will be the husband Callie deserves."

Time to let go of the fear. "I believe you," I said. But speaking something does not make it so. Even as I watched him leave, a stubborn jab of worry pricked at my resolve.

He must have passed Callie on the way out, because the elevator delivered her in a matter of minutes. I heard the "ding" and met her in the narrow hallway with a book as she got out. "Oh, honey. You look so beautiful." She had on a layered georgette dress in pale blue that really set off her coloring, and a matching crownless hat with a dense, narrow diadem of lilies of the valley. "So beautiful."

She almost smiled, but caught herself.

"I have something for you," I said, handing her the copy. "Or did Wade show you his?"

Ignoring my inadvertent double entendre, she frowned. "He didn't show me anything." She looked it over, skeptical, then eyed me askance without comment.

"I know it's the world's worst example of 'Do as I say, not as I do,'" I told her, "but that's going to change, I swear." I raised my hand as if I were in court. "As of now, this little book is my personal guide to recovery. I will be the best mother-in-law in the whole, wide world to Wade. I swore it on a solemn oath. And I told Wade to call me on it whenever I stepped out of line."

Callie gave me an I'll-believe-it-when-I-see-it look and dropped the book, unopened, into her straw bag.

So much for that idea.

I was rescued from further awkwardness when the elevator said "ding" and the doors opened to reveal three of Callie's chattering attendants. Holding on to their hats, they admired ours as they got off. Suddenly the little hallway wasn't big enough for all our brims.

I made a strategic retreat to the private dining room where everything was now set up.

Diane passed me on my way in. "I'm off to the bathroom before things get going."

Checking the place cards one last time, I saw that Diane had swapped mine with Peach's, whom I'd put between me and Callie in the interest of détente. Determined not to "push it," I was swapping them back when Mama walked in wearing a vintage emerald green hat and suit I recognized from the Jackie Kennedy era. It still looked like a million bucks on her.

I heard my sisters out in the hallway gushing over Callie, and felt a stab of jealousy at Callie's delighted responses.

"Whatcha doin'?" Mama asked, her pale blue eyes zeroed in on the card I'd just replaced. "You're not sitting next to Callie?"

I scrambled to come up with an excuse she'd buy. "Peach is so excited to be the flower girl that she considers Callie her own personal bride-to-be. I don't mind moving over. I put you to Callie's left. Her maid of honor is on the other side of you. You remember Angie, her sorority roommate."

I'd put Abby between me and Linda, safely beyond Mama's inability to conceal her disapproval.

Speaking of which, Mama clearly wasn't buying my explanation, but she let it lie. "Whatever floats your boat." Translate: "I brought you up better than to do that. It's not by the book, and you know it."

To my relief, she changed the subject. "Have you heard from Linda yet?"

"Just the one phone call after she got in Wednesday. She was so jet-lagged, we've all left her alone. But she'll be here today."

Boy, was it going to be good to see her again. You never know how much you'll miss somebody till they go away, and the three weeks Linda had been overseas seemed like three months.

Speak of the devil, she walked in.

"Aaah!" I headed for her, open-armed.

Caught in a hat-wary hug, Linda spoke over my shoulder to Mama. "Hey, Miz Peyton. Callie asked if you'd come out and help her welcome the guests."

Mama shot me a brief "aha" look. "Sure. I'm on my way."

She suspected something, but Mama was the last person in this God's green earth who needed to know about Callie's and my estrangement. She'd probably try to jerk a knot in both of us, which would only make things worse. I'd already done enough to take the bloom off Callie's rose. No way was I letting Mama stir things up.

But no sooner did Mama leave than I heard her demand, "Callista, why are you avoiding your mother?"

Fists raised, I skrinched my face shut. "Damn." Just what I needed.

"Never mind," Linda said quietly. "Callie brought this on. Let her deal with your mama."

Linda's absence had definitely cured our boredom with each other. I was beyond ready for the five of us to spend some time together. "What's Brooks up to today?" I asked her.

"Playing golf with the idiot groom and that idiot husband of yours," she said.

"And my idiot boyfriend completing the foursome," Diane said as she joined the circle. "He just called me on my cell and said the humidity was worse than Houston. It's huge for a Texan to surrender a superlative, even a bad one."

"Odd," I said as she and the others exchanged mandatory hugs. "John didn't mention they were coming,"

"They just decided," Linda told me. "I can't believe they're actually playing today. It's ninety-five in the shade. Good thing Brooks is a doctor. Assuming he doesn't faint first."

"What *is* it with men and golf?" Diane complained.

"Hit the ball, drag Martha," I quoted from one of my favorite golf fanatic jokes.

Linda shifted the conversation back to us. "Sorry I didn't call or come over since I got back. It's taken me this long to get out of the molasses and straighten out my days and nights. But boy, was it worth it. We had the time of our lives."

"And lost weight doing it," I said with a look of approval. She looked trim and compact in a navy blue blazer, spectators, and a white pleated skirt. "How'd you manage that?"

Linda's expression glowed. "We walked and talked, and talked and walked for days and days and days. Just like when we were courting. And rode bikes. It was so gorgeous there. With all that exercise, even the ale and soda bread didn't go to our middles."

She picked up one of the little books. "These came out fabulous. Nobody would ever guess you did them yourself." She opened it and read aloud, " 'For my precious daughter Callie, who means the world to me.' " She turned to the first page of text. "Wow. Good job."

Linda pointed to the list of authors. "You didn't have to put our names on it. It was your brainchild."

I shook my head. "Without y'all, it would only be six sacred traditions. And I never would have come up with the idea in the first place if it wasn't for Diane."

"Baloney," Diane said. "It was all you."

"All God, really," I allowed, "for arranging to have your MIL call when we were on the phone."

I heard Peach's voice, high with excitement, from the hallway and looked up to see her zoom in ahead of Teeny and Pru, all of them in pastels with matching hats.

Together again, at last. One of the missing pieces in my life slid quietly back into place as their presence soothed my banged-up heart. We had another group hug-in, then turned our attention to Peach, who looked like a buttercup in her adorable yellow jumper, white blouse, and yellow hat banded by green ribbons that hung down the back.

Full of herself, Peach flicked the ribbons. "Like 'em? They're just like Eloise at the Plah-za."

"I think we've created a monster," Pru said with a smile.

Peach preened. "Teeny said she would take us all to the Plah-za for tea this summer. Won't that be fun?"

"Yes it will," I said. "Maybe if you ask Callie, we can get her to come, too." Okay. So I wasn't above using a small child.

Peach put her tiny fists on her nonexistent hips. "Not till after the honeymoon, silly."

"Oh, of course," I said, dead serious.

As I showed Peach to her place of honor, my sisters and nieces and Callie's bridesmaids started drifting in, and *The Twelve Sacred Traditions of Magnificent Mothers-in-Law* became an instant sensation.

"Jane," my sister Kay said across the table. "Tradition One was made for Scott's mother."

Jane nodded. "And Number Three was definitely made for Art's." (My sister Nina's wretched MIL.)

Nina kept reading as she said, "Yeah, well I think Jim and Taylor"—my brothers—"could use a copy of this, too. Their MILs leave a lot to be desired."

Callie's friends joined in, and pretty soon, Magnificent MIL traditions and anecdotes were flying across the centerpieces like volleyballs, but Callie stayed out in the hallway with Mama till the elevator brought up the last guest. Only then did she come inside.

"Callie, your mother is a genius," Callie's childhood friend, Susan

Ratcliff, said as Mama and Callie took their places. "These are price-less."

"Mrs. Baker," her maid of honor asked me, "do y'all have any more of these? I'd be happy to pay for them. I can think of a dozen friends who would love to give these to their mothers or mothers-in-law."

All the attendants jumped on that idea like a flock of ducks at a Japanese beetle convention.

"Well, I hadn't really thought about doing more," I told them, flattered but uncomfortable to have the attention centered on me. This was Callie's weekend to shine.

Teeny and Diane responded in unison, "We can do more."

"Callie," her graduate school roommate said, "do you realize how lucky you are to have such a brilliant mom?"

Callie managed a prim smile. "Absolutely."

"I mean, really," her roommate gushed. "Most mothers don't know how to cut the apron strings, much less make a rule requiring it. This is genius."

"Mama's always been really creative," Callie allowed, but I could tell she wished the conversation would shift to something less awkward for her.

So I obliged by tapping my water glass with my knife and standing as the servers arrived with our plates. "Ladies, if you will look above your places, you will each find an envelope. On the card inside are some words of wisdom for marriage from Callie's godmothers, both of her grandmothers, and two of her great-grandmothers. This has been a tradition passed down for generations. After lunch, I'd like for you each to read yours aloud for Callie. But for now, may we return thanks?"

We bowed our heads, and the servers paused. "Dear Lord," I said, "we thank You for the sacred institution of marriage. What a blessing it can be when we keep You at its center. We ask Your blessing on Callie and Wade, and on this food. Amen."

Conversation erupted immediately, and we all enjoyed our lunches. As the desserts and coffee were being served, I motioned to Mama to start reading the cards. She tapped her glass till everybody quieted down, then cleared her throat. "Oh, good," she said as she pulled out the card. "This is one of mine. 'You have to love your husband, but not every single day. Just most of them.' "

Everybody laughed, including Callie. Callie's maid of honor went next. "If you have to throw something at him, throw a wet washcloth. It gets the point across without doing any damage or making too much of a mess. If you're really mad, wet it with refrigerator water." Another good laugh. "That was from Callie's grandmother Baker."

Pru went next. "Never wake up your husband in the middle of the night to hash over something he did that bothers you. He might fall asleep on the job the next day and get fired, and then where would you be?"

Pru laughed at the archaic presumption in that one. "This blast from the past is compliments of Callie's maternal great-grandmother Powell."

Around we went, enjoying pithy sayings like "He heard you the first time," and "If you do it for him, he never will," and "Men don't think PMS is a hormonal aberration, they think it's a terrifying glimpse of the real you." Or "The way to a man's heart is still through his stomach. Or lower." And "Men suffer from selective blindness: That's why they don't pick up dirty dishes or empties. They actually do not see them." "If you want things done around the house your way, do them yourself. If you want your husband to help, you have to be willing to let him do it his way, as long as public health issues aren't involved."

But I think my favorite was one from my Granny Peyton, who was definitely a woman who kept up with the times. "Men mark their territory in many ways: some with dirty clothes, some with papers, some with shoes, some with nail clippings. If it's nail clippings, try putting them in a crystal box and telling him it's a shrine to his DNA. He may find that amusing enough to make future deposits himself."

By the time we were done, everybody had loosened up, even Callie. She actually looked at me with a convincing smile. And she was pleasant the whole time she stayed to help Diane and me take down the decorations.

It felt so good not to be walking on eggs around her.

After we'd carried Diane's decorations and one of the centerpieces to her car, which was between mine and Callie's, Callie leaned in Diane's window and asked, "So, I can't wait to see that cowboy of yours."

Diane made a fierce face and said in a dead-on West Texas accent, "Stay away from him, you hussy, or I'll have to call you out into the street with my six-guns."

Grinning, Callie lifted her hands in surrender. "Honey, one man's enough trouble for me. Why in the world would I want yours?"

"Keep that in mind when you flaunt your gorgeous self in front of mine this weekend," Diane said as she put her car into reverse.

"Remember," Callie told her, stepping back, "tonight's super casual. Come comfortable."

"I will, and I thank you," Diane said in her regular voice. "I'm way past my pantyhose quotient for this day."

"Ditto," I said. My control tops had decided to go to half-mast, with the waistband bisecting my tummy in a most unflattering way. I should have known better than to try a new brand without a dry run.

As Callie waved Diane off, I opened the back door of my car and waited for the heat to escape, then I knelt to situate the bouquet safely in the floorboard.

Now that there were no witnesses, Callie immediately reverted to her cold, hostile ways. "Thank you for the party," she snipped. "And the favors. I know you went to a lot of trouble."

No compliments. No warmth. Just the bare social necessities.

"Please ask Daddy not to wear that pink madras shirt tonight," she told me. "Wade's wearing one just like it."

With that, she turned and went to her car, then left me alone in the empty parking lot.

She hadn't softened one iota. She'd only been pretending to keep the others from suspecting anything.

I got into the driver's seat, cranked up the engine and the air-conditioning, locked my doors, then cried my makeup off.

. . . .

THAT NIGHT, THE rehearsal and rehearsal dinner came off with only a slight hitch: Wade's daughter and two sons acted sullen and ungracious at dinner, but at least they came. Our son Jack stepped in like a perfect big brother, alternately making Callie laugh and jollying up her reluctant stepchildren.

As for my family, my sisters and brothers and spouses and others and nieces and nephews—all twenty-four of them—descended on the rehearsal dinner en masse, and I spent the entire night playing family catch-up with everybody while my only-child spouse patiently acted as host.

Nobody suspected that Callie hated me, and a good time was had by everybody but me.

After collapsing into bed at midnight, John and I slept eleven hours, then wakened to a perfect wedding day for an imperfect wedding, if ever there was one.

· 24 ·

There are only two cures for heartache: Get over it, already, or die.
—LINDA'S *BUBBIE*

The present. Callie's Big Day, Saturday, June 17. 2:45 P.M. En route.

. . . .

*C*ALLIE'S WEDDING DAY. T-minus seventy-five minutes and counting.

After all the months of parties and preparation, there I was on the way to the wedding, the actual, very-ever mother of the bride, right down to my pantyhose, lace hankie, and dyed shoes that matched the simple emerald-green dress Teeny and Diane had made me just for the occasion.

All morning long at the hairdresser's, I'd prayed my thought-voice hoarse, begging God for a special dispensation of joy so I could truly be happy about what was taking place. So far, though, I was still secretly miserable and oddly detached at the same time.

We pulled up to the red light at Peachtree. "Have you heard from Jack?" I fretted.

"Not since we finished lunch at the Varsity with Wade, all of an hour ago." John's dry wit let me know I was obsessing. "He'll be there."

Better I should obsess about my son than what my daughter was going to do in a little more than an hour. "So you haven't heard from him."

John patted my thigh. "Hon, he's thirty years old, an executive, and one of the groomsmen at his only sister's wedding. He'll be there on time."

I *really* wanted to call just to be sure, but managed to quell the urge.

Hard as I tried to relax, my mother-heart had a mind of its own and galloped inside me, diverting all the blood supply from my fingers and leaving me clammy with ice-cold hands. Meanwhile, my brain had gone completely ADHD, unable to focus, much less get a grip on myself.

This was Callie's day, and I had resolved to make the best of it in spite of Nora Green and Wade's heart condition and Callie's blissful naiveté. The consequences of Callie's decision were hers to bear. My job was to love her and be there for her no matter what. So there.

I tried rubbing my hands together to get some heat into them, but nothing doing.

Some people's bodies speak for them, a psychiatrist friend of ours once said. How I wished mine would just shut up, thank you very much.

If wishes were horses, then beggars would ride.

I decided to give meditation a try. I slowed my breathing and envisioned myself watching the sunset in a comfortable folding chair at Perdido Beach, with a glass of chilled white zinfandel in my hand and my feet in the warm Gulf waves. But Chicken Little kept popping up just offshore with cries of doom instead of "Help!" So I added a mental rosary of "I am happy. I am calm. I am happy. I am calm. I love my daughter and trust her choices. I am happy. I am calm . . ."

By the time we stopped for the red light at Lindbergh (the second in a row—an omen?), I realized that the more I chanted, the more wound up I got.

St. Philip's Cathedral loomed straight ahead. Two blocks from the church, and I was a wreck inside.

Please, God, please, I prayed for the jillionth time. *Send me Your peace, the peace that passes all understanding, so I can share Callie's joy without reservation.*

I sensed a familiar inkling of divine amusement.

Okay, maybe with a little reservation. I'm only human. But I need help. Not for my sake, but for Callie's. Lord, we're down to the wire, here.

In a flash of insight, I realized I'd let my fears about marrying a man I wasn't in love with rob my wedding day of the joy I might have had. Now, ironically, my fears for Callie were poisoning her wedding day, too. I couldn't let that happen. *Wouldn't* let that happen!

The light turned green.

Glory to God, my heart began to slow, and peace suffused my chest like inner sunshine, spreading its warmth down my arms and out to my fingertips. I didn't move, afraid I might be imagining it.

But I wasn't.

I felt like somebody had just freed me from a plaster of paris self-suit that was three sizes too little. As we passed Christ the King, I closed my eyes, leaned back against the seat, and breathed, really breathed. Slow and easy.

Thank You, thank You, thank You, Lord!

When we reached St. Philip's, John glanced over as we waited for an opening in the traffic so we could turn left into the dropoff entrance. "You okay?"

"I'm great," I said, grateful that I felt and sounded like myself again, not the worrywart I'd become. "At long last."

The warmth inside me began to sparkle.

I leaned forward to look at his handsome profile. "John, our baby girl is marrying a man she adores, who adores her right back. A good and decent and responsible man." I hoped.

The corners of John's eyes crinkled adorably with his smile. "I knew you'd come around. You always do." Traffic broke, allowing us to head uphill to the main entrance.

"Nothing like cutting it close," I said. "You'd think that after all these years, I would have learned. Why does it always take me so long to let things go?"

John patted my thigh. "You just have to gnaw on stuff for a while. It's your way. But you've never, ever let down any of us who love you. I don't know many husbands who can say that about their wives."

My soul, my soul, the precious man actually believed it.

Certain that I'd start crying and ruin my makeup if I told him what was in my no longer aching heart, I shot him a seductive look instead. "When we get to Ansley, I'm gonna dance with you till the band goes home. We are gonna have some fun tonight."

"Can't wait." He pulled up at the front door. "Here we are."

"Yep. Here we are." I held on to the moment for a little longer, smoothing the cowlick that sent his neat haircut to one side of his forehead. "What are you thinking? And I'm not talking physics."

Hands on the wheel, he took a long breath and stared through the windshield with that look of quiet contentment I knew so well. "That it's time."

After thirty-three years with his verbal economy, I knew he didn't mean hours and minutes; he meant the cycles of our lives.

"Kind of like having a baby when you get to nine months, isn't it?" I said.

He grinned. "A lot like that. Harder for you than it is for me."

Can we say, adorable?

I unhooked my seat belt, then leaned over and kissed him, soft and slow like it was the first time, which caught him by surprise.

"What was that for?" he asked with a wry smile when I retreated.

"It was time." Wiping a dainty fingertip below my lip to repair the damage, I got out. "I'll be in the bride's room till you come get us for the ceremony."

My sisters, sisters-in-law, and nieces had agreed that it would be insane if they all tried to see Callie before the service, so it was just going to be me and the grandmothers and my best friends helping the girls get ready.

"Jack and I'll ride herd on your family," John said without one micron of martyrdom. As an only child marrying into a big family, he'd been appalled at first by the commotion and conflict inherent in our gatherings, but over the years, he'd grown to love my siblings and most of their spouses.

Precious man.

I closed the car door and headed inside, eager to see Callie. The vestibule was a bower of gorgeous white flowers that were almost obscured by so great a host of relatives. It took me ten minutes to greet my way through everybody before I ran into Diane's gorgeous cowboy Cameron and made a point of taking him aside. As usual, he looked drop-dead great, ruggedly elegant in an understated suit that looked custom-made. "Howdy, pardner. You sure clean up nice."

He cocked a "Gee shucks" grin. "Dah-ann appointed herself my wardrobe consultant. Ah gotta admit, wearin' a suit isn't so bad when it fits right."

I leaned in. "Speaking of Diane, what's the June gift-of-the-month?"

He looked briefly taken aback, then shook his head with a smile. "I keep forgettin' that the lot of y'all come with the deal with her."

I smiled. "That we do." I wasn't about to let him off the hook. "So, what's the gift? I promise, I won't tell her. Or have you already given it to her?"

"Not yet. Ah been waitin' for the right moment." He looked from side to side to make sure she wasn't around, then drew a tiny black velvet box from his pocket.

Uh-oh!

Sure enough, he opened it to reveal one of the most gorgeous rectangular rubies I'd ever seen, at least four carats, flanked by two brilliant teardrop diamonds. A low whistle escaped me. I looked up into his face, which brimmed with optimism and pride. "Wow. It's smashing. What is it?"

"A ruby. Mah great-granddaddy won it in a poker game and had it made into a ring for mah great-grandmama. It used to be bigger, but Ah had it recut for brilliance, just for Dah-ann."

A family heirloom. Double uh-oh. "I guessed it was a ruby. Maybe I should have been clearer. Is there any special significance to this gift?"

Cameron went ruddy beneath his tan. "Ah been proposin' to Dah-ann every time we've seen each other for the past year. Thought maybe this might get her to take me seriously." He motioned to my gathered family. "You know . . . weddin's and all." He sobered. "Ah don't want to take her away from y'all. Ah just want to marry her. We can work out the logistics later."

How, I couldn't imagine. Cameron was rooted to his ranch in

Austin, and Diane had made it clear she intended to keep living in Atlanta and working for Teeny. But this was one engagement I had no intention of getting into the middle of. I closed the ring box and pressed it into his hand. "I think you're the best thing that's happened to her in a long time, and I know she does, too. Good luck."

Cameron shrugged. "It's a long shot. We'll see. If I have to settle for the way things are, then so be it."

I looked at my watch. "Yikes! I was supposed to be downstairs half an hour ago." I gave him a quick hug. "Don't worry. Your secret's safe with me."

On my way, I passed Jack and approved the new suit his California girlfriend-of-the-month had helped him choose. When I finally reached the bride's room, I ran into John's mother coming out.

"Hi, sweetie." She gave me a brief, hair-and-dress-wary hug. "You look almost as gorgeous as Callie."

"So do you." John's mama was ageless. "Where are you headed?"

"I'm off to the drugstore to get Wade some Seltzer-Al. Callie said he had three sausage patties, grits, and a Mexican omelet at the Hickory House for breakfast, and he came home from lunch acting like Napoleon, with his hand clutched to his stomach. I sure hope he didn't get hold of a bad batch of eggs."

A Mexican omelet? Add that to his lunch, and . . . I leaned in close. "Maybe you ought to get some Depends, while you're at it. He had three Varsity chili dogs and onion rings for lunch."

She colored slightly from embarrassment. "Listen to you. My gracious." Then she headed for the parking lot. "I'll see you later."

Inside the bride's room, I found everybody in a happy chatter of preparation. I didn't see Callie, but Teeny and Linda and Diane—all in color-compatible pastels that were pretty without being overt—descended on me immediately.

They didn't have to ask how I was feeling.

"Look at you." Linda rearranged a tendril of my beauty parlor hairdo. "Gorgeous. You look like Callie's sister, not her mother."

"Liar," I said with a grin. "But keep it up."

"Have you lost weight?" Diane asked. "Or is it just the dress?"

"About time you noticed. I lost eight pounds in the past two weeks." I smoothed my slightly flatter tummy. "Must have been the parties."

"No fair," Linda said. "Most people gain weight at parties. If you weren't my best friend, I'd have to hate you for that."

Teeny stepped back for a long, satisfied look at me. "The dress is perfect on you."

I smiled. "It's by my favorite designers."

"Hey, George!" Pru called from across the room, where she held a curling iron tightly in Peach's baby-fine hair. "You look great."

"Thanks." I waved. "Hey, Peach."

Peach waved without looking up.

"Callie's in the bathroom," Diane said. "You just relax and visit. We'll take care of everything else."

"Y'all are the best."

They went back to acting as fetchers and general ladies' maids for Abby and the three girls who'd been Callie's undergrad, sorority, and post-grad roommates.

Taking everything in as she sipped champagne, Mama sat happily ensconced in a corner chair with her jacket and high heels off, and the waistband of her pale yellow cutwork suit unbuttoned. "Hey, honey." She waggled her sensible manicure my way. "Goodness, but we've got some handsome women in this family. You look mah-velous."

Mama, imitating Ricardo Montalbán? "How much champagne has she had?" I quietly asked Diane.

Diane shrugged. "I wasn't keeping track. But I'll take her some canapés and make sure she doesn't overdo."

"Thanks."

"Hey, Georgia." Abby waddled over wearing the reasonably subdued (by her standards) dress she and Callie had found at a consignment shop in Virginia Highlands. It had a layered, sort of medieval-Victorian thing going, but it wasn't too tight and blended with the other girls' simple light green sheaths. At least she didn't look Goth.

She touched her short, spiky, no-longer-neon hairdo. "How do you like it? In honor of the occasion, I put a temporary over the purple." She'd even foregone her nose ring.

"You look wonderful."

The baby had definitely dropped since the rehearsal dinner. I almost said she was big as a mama tick—one of my daddy's favorite third-trimester descriptions—but caught myself in time. "Bless your heart, looks like you're growing a linebacker in there."

"They amended my due date to a week from now." Abby braced her palm against the small of her back in that universal gestating stance. "I don't think I'm gonna make it that long."

Uh-oh.

Chicken Little cranked up with, *Her water will probably break during the service!*

I gave Abby's shoulders a gentle sidelong hug. "Just as long as you don't have him during the ceremony." Dumb thing to say! As if she had any control over it.

Abby grinned. "I'm past ready to have this kid, but I promise not to let anything happen till the newlyweds are on their way."

She rubbed her belly with a deep sigh. "Well, time to let Mama do my makeup like a regular earthling." Thank goodness, there would be no black lipstick in the wedding photos. Abby gave a mock shudder. "At least it'll keep her from driving anybody else crazy."

We'd long since stopped trying to correct each other's kids when they griped about their mothers, so I let the comment pass. "Okey-dokey."

Suddenly awkward without anything to do, I looked at my watch. The photographer was doing all the "his and hers" portraits separately beforehand. We needed to get ready.

Callie didn't even have on her dress yet. Her elegant, modest wedding gown—with a zillion tiny, time-consuming little satin buttons down the back—hung ready above spread-out sheets. It perfectly suited her taste and personality.

Pregnant matron of honor aside, she'd done such a good job on the wedding. Nobody would have ever guessed it was a shoestring operation, with many of its elements donated as wedding gifts by Wade's friends in the business.

"Hey there, my good-godmother Georgia!" Peach bounced in front of me wearing the long satin slip that went under her yellow dotted Swiss flower-girl dress. She looked like a fragile little fairy and was clearly enjoying the feel of the ringlets Pru had coaxed into her hair.

"Hey there, Miss Peach Fouché." I stooped to her level. "You're lookin' mighty gorgeous. Where are your flowers?"

She switched from bouncing to ballet. "Over in that basket. But they're not really flowers," she said with a hint of pique. "They're just rose petals." She executed a graceful arabesque. "I'm supposed to scatter them down the aisle. Not too many all at once," she mimicked Pru's inflections, "just sprinkle them out even."

She came down to earth, literally and figuratively. "Flowers can stain, you know. I warned Callie they could ruin the bottom of her dress, but did she listen to me?" Her voice went up on the last, then dropped for a dramatic, "No." Peach shook her curls, then resumed her dance. "She said she didn't plan to wear it again anyway, but she promised to have it cleaned so I could use it someday if I wanted to." She granted me a smile. "You sure have a nice daughter." With that, she arabesqued her way back to her grandmother.

Callie came out of the bathroom wearing her ancient pink-chenille kimono open over a risqué ensemble of white wedding underwear, complete with a lace garter belt over matching bikinis, and old-fashioned stockings with lace tops. "Mama," she acknowledged, her tone still cool.

Enough of that. "We need to talk." I grabbed her arm and led her back into the bathroom. "Come with me, my darling, my dear."

After I closed the door behind us and turned on the water to give us a little privacy, I took both her hands and peered into her averted face. "Callista, my precious one-and-only daughter, this is your wedding day. Never mind what I did."

That earned me a sharp glance, but I wasn't about to give up.

"You have two choices," I told her calmly. "You can live this day fully, steeped in joy and gratitude, or you can choose to stay mad at me and cheat yourself out of what's supposed to be the happiest day of your life. And if you choose to cheat yourself, I hereby refuse to take the blame."

That surprised her.

"What I did," I went on, "I did out of concern for you. I had nothing to gain for myself, and everything to lose when it came to our relationship, but I could not stand to see you marry a man who might be living a double life."

She inhaled slowly, then blew it out, finally meeting my gaze. "I know that. I *know* that." Conflict washed across her features. "I also know Wade isn't leading a double life. Mama, there's something I need to tell you. Those pictures in the report—"

She didn't owe me an explanation. "You don't need to tell me anything but that you forgive me, and you're ready to move past this." I squeezed her beautifully American-manicured fingers. "Sweetie, I beg of you, let yourself be happy without reservation on this, of all days."

I could almost see those Bigbrain wheels turning in her mind. "Oh, Mama." In a wrenching gesture, she started to cry and snatched me close. "I hate being mad at you," she said over my shoulder. "And I hate that you're not happy about my marrying Wade."

I clung to her just as hard. "It doesn't matter what I think. Time will tell. You have to do what you know is right, and if that's marrying Wade, so be it. Your daddy and I only want you to be happy, and that includes today."

She drew back so I could see her heartfelt conviction. "I will be happy with Wade."

I bumped her hip with mine. "Make that present tense, and you've got a deal."

"I *am* happy with Wade," she said, relief washing over her expression. "And this *is* going to be the happiest day of my life. So I forgive you. So there. End of story."

"Hallelujah, amen!" I seconded. Then I dampened a paper towel before turning off the water. "Here. Your mascara's running. Let me fix it."

Ever independent, she took the towel from me. "No. Let me."

When we came back into the bride's room grinning, arm-in-arm, the subtle undercurrent of tension caused by our estrangement vanished.

Abby lumbered over to Callie. "Everything okay now?"

"Absolutely okay." Callie smiled so hard it made me think of her third-grade school portraits where her grin-slash-grimace looked like she was in a contest to see who could show the most teeth.

We all helped her into her wedding dress, then Diane set the veil in place.

The Callie who stood before us was no child. She was a grown woman, and gorgeous beyond anything her father and I had contributed.

I know I'm prejudiced, but I swear, she was well on her way to being the most gorgeous bride the world had ever seen. "Oh, sweetheart, you look magnificent."

Even her attendants stood in awe.

I flashed through the past twenty-seven years, from her sweet scent and softness when I'd first cuddled her in my arms, to her boundless energy as the chubby brunette toddler who gave new meaning to the word *independent*, to her poise as a prissy vision in pink—complete with hat and gloves—on her sixth Easter Sunday. Then the sun-browned ten-year-old tomboy who caught her first big bass from the lake. And the self-conscious thirteen-year-old talking to the fourteen-year-old boy who'd finally gotten up the nerve to call her. And the stunning summa cum laude graduate at Georgia Tech.

"Mama? Are you okay?"

"My daughter, mine," I breathed. "You're so beautiful, I think my heart may break."

She laughed. "No broken hearts today. You, my mother, mine," she said, searching my face with delight, "look . . . absotively, posilutely happy."

She hadn't called me "my mother, mine" since our fight. "I am happy, sweetie. Down to the bone. And so proud of you."

That sent Mama way past her limit for mushiness. She got up—rock steady on her feet, I was glad to see—and crossed through the pandemonium with a small, flat box wrapped in white with no bow. "Okay. Enough of that." She lifted an eyebrow and blared out, "Did you two ever get to have that mother-daughter sex talk I never had with Georgia?"

Conversation halted abruptly, followed by explosive laughter.

Callie went red as a UGA Bulldog football blanket, but nothing my mother did these days shocked me.

Mama laughed. "Sorry. I just couldn't resist."

"Nana." Callie gave her an embarrassed nudge.

"Here. Maybe this'll make up for it." Mama handed the gift to her. "Something old from your old grandmother." As Callie took it, Mama said, "I was going through my things last night looking for something special to give you. Had a regular nostalgia fest, pulled out all my old pictures and papers. Wrecked the house completely, but it was the next best thing to seeing your granddaddy again. When I found this, I knew it was just right."

Callie kissed her grandmother. "I can't wait to see what it is." She opened the wrapping and found a silver frame that held a poem typed on aging paper with "Happy 25th Anniversary" written at an angle in my father's bold handwriting.

Why hadn't I seen this before?

I read the words over her shoulder:

Boundaries

> *We've built our walls adjacent, you and I.*
> *They're intricately fit, both "just-so" high,*
> *Each stone selected, weighed, and turned about*
> *To keep what's inside in,*
> *What's outside out.*
> *But trust and time have eased away the line*
> *That marked your wall as yours and mine as mine.*
> *They've leaned together, formed a bridge instead,*
> *Old lovers sleeping back-to-back in bed.*

"Mama, that's beautiful," I breathed. Goosebumps.

Callie pressed the poem to her heart. "It's perfect, Nana. Just perfect."

"So much for something old." Mama pulled a small velvet drawstring bag from her purse, then handed it to Callie. "You can't wear it, though, so here's a little something old *and* blue that you can."

Callie opened the drawstring and poured out a large, exquisite male cameo in classic Greek style on a deep, smoky blue background. A simple frame of old gold surrounded it.

"It's very rare," Mama said. "Good male cameos are hard to find, especially in that color. My grandmother gave it to me on my wedding day in 1943." She tapped her bra between her breasts. "It didn't exactly go with my wedding dress, so I wore it right here, underneath."

Callie pinned it to her own bra.

Mama beamed. "My grandmother Harris got it from her grandmother on her wedding day just after the Civil War. It came from the China trade on the great sailing ships. You can pass it on to your granddaughter some day."

And I'd thought we Episcopalians didn't have female rituals of passing. I sensed the unbroken line of women who had gone before the three of us, and swelled with pride.

Beyond words, Callie crushed Mama in a bear hug, then pulled away to show her friends. "Y'all, look what Nana gave me for something old and something blue. It's the most romantic thing ever!"

Mama turned to me. "Sorry about that, but you were the skip generation."

"I'll get over it." I cocked my head. "I didn't know Daddy was a poet."

Mama let out a satisfied sigh. "That was the only poem he ever wrote. But once your father mastered something, he moved on to newer things."

I focused on Callie as she reverentially displayed the poem and the pin to her attendants. "You've got four other granddaughters. What made you decide to give these to Callie?"

"Ever since she was a little girl, I've known that she was the one who should have them." Mama put her arm around me and smiled at Callie. "She has your appreciation for what really matters."

My heart swelled with the compliment. "Thanks."

A loud knock sounded at the door. "Photographer! Y'all ready for the photos?"

The girls scattered to their final preparations in a flurry of protests.

Linda opened the door a crack to tell him, "Give us five more minutes."

We all scrambled to clean up the room and hand out flowers. No sooner was that done, than another knock sounded, more tentative. "Callie? It's your daddy."

"Would the rest of y'all mind going out into the hall for a few minutes?" I asked. "I want to give Callie some time alone with her daddy."

They poured past John, blocking his view, until I was the last in the doorway. "Take a look at your daughter, sweetheart," I told him as I stepped aside to reveal her standing there.

John's face went slack in awe.

I kissed him lightly. "She's all yours."

He cocked that sweet half-smile. "For a few more minutes, anyway."

"How's Wade holding up?" I asked him.

John shook his head, brows lifted. "Waiting for the Seltzer-Al to kick in. But Mama embarrassed him half to death with those Depends."

"Oh, John, she didn't." I told you my mother-in-law was great.

He grinned. "Oh, yes she did." Then guilt erased his sparkle. "I shouldn't have taken him to the Varsity, though. That was stupid."

"Better the Varsity than a strip club." I glanced at my watch. Five till four. We hadn't planned to start till quarter after. "The photographer said he'd need at least ten minutes to take the prewedding shots."

"Give us five, then." John gave me a peck.

When I closed the door, he was reaching out for Callie as if she were some magical creature made of light.

My heart echoed my great-grandma Sibley's favorite affirmation: *We done good with this one. We done good.*

Eyes brimming, John came out when his five minutes were up. After Callie's portrait and all the bridesmaids' pictures were taken, we all trundled to the packed chapel on schedule, Callie and John tucked just inside the main sanctuary, out of sight, to wait for her grand entrance.

Inside the chapel, the string quartet from Oglethorpe sounded concert-worthy, and Wade had outdone himself with the flowers along the aisles and at the altar and framing the entry.

Except for Wade's daughter Laurie—sulking in the first row of the groom's side after threatening to boycott the ceremony—the only other person in the room who didn't look happy was Wade. His palm held just below his rib cage, he smiled like a man whose shoes were two sizes too small.

Clearly, the Seltzer-Al hadn't helped.

Oh, please, Lord, don't let him throw up—or worse—during the cere-mony!

Standing there beside him, both his sons had the good grace to act pleasant, despite their objections.

Almost half of the bride's side was crowded with my sisters and brothers and best friends and their others. The rest of the chapel was filled with our friends and Wade's and Callie's.

Waiting for Jack to escort his grandmothers to their places, then come back for me, I felt as if I were watching things unfold in the fairy tale of flowers and dark wood and stained glass of the chapel on TV instead of being there. Still, it struck me that in less than thirty minutes, everything would be different between Callie and me and John. For always.

That sudden realization set loose a flock of butterflies inside me.

Then there was a minor commotion behind me. I turned to see Rachel and Sol hurrying toward us, Sol in emerald green dressy African attire, and Rachel in a gorgeous deep purple Nigerian outfit livened with shiny gold motifs, her hair bound up in an artful turban of the same fabric. She had on very little makeup, but still looked gor-geous, her eyes and coloring intensified by the purple.

John followed my line of sight, then exclaimed in an unprece-dented show of enthusiasm, "Sol!" He fairly leapt from Callie's side to grab Sol's hand and all but shake his arm off. "What an honor. Thank you so much! So much!"

Weird. Had John invited them? Without telling me?

Before I could pursue the thought, Rachel rushed up to me and hugged me like we were long-lost friends. "Georgia!"

The guests turned curious glances toward the sound.

Rachel whispered into my ear, "Please pretend you invited us. Please. I just *had* to get out of Africa. I haven't had a manicure or a pedicure or a decent haircut since we left, and we've been eating native mystery food in Sol's orphanages and clinics. Yuk." She shuddered.

Definitely not the life she'd anticipated. How beautifully ironic. Still, I took pity on her and made a great show of saying, "I'm so glad y'all could make it after all."

Fawning over Sol like a golden retriever puppy, John leaned close to murmur something, after which Sol nodded, and they parted—John to Callie and Sol to hug Rachel from behind.

"How do you like my bride's new look?" he asked. "I've been showing her how the rest of the world lives and teaching her to simplify, and she's doing beautifully."

Rachel, simplified? Not likely. Coming up with a unified theory of physics would be easier.

Jack arrived to escort me to my place beside Mama on the front row, but I diverted him to the Rosenwassers. "Honey, there's room for Sol and Rachel on the second row beside your Uncle Taylor and Aunt Angie. Please make them feel welcome. They've come all the way from Africa to be with us."

Rachel shot me a look of raw gratitude.

Jack took her arm and murmured deferentially, "I'm so pleased to meet you. Mama's told us all about you and Mr. Rosenwasser."

Thank goodness, he didn't elaborate further. The Rachel stories I'd regaled him with had been had been anything but complimentary.

A stir of conjecture passed through my family when Jack escorted them to the bosom of the Peyton clan, then returned to collect me.

The handsome young man who had once been my little Lego addict offered me his arm. "Show Callie how proud you are of her," Jack murmured for my ear only.

My chin up high, I took his arm and did just that.

There were no guarded looks among the people I greeted on my way down the aisle. Regardless of what the future held, my daughter and her husband would start their life together supported by many friends and family. I was genuinely thankful for that.

Leaving room for John, I took my seat beside Mama.

Then the string quartet struck up with Bach, and we all craned in our seats to see the bridesmaids make their way to the front. Last but not least, Peach acquitted herself perfectly of her responsibility as flower girl. After reaching the wedding party, she doubled back to sit in her daddy's lap, who beamed like any proud papa.

The string quartet fell silent, then the organ began the processional from Lohengrin, setting every hair on my body aright.

"May we all rise?" our good friend, the dean of the cathedral, asked.

I don't remember standing. All I remember is the sight of John and Callie framed by the garlanded arch of the doorway.

And the way Wade's pained expression turned to wonder at the sight of his bride.

An audible murmur of admiration swept through the chapel as my proud husband led our daughter toward one of the most important rites of passage in her life.

Our Callie. So beautiful.

Then something niggled at my brain, drawing my eye past Callie and John to the last pew across the aisle, and an all-too-familiar face.

Nora Green, looking way too good for comfort!

What was *she* doing there?

A bolt of alarm sent me grabbing the back of my pew for support. All my noble resolutions tumbled into darkness.

Callie took one look at me, then followed my line of sight to the woman Wade had been kissing in all those clandestine photos. Her smile went brittle as a shattered mirror.

Meanwhile, John—Mr. Oblivious—kept grinning with pride as he approached the man into whose hand and life we would entrust our daughter.

Callie shot me an oblique look as she passed, one I couldn't decipher accurately. Apology? Surely not.

"Who gives this woman in marriage?" the dean intoned.

"Her mother and I do." John leveled a sober look at his best friend. Then he turned to join me in the pew.

I dared not look at him, even when he took my ice-cold hand in his.

The ceremony that had seemed fast-forward suddenly went into slow motion.

"You may be seated," the dean instructed. I plopped down like a robot whose knees needed oiling.

Calm, I ordered myself. Stay calm. For Callie's sake. Believe that everything's all right, for her sake. Find the peace somewhere.

Lord, please, grant me Thy peace, I pleaded. *You did it before. Please, bring it back.*

I felt as if my prayers weren't making it past the ceiling. Yet somehow, I managed to keep from betraying what I felt—except for the subtle tremor at the edge of my forced smile nearest John.

He took note and put his arm around my shoulders in a protective gesture that was more than welcome.

Wade looked flushed as he faced Callie for the opening passages of the ceremony. Then he and Callie followed the dean to the altar, trailed by Abby and Wade's eldest son Tom.

Callie handed Abby the beautiful bouquet Wade had made her, then took his hands for the exchanging of rings and traditional vows.

Wade's voice remained strong and firm as he faced Callie, despite the subtle exaggeration of the wrinkles on his face and the beads of sweat that broke out on his brow.

Maybe he *had* seen Nora Green.

Nothing had changed since the talk I'd had with Callie, I kept telling myself. She'd seen those photos of Nora and chosen to marry Wade, anyway. Either she knew something I didn't, or she had chosen to overlook and forgive. Nora Green's presence made no difference, really.

The only trouble was, it did to me.

And then the dean was saying, "By the authority vested in me by the Episcopal Church and the state of Georgia, I now pronounce you man and wife."

Wade started to bend sharply forward, then checked himself.

"You may now kiss your bride."

Please, not a soap opera kiss! I'd seen far too many lately.

Much to my relief, Wade gave Callie a chaste kiss on the cheek.

Then the newlyweds turned to face the congregation, and the dean said, "Ladies and gentlemen, it is my honor to be the first to present to you Mr. and Mrs. Wade Bowman."

The organist struck up with the joyous peals of Widor's "Toccatta," full blast.

Wade tried to look joyous, but his grin was forced, and his flushed face had gone ashy. They made it as far as the main aisle before his smile turned to an agonized grimace. He gasped and rooted to the spot, bringing Callie to a surprised halt.

She turned to him in confusion.

He peered at her with a look that said good-bye. "Pain," he ground out, sinking to one knee, his left fist clutched to his heart.

"Daddy!" Laurie cried.

Everybody froze in disbelief.

Eyes clenched shut in agony, Wade collapsed against Callie, who dropped her bouquet to support him. "Wade!"

Peach shrieked like a wounded animal to see yet another adult struck down before her.

"Dear Lord, no," John breathed out, pale as his best friend. Then he leapt forward to help.

I was right behind him.

"Brooks! Help!" Callie's desperate cry was all but drowned out by the organ.

Already on his way, Brooks tossed Linda his car keys. "Honey, please bring my bag from the trunk."

"Somebody call 911!" Callie pleaded.

Half the congregation pulled out cell phones and did just that, then several voices yelled into their phones over the thundering organ, "I have an emergency at the chapel of St. Philip's Cathedral in Buckhead."

Grimfaced, Linda and my two brothers hurried toward the door.

"We'll bring the paramedics when they get here," Taylor called back to us.

Pru and Bubba cradled Peach and tried to soothe her sobs.

After that spurt of pandemonium, deathly silence fell on the congregation, but the organist kept right on playing, the joyous strains now macabre. The dean headed over to clue him in.

Mama knelt in her pew and started praying, a posture quickly taken up by the rest of my family and many of the guests.

I went to my knees on the stone floor behind Callie. *God, I didn't mean it when I said that about having something happen to Wade. You know I didn't mean it.*

The organ stopped in mid-arpeggio, then the dean emerged to announce over his lapel mike, "If everyone will please remain seated, let's let the doctor take care of this."

"Okay," Brooks said to Wade. "What's going on?"

"Pain," Wade bit out. He tapped his sternum. "Right here. Had indigestion all afternoon. Just indigestion, though. Trust me. I—"

"Maybe indigestion, maybe not," Brooks interrupted. "Why don't you try to relax and let me do the diagnosing? At our age, it's better to be safe than sorry."

He slid his arm under Wade's shoulders. "Let's get you flat and elevate your feet," he said, helping Callie ease him down onto her skirt.

"Aagh!" Wayne curled in agony, raising his head. "Hurts worse that way!"

"Okay." Brooks eased him back into her lap. "Believe it or not, that's a good sign."

Still sweating and clammy, Wade chuffed a few breaths. "Better. Still feels like there's a sword in my chest." Puff, puff. "And a boulder on top of it."

The dean joined our huddle, praying almost inaudibly.

Oblivious to the fact that perspiration from Wade's close-cropped gray hair stained her gown, Callie stroked his forehead with her lace handkerchief. "It's okay, sweetheart. Just rest. You're gonna be fine."

"Nothing like ruining your beautiful wedding," he gritted out while Brooks took his pulse.

"It's *our* wedding, not mine," Callie said stoutly, "and you haven't ruined a thing. We're married, aren't we?"

Shame washed across Tom's face as he grasped his father's hand. "Dad, I'm so sorry I acted like such a jerk about all this. We all did. We made things so hard for you." His voice broke. "I'm so sorry."

"So am I," Wade's other two said almost in unison, as if their father was on his deathbed, which I fervently prayed he wasn't.

"Please forgive us," Laurie begged. "Don't die."

"Whoa." Brooks spoke with the measured calm of a professional. "We're getting way too serious here. Nobody said anything about dying. We don't even know what's really going on."

"Their mother's . . . superstitious . . . about deathbed absolution," Wade defended.

I noted that Callie was hyperventilating, so I bent behind her and clasped her shoulders. Tense with worry, John put his arm around me, linking us all together. "Breathe slow, through your nose, sweetie," I whispered to our daughter with a calm I didn't feel. "It won't do Wade any good if you pass out. Focus on your breathing. Nice and easy." I demonstrated. "In, and out." Slow inhale. Slow exhale. "Nice, and easy."

Keeping her eyes on Wade, Callie nodded and matched her breaths to mine.

We heard an approaching siren in the distance.

Ours. Please.

Brooks turned to Wade's kids. "I need to ask your dad some personal questions. Could y'all please wait outside in the hallway? Just for a few minutes, then you can come back in."

"Are you nuts?" Laurie fired back. "No way am I leaving my father when he might—"

"Laurie, put a sock in it," Tom demanded. "You're just making things worse. The doctor needs us to go, so we're going." Flanking her, the two brothers all but picked her up and moved toward the vestibule.

Laurie fought them, then after only a few yards of progress, dug in like a mule in clover.

"Don't worry," Brooks promised. "I'll call you right away if anything happens before the ambulance gets here."

"Ambulance?" Wade tried to sit up in protest, but Callie held him firmly in place.

"Wade Bowman, you stay right where you are," she ordered in top wifely form.

"I'll see your children out," the dean volunteered. He asked Brooks, "Would you like for me to clear the chapel before the ambulance comes?"

Brooks looked to Callie for her okay.

"Good idea," she said, showing incredible grace under pressure. "Ask everybody to go on to the reception, please. We'll let them know as soon as we find out anything."

The dean nodded, then headed for Wade's kids. "Ladies and gentlemen," he said through his lapel mike, "the bride and groom have requested that you all go on to the reception. They'll let us know as soon as they find out anything." He motioned for the attendants to exit. "In light of the circumstances, we'll dispense with the formalities and ask you to leave as quickly and quietly as possible."

Amid a clunking of kneelers and low murmur of concerned voices, Diane came over and looked at our little family in sympathy. She wasn't wearing Cameron's ring. "Do you want any of us to go with y'all to the hospital?"

Callie shook her head. "No, thanks. We'll be fine. But I'd really appreciate it if y'all'd go make sure everything's okay at the reception." She handed her godmother her bouquet. "Put these by the wedding cake." She scanned the worried looks aimed her way as the guests left the chapel. "I know everybody's upset, but try to get them to enjoy the food and the band."

"Bride and groom's orders," Wade ground out.

Diane clutched the bridal bouquet, the irony of having it lost in her concern. "Don't worry, Callie, darlin'. We'll make sure everything goes smoothly and y'all get plenty of pretty pictures of the cake and everything."

Eyes welling, Callie nodded in gratitude.

"Do you want us to leave, too?" I asked my daughter. "We can—"

"No!" She gripped my arm. "Please stay with us. Please."

Brooks waited till most of the pews had cleared to lean close and ask Wade, "Have you taken any . . . new or unusual medications in the past twenty-four hours?"

Wade's pallor abruptly shifted to a dusky flush, but his lips clamped into a straight line.

Callie answered for him. "Yes." Her voice cracked with guilt. "Last night." She shot me a pained look, then said softly, "Someone had given me some pills"—her voice dropped to an agonized whisper—"Viagra, and we tried it."

Wade groaned that she'd had to expose that particular bit of information in front of us. "It was all my idea, not hers."

I'd be lying if I said I was shocked by Callie's revelation, but I worried what John might be feeling. His grave expression had become unreadable.

Callie turned her face heavenward, tears leaking from her closed lids as she murmured, "Oh, God, I am so sorry. I never should have given in and let him take it. I knew what we were doing was a sin, but—"

"Callista Lundeen Baker . . . Bowman," I said firmly, "get a grip on yourself, young lady. The last time I looked, God wasn't in the habit of smiting people who had sex before marriage. If he was, more than half the country would be dead as a doornail."

"It's not her fault," Wade defended. "It's mine, completely." He looked to us. "I didn't want her to marry me without finding out what she was getting in that department. But I was so nervous . . . and she had those pills—"

I cut him off with a quote from *Gone with the Wind*, "Cap'n Butler, you don't want me to hear such things." I turned back to my daughter. "For all we know, this is just indigestion. Regardless, what happened, happened, and we're here for you both with love, not judgment."

Wade looked up at Callie. "I told you your mama was great."

Linda arrived with Brooks's bag at the same time the siren came to a halt just outside. She handed Brooks his keys, then his stethoscope, which he immediately put to use.

"Any unusual symptoms," he asked Wade, "or . . . manifestations after you took the medication?"

"None. The pain didn't get bad till after I ate lunch." Wade's features eased. He risked a deep breath. "Whew. It's finally fading. Much better. Can I get up?"

"Not yet," Brooks ruled. "Any stomach problems before this?"

"Just some gas and indigestion."

"Try to relax. We'll know more after we get you to St. Joe's. They have a great cardiology setup."

"Should we give him aspirin?" Callie volunteered. "I heard on a commercial that three aspirin can help if it's a heart attack."

Wade tightened his grip on her hand. "It's okay, honey. I take the recommended dose every day. And there was aspirin in the Seltzer-Al I took right before the service."

"Great if this is a heart attack," Brooks said. "Not so great if you're having a gastro-intestinal bleed."

"But this is just indigestion," Wade countered. "Really. I don't get it often, but I know what it feels like, and this is it, only times ten."

Brooks remained skeptical. "What did you have for lunch?"

John answered for Wade. "Three chili dogs, a Special Sandwich, and onion rings. And a Big Orange. At the Varsity. I took him."

For Wade's own good, I felt compelled to add, "Not to mention the sausage and Mexican omelet he had for breakfast."

John winced. "Sorry, pal. I should have taken you for a steak and a baked potato, instead."

"It's not your fault." Wade exhaled hard, then confessed, "I was fairly okay after that. It was the three brats and that last can of sauerkraut I had at home that pushed me over the edge."

Callie recoiled. "Wade!"

He looked sheepish. "Sorry. Hey, I'll never fight fire with fire again. I swear."

Brooks let out a long, low whistle. "Maybe it *is* just indigestion."

"That's what I've been tellin' you," Wade grumbled.

Linda motioned to me. "I'm going to the reception with Abby and Osama. Call me when you know anything."

"I will," I promised.

"You're not off the hook, yet," Brooks told Wade. "In light of . . . everything, I think we should err on the side of caution. Your heart rate's way too high, and there's a lot of noise inside your belly. We need to give your heart and your guts both a thorough checkout."

The sound of rattling wheels preceded two EMTs with a stretcher into the now-emptied chapel.

Brooks got up to meet them a few yards away, speaking low in medical-ese. I caught, ". . . diaperetic . . . pulse irregular at 148 . . . No nitro. He took . . . Alert cardio at St. Joe's . . ." which didn't sound good.

Once they were briefed, the EMTs helped Wade remove his suit coat and shirt so they could stick on a bunch of electrodes to transmit his EKG to the hospital right away. Then they transferred him onto the stretcher, covered him, hooked up the leads, and started an IV. "We're putting you on saline, and we'll be giving you something to get your heart rate down," the EMT explained.

Callie hovered beside Wade, holding his free hand while the EMTs strapped him to the stretcher, then raised it to transport him.

Brooks handed John his keys. "Would one of you mind driving my car to the hospital? I want to ride with Wade."

John and I both spoke at once. "Sure."

As they all started down the aisle, fluids aloft, I called after Callie, "We'll bring your clothes to the hospital so you can change."

She nodded, then the entourage left us alone in the chapel.

Finally, I could collapse. I fell into John's arms, too frightened to cry. "Oh, John, he's got to be all right."

"You heard what he ate after I dropped him off, honey," he soothed, holding me secure. "I'm sure it's just indigestion." But he didn't sound convinced.

"Hold that thought," I said into his chest.

He barked a dry chuckle. "And here I was, guilty as hell because I'd made a fleeting wish way back when that he'd get just sick enough to keep him from marrying Callie."

"I did the exact same thing."

He sighed. "We are two evil people. We deserve each other." He gave me an extra squeeze, then let go. "Come on. Let's get Callie's stuff. She'll ruin her dress for sure in the emergency room."

I followed, feeling like I was moving underwater. "Oh, John. Their honeymoon."

"Never mind the honeymoon," my husband said dryly. "They already had it last night."

I would have laughed if I hadn't been so worried. "Let's get her clothes and get out there. The girls will take care of things at the reception."

St. Joseph's Hospital, Dunwoody.

IF BROOKS HADN'T come out to get us, we never would have been able to get past the security doors in the acute cardiac unit. As it was, more than an hour had passed before he motioned us inside. "He's stable, and the tests have been run, but Callie's still worried sick. Maybe y'all can calm her down."

We followed him halfway to Wade's room when Brooks got a page. Frowning, he stepped to a nearby phone. "Y'all go ahead. They're behind curtain number three. I have an emergency at Piedmont. I'll check back with you later."

We thanked him and went to find the newlyweds.

Wildly out of place in her wedding gown among the tubes and wires and monitors and machines, Callie fled to us the minute we walked in. After a lot of hugging and reassuring, I heard someone else come in and turned to see who it was.

Nora Green stood there, bold as brass!

Instantly, I stiffened, as did John.

"Mama, this is Nora Green," Callie said, calm as you please. "Wade's half-sister from Santa Barbara."

His *sister?*

John shot me a rueful glance.

"My mother died of breast cancer at fifty last January," Nora said quietly. "We had no idea Daddy's real name was Bowman, or that he had a son. Only that he'd been married before. Not three months after we lost Mama, Daddy died of a massive heart attack. He'd never been sick a day in his life, then he was gone, and I was an orphan." She looked to Wade. "But when I went through his papers, I found some letters from Wade."

Her expression glowed with quiet gratitude. "It was like a miracle. I'd been so alone. Then suddenly, I had a brother."

"It was like a miracle for me, too," Wade confirmed. "We corresponded over the Internet at first. Then Callie suggested we send her a ticket to come see where Dad was born and meet us. After we picked her up at the airport and took her to her hotel, Callie gave us the rest of the week together to get to know each other."

"Wade's half-sister!" John pumped Nora's hand so hard she almost fell over trying to keep her balance.

So Wade hadn't been leading a double life. And I had been wrong, wrong, wrong. I couldn't blame Callie for not telling me the truth.

Relief and regret flooded me in equal measure.

Callie smiled at Nora. "We hit it off so well, we invited her to the wedding." She turned to me. "I should have told you sooner, but I was so mad at you over our fight."

Nora's expression sharpened, but she said nothing.

"I tried to tell you this morning after we made up," Callie said, "but you cut me off."

That I had.

Nora extended her hand to me. "I'm so glad to meet you. Callie has told me so many wonderful things about her family." Her shake was honest and firm. Then she turned back to Wade and Callie. "I think I'll go back out to the waiting room and give y'all some time together." She hesitated. "You'll let me know if anything comes up? Please."

"Absolutely," Callie assured her.

Visibly relieved, John directed his attention to our daughter. "Why don't you let your mama help you change? I'll stay with Wade till you get back."

"Go," Wade urged her. "The EKG and enzyme levels were normal, and my pulse is down. The doctor said they won't have the results of the angiogram for a while yet."

Red flags went up. "They did an angiogram?" I asked in what I hoped was an offhand tone. They didn't do those for simple indigestion.

"Just to be sure," Callie said. "The cardio-radiologist had two critical cases ahead of us to read, so I don't know when we'll hear anything. But it's good to know Wade's not considered critical." She started toward me, then paused to ask Wade, "Promise not to get sick or anything while I'm gone?"

"Word of honor." He turned to John. "Unless your daddy feels the need to give me a proper drubbing about last night."

"You're married now," John clipped out. "No drubbing. For that, anyway."

"Great." Wade definitely sounded like his old self. "Go get comfortable, honey."

Callie went reluctantly, but she followed me into the hallway, where Brooks was waiting to tell her, "I have to do some surgery at Piedmont, but don't hesitate to call me anytime if you have any questions. Your mama has my private number. Wade's in good hands here. Dr. Lofton is top-notch."

I didn't want to upset Callie by asking him why they'd done an angiogram.

"Thanks so much for everything, Brooks." Callie hugged him. "And please tell Linda to let the others know how much I appreciate their taking over the reception."

Brooks grinned as he headed out. "Rumor has it, Abby's been boogying down with Osama ever since the band cranked up, trying to bring the baby."

Noting the clothes on Callie's arm, Wade's nurse approached us. "Let me take you to the on-call room to change. We're so busy tonight, there's no way the residents will need it." She led us down the hallway to a small room with a rumpled bed. "Take your time," she told me, "but there's no lock on the door, so you might want to stand guard, just in case."

"Thanks."

I wondered if Callie was going to break down once we were inside, but she didn't. She took off her veil and folded it neatly, then came over and turned her back to me. "Get me out of this thing. Definitely not designed for sitting in hospital chairs." Her voice was weary, but steady.

I started freeing the long line of little silk buttons from their loops. "How are you holding up?"

"Terrified. Tired. Embarrassed. Guilty."

"Guilty?"

"About last night. I never should have—"

"This is your mama speaking," I told her. "Terrified is okay. I don't blame you. Tired is okay. You should be. But embarrassed and guilty? Sorry, but you must stop that immediately. Do you think you're the only Christian woman who slept with a man she loved before the wedding night?"

"I broke my vow to God. I knew better than to do it." She looked so miserable. "You taught me better."

Feeling like a total hypocrite, I decided to come clean. But I didn't have to tell her my first time was with my high school heartthrob, Brad, not her father. "I'd call that a classic case of 'Do as I say, not as I did.'"

Callie stilled. "What?"

"You heard me. Except for the Viagra, you haven't done anything I didn't do myself."

She turned, pulling the button from my grasp, and peered at me with a skeptical eye. "I don't believe you. You're just making that up to make me feel better."

"Honey, I'm not making it up, and I'm not proud of it, either. But it's the truth."

I could see she wasn't convinced. "You? Miss Straight Arrow?"

"I could say the same for you, my daughter, mine."

Some of the anguish on her face eased. "I shouldn't feel better hearing that, but it helps." She qualified, "*If* it's true."

"It's all too true." I met her eyes without flinching. "Promise me one thing, though, woman to woman," I asked. "Please don't ever say anything about this to Wade or your daddy. It's none of Wade's business, and it would only hurt your daddy to know I told you. Nobody in this world deserves less to be hurt."

She hugged me. "Woman to woman, your secret's safe with me."

"And yours with me." I turned her around to finish unbuttoning her. "Now let's get you back into your regular underwear and those jeans you wore to the church."

When she got down to her bra, she clutched the cameo. "I want to keep this on. For luck."

"Sure, sweetie." After hearing how Wade's daddy had died, I had a feeling my new son-in-law could use some luck.

I carefully folded Callie's dress, unmentionables, and veil into a compact rectangle of satin, then we returned to cubicle three. John and I had just decided to go on to the reception when we heard a ruckus from the end of the hall.

"I am his wife, I tell you, and nobody is going to keep me from going back there!" a strident woman's voice all but shouted.

Madelyn! I'd recognize that sharp edge anywhere.

What in blue blazes was *she* doing there?

"Ma'am! Ma'am," the nurse argued, "if you don't return to the waiting area, I'll have to call security."

"Call them. My husband's a surgeon here, and I can promise you, he won't take kindly to my being treated this way!" I heard curtains jerked roughly aside as Madelyn started working her way toward us.

"Stop that!" the nurse snapped, unintimidated. "These people are very ill, and you're disturbing them!" Her tone escalated. "Y'all cannot go back there! Mr. Bowman already has too many visitors, as it is."

"We're his children," Tom's voice said. "We have to see him."

With that, our curtain was jerked aside, revealing none other than Wade's first wife, with her children not far behind.

"Oh my God," she cried dramatically. "The kids called me, hysterical. They said you had a heart attack at the wedding, and these people wouldn't even let them see you." She closed the curtain behind her, shutting them out.

So much for the children. They murmured in protest, but didn't come in.

Madelyn being all about Madelyn, it came as no shock when she blurted out, "Wade Bowman, I'm your wife! You cannot die without forgiving me."

For a minute I thought that Callie might come out swinging—I certainly wanted to—but instead, she put herself between Wade and his ex, one hand fisted at her side and the other pointing toward the waiting room. "Get the hell out of here," she growled out. "You are *not* his wife. Like it or not, I am, and you have no right to come back here.

You forfeited that when you walked out on him and took his kids, then tried to turn them against him."

The kids fell silent beyond the curtain.

Callie wasn't finished. "I cannot believe you would endanger Wade's health just to soothe your guilty conscience."

The harried nurse bustled in, providing Wade's kids with an opportunity to sneak in behind her. "I am so sorry, Mr. and Mrs. Bowman," she said. "I've called security."

"No. No security," Wade said in weak, rasping tones, suddenly looking very much like a man on his deathbed. "I need to make my peace with this woman, with my children here to see it." He motioned Madelyn forward with a limp hand. "Closer."

Callie's gaze sharpened. No slouch, she immediately caught on to what Wade was doing, which was more than I could say for myself. "Don't try to talk, darling," she emoted. "You know what the doctors said. Save your strength."

"No," he rasped. "I need to clear the air, settle this." He sent the nurse a look of supplication. "Please. I have to do this, before . . . I *have* to do this. If I don't, I'll get really upset." He grabbed at his chest. "Aaagggh!"

Alarms started beeping.

Only I could see that Wade was pinching the poo out of himself with his other hand.

The nurse relented. "All right, but I'm calling your cardiologist, and these people need to be out of here in three minutes flat." She briskly retreated.

Her kids close behind her, Madelyn shot Callie a triumphant glare and moved in, taking Wade's hand. "Wade, how bad is it, really? Tell me the truth."

"It's just indigestion," he protested feebly through convincing agony. "Really."

Callie stepped beyond his line of sight and motioned to Madelyn, shaking her head as if we were keeping some dreadful truth from him.

Wade gazed wanly up at Madelyn and let loose with the loudest, longest, foulest fart I had ever beheld, especially ironic in light of his "clear the air" comment.

Shows what a Mexican omelet, two chili dogs, a Special, rings, three brats, and a can of sauerkraut will do to you.

Poisonous miasma enveloped the bed, which only served to confirm Wade's indigestion, but Callie covered by grabbing him. "Wade! Speak to me." Wild-eyed, she turned to Madelyn. "That sometimes happens when people . . ." Back to Wade. "Are you okay?"

John shot me a wide-eyed glance, lips glued shut over a dropped jaw. It took all my self-control not to laugh or run gasping from the room.

"Madelyn," Wade wheezed.

Eyes watering, she fanned at the stink, but moved in closer.

"I'll forgive you," he said loudly enough for the kids to hear, "but only if you tell the kids the truth. Here and now."

"Anything, as long as you forgive me."

Her lack of hesitation brought to mind what Wade had said about her deathbed superstitions.

"Kids?" He played it to the hilt.

They crowded closer. "We're here, Dad."

He peered at Madelyn. "Tell them."

She chewed her lower lip, then averted her eyes as she spoke. "Kids, when I told you it was your dad who cheated, I wasn't telling the truth, exactly."

"Madelyn," Wade gasped out in feeble indignation, "the truth."

"Okay, I lied," she admitted. "We had been struggling financially for so long, and I wanted more for y'all—"

"Madelyn!" His voice sharpened.

"Okay, so I wanted more for myself, too," she admitted. "Your father had to work so hard to make ends meet as a florist. And Sonny was in love with me, and he was a doctor who could offer us real security. And he was crazy about you kids, since he couldn't have any of his own, so when he asked me to marry him . . ."

"And when was that?" Wade prompted.

"We . . . I was thinking about leaving your father."

Wade feigned another attack of pain.

"Okay," Madelyn blurted out. "We had an affair. There. That's the truth. It was me, not your father, who had the affair."

Laurie recoiled. "Mama. All these years, you lied to us? Made us think Daddy was the one who broke up our home, when it was you? What kind of person does something like that?"

The boys glared at their mother in outrage.

Madelyn had the sense to look ashamed. "I had to. That was before no-fault in Georgia. I knew Wade would never surrender custody, and that y'all would blame me—and Sonny—if I told the truth. I had to lie, to keep you. I had to." She jerked free of Wade's hand, angry now that her lies had been exposed. "You promised you'd forgive me. Do it."

Wade dropped the act, looking from one child to the next. "I loved y'all too much to put you in the middle of an emotional tug-of-war, so I let your mother get away with what she did. It was easy to forgive you for believing her," he said in his normal voice. "But I didn't forgive her until Callie helped me see that my bitterness was only poisoning me. So I finally let go of it."

He took his daughter's hand. "I'm asking you to do the same for your mother now. I'm not minimizing what she did, just asking you to love her anyway. She loves you the best she can. Please don't go from blaming me to blaming her."

Proud enough to bust, Callie edged Madelyn away from her husband. "Do you see now what an amazing man your father is?" she said to his children. "How could I help but love him?"

Anger at their mother, betrayal, and anguish warred in the kids' expressions, but it was Laurie who spoke first. "Callie, I'm so sorry I was hateful about you and Daddy. I see, now, why he loves you, too."

Tom glared at his mother, clearly a long way from forgiveness. "I'll try to forgive Mom, Dad. That's all I can promise for now. I'll try." He looked to Callie. "I'll make it up to you, honest."

"I know you will," Callie said.

"Can you forgive me, too?" his younger brother asked her.

Callie laughed. "My wedding gift to y'all is a fresh start. How's that? We were friends before I started dating your dad. That's all I'd like to be now: friends."

Madelyn took the offensive. "I think you're being awfully cavalier for a woman whose husband is in cardiac intensive care."

"What in blazes are all these people doing back here?" a tall doctor scolded as he pushed his way into the cubicle with a chart and clip-board heavy with papers. He recoiled from the smell and looked around for the culprit. "Good lord."

Wade shrugged. "Sorry."

"Dr. Lofton, these are my parents," Callie introduced. "And these are Wade's children and ex-wife. Dr. Lofton is Wade's cardiologist."

Dr. Lofton was in no mood for a family reunion. "Everybody but the real Mrs. Bowman needs to leave. Now."

To Madelyn's shock, Wade sat up and grinned. "Don't kick them out. They've come to my deathbed, and we've made very good use of the time." He pointed to the chart. "What's the verdict? It's just indi-gestion, isn't it?"

The doctor glanced balefully at the rest of us before proceeding. "It's a good thing for you that it is. Heart attacks are no place for com-pany. We couldn't even get a crash cart in here with all these people."

"Indigestion?" Madelyn's voice went even shriller. "You let me think you were dying! Tricked me into telling the truth! You sorry son of a bitch! I ought to finish you off myself!"

Tom gloated. "Calm down, Mom. He told you it was just indiges-tion. I heard him."

"Yeah." Laurie took one of Madelyn's arms as her brother took the other. "See you later, Dad." They hustled her out.

"Let me go!" Madelyn protested. "See how tricky he is? He tricked it out of me. How low can you be?" Her voice grew fainter till we heard the waiting room doors close behind them, and the unit fell blessedly silent.

"You were married to that?" Dr. Lofton asked Wade, who nodded. "It's a wonder you didn't have a heart attack then."

Wade grinned. "I told y'all it was just indigestion." He drew Callie close beside him. "C'mere, wife. Maybe we can make a later flight to Bermuda."

"Not so fast," Dr. Lofton said. "It's a good thing you had that at-tack of acute indigestion. Otherwise, we wouldn't have done a thor-ough workup on your heart, and you might have had a heart attack for real. Your angiogram revealed a sixty-percent distal occlusion in one of your descending anterior coronary arteries."

All the color drained from Callie's face. "Oh my God."

"The good news is," Dr. Lofton told Wade, "none of the blockage broke loose, and it's in a position where we can use cardiac catheterization to clear the artery and put in a medicated stent. I've scheduled the surgery for seven tomorrow morning." He handed Wade the thick stack of disclaimers on the clipboard. "If you'll read through these and sign where it's highlighted. Assuming things go well, we'll let you go home tomorrow night, but with a portable monitor for the first few weeks."

Undone at last, Callie started to tremble and threw her arms around Wade. "You said it was just indigestion!"

The gruff doctor softened. "We have excellent equipment and medications for these procedures. If everything goes as I think it will, Wade will be better than ever afterwards. My surgical statistics for this procedure are as good as any in the country, and I can confidently tell you that, barring unforeseen complications, he has a better than eighty-percent chance of feeling a lot livelier afterwards than he did before."

"I like those odds. Sign me up," Wade said over Callie's shoulder. "When will I be able to travel?"

"I'd put off that honeymoon for a month or so, just to make sure everything's copacetic."

Callie's sobs escalated.

"It's been a long day," Wade explained, stroking her hair. "Our wedding. Church full of people. We didn't plan to go back down the aisle with me on a stretcher."

"I saw the dress when you came in," Dr. Lofton said dryly. He dropped his voice. "Would you like for me to write her something to relax her?"

"I'm right here," Callie said, her voice muffled against Wade's shoulder. "Kindly do not speak of me in the third person in my presence. And no, I do not want something to calm me down. My husband has a sixty-percent distal occlusion in his descending coronary artery, and we're missing our wedding reception. And our honeymoon! I'm entitled to be miserable, at least for a while."

She drew back to glare at Wade, the remnants of her makeup

smeared from hither to yon. "And you, mister, are going to do exactly what the doctor says and be better than ever, or I will never forgive you. I don't care if it poisons me. And no more sausage and sauerkraut. Or chili dogs."

Wade gazed at her ruined face with adoration. "Whatever you say, my precious raccoon." He lovingly wiped a streak of mascara from her cheek with his thumb. "Feel better, now?"

Callie answered with a petulant no, but I could tell she did.

"I think that's our cue to head on over to the reception," I said. It felt like midnight, but was only nine thirty. The party would still be going. "What, if anything, do you want me to tell everybody?"

Callie didn't hesitate. "Tell them it was only acute indigestion, and a good thing, too, because they found a sixty-percent distal occlusion in his descending coronary artery, so they're going to ream him out first thing tomorrow. Please ask everybody to start praying for him and keep it up till he's all well."

"I'm right here," Wade mimicked with humor. "Kindly do not speak of me in the third person in my presence."

Callie whacked him in the chest. "You."

Dr. Lofton raised his palms in alarm. "No hitting in the chest, please. At least not till we get that artery cleared."

Callie drew back, abashed. "Oh, I'm so sorry."

"So it's okay for her to abuse me," Wade teased with a smile, "as long as it's *after* the Roto-Rooter job."

"Works for me," the doctor said.

"May we come sit with you in the morning?" I asked Callie.

"Please," she answered with gratitude.

"What time should we get here?" I asked the doctor.

"We'll probably take him to preop at six thirty." He backed away, clearly glad to escape us loonies. "See you in the morning, Wade."

"I'll be there."

"Six thirty it is, then," I told Callie. "I'll bring muffins." She loved my homemade blueberry muffins. Baking was good therapy, and I probably wouldn't be able to sleep, anyway.

I gave her a kiss. "Call us if you need anything, any time of the night. We'll be here right away."

"Thanks. I think I'm just going to climb up in this bed with my husband, strictly for some huggin' and some sleep."

"Sweet dreams." John kissed her forehead, and we left the two of them alone at last. As alone as you can be in a cardiac unit.

I waited till we got to the car to call Linda, who answered without a greeting. "Hey. How is he?"

Caller ID still unnerved me. "Fine, for now. It was an acute attack of indigestion."

Before I could relay the rest, she muffled the receiver and shouted, "It was just an acute attack of indigestion!" When she uncovered the receiver, I heard cheers and applause. "Are they coming over?"

"No." Suddenly, all the moxie ran out of me. "The workup showed a significant blockage in one of his coronary arteries, so they're going to clear it and put in a medicated stent with a cardiac cath first thing tomorrow."

"Oh, Georgia." Linda's voice went thick with sympathy. "Is there anything we can do? Anything at all? Just name it."

"Yes. Pray for them. And have a good time at the party. Thanks so much for handling all that for me." We were approaching Peachtree Battle, and I motioned for John to turn toward home. "I'm so worn out, I just want to go home and get into bed."

"Amen to that," he seconded, taking the shortcut behind the little building that had been my kindergarten.

"We'll all be praying," Linda said, "for all of y'all."

"Thanks. G'night." Eyes closed, I leaned back into my seat and was sound asleep before I knew it.

John shook me from my warm oblivion. We weren't moving, and I breathed in the familiar scent of our garage. "Sleeping Beauty, I'd love to carry you to bed, but I have a sixty-one-year-old son-in-law, so I'm too old and too tired to pick you up."

"In that case," I said without opening my eyes, "I'll have to kick you to the curb and find a younger man."

"Be my guest." He tugged at my hands. "C'mon. You're all un-hooked."

Glad for the help, I swung my feet out and let him pull me upright beside him.

He put his arm around me and headed for the stairs. "Bed. Now."

Punch drunk, I didn't even wash my face before closing the blinds and falling into bed, but John headed for the kitchen, where I heard a faint "pop." No sooner were my eyes closed than I felt him climb in beside me. "Don't go to sleep yet," he coaxed. "I have a surprise for you."

I rolled over and cracked one eye to find him standing beside the bed in his boxers holding a tray with two flutes of champagne, a red rose in a bud vase, and a thick ivory envelope with his name engraved on the outside, already opened.

When my husband went to trouble like that, it was always something seriously special, so I sat up. "Okay. Let's have it."

He then put the envelope in my left hand and the champagne in my right. His own flute in hand, he set the tray on the bureau, then crawled in beside me. "I had planned to do this when we got home from the reception," he said with that boyish shyness he showed only to me. "Look inside." He handed me my reading glasses from the bedside table.

Yawning, I pulled out the note inside and struggled to focus. Below a gilded, colorful engraved crest, elegant engraving announced, "On behalf of the Deans, Faculty, and students of the Santa Barbara campus of the California Institute of Technology, we are honored to extend this invitation for our esteemed colleague, John Robert Baker, Ph.D., to accept the first annual Sol Wasserman Cold Fusion Visiting Chair at this university, with all its appurtenant honoraria and accommodations, commencing September fifth of the upcoming scholastic year."

I tingled all over. So that was why he'd been so excited to see Sol at the wedding.

"It comes with a car, a furnished house on the beach, a $350,000 stipend, and amazing grant money," he said in a voice fresh with pride and possibilities.

Three hundred and fifty thousand! On the beach!

"John, I'm so proud. When did you find out?"

"A week ago."

I set my champagne aside and pounced on top of him, spilling his as he fell beneath me. "You kept this from me for a whole week?"

"I wanted to wait till you weren't distracted." His eyes twinkled. "I'll be working with the best. And you'll be there with me. It doesn't get any better than that."

Two weeks in Maui, then Isle of Palms for another week—with Wade and Callie after all, God willing—then a year on the beach in California. Suddenly the world looked new again.

I paused. "I reckon I can manage without my Red Hat Club for a year."

"Won't have to." He grinned. "Thanks to Teeny, y'all are gonna take turns meeting here and out there."

I might have known. "Leave it to Teeny."

"Oh, and she's opening a new Shapely plant near Austin," he went on, "and putting Diane in charge of getting things up and running."

"Agggh! That's perfect!" But how come he got the scoop instead of me? "When did you find out? And why didn't Teeny tell me?"

He smiled. "She'd planned to surprise you at the reception. When we didn't go, she called you while Callie was changing, and I answered your phone. I was going to tell you, but Madelyn came in." He snapped his fingers. "Oh, and Diane accepted Cameron's proposal."

"At long last." I snuggled closer. "Except for geography, they're perfect for each other." Thanks to Teeny, it just might work out. Much as I hated for Diane to move, I knew we wouldn't lose touch.

"They're getting married after we get back," he went on, clearly enjoying the fact that he got to tell me, "and before we head for California."

I bristled just a little. "Anything else you know that you haven't told me?"

"Not a thing." He closed his eyes and relaxed.

Happy, happy, happy, I turned off the light, then settled under his arm in the dark, my ear to the comforting rhythm of his healthy heart. "Did I ever tell you how great you are?"

"All the time," he murmured. "But it's always nice to hear." He groped for the sheet, then pulled it over us. "Now go to sleep, woman. I set all three alarms for six, so we won't be late to the hospital."

"You are the greatest," I repeated as I drifted toward dreams of Hawaii.

"And so are you, my bride" was his lullaby. He hugged me closer. "I just pray that Callie and Wade will be able to know what this feels like."

"They will," I murmured from halfway to paradise, believing it for them. "They will."

· Acknowledgments ·

MY LIFE IS blessed by so many good things—not the least of which is the privilege of earning my living by writing for wonderful readers like you. It's hard to whittle my thank-yous down to a page or so, but for this go-round, I'd like to start by thanking every single person who has bought or spread the word about my books. Bless you! Every single sale matters to my career, especially the advanced and first-week sales that help put me on the all-important bestseller lists, so I can keep writing books that bring hope and laughter to my readers.

Next, I'd like to thank my ex-husband for twenty-seven happy years of marriage. What happened after that doesn't erase the long, good years we shared and the "Norman Rockwell" childhood we gave our son. I'd also like to thank my ex's present wife (my "wife-in-law"), a precious, hardworking Christian friend who lives her faith with all her might in every breath. She and her late husband were always special to us when our kids were growing up together at New

Bethany Baptist Church, and Blair and Joel and Laura are every bit as wonderful and committed as their parents. My ex and our son are lucky to have the Bailey Bunch as their second family. I wish them all God's best in their lives.

A huge thank-you, though posthumous, goes to my precious mother-in-law, Margie, who lived across the street for thirty years. I loved her to smithereens, and I still do. Our son didn't even have to pack a bag to run away from home. Everything he needed was right there at Mimi and Papa's. It was Margie's love that inspired me to write this book about having and becoming mothers-in-law. I learned from the best, and now that my son and his wonderful wife and my grandbabies are across the street from me, I'm trying hard to fill Margie's shoes.

Next, I'd like to thank my agent, Mel Berger, for his indispensable help in my career, and my editor, Jennifer Enderlin of St. Martin's Press, for sticking with me through the difficult birthing of this book. Some stories come to life easier than others, and this one was a long, hard labor, but we all love the result, and I hope you will, too.

Special thanks go to Dorothea Benton Frank, Cassandra King Conroy, Nancy Thayer, and Linda Lee for taking the time to read my books and share such generous praise. Bless you!

Thanks, also, to the ladies of the Red Hat Society state and regional get-togethers who have brought me in to tell how a Southern Baptist Sunday-school teacher ended up writing historical romances then switched to "hell hath no fury" hardbacks that made the *New York Times* Best Seller List. They all treated me like a queen, and what fun we have had. I rarely traveled as a child, but I always dreamed of seeing faraway places, and now I get to do so as an honored guest! Though my books aren't endorsed by the society, the Red Hat ladies are fabulous, and I heartily recommend the organization to any woman who's sensible enough to enjoy dressing up and acting silly on occasion.

I'd also like to thank my pals at Maaco in Lawrenceville, Georgia, for giving my precious Queenie car a glamorous makeover. Great job, guys! Nobody would ever guess how many minor insults she's endured at my hands (always under fifteen miles an hour!). She looks brand-new. Wish you could do the same for me, but I don't think a baked-on finish would work.

As always, thanks to Glen Havens, M.D., of the Ark for helping preserve my sense of humor. And to R. Marvin Royster, M.D., of the Peachtree Orthopedic Clinic for my fabulous new knees—a genuine miracle! I can finally exercise, which I love doing at the Curves in Flowery Branch, Georgia. What a difference it makes, being able to live without all that pain. If you need your knees done, Dr. Royster is the best.

To my amazing Jawja Hattitudes—Bonnie and Cathy, and Holli and Joan and Liza and Rosie and Sara and Vicki and Willow Heart—y'all are the best bunch of wild women I've ever hung out with. Thanks so much for your friendship. Nobody can fill Cindy's shoes, but I'll give it my best, because that's what every one of you deserves.

For precious Betsy K. Thanks for your sweet friendship and all your help with redecorating and reorganizing. I miss you like crazy. Our loss is Chicago's gain, but Delta is ready when you are, sweetie. Come see us.

And special thanks go to my church, Blackshear Place Baptist in Oakwood, and all the caring people who welcomed me back to Georgia: Doug and Suzann Bonds's terrific 8:00 Small Group Bible Study and Wade and Mary Ash's 9:30 Singular 45 class, who made me feel welcome and accepted; Pastor Jeff for the inspiring messages every week; Dave Chappell, who ministered wise counsel and caring when I faced some really thorny practical issues; and WOW Women's Bible Study for keeping me in the Word with joy.

In spite of the inevitable pain and problems life brings, I can honestly say this is the best time of my life, and I have so many more stories clamoring to be told.

Watch for my humorous, heartfelt little handbook, *The Twelve Sacred Traditions of Magnificent Mothers-in-Law,* coming in spring of 2009, a perfect gift of happy hints for every bride, mother-of-the-bride, mother-in-law, or daughter-in-law.

Turn the page for a sneak peek at Haywood Smith's
new novel

Ladies of the Lake

Available now

· 1 ·

There's nothing wrong with this family that a funeral or two wouldn't fix.
—MY PATERNAL GRANNY MAMA LOU

. . . .

I HAVE SOME family secrets to tell, but first, I need to make one thing crystal clear: With two glaring exceptions, my mother is a true Southern lady of infinite grace and discriminating taste.

The first exception—and by far the least—is the fact that as soon as the four of us girls were safely on our own, Mama moved to a double-wide in Clearwater, Florida, where in short order she married, then buried, two "diamonds in the rough" who smoked cigars. Good men, but phew. Only recently did she find the second great love of her life besides Daddy: retired rabbi David Rabinowitz, who loves her back just as much as our sainted daddy did.

The second, and worst, exception is that Mama (who hated being named Daisy) broke her own vow to give her daughters normal names and succumbed to the centuries-old tradition of christening all female descendants of our direct ancestor Lady Rose Hamilton with floral names. Mama said she wasn't afraid of the ancient "unlucky in love" curse that's supposed to fall on nonfloral daughters, but Daddy, romantic that he was, loved the idea of siring his own little bouquet, so Mama finally gave in, sparing herself the infamy of breaking the chain of ages. Her only rebellion was naming me, the firstborn girl, Dahlia instead of Rose.

Frankly, I would have preferred Rose. Weird names like mine made me fair game for the Susans and Patricias and Nancys and Cathys of my era. Not to mention the fact that I still have to spell out Dahlia for everybody.

I was unlucky in love, too, so maybe there's something to that curse, after all.

Two years after I was born, feisty, colicky Iris arrived. After another two years, we were blessed with precious Violet, an angel-child from her first breath. I was eight before placid baby Rose was born and Mama made her nod to the woman who started the whole tradition back in England.

We've forgiven Mama for our names, but Mama hasn't been able to forgive our grandmother for her shortcomings, which were many, as you shall see.

My three sisters and I had the privilege of growing up in Atlanta during that golden illusion of domestic innocence between World War II and the sixties. For us, magic was real and had a name: Lake Clare. We didn't know and didn't care that the lake was Old Atlanta's premier summer watering hole, its rustic homes handed down from generation to generation, among them our great-grandparents' impressive three-story Hilltop Lodge and Mama's tiny Cardinal Cottage. We only knew we loved spending our summers in the little log cabin just down the hill from our beloved great-grandmother and our black-sheep grandmother Cissy (short for Narcissus), who was so vain she never let anybody—even Mama— call her anything but Cissy.

We never suspected how much Mama hated it at the lake, or why. All we knew was that there, in the cool beauty of the mountains, we could go barefoot, drink café au lait instead of milk with our eggs and bacon, and spend our days swimming and exploring and playing. And, in Iris's and my case, fighting. We were so busy, we never suspected the secrets that hid in the shadows of Hilltop.

....

THE LAST TIME my sister Violet and I saw Cissy was two years ago, and she was trying to kill us—and enjoying herself immensely.

But that was Cissy for you. She never had been anybody's idea of a grandmother—or a mother, for that matter.

It was just before Christmas, and Violet and I were on our regular holiday run up to Lake Clare, bearing gifts and a perky little decorated tree along with the food we and my other two sisters took turns delivering every month. Normally, Violet and I really look forward to our December drive from her place in Clarkesville to the northeast corner of the state. We both love the bare-bones splendor of the mountains in winter, and the trip provided welcome escape from the pressures of the season and a chance to visit.

But this time, an unexpected Canadian Clipper had barreled down on us, sending the temperature plunging in the cold, hard drizzle. By the time I picked her up and got back onto Highway 441, the Bank of Habersham sign said 31 degrees, and the pine trees were already bowing slightly under a coating of freezing rain.

"I should have let you drive," I fretted, slowing down to fifty. There wasn't much tread left on my ten-year-old Mercury Sable's tires, but the home-building crisis had put a serious dent into my developer husband's income and his ego, so I'd used the car maintenance fund to buy him a new golf club for Christmas to cheer him up. "These tires are okay for regular driving, but not ice."

"Nothing's okay for ice," Violet said without alarm. "But we'll be fine. WSB said it wasn't going below freezing, even up here." As always, her blue eyes and soft expression radiated calm and reassurance.

It took a lot more than the prospect of running off the road to ruffle Violet. Of the four of us Barrett sisters, she was the most stable and well-rounded.

"Oh, gosh." Violet delved into her huge purse. "I almost forgot to call Cissy." We were nearing the fringes of the cellular network, and it wouldn't do to arrive unannounced in our grandmother's isolated mountain realm. Even when we called ahead, there was no guarantee what we'd find when we got there.

After dialing, Violet stuck her finger in her ear (we all have midrange nerve deafness) and waited, then hollered, "Cissy? Hello? Cissy!" She frowned at the phone and muttered, "Still plenty of signal. She just hung up."

Our grandmother Cissy was almost as hard of hearing as she was crazy, so even the special amplified phone we'd gotten her didn't make communicating much easier. You have to pay attention to the other person for it to help, something Cissy never had mastered.

Violet dialed again, waited, then hollered hello again. After a brief pause, she brightened. "Hi! It's Violet! We're on our way with your groceries!" Pause. "Violet! Your granddaughter!" Her soft alto voice wasn't made for yelling. "No, Daisy is my mother! I'm Violet!" She gave the thumbs-up (Cissy had remembered Mama, at least), but she crossed her eyes at me when she did it, which made me laugh. "Dahlia and I have your groceries!" Pause. "Dahlia! Your granddaughter Dahlia! We're coming with the groceries!" A sigh of resignation and renewed volume. "We're on our way with the groceries! Your groceries are coming today!" Her lips folded briefly. "No, we're bringing groceries to *you!*"

The routine was so familiar, I could hardly keep my tickle box from tumping over, which would only set Violet off, too.

Violet enunciated every word emphatically. "We . . . are . . . bringing . . . your . . . groceries . . . today!" She frowned, then gave up and flipped the phone shut. "Boy, that wears me out. I have no idea if she ever connected with what I was saying before she hung up on me."

Based on experience, things wouldn't be much easier when we got there, even though Cissy seemed to be having a fairly good day. I mean, she'd remembered Mama, which was something.

Beside the road, pine saplings were bent double now. I gripped the steering wheel. "Let's get her the food and get back home ASAP."

"Works for me," Violet said.

Thirty minutes later, I was relieved to turn off the slick pavement onto the rough tar and gravel road that led over the mountain to the family compound where we'd spent our summers as children. The way was steep, but offered a lot more traction than the highway's slick blacktop. It took us another twenty minutes to navigate the cutbacks up and down the other side, but at last we reached the single-lane dirt road at the edge of Cissy's fifty-three acres, and scraped our way through ice-laden rhododendrons and mountain laurels down to the turnaround at Hilltop Lodge.

"Let's take the stuff to the side door, so it won't get wet," Violet said as we broke out the umbrellas and hurried to unload.

Nobody ever used the side entrance on the verandah, but there was no protection from the elements at the kitchen door, so I agreed. I didn't hear Foxy (Cissy's mangy old red mongrel that she insisted was at least half fox), but the dog was as deaf and ancient as she was, so I didn't think anything of it.

Worried that a huge branch might break off and kill one of us any second, we skirted the thick laurel hedge that shielded the little vegetable garden and the kitchen door, then carefully picked our way up the mossy flight of native quartz stairs to the verandah.

Built in 1919 from virgin timber as a hunting lodge, the rambling old two-story place had sunk and sagged till it seemed to have grown up out of the sodden drifts of leaves like a giant mushroom fantasy, with thick moss on the log walls and curling shingles. Down the slope of the orchard beyond, Lake Clare lay shrouded in mist like a Turner painting.

I put down the gifts and groceries on the ancient wicker settee, then turned to gaze across the lake and breathe of the cold, clear air, mold be damned. No other place on earth had the power to calm me like this one.

Sending me half out of my skin, Violet shattered the quiet with an ear-piercing rendition of the distinctive five-note whistle that had been our family's summons for generations.

"Violet!" I scolded, heart pounding. "You scared me half to death."

She just smiled her graceful little smile, but I knew her calm façade hid a streak of mischief a mile wide.

We listened for some sign of life inside, but there was none.

Violet whistled again, but this time, I was prepared.

After the brief echo died, we heard nothing but the rain and the ominous creak of ice-coated branches from the surrounding forest.

I jumped at the crack of a breaking branch in the big hemlock by the kitchen, but when I whirled toward the sound, there was only the soft whuff, whuff, whuff, *whump* as it fell through the foliage to the ground.

"She's probably holed up under the electric blanket," Violet said. "I can't blame her." The screen door was hooked, so we picked up our umbrellas and headed back out into the rain toward the kitchen door.

When we got there, we found its screen hooked from the inside, too, so we circled around to the terrace. Violet and I both peered into the sliding glass doors that made up the corner of the master bedroom—a six-ties renovation the Captain and Cissy had made that included a sunken tub (the only one in the whole house) overlooking the terrace, the veran-dah, and the path to Mama's now-derelict guest cottage. Amid the piles of old magazines, clothes, newspapers, and junk, Cissy's unmade bed was empty except for the black plastic mesh hair protector she wore to keep her French twist in place as she slept. She was a dead ringer for Queen Nefertiti with it on.

The sunken tub was full, a film across the cloudy, hard well water.

"Uh-oh," Violet said. "Her boots are gone." Summer, winter, rain or shine, Cissy wore those bright green rubber barn boots whenever she went out.

I checked the pegs by the hall door. The rest of her "uniform"—a tall-crowned, floppy denim hat stuffed with newspapers to keep it from coming down over her face and the Captain's WWII trench coat and wool army trousers—was missing, too. "Oh, lord. She's gone out in this weather." I scowled. "Perfect. We'll have to call Mountain Patrol to bring the search dogs." Again. So much for getting home before dark.

It never occurred to Violet or me that this time, something might have actually happened to Cissy. As our other grandmother was wont to say about people as difficult as Cissy, "The Good Lord wouldn't have her, and the devil's gettin' too much use out of her to kill her."

The Mountain Patrol had to be getting sick of finding Cissy when she got lost (which was often), but she was so fiercely determined to live out her last days in her own home that even the authorities didn't want to mess with her. They'd tried carting her off to a nursing home once, but she'd escaped three times in less than a week, leaving rampant destruc-tion in her wake. So they, like us, left her pretty much alone, except for the visiting nurses, who—thanks solely to her—had the highest turn-over rate in the state. Maybe even the whole Southeast.

"She might have just gone to get the mail," Violet suggested. "Let's check the boathouse." Which was where the postal boat delivered.

Wary of falling ice and debris, we headed down that way.

"Damn." I scowled when we found no sign of her there. God forbid, we should have to spend the night in Hilltop with the mildew and the fleas and who knew what else. And if we had an ice storm, there was no telling when we'd escape. I shuddered at the prospect, but at least we'd brought a HoneyBaked Ham we could eat without fear of ptomaine. "Crap, crap, crap. We'll have to call the patrol."

"At least we know she hasn't been gone long," Violet said. "She answered the phone when we called. Let's look awhile longer."

We were almost back to the house when the first shot went off.

At first, we both thought a tree had snapped, so we frantically scanned the oaks and white pines overhead to see which way to run.

Only when the second shot blew a huge hole in the furled rhododendrons not three feet from Violet's shoulder did I realize what was happening. But sound plays tricks on the steep slopes beside the lake, and I couldn't tell where it had come from.

"Run!" Violet shrieked, dropping her red umbrella in the path as she took off for the neglected orchard's open spaces.

Hearing the click of reloading nearby, I dropped my umbrella, too, and launched myself toward my sister, barely catching her raincoat in time to drag her down into the vinca minor beside me. "Stay down."

It never even occurred to me that it might be somebody besides Cissy shooting at us. A crack shot, she had hunted with Hemingway in Africa and taught us all how to use and clean a shotgun. Even with cataracts and arthritis, she posed a very real threat.

"Head for the basement," I whispered to Violet. It was hidden from the yard by an overgrown hedge that offered the closest cover, and the doors hadn't been lockable in decades.

When the third shot blew Violet's umbrella to bits, showering us with red nylon confetti, we screamed and flinched in unison, then made a break for the hedge.

"We got rid of all her guns," Violet panted out as we cowered behind the ancient tractor stashed behind the hedge. "We both went over every square inch of that house. Where did she get this one? Nobody in the county would be stupid enough to sell her one!"

"I don't know," I snapped, in mortal terror for my life. "Maybe Santa Claus gave it to her."

Another blast sent my umbrella soaring, sieved with holes. "Hah!" Cissy crowed from somewhere nearby. "Got the other one!"

Better my forty-five-dollar Brookstone umbrella than me. My son thought I was an old stick-in-the-mud, but he'd miss me if I was gone. And he'd be mortified to have to tell everybody his great-grandmother had killed me.

I peered gingerly over the tractor and was hugely relieved to see no sign of Cissy, so Violet and I picked our way over to the only pair of functional French doors that led into the basement, and tried to pull one open. When we did, ice cracked and fell from the wisteria and honeysuckle that covered it, so we retreated back to the tractor.

Then we heard a rustle from the woods, followed by heavy steps treading up the path toward the house.

"Vile rapists!" Cissy's voice rang out. "My womanhood is all I have left for them to take, but they shall not have it, my Captain." Our step-grandfather the Captain had been dead for fifteen years. "I know I sought the ideal lover many times before we met," she went on dramatically. (She did everything dramatically.) "We both dipped our oars into many a lake of passion, but all that's over now." I heard her start up the stone stairs, followed by the click of Foxy's labored pace behind. "It was war. But my chamber of treasures opens to no one but you now, my darling. No one but you." She started toward the side door.

Gripping each other's hands, Violet and I pressed ourselves hard against the stone foundation under the verandah so she couldn't see us.

Several steps onto the floorboards, Cissy halted, and I heard her open the breech, slide in two more shells, then snap it shut. "Filthy rapists. I'll kill every man-jack of them if I must, but I shall not be defiled."

Her steps came closer above us, then stopped directly overhead. "Here, now! What's this?"

Violet and I both winced and tightened our hold on each other, expecting the worst.

Cissy's strident tones abruptly became almost dainty. "Presents. How lovely. Look, Foxy. Santa Claus has been here." A rustle of wrapping paper. "From Violet. From Dahlia. Who the hell are they?" More rustling. "From Iris and Rose." Her voice sharpened. "What, they're too cheap to get me a gift apiece?" Another rustle. "Rose. Rose." There was recognition in the way she said it. "That child is the spitting image of my mother, Foxy, only she lacks backbone. Isn't she a nurse or something?"—no, a preschool director—"I do believe she is, a talent she undoubtedly got from me—all those years in the Red Cross, you know." Just as abruptly, she became suspicious again. "They weren't so picky about official training back then. The government's absolutely destroyed individual liberty in this country. It's those industrialist whores, the Republicans, who did it. Ike, indeed! Rapists, all of them."

After a hard thump, we heard cans rolling on the verandah and the sound of something being dragged. "Foxy, no," Cissy ordered. "Put that ham back!" So much for safe eating. "Obey me, cur!" She swatted at her pet, who sounded a feral growl that made me wonder if she really might be part fox after all.

After a brief scuffle, we heard tinfoil ripping, then the smack of meat on the boards. "There. That should tide you over till supper. Come." Cissy's boot steps schlepped toward the French doors to the two-story living room. "Let's bring these presents in, then clean our gun. Only the basest sort would put a gun away dirty."

The phrase took me straight back to pistol practice and skeet-shooting sessions in the orchard with Cissy that were our rite of passage from childhood to adolescence. "Every woman should know how to handle guns, dear," she had confided to each of us in turn. "Men find it incredibly sexy."

Mama had been horrified, but Daddy had said learning gun safety was a good thing. I'll bet he never dreamed we'd end up being her targets.

Cissy's voice grew fainter as she went inside. "Can you believe they just dropped these boxes at our doorstep like a bastard child in a washbasket?" She clumped to open the side door. After a plink and skreek of rusty screen-door spring, she came back out. "They didn't even bother to ring the doorbell or let me know they were here," she fumed as she started moving things inside. "Not so much as a hello. Probably those sneaky Christians. I am nobody's charity case. Thank the Buddha and the Great Creator for Transcendental Meditation, that's all I can say. Without it, those sneaky Christians would drive me insane."

A pause.

"What do you mean, the grandchildren, Captain?" Pause. "Oh, they did, did they? The little ingrates. It's why I'm glad I never had any more children of my own. No respect for their elders. And I'll bet one of those presents is another cursed cotton nightgown. Same thing every year, underwear and coarse cotton nightgowns I wouldn't inflict on the maid.

I've got a chest full of those wretched things upstairs, but they're not the ones I like. I've told them a hundred times, I like the nylon Madame Lillie peignoirs and the Madelaine silk-knit tap pants with six-inch legs, but do they ever listen? No."

Never mind that those hadn't been made for a generation.

"Should we make a run for it?" Violet whispered tightly as Cissy continued her delusional conversation in and out of the door with small loads from the boxes.

"Not yet," I breathed into her ear. Cissy was so deaf, we could have spoken normally without fear of being overheard, but both of us were too rattled from being hunted. "She still has the shotgun. Let's wait till she closes up and goes to her room. Then we can sneak across the path and cut through the woods to the car."

A bolt of adrenaline sent me groping for keys in the pocket of my coat, but they were there, thank God. "Whew!"

"Double whew," Violet said in a more conversational tone.

It seemed like hours, but was probably only about ten minutes before we heard Cissy retreat to her room.

With painstaking care, we crept back out into the freezing rain, made our way to the path, sprinted across its ten-foot span into the woods, then beat it for the car. I clicked open the doors, and we jumped in. Then I started the engine and threw the car into reverse, backing out with such force that I didn't realize I hadn't taken off the emergency brake till I whipped into the turnaround at the blackberry patch, and the smell of burning rubber caught up with us. With tingling fingers, I reached for the release and popped the hood instead. "Oh, damn!"

"Don't panic," Violet said. "Put your foot on the brakes and take a deep breath. I'll get out and close it. Deep breaths."

I did as ordered, managing to find the proper release and pull. Violet got back in and away we barreled, heedless of the branches lashing at my car as we bounced up the rutted road toward safety. Halfway up the hill, we both burst into a hysterical mix of laughter and tears.

"Can you believe that? Can you?" Violet asked. "She really tried to kill us!"

Jouncing and lurching, I pleaded, "Oh, please, don't make me laugh. I'll wet myself."

"Merry Christmas!" Violet said, hilarious.

"No, really, don't," I said, wracking my memory for the nearest rest-room and remembering that the one at the River Road convenience store had holes in the floor and smelled of sewage.

"Under the circumstances, inappropriate laughter is perfectly under-standable," Violet said. "It releases the tension." As dean of women's athletics in her little college, she counseled lots of her students, but I was in no mood to be counseled.

"Don't give me that psycho-pop lala. Cissy really, truly tried to kill us. We need to call somebody. Have something done. She's dangerous. Next time, she might kill one of the nurses. Really."

Violet sobered. "Who do we tell? Mountain Patrol? They don't have a SWAT team."

"Nobody said anything about a SWAT team." We reached the tar and gravel road, and I increased my speed to a reckless thirty. "But some-body has to do something."

"Maybe we should do what Rose suggested and have State Game and Fish dart her for real," Violet said. Our baby sister, Rose, was a certified angel, but she had a wicked sense of humor underneath.

"That would be perfect except for the fact that sedatives make Cissy psychotic," I reminded her. "Extremely intelligent and psychotic, or have you forgotten the Ativan incident at the nursing home? Or the time she climbed naked out on the ledge at the hospital after her breast cancer surgery?"

"This really isn't a police matter," Violet said. "It's mental health."

"Yeah, well, call it what you will, I don't want anybody to get killed dealing with it, not even Cissy. We'll phone the sheriff from the conve-nience store on River Road." Holes in the floor or not, I'd have to use the bathroom there.

A thought occurred to me. "Maybe Iris might have an idea what to do." Iris loved telling people what to do, under the guise of concern. "I mean, I certainly don't want to take responsibility for what might hap-pen. The more, the merrier," I suggested.

Usually, that was Iris's corporate-minded modus operandi, not mine.

Normally, Violet backed me up a hundred percent, but this time, she shook her head. "Honey, this is a job for the sheriff. He gets paid to han-dle things like this, so let's let him."

I tried to convince her otherwise all the way to the convenience store, but even though she validated my point of view, she wasn't persuaded.

So we called the sheriff, who spoke with us personally and told us not to worry, he'd take care of it, then insisted we go back home before the roads iced up. I made him promise to call and tell us what happened, which he did.

Three hours later as I neared the Perimeter in Atlanta, my cell phone rang, displaying a Clayton exchange.

"Hello?"

"Mrs. Cooper?"

"Yes. Is this the sheriff?"

"One and the same. Everything's fine." He sounded almost offhand. "We contacted a friend of hers on the lake, and he went over and talked her out of the gun and ammunition, so everything's back to status quo."

I was horrified. "You sent a civilian into harm's way with an armed crazywoman?"

He just laughed. "Well, technically, he's a deputy, and your grandmother sets great stock in him. It was his gun; apparently, your grandmother snuck over to his place and took it. He's promised to keep his arms under lock and key from now on, and make sure she's unarmed before y'all come up for your regular visits."

"But—"

"I'm sorry, but I've got another urgent call coming in," he said. "Y'all have a merry Christmas, and don't hesitate to call if you need any more help with Miss Cissy. 'Bye, now."

I hung up, never dreaming it would be two years before I got back up to the lake, or that I'd be divorced and alone.